I0831149

Gwyn's Kingdom - The Electric Moon

If you were to leave the world for a while, you'd likely forget it, and it would likely forget you.

But . . . yes, indeed, there are exceptions.

There are things that leave a mark so deep, that even when gone and forgotten . . . they can't be ignored.

Contents

Mt. Scott

Myrrh

The Moonless Forest

Franz & Delilah

Edenshire

The Rusted Forest

The Burrows

The Western Kingdoms

SILVANIA

Bordeaux

e Cashmere Caverns

The Northern Kingdoms

NGTON

N

W

E

S

Gwyn's Kingdom

DIA

The Eastern Kingdoms

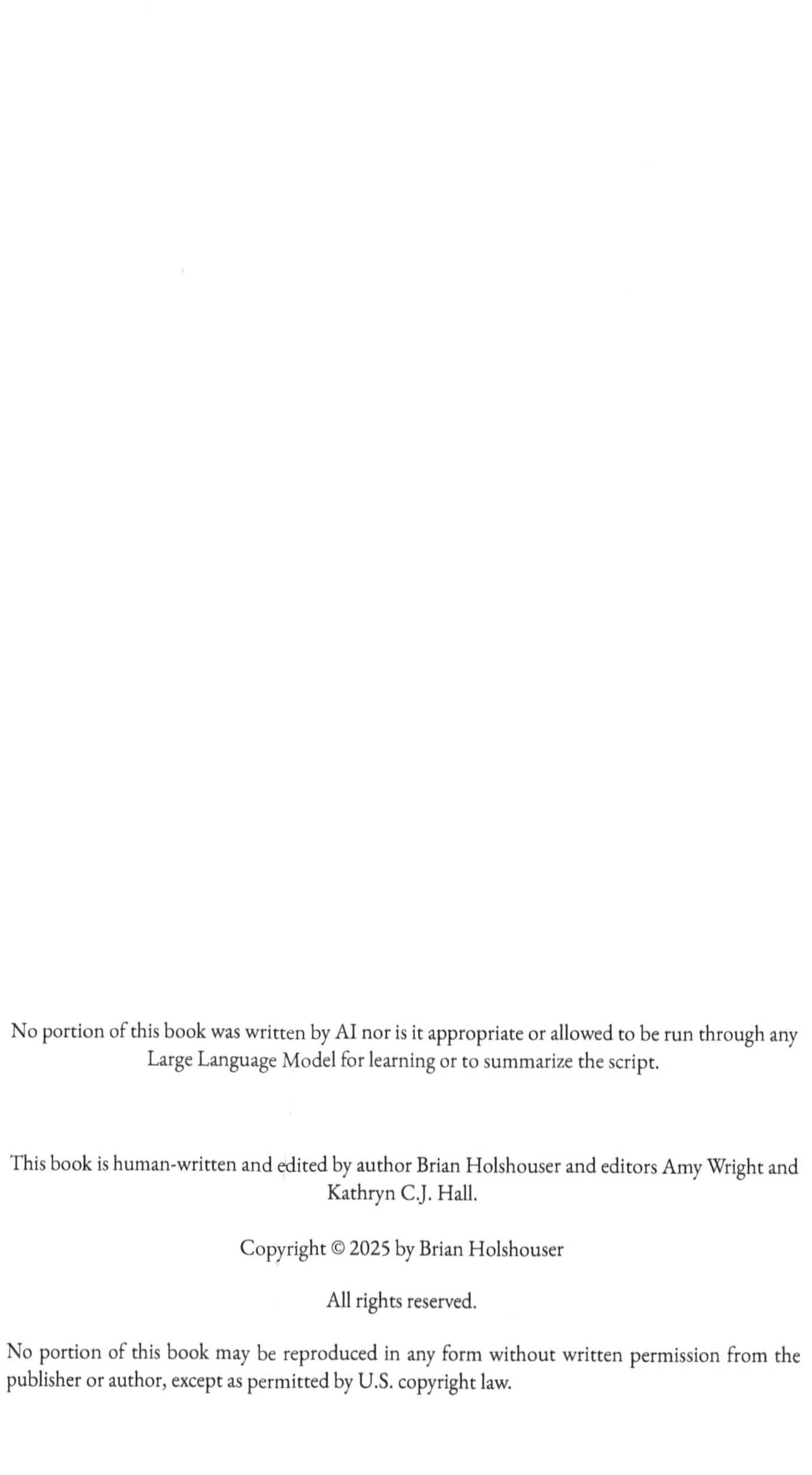

This book is human-written and edited by author Brian Holshouser and editors Amy Wright and Kathryn C.J. Hall.

So in that day
When flowers bloom
You'll hold the heart
Of the Moon

CHAPTER 1

Gwyn

Nestled deep within the rural lands of the Western Kingdom was a small stone cottage. Inside, a young girl sat, swinging her feet off a bed—her green eyes staring out the window toward a forest. The house was tucked along an ancient cobblestone road by the Rusted Forest, its surface coated with dust accumulated over time from light travel. If you followed the lonely road long enough, it would eventually take you to the circular city of Pantheon.

Like many cities of the world, it was far removed from anything supernatural. Such things were reserved for books, songs, and tall tales. Though some old songs and stories whispered of magic, the people of Pantheon dismissed it.

The cottage faced away from the road where thick trees served as a curtain, as if it would rather look at the forest. It was a nice home—simple and peaceful.

The small girl sitting on the bed was named Gwyn. She knew only happiness in her young spirit. Sorrow had no place in her heart.

She was swinging her feet back and forth while watching her grandmother sew. Her grandfather, George, was teaching her how to roll a copper coin over the back of her fingers.

"Practice this, and it'll make your fingers nimble like your grandmother's!"

Her grandmother, Enna, had fingers that were indeed quick and nimble, proving as much as she mended a torn, dark green cloak. When it was finished, the stitching was nearly perfect and unnoticeable.

Gwyn waited patiently—or at least as patiently as a child can wait—while attempting to roll the copper coin across the back of her tiny, slender fingers. Her other hand was busy twirling a lock of black hair. To simply say her hair was black would not do it justice, for her hair was a dark, shimmering black, like wet ink. It was full and luscious, nothing like the hair of her grandparents, which was coarse and grayed.

Gwyn thanked her grandmother, hugged her tightly, and wrapped herself in the green cloak as she went outside to play.

She ran through the front yard, past the flower beds that were carefully planted around trees. She listened to the crunching sounds from the pebbled walkways that extended from the cottage through the yard. She lightly splashed water from one of the nearby bird baths, then jumped and rang a wind chime before leaping over a gazing ball and running into the Rusted Forest, her cloak trailing in the wind behind her.

It was a sturdy cloak, perfect in Gwyn's opinion. In the winter, it kept the frostbitten wind at bay, but she wore it through all seasons. It was made well enough to resist thistles, briars, and other sharp things from tearing into Gwyn's fair skin. She appreciated the protection while adventuring through the ancient forest. It gave her a sense of confidence. "I'm a bit braver with it than without," she told her grandmother. The right clothes can have that effect, and this was the right cloak for Gwyn.

Her grandmother had always told her 'not to wander too far' but never gave specifics as to what 'too far' exactly meant. To Gwyn, this lack of detail meant that the discretion was left up to her as to what it really meant.

Gwyn had received the green cloak from her Uncle Franz and Aunt Delilah for her eighth birthday.

"It's the first of many gifts," her uncle told her, placing it on her shoulders with great pride.

She loved it instantly: the dark green material, the pockets inside, the way the fabric felt when she'd rub it between her fingers. Even the smell was comforting in a way she couldn't explain. She had her grandmother hem it to her size so she could wear it because it was so large. Every few months, her grandmother would have to resize it as she grew.

Gwyn knew where a creek ran in the woods behind their home. It was past the plowed gardens in their backyard, where a scarecrow stood. She'd learned how to fish in the deeper parts of the creek to help with dinner or trade at the markets in Pantheon.

Pantheon was a large city with limits widespread and thin populations on its far-reaching outskirts. Their cottage was barely within the rural limits. The inner city was buzzing with modest, hardworking people. Many of them spent their time running shops or haggling in the markets that were scattered about the city's inner rings.

At the nearest market, Gwyn knew several people well. Mrs. Miller sold common goods like flour and salt; Barney the Butcher was goofy but made her laugh; Fishy Frank, as they called him, dealt in and smelled of fish; and so on.

Her grandfather showed her how to clean a fish once, which she wasn't fond of. She watched him, but the process made her stomach turn.

Although the creek was a bit of a trip into the woods, Gwyn had secretly gone much farther on her own.

She had an idea of where mountains were to the far north, though she could only see tiny peaks of them in the very far distance from tall hilltops or the tops of tall trees if she went very far north.

She'd also found the foundations of what looked to be old buildings or houses from long ago. Whatever they were now lay in ruins, like forgotten ghosts buried deep in the forests. Gwyn saw many wonderful and strange things there.

She never told her grandparents about what she had seen. She was afraid they wouldn't understand her desire to explore and would only worry or make her stop going altogether. So she kept it a secret.

At the age of ten, her grandfather thought it wise to teach Gwyn how to shoot a bow. She thought it to be terribly awful at first, but her grandfather insisted she learn.

During her third lesson, she had managed to pull the bowstring back far enough to launch the arrow. When she released it, the bowstring struck the skin of her forearm above her leather arm guard with a loud snap, sending a sharp pain across it.

A line of blood slowly surfaced across her pale skin.

As she watched it, something began to stir inside her. An overwhelming flurry of fiery energy burst through her chest. Every pulse of pain billowed the growing flames. The desire to give up vanished, replaced by a flame that was spreading uncontrollably through every inch of her body.

She could feel power—insisting, demanding—that she press on. It replaced the pain, and as if in a trance, her cautions were set aside, and her burning will was brought to the foreground of her mind with an intense and deadly accuracy.

Something in her green eyes gave it away. Her grandfather's demeanor changed. He pleaded with her to put the bow down and go inside, but Gwyn didn't hear him. With strength she couldn't explain, she removed her grandfather's grip from her arm, withdrew an arrow, and quickly nocked and released it. The bowstring lashed, leaving another bloody line slightly crossing the old one on her arm. However, her arrow struck the scarecrow, sinking deeply into its hay-filled burlap skin. She fired arrow after arrow, the string biting at her flesh with every shot.

Finally, with an empty quiver, her mind returned. Her grandfather was cautiously staring at her from the ground. She didn't realize she had brushed him aside with such force. Exhausted, she skipped dinner and went to bed.

The next morning, Gwyn skipped breakfast, grabbed her bow and quiver, and went outside to practice. One shot at a time, she slowly learned to avoid slicing her arm with the bowstring. Her confidence and accuracy grew with every arrow. It wasn't long before she became quite skilled with a bow.

Her grandfather was an old craftsman who had spent years whittling away at carefully chosen pieces of wood, making things like fine bows and walking sticks. For her twelfth birthday, he gave Gwyn her own handcrafted bow. Gwyn could draw the string with ease and release a deadly shot. She practiced nearly every day, often into the dim, cascading orange light of sunset, and sometimes late into twilight.

Her aim was good—better than fair. It was natural for her. It was the first skill she had chosen to learn out of self-discipline and became one that she loved and took with her everywhere.

Gwyn had been homeschooled off and on by her grandparents. In seasons they could afford it, they sent her to the school at a church up the hill. It was there that Gwyn realized she was different from other kids. It wasn't clothes, jewelry, or ribbons and bows that made her different; it was that other kids had parents—not just grandparents, but a mom or dad who would come to pick them up and talk to teachers.

She found that some of the other kids thought that only having grandparents was odd. Some of them made fun of her for it. One large boy named Matthew was often the instigator of the insults, once pushing her around the playground while asking her what she did to her mom and dad. The concept had never crossed Gwyn's mind much before, but now it seemed like she was inadequate and should know the answers to such questions.

She thought a lot about the issue. She often dwelled on the fact that she didn't have a mother or a father, but only had grandparents.

Was it normal? Where are they? Why did they go? Questions like these nagged at her curious mind throughout the day. She found that shooting her bow helped to clear her head from it.

Gwyn contemplated asking her grandparents but for some reason feared the answer. Besides, she thought, if they haven't told me by now there's sure to be a good reason for it.

As kind as this sort of thinking often goes, Gwyn wasn't doing herself any favors. Inside she wanted to know the whole of it and it ached her more every day.

"Put your bow and arrows down and get ready for school," Enna told her one early morning. Gwyn remembered the walk they took up the hill on the cobblestone street that morning. The air was fresh, cool and crisp with a hint of winter pine in it.

At the top of the hill, the cobblestone street widened and wrapped around an old wishing well in the middle of an abandoned town square. Her school was in a church further ahead. Here, only a few small, rotting buildings remained after walking through a withered overhead archway. Her grandmother had told her about wishing wells and gave her a small silver coin. "Here you go, make a wish!"

Gwyn tossed the coin in and squeezed her eyes shut.

"I wish I knew who my parents were," she whispered softly, yet not quite softly enough. Her grandmother had heard. Gwyn had a feeling she did, too, by the look on her grandmother's face when she opened her eyes.

Gwyn was thinking to herself in bed that night when she heard whispers coming from down the hall. She knew her grandparents were usually asleep by that time and thought it odd that they were talking.

She quietly tiptoed down the hall toward their room. The soft glow of candlelight flickered from under the door as she pulled up close and sat quietly to listen.

"Not yet, Enna ... Not yet... Not this young!" she heard her grandfather tell her grandmother.

"Tis it not time? Then when!? She deserves to know."

"Well..." Her grandfather paused for a deep breath, then said, "Well... Maybe... Well, just maybe... But I think a year or two would be better, personally. Honey, is it truly right?"

Her grandmother sighed. "Sometimes we hurt the ones we love because we're trying too hard to protect them."

Gwyn knew the words were meant about her. But what did she not know? And why?

"Darling... you'd best send the letter. You know they'll know much better what's proper and not... much better than us."

"Yes... of course. I'll send the post tomorrow, then. But you know what this means, don't you?"

There was a sigh before her grandparents whispered a soft "Good night" to each other.

With that, the candlelight went out, the whispering stopped and Gwyn quietly snuck back to her room.

She lay in bed but couldn't sleep. Her mind was wandering.

When Gwyn finally did fall asleep, she had a strange dream about shooting an arrow into a wishing well. The arrow was shiny as it flew and struck the silver coin she had used to wish to know her parents. The coin shattered into several small shards with an explosion of indigo veins of electricity. She looked up, and all around her were kids from her school with their parents next to them. They all laughed and pointed, condemning her, telling her that she should have kept her wish. What a fool she was to have broken it!

She woke suddenly and realized that she could feel her heart beating heavily in her chest, pulsing throughout her body. As she swept the hair from her face, she noticed that her forehead was drenched with cold sweat. It was a silly dream, really, and she knew as much; it just seemed so real. She rubbed the sleep from her eyes, attempting to shake the flustered state the dream had left her in.

She got up, grabbed her cloak, bow, and quiver, and snuck out the back door of the cottage. She made her way through the familiar woods. An odd whoosh in the trees made her pause for a moment, but only a moment. Soon, she found a large, tall tree she'd learned to climb years ago. She expertly scaled it, ascending the tiers of branches, stopping only when she came to the highest branch that she knew would support her weight.

Through the canopy of leaves, Gwyn looked up, and her eyes locked onto the bright moon. But it was not just the moon she saw, for tonight, shining brightly in the sky, was the glow of the majestic Electric Moon.

CHAPTER 2
The Electric Moon

In the world now, the moon was different. It had two phases: the normal, white moon we all know and love, and a glowing indigo ball of energy with pink waves of lightning slowly crawling across its surface.

The second phase was known to Gwyn and commonly as the 'Electric Moon'. The moon switched phases every other day, from electric to white—always full, always awake at night, in one form or the other.

Why the moon changed like this was unknown to Gwyn. Her school had only ever taught her that it did change and never had answers to the question of 'why' when it came to the moon and its phases.

High in the tree, she was staring at the Electric Moon. She didn't know why but it helped to calm her. Wrapped in her cloak, she felt warmer in the cool evening air while gazing at it. It was as comforting as a freshly baked pie in the fall or hot cider and chocolate in front of a fireplace in the dead of winter. The sight of it warmed her from within. It may have been the very night she fell in love with gazing at it. She felt a special connection to it.

After some time had passed—much longer than Gwyn realized—a large owl landed on a branch a few feet above her. Her heart nearly leapt from her chest, and her hand instinctively went for her bow and arrow. But sitting on the branch made her movements awkward, and she was forced to move a bit slower than usual.

"No need for that, young miss," said the big brown owl with a slight roll to his voice.

"You . . . you can speak?" she asked in awe.

"Of course!" the owl hooted. "I have been around for a long, long time! I'd find it rather a bore if I'd never learned to speak, but even worse if I'd never learned to listen!"

"Oh... I'm sorry; it's just I've never heard of an owl speaking before."

"And perhaps you never will again!" said the owl, followed by a long, rolling hoot.

Gwyn resituated her bow and apologized for drawing it.

"It's quite alright," the owl assured her. "But why come all the way up here? It is so far from the ground?"

"I... I..." she stumbled over her words to remember a reason. "I had a bad dream... just thought it'd be calmer up here... I guess. That's all." She felt silly giving a reason for what she was doing, but knew it all made sense somehow. Eager to move away from the awkward answer, she asked the owl the same question. "Why did you come all the way up here to talk to me?"

"Hoo! Silly girl, is it not common for an owl to perch high up in a tree? Perhaps I live here! Perhaps it is my home that you have trespassed in!"

Gwyn suddenly felt embarrassed by the thought of being in someone else's home without permission. "Oh, I'm sorry. I didn't..."

"Wohoo! No need—just remember, things are not always as they seem. But I will tell you this: I came here to see what kind of thing was in this tree tonight. You see, I was flying very high when I saw your eyes. To me, even miles up, your eyes were like beacons of a lighthouse tonight. And even more, I thought I saw... No, I know I saw . . . it."

"...What?" she asked.

The owl leaned his head down and peered at her. In the reflection of his big, round, dark eyes, she could see her own. They were big, green, and shimmering, gleaming with the reflection of the Electric Moon in them. The image was captivating to her.

"Magic..." whispered the owl.

"Magic?" she whispered back.

"Yes," whispered the owl. "Real magic."

"Why are we whispering, Mr. Owl?" asked Gwyn with a brow raised in curiosity, still staring at her reflection in the owl's big, round eyes.

"My dear, sweet young child, because, there are those who abuse and fear such things, and you never know who, hoo hoo... is listening."

The owl pulled his head away from her and looked straight ahead. "...And for good reason, too. Magic can be a dangerous business. It has done a lot of harm to the world."

"But, Mr. Owl, I don't even know what it is. How could I be dangerous?"

The owl hooted and ruffled his chest feathers and stood himself up as if preparing to tell a story. "The truth is, magic is a whole handful of things. Not knowing about it, like you, is possibly even MORE dangerous! You see, it could be used to move the wind. I've seen it used to light a fire out of thin air. I've seen arrows and spears stop in the air and drop to the ground as if they struck an invisible wall. But I haven't seen that look in your eyes in quite some time."

Gwyn thought about what the owl was saying, then asked in a whisper "What is in my eyes, Mr. Owl?"

"Oh ...Oh, I wouldn't tell! For even an innocent child may grow up with the poorest intentions, one day. But I will tell you this: be careful with it. I urge you, no, I beg you—if you find it..." The owl leaned down close to Gwyn—his huge, dark, round eyes focused intently on hers—and whispered, "...Be sure that you use it for good. For there is also a light within you, child."

The owl stood back up and stared into the distance. "There is plenty of evil in this world these days; it would be nice to see some good in it."

Then, with a round of purring owl noises, the owl leapt off the branch and flew away.

CHAPTER 3
Friends and Foe

During recess at school one day, Gwyn was sitting at a table outside, working on a math assignment, when she heard Matthew—the biggest kid in school—saying something behind her.

He was laughing at a boy with dark hair and freckles, calling him a "freckled-faced freak." At first, Gwyn thought Matthew was talking to her, given how close he was. But when she looked up and saw the small, freckled boy, the situation became clear. She had often been pushed around and made fun of by Matthew, mostly because she only had grandparents, and they were old with no proper mom or dad. The unnecessary meanness made no sense to her. As far as she could tell, she was no different from any of the other kids.

Gwyn watched for a moment, trying to think of something to do. But while she was thinking, Matthew violently pushed the dark-haired boy—who was much smaller than he was—hard enough that he fell backward. The boy landed hard on his back, skidding across the gravel beneath him.

She saw fear and anger in the freckled boy's eyes as he lay on the support of his arm, breathing heavily. Before he could get up, Matthew ran and slammed his heel down into the boy's ribs, causing a loud thud as a row of awed noises came from a gathering crowd.

Before Gwyn knew what she was doing, she had stood up, made her way behind Matthew, and had thrown every ounce of energy she had into his back, using the point of her elbow as a weapon. The blow was shockingly hard—so hard it temporarily broke the trance she had snapped into to deliver it and brought Matthew to his knees in pain.

It also caught the attention of Matthew's running mates—three tall boys, all a bit smaller than Matthew, who quickly started heading toward Gwyn.

Matthew quickly spun around, lunging from his knees while swinging a fist toward Gwyn. She reacted instinctively, but not fast enough, and felt a connection. It was a stiff blow to her ribs. The force of it took most of the wind from her lungs, causing her vision to blur. But it knocked her back, not down.

Then, without thought, without will, without any explanation at all, somewhere in Gwyn's mind, she realized she was still holding the sharp pencil she had been using for her math assignment. During Matthew's next powerful swing, she jumped back, spun in the air—arm extended, wielding the pencil like a knife, and caught Matthew's fist mid-swing. She felt the pencil pierce and sink deeply into his flesh as their fists met with extreme force.

The whole thing happened in roughly a second, causing the growing crowd of onlookers to gasp again in surprised awe.

Matthew let out a violent scream and squeezed his now-bloody hand at the wrist with his other. The pencil had gone fully in and through his palm, sticking halfway out one side and halfway out the other. Lines of blood ran down his arm as he stared at it in shock.

Gwyn slipped out of the trance that once again had taken over her actions and realized the whole of what had just happened. Too stunned to move, she stared at Matthew's bleeding wound as he squeezed his wrist in pain. She then turned and looked down at the freckled boy, who looked as shocked as she felt.

She was so stunned—she didn't even try to move when two large arms locked hers tightly behind her back. By the time her senses had almost returned, two more hands were pulling her black hair, hard. They gripped it so tightly she heard strands rip and tear out with a sharp pain.

If Matthew's screams hadn't summoned the teachers, she probably would have suffered a lot more than a bloody lip. Unfortunately, while still in shock and restrained by two boys much larger than herself, one boy did manage to land a blow before teachers could stop him.

She heard a loud crack with a jolt of pain through her jaw; then everything became a dizzy blur of adult voices for a moment. She began to realize she was now on her hands and knees as her wits began to return. She stood up and brushed the dust from her green cloak, not even aware that her lip was bleeding. In fact, while the teachers were busy expelling four bullies for hitting a girl, she walked over to the freckled boy, who was propped up on his scraped elbows donning a look of shock on his face.

She extended her own scraped hand down to help him up and said, "Hi. My name's Gwyn."

"Jack," the boy said, his voice a mix between shy and shaken.

Jack took her hand but was still hesitant to get close to Gwyn. After all, he had just seen her—a small twelve-year-old girl—bring a much larger bully to his knees. Not to mention seeing the way she casually got up and dusted herself off as if nothing had happened, even after taking what looked to be a powerful blow to the face. She hadn't even wiped the stream of blood running from her lip down her cheek before offering to help him up.

It might have been any one of these things that made Jack hesitant, but he'd also seen a strange look in her eyes as she was fighting Matthew. It was only there for a moment, but he was sure he saw it. It was almost as if her pupils were a little too large, or her eyes were too big, or perhaps just too fierce; and there was a slight glowing light behind them. He knew it happened, but it happened very fast.

"Thanks," Jack said, before grabbing his book bag and quickly walking off.

She felt a bit cold-shouldered by his decision to withdraw from the conversation without more to say, so she stood there, thinking silently to herself as she watched him leave.

"That was very brave of you," said a small blonde girl about her age.

"Oh, thank you. I don't know if it was the right thing to do though," Gwyn retorted.

"Don't worry. It was. We all wish we could be that brave."

"I don't know what came over me. I wasn't always so brave... if that's what it was."

The blonde girl smiled. "And don't worry about Jack, he'll come around. He's just a little shocked. Not to mention, probably embarrassed."

"Embarrassed?"

"Well, most guys don't have girls come save them, you know?"

Gwyn thought it over and realized the blonde girl was right, and nodded in agreement. She knew the blonde girl by face but had never actually spoken with her. In fact, the more she thought about it, she had never seen the blonde girl speak much to anyone.

"I'm Gwyn, by the way. Thanks for... well... thanks."

"My name's Chele—Chele Ash. Here's some cloth for your lip," she said, handing her a blue handkerchief.

She took the cloth but thought it looked too nice to stain with blood. "Thanks," she told Chele, humbled by her kindness.

"No problem. I'll see you around," she said, then smiled, turned, and headed up toward the church.

Gwyn spent the next week doing something she had never done before at school—attempting to make a friend. Slowly, she earned Jack's trust through small talk, witty comments, and plenty of smiles; and with his trust came friendship.

She found that Jack had been raised in an orphanage and had never known his parents either.

It wasn't long before Chele started joining them as well, whose presence Gwyn found rather pleasant. They started working on assignments together and soon were spending breaks and lunches talking and joking about things like friends do.

Chele, who was very quiet and shy at first, proved to be quite intelligent in many areas of school, making things for Jack and Gwyn easier and more fun than it had ever been.

Gwyn's reputation had changed at school. No one made fun of her anymore, and she got the sense that some people were a little scared of her—avoiding eye contact in the halls, quickly moving out of her way without being in it in the first place.

She overheard rumors about how people had seen her fly for a moment. She had even heard a version where she cut off Matthew's hand, and someone once even said she made him eat it.

Gwyn, Jack, and Chele laughed at the rumors, especially when someone said she had tied all four of the boys up and took turns giving them all beatings until they agreed to leave school.

It wasn't long before Gwyn invited Jack and Chele over for dinners and play dates. Soon, they became close with her family and shared in their jokes and helped with their chores. This was embraced by her elderly grandparents, given their old age had made things harder on them.

Her grandpa taught them several tricks to making bows and arrows. He showed them where the bow should come from within the rings of the tree, which trees made the best bows and arrows, and how to string and tiller the limbs to perfection. It was an art he took pride in, selling his bows to local hunters and tradesmen who took them to cities around the world to sell.

Although bows and arrows were a great source of income for the family, their gardens and fish provided food and income as well. They had wheat for making breads and cakes, corn for making animal feeds, tomatoes, melons, and other various fruits and vegetables, both for using and to sell.

Gwyn teased Jack about his freckles from time to time, and he teased her about her hair being too black and frumpy and only good for pulling. But the truth was, her hair was very flowing and not frumpy at all, and his freckles suited his face rather nicely—or so, at least, they thought as much about each other.

Enna told her she should teach Jack how to cook, and that a young man's not worth a flying fish if he can't cook it. The analogy was odd, but Gwyn got the point and agreed it was best to teach him how to cook.

"Here, I'll show ya how to make bread," Gwyn told Jack, first teaching him how to measure properly. "Take a scoop of yeast and put it in a bowl." She set a bowl on the counter and gestured to it.

Jack shrugged and scooped up a large cup of yeast from a gunny sack and poured it quickly into the bowl, kicking up a cloud of yeast in the process that tickled his nose. He repeated the process with flour into a separate bowl he sat on the counter.

"Okay, now pick up the bowl and bring it to the tap. Just put the bag of flour on a shelf in the pantry," Gwyn told Jack, starting to make her way past the pantry. Jack lifted the bag of flour over his head with his free hand and tried sliding it securely onto the shelf, but his nose was now itching, and he couldn't stop himself from closing his eyes as he let out a huge sneeze. As he did, he made sure to turn his head to avoid getting it into the bowl of yeast, but the bag of flour on the shelf slipped and fell on its side, raining flour all over Jack while he quickly fought to sit the bag back upright. The incident left him covered in white flour.

White lines crossed his now flour-covered face and body as Gwyn tried not to laugh. She held her hand in a fist over her mouth as she looked the white, powdery boy up and down. The image almost looked unreal, as she'd never seen a human that was completely pasty white.

Chele had just arrived at Gwyn's to help teach Jack to make pies and came in through the back entry near the pantry. Before anyone saw her, she spotted the ghostly white Jack standing near the pantry, let out a chirp of a squeal, then turned and ran back home. The squeal startled Gwyn, and she jumped and turned to face the door and let out a small scream herself. Once she realized it was Chele running from what she probably thought was a ghost, they both burst into laughter.

"Oh wow! She thinks you're a ghost!" Gwyn said, while holding a stitch in her side from laughing. Jack, still covered in flour—who fortunately was a good sport about the whole thing—raised his arms and started making ghost noises before he found himself laughing again. She helped him clean up and spent several minutes knocking and shouting at Chele's door to convince her that they weren't a ghost coming to get her. Chele felt rather silly and blushed once they had explained the whole thing to her.

When it was all said and done, Chele had taught them both how to make wonderful pumpkin, apple, and cherry pies.

"The secret is in the crust," she told them.

Gwyn also showed Jack how to shoot a bow, although he wasn't very good at it, and on his third attempt to stick a scarecrow, he aimed too high and sent an arrow into her grandpa's workshop window, causing it to shatter.

"Oh... err. It's fine... It's fine," she assured him. She then let out a mournful sigh and held her head down.

Jack looked at her with concern. "What?"

"Well..."

"Gwyn, what?"

"It's just, my granddad... He'll probably trim your fingertips so you can't shoot anymore... but it won't hurt much. Could be a lot worse, really," she said with a serious demeanor and look on her face. It was a fine bout of acting, she thought.

Jack waited, assuming she was joking at first, but the joke never came, and his eyes suddenly went big with terror. "What!"

Then, slowly, he saw a smile creep onto her face. "Oh! Crud, Gwyn! That's not funny!" Jack yelled, then let out a sigh of relief. "Well... I may be a rotten shot with a bow, but I can set a trap to catch a bear if I wanted!"

Jack showed Gwyn how to tie proper knots and set traps for small game. Although he could definitely catch a rabbit, Gwyn doubted his claim to catching anything much larger, but she didn't call him on it.

They learned several things from each other and spent a decent amount of time exploring the strange things deep in the forests. Both of them posed theories about what was once there or what this and that did.

"Probably a place where ghosts go when they die," Jack said. "But I wouldn't go there if I were a ghost."

"I guess we shouldn't tell Chele if it is," Gwyn joked.

Having friends around was a rather nice change, Gwyn thought. Neither she nor Jack had parents or needed them, and life was fine without them—or so it seemed for the time.

Gwyn's grandparents also didn't seem too upset about her run-in at school. In fact, if it weren't for a dried streak of blood on her face and messy hair when she came home the day of the fight, they probably wouldn't have known anything had happened—at least, until the teachers said something to them. It seemed to her grandparents that Gwyn was fine and did the right thing. And other than some bruised ribs and a sore jaw, she was fine and healthy.

Gwyn hadn't, however, told anyone about the owl she'd met in the tree. Honestly, she wasn't convinced she hadn't dreamed the whole thing.

But the memory of it still stuck with her, nagging at her conscience from somewhere in the back of her mind. She made it a secret and buried it deep in her heart—and there it lived quietly and mysteriously as it had been since the night it happened.

CHAPTER 4
Birthday Surprises

Gwyn's thirteenth birthday came around, and her grandparents decided to have a party for her. Of course, she invited Jack and Chele. She found out that Chele had lost her dad in a construction accident when she was little and now lived with her mom and grandparents.

"We're going to the park!" her grandmother told her. "We have a surprise for you there."

Gwyn grabbed her bow and arrow, but her grandmother asked her to leave it. She did, but it felt weird without it. Her grandfather stayed home to do chores and prepare dinner for when they came back.

The four of them made their way up the hill, past the wishing well and school, and on into the outskirts of Pantheon. Gwyn had been at the entrance to the village many times—it was where the market was. But they walked further still, taking a carriage some way in, her grandmother handing over four golden coins she called denari to the driver. Although it wasn't too cold, there was a definite chill in the air as they boarded.

The carriage ride went on for some time, and Gwyn, Jack, and Chele peered out the windows, looking at all the buildings and houses they had never seen before. The town seemed to grow larger and busier the further they went.

Jack and Chele handed Gwyn a small sack with a bow on it. Inside, she found pink-framed sunglasses with rose-colored lenses. She thanked them and put the glasses on for a bit, but grew tired of the pink hue they gave the world and lifted them to her head.

The road eventually veered off from the market streets and went past a structure that caught all of their attention. It was a large, glowing crystal, at least twelve feet tall, supported by a concrete base. It was an indigo color and glowing, with pink veins of lightning slowly crawling on the surface.

"Grandmother, what is that?" Gwyn asked.

"Well, that's a Xi crystal—they power lights, grinding wheels, and some other things. Without them, the city would be dark at night. Well, we'd be stuck with candles and torches for everything anyway."

Gwyn had heard about Xi crystals in school before but had never seen one and didn't expect it to look so marvelous. She knew they routed some form of connection underground to power lights, mostly. Even their house had a few lights powered by Xi crystal energy, but the sight of it was almost like looking at the Electric Moon to Gwyn. Suddenly, the memory of her own eyes reflecting in the owl's giant, round ones flickered past her mind's eye, and she began to think about that night and what the owl had told her.

The carriage rolled on for some time, but Gwyn said nothing else and sat and thought quietly to herself until it came to a stop. The sudden stop shook her from her thinking, and she and her friends stepped out of the carriage to find a wooden fence around a wonderful, large, colorful playground.

There were swings, bright red teeter-totters, large wooden forts, towers with ropes to swing from, slides and structures built in the shape of animals that you could crawl in. Going to the park was rare for Gwyn and made for a pleasant treat.

But there was also another surprise there: her aunt and uncle, Franz and Delilah. She felt a rush of excitement at seeing them and ran up and hugged each of them.

Her uncle had long, dark hair and wore a white shirt and dark pants with a long, dark leather coat and boots. Delilah wore a white dress with leather boots and a jacket and had blonde hair with thick, wavy curls in it.

Discussions about how fast Gwyn had grown, her learning to shoot a bow, and the mending and hemming her cloak had endured went on for several minutes. Then her grandmother broke the news of her fight, although her account of the story was definitely different from what had actually happened.

"Gwyn got a bit roughed up by some bully. Busted her lip. But she didn't even cry. Lucky for her, when the bully tried to hit her again, she held up her pencil, and he stuck his hand on it."

Gwyn's aunt and uncle looked very concerned, and her uncle put a hand on her shoulder.

"I'm fine. I didn't get hurt," she assured them, feeling a bit embarrassed. Then Gwyn, Jack, and Chele took to the playground.

Her uncle maintained a worried look as he shook his head. "Just want you to be safe."

After some time, Gwyn slid down a large slide and landed close enough to hear her aunt and uncle talking with her grandmother. They were sitting at a picnic table not far from the slide.

"...It's a good time. She is old enough now; it'll be perfect. We'll let you know when we can come get her. It may have to be closer to summer, though."

Her eavesdropping didn't go unnoticed for long, as Delilah soon waved her over. "Come here! We have a gift for you!"

"Okay, hold on. Let me get my friends." Gwyn called Jack and Chele over, and her uncle set a nice, suitcase-shaped box in front of her.

"Well, this is something you'll need to be careful with, although it is very durable," Franz said. "We've given it a lot of thought, but we think it's time for you to have it. And learn it, too, if you want to. Of course."

Gwyn found latches on the side and found the case opened smoothly on hinges. Inside was a beautiful lap harp. The wood was white with some blue and pink lines throughout the grain. It was carefully hand-carved, and the fresh polish on it smelled sweet as the scent of it rose up from the case.

The wood's design was sleek but sturdy and begged to be touched and played.

She lifted it from its case and placed it in her lap. It was lighter than she had expected. She gently swept her fingertips across all of the strings, and the air filled with beautiful, angelic notes.

"Gwyn, that's amazing," Jack said, whose eyes begged to play it.

But Gwyn was not quite ready to share, and she plucked and figured out simple tunes and lullabies from the harp. She plucked a lullaby her grandmother had sung to her as a babe:

Sweetest star
From afar
Can I reach you where you are
To make a wish
I'll blow a kiss
And somehow we can meet again
Someday when that morning comes
Rays in your eyes from the sun
So in that day
When flowers bloom
You'll hold the heart of the moon

Though the song was simple and the notes were few, Gwyn suddenly felt as if the song brought her vision into another world. There were waves of energy swirling around her, and the strings of the harp danced like majestic banners braided and wound with golden lace. Every note went into the air like the waves of an ocean, each tone carrying its own brilliant color. It only lasted for a moment before the voice of Jack startled her back to normality.

"Where did you learn to play that?"

"I... My grandmother sang it to me."

"Oh my dear, you are mistaken," Enna quickly chimed in. "I must say that it's rather beautiful."

"Gwyn... Delilah and I want to tell you something," Franz said. "We'd like to have you up for the summer. There's a school for music near us, and we know someone from it that can teach you how to play—if you want to," her uncle told her.

Gwyn's heart leapt with excitement at the thought. Moving west with her aunt and uncle for a summer? Of course that sounds fun, she thought!

Then her eyes fell on Jack. Then Chele... Suddenly, the idea of having no one to hang out with anymore seemed less exciting, even if it did mean she would learn to play the harp properly.

"I... I'll have to think it over," She said, placing the harp in Jack's hands so he could play it. She thanked her aunt and uncle and took to clapping and singing with Chele as Jack awkwardly figured out notes to songs. After Jack had had his fill, Chele played it for a while as well, then turned it back over to Gwyn.

After spending a good while at the park, Enna insisted that the six of them head up the road for some warm drinks.

A quick walk up the road led to a large place called the Red Cedar Tavern. Inside, the air was filled with the rich aroma of baked bread, coffee, freshly brewed teas and ciders, and honey-roasted nuts.

"Here," Franz said, handing Gwyn a stein of drinking chocolate. "It's a special blend for a growing girl."

Gwyn drank from the stein and felt a warming sensation rush through her. "Wow. What a strange drink."

They each had their fill of roasted nuts, garlicky basil breads and cheeses, and washed it down with hot cocoas, apple ciders, and peach ciders. Chele and Gwyn discovered pumpkin spice and added it to their drinks liberally.

After a time of indulgence, the conversation quickly turned to a more serious topic. "You know, Gwyn, you really do need to be careful," Franz said from across their table, where he was sipping a frothy mug of hot cocoa.

She opened her mouth to respond but then closed it. She knew she'd been misunderstood, but suddenly felt strange. She almost felt sick; however, she also felt a strange sense of strength within her.

"It's not like she did anything wrong," Chele said. "She was helping Jack."

Everyone's eyes turned toward Jack, who was staring into his steaming mug of chocolate. After a moment, he looked up, took a deep breath, and said in an embarrassed tone, "Yeah... She was saving my hide. No one did anything wrong but me—letting Gwyn get hurt."

A look of confusion and surprise crossed her grandmother's face.

Franz lifted his mug of cider and gestured toward Jack. "Well, then, it sounds like something has gotten lost in translation. But it's good for the truth to come out!" he said before taking a drink. "I simply want to know that you're safe, Gwyn. Safety is a priority for things that are precious... and you are, indeed, very precious." With that, he laid a hand over her hand that had been resting on the table. He then looked up at her and smiled—a warm smile that revealed years of crow's feet near his dark brown eyes.

For a moment, Gwyn thought it must be what it feels like to have a father. She stared at the fingerless dark leather glove her uncle wore and admired its craftsmanship. It had finely crafted metal buckles and leather bands that laced the sides... His long fingers engulfed her hand with ease. She then looked up at her uncle and kindly smiled back.

Shortly after they left the Red Cedar Tavern, the carriage returned to take them back home. The driver stepped down from his wooden perch and opened the door for them. They all bid their farewells to Franz and Delilah as they boarded. Delilah managed to pull Gwyn aside just before getting on and dropped down to meet her eye level. "Gwyn, please reconsider and come over next summer. I saw how you didn't want to leave your friends, but I'm going to talk with your uncle and see if we can't have the whole lot of ya! Okay?"

She thought Delilah's words were as sweet as honey. Something in her chest felt lighter hearing that her aunt knew how she felt, and she smiled and nodded. Her aunt kissed her on her forehead and said, "Do be careful, Gwyn."

She hugged her aunt and climbed into the carriage with her harp. She tucked the case under the seat, pulled the window curtain back, and waved goodbye to her aunt and uncle. They smiled and waved until they shrank into the distance.

The sun was now starting to set, and the four of them settled in for the long ride back home.

"Your aunt and uncle are very nice," Chele said to Gwyn. "I've never met any of mine. They live so far away."

"Yeah, Gwyn, you're lucky! That harp must've cost a fortune!" said Jack.

Gwyn smiled, looked at both of them, then to the floor. "Yeah," she agreed, but her mind was somewhere else. She still wasn't feeling quite right, and the thought of moving west kept popping into her head. She wondered if moving had anything to do with what she had overheard her grandparents talking about. She also kept working out ways in her head to make sure Jack and Chele could come, too. But her mind was realistic and also played to the possibility—and likelihood—that they wouldn't be able to go, especially for a whole summer.

Gwyn was consumed with her thoughts and sank deep into them. It wasn't until several minutes later, when Jack said, "Thank you, Gwyn," that she went from blankly staring at the floor to jumping straight up in her seat from the startlement.

"Huh?" She looked up to find Jack looking at her.

"I... wanted to say it properly. Thank you... for saving my butt on the playground. I would've been toast without you."

She wasn't exactly sure why, but her face flushed with embarrassment. She thought about what Chele had said—about him being ashamed to have a girl save him. She figured that if it had taken Jack this long to properly thank her, Chele must've been right.

Had I embarrassed him? She wondered. She never meant to hurt his pride. In fact, she wasn't sure what drove her to do it in the first place, and that left a loophole as far as she was concerned—a loophole that allowed her to claim it wasn't just for him.

"It... It wasn't just for you," Gwyn said out loud. "I did it for myself... and everyone. Matthew deserved it." She hoped saying these things would make Jack feel better.

"Oh..." Jack said, then looked at the floor.

She immediately knew she hadn't helped the situation. "Well... okay. I did do it for you. I just didn't want you to feel like you owed me anything for it, that's all," she added quickly.

Jack lifted his head and smiled.

The cabin of the carriage grew quiet and dark as night fell upon them. They had all closed their eyes and started to fall asleep. Even Grandmother Enna had long since drifted off.

It wasn't until the carriage came to an abrupt stop that they all woke with a startle.

"Whoa! HOO!" they heard the driver yell. Gwyn pulled back the curtains but didn't see anything. She could hear men speaking in low voices.

"There's a toll here tonight, old man—pay up, or we'll take your teeth instead. We hears there's a market for 'em these days."

"We're being robbed!" Jack whispered. Gwyn reached for her bow, but her heart sank to find it wasn't there. A few seconds later, the door swung open, and a masked man holding a lantern stood there. His eyes were dark and lined below the brim of an old hat.

"Good evening, ladies and gents. Please hand over your precious cargo, and we'll be out of your hair in no time," the masked man said in a rough voice, billows of steamed breath puffing from behind his mask. Surprisingly, no one moved as they stared at the robber.

"Fine, we do it the hard way." The masked man grabbed Enna by the wrist and yanked her onto her knees. He then held up a short sword and went to place it to her neck, but Gwyn's mind had snapped. Before she realized what she'd done, she found her foot had kicked the robber's throat, knocking him back. She kicked his hand, sending the blade spinning back to stab his shoulder. He screamed, clutching the wound, and two other masked men ran around to see what had happened.

"That girl!" the wounded robber grunted, pointing at Gwyn. "That girl! She stabbed me! Kill her!"

One of the two masked men reached for Gwyn, but she kicked him in the nose before he could reach her. The kick made a loud crack, and blood poured down the robber's now-broken nose. The blood glistened as it dribbled to the ground in the dim lantern light. The other robber, however, grabbed her ankle and pulled sharply. Gwyn fell and slammed into the carriage floor on her side. She quickly reached under the seat and grabbed her harp case as the robber yanked hard again on her leg, pulling her from the carriage. As she came sliding out, she slammed the harp case into the robber's face, striking his left eye. The case made a loud ringing noise as the robber fell backward. He began screaming, holding his eye and writhed in pain.

Still, after successfully hitting the robber with the harp case, Gwyn slammed into the ground outside the carriage. The fall knocked the breath from her. Her harp again cried as the case hit the ground beside her in the dirt and grass. She quickly managed to get to her feet. She could hear the three robbers moaning and groaning in pain, confused by the counterattacks Gwyn had fearlessly made. She didn't know there was a fourth robber, and as Jack and Chele helped pull her and the harp back into the cabin, the fourth one threw a bottle that struck her above her right temple and shattered. She immediately began hearing a loud ringing, and she felt wetness pouring down the side of her face, dripping onto the floor. She fell to her knees, clutching the wounded side of her head. The driver must have sensed it was a good time to leave and took off at full speed.

She felt hands on her back as she held her pulsing temple. Her head was still ringing louder than anything she could hear, and she wasn't ready to talk yet. She could see in the pale moonlight from the windows that there was a puddle under where she was leaning, but she wasn't certain if it was her blood. She hoped it was the liquid in the bottle that had shattered. A deep breath revealed the reeking smell of whiskey that now filled the cabin.

"Gwyn! Are you alright!?" Enna demanded, asking as if she had asked the question several times before. Gwyn felt her grandmother shake her as she asked the question.

"Yes," Gwyn said with tears in her eyes. She slowly stood up and fell into a hug with Enna. She didn't care if her head hurt or if her ears were ringing. She was happy to have her grandmother alive. That's all.

Gwyn lay there, hugging her grandmother, and silently shed a few tears into her shoulder. She doesn't remember much more than that, other than it being very wet and cold—because she fainted.

When Gwyn woke up, she was back at home, looking at the log ceiling from her bed. Her vision was fuzzy, and her head was slightly feverish, but not nearly as bad as it had been when it rang. Her grandmother was sitting next to the bed, running her fingers through her hair.

"What happened?" Gwyn asked, looking around her room slowly. "How'd I get home?"

Her grandmother was next to the bed, holding her hand. "I'm afraid you fainted. You lost too much blood."

She wondered how long she'd been asleep. Hours? Days? Weeks? She'd heard stories of people falling into comas and missing long periods of time and feared it might have happened to her. She looked at her grandmother to see what she was wearing and saw a giant red blood stain on her shoulder where Gwyn had laid her head.

"That was tonight?" She asked.

Her grandmother smiled and nodded. "It was. Be glad you missed the several hours of panic between now and then. I'm so glad you're back with us now."

Gwyn felt her head and could feel that a bandage had been wrapped around it. "Is it bad?"

"Not anymore. You're all stitched up and ready to get better," her grandmother said with a smile, her eyes a little watery and bloodshot from lack of sleep and too much worry, as mothers often do.

A doctor came into the room with her grandfather and looked Gwyn over. He used a bright Xi light to shine in her eyes and asked her several questions about how she felt before telling her grandparents she'd most likely be fine. "She lost a lot of blood. I'm surprised she's awake."

Gwyn lay back and stared at her ceiling. She thought of the bandit for a moment and how he pulled a blade on her grandmother. She thought of how she reacted—how she bloodied several men without even realizing what she was doing—then decided thinking wasn't the best idea at the moment. "You should go to bed; you look worse than I feel. And don't worry, I had a wonderful time today. Thanks for my birthday." With that, she closed her eyes, felt her grandmother's kiss on her forehead, and fell into a deep sleep.

Her dreams shifted back and forth between armed bandits with swords chasing and fighting her, to playing the harp, to sliding, swinging, and drinking hot cocoa next to the Xi crystal.

CHAPTER 5
Halloween: Enchanting Rumors

It was late afternoon when Gwyn woke up.

The dream she was having was another repeat from the night before, only this time, when she woke, she thought her room had been shaking. She had felt it in her bed... or was it a dream? she wondered.

She carefully sat up, surprised to feel no pain, and made her way to the kitchen. Her grandparents were already awake and had a nice lunch ready to eat. Gwyn sat down at the table and ate small bites from a piece of toast with honey butter on it. She mostly ignored the cinnamon oatmeal and slices of melon on her plate.

Her head felt surprisingly clear. She felt a bit funny wearing a bandage around it, but she figured it best to leave it on for a while.

"Did you sleep well dear?" asked her grandmother.

"Yeah... I guess," she said, speaking quieter than usual for fear it might make her head throb in pain.

Her grandfather, sitting across from her, opened a newspaper. He fiddled with it for a minute, glancing from article to article. "Heard you, uh, took on four ruddy bandits last night... by yourself," he said.

Gwyn swallowed her bite of toast, suddenly wondering if she was going to be punished for what she'd done. In hindsight, it all seemed rather foolish. Attempts to justify what she had done sounded silly in her head.

"George, let her eat. We had a terrible, rough night, and Gwyn had the worst of it," her grandmother said.

"I just wanted to hear it from the kid herself. She don't weigh more than ninety pounds, and that's wet! Hard to believe, that's all," her grandfather said before returning to his paper.

"Well, you know as well as I do, we can expect great things from our little Gwyn here."

Gwyn set her toast down, swallowed, and finally asked a question she'd been afraid to ask for years. "Where are my parents?"

The room went silent, other than the sizzling of a frying pan full of bacon that her grandmother was tending to. After several seconds, she asked again, "Where are my parents?"

George swallowed, looked up from his paper, and said, "Well, Gwyn..." He looked at her grandmother, then back to her. "We... don't know exactly."

She looked down at her buttery toast, picked at a crack in the wooden table, then looked back at her grandfather and asked, "Well... who does know, then?"

Her grandmother let out a sigh, took the pan of bacon from the stove, and set it on a potholder near the end of the table. "Gwyn, we don't really know much," she said, as if it was painful to admit. "Perhaps the ones to ask are your aunt and uncle. They'll be able to tell you a lot more than we can."

Gwyn wasn't happy with the answer, but it left her with a lead. So she simply said, "Okay," and went back to her brunch.

Later that day, Jack and Chele came over to visit. Chele had baked her a pumpkin pie that Gwyn thought tasted wonderful, and Jack brought a rabbit stew that she thought tasted awful. She set the food on the stand next to her bed and they discussed the previous night's events until Gwyn made it clear she didn't feel like it anymore. She then told both of them about the proposition her aunt Delilah had made to her.

Both Chele and Jack were excited, and Gwyn was surprised to find that Chele was certain she'd be able to go. Jack was convinced he could, too, if he could get a letter of consent from Franz and Delilah.

Gwyn also told them about the odd conversation she'd had with her grandparents that morning. Chele suggested that she write a letter to find out, but Jack said it was something to wait and ask in person. Gwyn decided to wait, given the nature of the question, but strongly considered writing as well.

By the next day, her head had healed enough to remove the bandage. She was relieved to find in the mirror that her hair covered the scar. Her grandparents were hesitant to let her go outside to play, so she agreed to stay close to the house and practice her archery.

The scarecrow she used for target practice was looking more like a giant pincushion than a scarecrow when Jack and Chele walked up.

"Sheesh, Gwyn! Give the poor fella a break!" Jack said as he strolled up with his hands in his pockets. He stopped and stood beside her, watching her take her next shot.

"It's about the only thing keeping me sane at the moment. Grandparents have me on house arrest for a couple of days. They wanna make sure I'm healed up before I wander off and hurt myself."

"Is it hard to shoot?" Chele asked, watching her nock another arrow.

"Not really, once you get the hang of it," She replied. "Any news?"

"Looks like I'm good to go next summer," Chele said excitedly.

"Chele, that's great news! Anything from you, Jack?"

"I ran it by the director. Gave me a form for your aunt and uncle to fill out. Said it had to be approved and all that, but I think I'll be good."

Gwyn's heart suddenly felt lighter than it had all day hearing the news. She had seven months, and then she would be learning the harp and living on the West coast with her aunt and uncle along with her best friends for a whole summer. The thought was exciting, like anticipating an upcoming vacation.

Gwyn returned to school after a few days. She wasn't sure how, but rumors of what had happened were already spreading. Some were so accurate that it was scary to hear how close she and her grandmother had come to dying. Others, like before, were wildly unbelievable. One version painted her as a demon that possessed the bandits. Another told of an ancient enchantress with magical powers. And one was so bizarre, she wasn't sure if it was even about her at all, given it had pirates and buried treasure.

Where the rumors started or came from was impossible to tell. Some people hadn't even gotten Gwyn's name right, and the heroine of the story had been changed to Jen.

She did her best to ignore the rumors and focus on her assignments and friends.

One day at lunch, Gwyn was working on an essay about the massive Xi crystal formations throughout the midwestern provinces when Chele sat down across from her.

"Halloween's coming up. I don't know if I'll dress up. I want to, but I don't know what to be." Chele said.

"Well, didn't you say your grandma had an old pumpkin costume?"

"Yeah, but, well that thing's frumpy and smells like the inside of Gammy's shoe."

Jack walked up to the table and sat down next to Chele with a bowl of steaming broth. "Talkin' 'bout Mrs. Tate's soup?"

Gwyn smiled and looked up from her paper. "Funny, Jack. The soup's not that bad. You're just mad because she can halfway cook a stew that doesn't taste like mothballs—hey, there's a thought."

"What? Mothball soup?" Jack asked.

"No, just go as a moth—or your favorite insect or animal."

"Oh!" Jack said. "Halloween costumes. The school's Halloween ball is in a few weeks. Don't freak out or nothin', Chele, but I am planning on going as a ghost!"

Gwyn chuckled, then looked at Chele, hoping she wouldn't be too upset that she had laughed.

"Well, Lord knows you've got practice at it, you pasty prat. If only one could learn to place a bag on a shelf, I'd have recognized that delightfully rabid mess of a face in a heartbeat," Chele said in a surprisingly pleasant tone.

"Mm-hmm," Jack said, placing a mouthful of soup into his mouth, though he stopped mid-chew to shoot a dirty look at Chele, suddenly realizing he'd been insulted. Since his mouth was too full of Mrs. Tate's soup to make a retort, he was forced to settle for a long, disgruntled growl.

Gwyn saw the revelation take place on his face and laughed. "Priceless! Ha! Okay, so what am I going to be, then?" Gwyn lowered her voice and leaned over the table. "I'm really thinking about playing up the rumors and going as an enchantress, but I'm not sure how to dress."

Jack threw his arms up. "Brilliant!" he said, shooting specks of soup across the table. Chele, however, averted her gaze. Her expression became rather blank as she looked away.

"I honestly don't have a clue how to dress for it. I was thinking about having my grandmother make a robe for it. My grandfather has some cool hats, too. Or I could weave a crown out of carnations. They're dying off anyway."

"No," Chele said. "A robe's not bad, but you'll need more than that. Enchantresses are supposed to be powerful and usually beautiful, but dress for battle... according to lore, that is. Try a two-piece with armor—maybe a pointed hat or helm and spiked pauldrons."

"A what?" said Jack.

"A pauldron—shoulder armor. Just come over after school, and I'll draw you a picture."

"Okay, perfect!" Gwyn said. Then they finished lunch and returned to class.

Later that day Gwyn arrived at Chele's house and knocked on the wooden front door. Chele answered and ushered her through the common room to her own. There, Chele had a large drawing board. On it, she'd drawn a marvelous picture of a woman wearing unique outfits crafted for movement and battle. They were made of what appeared to be a spiky, leathery two piece that worked into a long skirt with a slit up the side. The top part connected to a pointed piece of armor that covered her left shoulder.

"Wow, Chele. Did you draw this?"

Chele nodded, smiling shyly.

"It's impressive. Where did you get the idea from?"

Chele looked down and off to the side. She grabbed her left arm with her right. "Well... there are books... at the library. I know it's weird, but I read them sometimes."

"That's not weird, Chele. Besides, it looks incredible. A little more skin than I'd like to show, but incredible."

"I could tone down the design a bit. It's just what I remembered seeing," Chele said, then quickly added, "in the books."

"That would be perfect. It should be easy for my grandmother to make. She's got quite a bit of spare material from when she had the tailor shop in town."

Chele revamped the drawing and handed it to her to take to her grandmother. Gwyn showed her grandmother the drawing that evening, and she began taking measurements and picking out colors for it.

Halloween came, and Gwyn, Chele, and Jack met up by the old wishing well to walk to the ball together. Jack was true to his word and dressed up as a ghost; Chele had dressed up as an angel, which went well with her light blonde hair; and Gwyn went as an enchantress with a large staff. Her grandmother had made a nice two-piece costume with a medieval look.

"I feel ridiculous."

"Don't Gwyn! You look great!" said Chele.

"Why woo woo wheel wawicwoowess?" Jack mumbled through his ghost costume.

"Uhh, what?" Gwyn asked.

Jack struggled awkwardly for a moment, then pried the headpiece from his ghost costume off and gasped for air. "Forgot to cut a mouth hole in this thing. I can't breathe! Put loads of stuffing in the head to make it puff out more."

Chele rolled her eyes, then reached down and pulled a knife from her boot. Both Gwyn and Jack watched as she took the ghost headpiece, rammed the knife through where the mouth hole should be, and twisted the blade to widen the hole. "There," she said as she gave it back to him.

"Holy cow! Since when did you carry that!?" Jack asked.

"Since the run-in with those bandits. My mom said it would be wise to learn to defend myself. The knife itself goes back several generations in our family." She held it up to show Gwyn and Jack. It was about half a foot long with a silver blade and a white, round, pearly handle. Gwyn thought it looked majestic.

A chill blew through the fall air as they made their way to the Halloween ball.

The church had a large reception hall in the back. The room was lit with candles and decorated with jack-o'-lanterns. There was plenty of punch and snacks, and after they'd had their fill, they sat at a table in a corner.

The three sat down and watched as several couples danced to songs played by a live band from the inner city of Pantheon. Gwyn received several freaked-out looks from people as they passed by, knowing her costume fed into some of the rumors.

"I got a letter back from your aunt and uncle today," Jack said.

"Oh! Pray tell!" Gwyn asked.

"Took the form straight to the director. He said I'm officially orphanage-free for next summer!" Jack threw his fist in the air, then played an air guitar for a moment.

Chele smiled and rolled her eyes. "Try not to wet yourself with excitement, will you?"

Gwyn spewed the drink of punch she'd just taken and clutched her side laughing.

"Lay off, will you! I've never lived outside of the orphanage."

Gwyn suggested they make a round of trick-or-treating, and the three of them each slowly filled a pillowcase full of sweets. They then strolled through her grandparents' pumpkin patch, each of them picking out a pumpkin.

Afterward, they returned to Chele's. Gwyn and Jack carved a jack-o'-lantern while Chele used an extra one to make a pumpkin pie. She also baked the seeds, which they ate and spat off the back porch until late into the night. There, they told ghost stories until Chele turned pale and discussed the exciting summer they had to look forward to.

It was the best Halloween Gwyn had ever had.

After Halloween, Gwyn, Jack, and Chele focused mainly on their studies at school. Gwyn played her harp a bit in her free time but was excited about going to a school to learn it properly come summer. She had already figured out how to play a lullaby called Twilight's Kiss. It was a very old song—one her grandmother used to sing to her at night:

Winter never felt like this
Summer's warmth can leave a hint
Spring and Fall come closest yet
To the gentle touch, of twilight's kiss

The notes rang beautifully out of the harp when she played it, but she still wasn't confident enough to show anyone yet. She had found a place at a bend in the creek where she enjoyed practicing. No one seemed to know she went there to practice, and it was private and peaceful to her.

The next holiday came: a day of giving thanks. They celebrated mostly at Chele's house. Franz and Delilah also came, though a bit later than everyone else.

There was so much food on the table that there was hardly room for plates. Chele and her mom had baked pies, custards, stuffings, rolls, potatoes, pumpkin bread, jams, apple butter, fluffy pink stuff, casseroles, puddings, two chickens, and a ham. All of the families had pitched in to pay for the food, and Jack and Gwyn had caught and sold fish in Pantheon's market to help as well.

It was a feast, and everyone stuffed themselves liberally.

Afterward, they all played games til they ached miserably and had to rest.

Franz and Delilah made their goodbyes and then made their way to the horses they had ridden in on. Delilah waved Gwyn over as they were preparing to leave.

"What is it?" she asked.

"You have to promise to wait until Christmas, okay?" Delilah said as Franz pulled a long package out from the trunk of their carriage.

Gwyn's eyes widened as she nodded. Whatever was in the package, she knew would be amazing. She hugged and kissed her aunt and uncle, then waved goodbye as they rode off.

Winter came and cast a thick layer of fluffy snow onto the ground. Gwyn counted the days left before Christmas and waited anxiously to open the package, often staring at it as she rolled a copper coin over her knuckles.

Several times, she caught herself almost opening it. She just couldn't wait! But she did, anticipation growing with every day.

Finally, Christmas Eve arrived, and Gwyn had Chele and Jack over for the night. Gwyn's grandparents had signed a form to allow it for Jack. They decorated a tree, sang ancient carols, and drank hot cocoa.

By night, Gwyn's anticipation had grown even more. She squeezed her fists with excitement. She had hardly slept when the sunlight peeked in through her window.

She got up in such a hurry that she almost forgot to wake Jack and Chele up as she ran to the living room. Once there, she grabbed the package and tore the pretty wrapping open, revealing a long wooden case. She unlatched it at both ends, lifted a side, and revealed a beautiful white recurve bow. It was the most beautiful and majestic-looking bow she had ever seen.

Gwyn gasped and jumped back a few inches at the first sight of it.

"Whoa!" Jack said, unable to keep from gawking at it.

Chele also stared at the bow expressing awe on her face.

"I've never seen such a nice bow," Gwyn said, and she slowly slipped her fingers underneath it, as if she were holding a newborn baby for the first time.

She ran outside with her quiver, drew an arrow and released it. The arrow swiftly stuck into the head of the scarecrow, knocking a layer of snow loose from it as it rocked back and forth.

The bow was not only beautiful but shot better than any bow Gwyn had shot before. The string was taut, yet easy to draw and smooth to release. She put three more arrows into the scarecrow's head, all within a couple of inches of each other.

"Wow, Gwyn, that's amazing. You're making me wanna shoot," said Chele.

She let Chele and Jack have their turns with the bow, but neither of them was nearly as skilled with it as Gwyn was.

They finished exchanging gifts before making a snowman to use as target practice until it disintegrated from the abuse.

Jack and Gwyn had gone together and gotten Chele a set of throwing knives. She impressed both of them when she showed them she could hit the scarecrow almost every time from roughly twenty feet away.

Gwyn and Chele gave Jack a nice warm hat and a pair of gloves, but Gwyn told him he could use her old bow now that she had this one as well. It was indeed a merry Christmas.

The holiday break lasted nearly two months because of the snow.

Gwyn and Jack designed an arrow that allowed them to shoot fish by tying a fishing line onto an arrow so they could pull the arrow back after shooting it.

They broke a hole in the ice on the creek and shot several fish. It took a while for Gwyn to figure out how to shoot something in the water, but she soon became a dead aim. The snow on the ground allowed them to stock up several fish before taking them to the market to sell. Barney the Butcher bought all of them at a good price. He joked they made good defense weapons against bandits, poking around the air with 'em like swords.

Chele used the fishing string on a throwing knife to some success as well. Although she had to learn how to pierce the fish just right, or it would cut it in half. She liked the idea so much that she braided a rope out of the nylon string and started practicing throwing the knife, then pulling it back by the string and catching it by the handle.

Gwyn suggested that she put a sheath on the blade until she got better. It was good that she did, too, because Chele caught the knife by the blade end several times at first, but soon figured out how to pull it back and catch it by the handle. The three of them made a small fortune fishing and hunting small game that winter.

"Twenty-two gold denari! I've never seen so much money in my life!" Jack said as they walked home from the market.

"We're pretty much the only ones around with fresh fish right now," Gwyn replied.

"We'd have more if you hadn't given some away," Jack said.

"The Stricklands had a hard crop this year. They're good people. I'm glad we helped them," Chele said.

"Yeah... I'm sorry. I'm getting all greedy with all of this money. I know better than anyone what it's like to starve out a winter," Jack said.

Gwyn and Chele gave five gold pieces each to their families and split the rest.

When winter passed and school began again, they had all taken up the skill of crafting arrows. They were a bit expensive to buy, and once they got the hang of it, not too hard to make. Grandfather George showed them how to make sure an arrow was straight using heat and how to fletch feathers to help stabilize them.

Gwyn and Jack practiced archery every day, as Chele practiced knife throwing alongside them. Chele had set up a wooden target next to the scarecrow in the crop field. She had become quite impressive with her throw-and-return technique. She had even added to it by pulling the knife back and sending it to the target again without even touching the blade.

Jack showed her a strong braid he knew that allowed the line to flex a bit more but made it stronger.

After they practiced, Gwyn, Jack, and Chele worked on the crops. They planted melons, tomatoes, potatoes, sunflowers, corn, and several types of herbs and peppers.

CHAPTER 7
Journey to the Farm

wyn was largely busy with school and chores during early spring. When she had the time, she would practice her archery or hang out with her friends.

Her new bow had taken her archery skills to a new level altogether. She had also learned a bit of Chele's knife-throwing techniques, though by April, Chele was far more impressive with them.

Gwyn had asked her grandparents a few more questions about her parents, but they never had an answer aside from saying they didn't know and it wasn't their place to say. She even asked her grandmother how she could not know what happened to her own child, and which of her parents was their son or daughter. But her grandmother did not answer. Instead, she turned and walked away with tears in her eyes, saying, "I'm so sorry."

She felt frustrated and confused and didn't like seeing her grandmother cry, so she stopped asking. She had taken every private opportunity to look through old drawers and cabinets for any information about her parents but could not find anything—not a single clue as to who or where they were. No pictures. No letters. No baby books. In fact, Gwyn actually found a few pictures of herself when she was very young, but she was with her grandparents—no mom or dad to be found in them.

One day, as she was searching through an old hope chest in her grandmother's bedroom, a sudden thought went through Gwyn's mind—a 'what if' kind of question that begged to be answered: What if she had been adopted? Had her grandparents played the part of mom and dad, perhaps because they looked too old to be parents?

"That doesn't make sense," said Jack after she explained her theory to him. "Why wouldn't they just say if that were the case? Besides, what do they have to hide? I mean, so what if you were adopted?"

"Maybe they got embarrassed because of their age," Chele said.

"It's a possibility, but it still doesn't make sense not to tell you," Jack replied. "Who cares if you don't have parents, Gwyn? I don't either, but it's not a big deal."

Gwyn shrugged and kept her head down as the three of them walked home from school. Once home, she marked her calendar, crossing off the current day. She was another day closer to the summer, which started mid-May.

April passed slowly, and May finally came. Gwyn received a letter from Franz and Delilah, telling them that they would pick them up at noon on the first Saturday after school let out—which was in a couple of weeks.

The three finished their final exams for school, packed their trunks for the summer, and, when Saturday came, waited at Gwyn's grandparents' house.

Noon arrived, and as the clock began to ring, a knock rapped on the door. Gwyn ran to it, opened it, and there stood her uncle. After exchanging welcoming hugs, Franz loaded the trunks into the back of a horse-drawn carriage, then, once everyone was seated, took the reins, and off they went.

This carriage was half-covered and quite different from the one they had ridden in for Gwyn's birthday. At first, the discussion was lively as they told stories of what they had done over the last several months. Gwyn didn't brag much about her skills with a bow but did tell her uncle how amazing her new bow was.

Several hours passed, and things grew quiet for hours inside the carriage. They stopped to take a short break and eat some sandwiches Gwyn's grandmother had packed for them, then continued their lengthy trip, going far west and slightly north.

It was after seven in the evening when they finally reached a set of tracks that were barely visible, veering off from the main road. Franz steered the carriage down the decline where the tracks led and followed them into some trees. The tracks looped around a couple of times through the trees, getting very dark at times, then suddenly exited into a large opening where a stone house sat. It was a good-sized house, and there was a large barn slightly down the hill from it, a large silo by the tree line, a few plowed crops, and some other small buildings likely used for storing tools or possibly a well.

The large open field looked as if it were completely surrounded by trees. The land itself was almost flat, but there was a bit of a rolling texture toward the middle behind the house.

"Let's go in, shall we?" Franz suggested.

Franz helped unload the trunks and led them inside. There, Delilah stood. She had already been preparing dinner, and the delicious smell of it filled the air. She was smiling and went straight up to Gwyn to hug her. She felt the warmth from her apron and could smell delicious foods on it.

The inside of the house was fairly normal. A piano, a fireplace, a painting of a man with a beard, and a few lit candles were placed about the living area. Gwyn sat on a green couch, and Delilah poured them tea and brought them biscuits and muffins to snack on before dinner.

After formal discussions had passed, Delilah quizzed Gwyn about what happened with the bandits, her friends helping recall the details.

"Do you remember when you lost control of your actions?" she asked.

"Well..." she thought about it for a bit. "I guess when I thought Grandmother was in danger."

Delilah gave Franz a knowing look. "Gwyn, do you remember everything you did?"

"Uh, well, err, kind of. I remember it, but it's a strange kind of memory—like I'm watching it happen and not exactly doing it. But at the same time, I am doing it. I mean to and all; it's just weird."

"Well, honey," Delilah said, then laid her hand on Gwyn's. "At least it's all over now. And if it weren't for what you did, there's no telling what would have happened." Delilah stood up and said, "It's time for dinner!" and they joined at the table.

The food was delicious. Gwyn had never eaten Delilah's cooking before and was now wondering why. She had potatoes with fresh herbs and cheese in them, a steak that was cooked to perfection with a perfect balance of seasoning, several fruits and steamed vegetables, fresh honey rolls, and plenty of teas—both iced and hot—to wash it down with.

CHAPTER 8
Sleepless

After dinner, they all made their way to bed. Franz and Delilah slept in a room across from Chele and Gwyn, while Jack slept in a bed in an annex that had been built outside the kitchen in the back. The annex had several windows, including a few on the ceiling, and a tile floor, but the bed was quite comfortable, and the view of the night sky was outstanding.

Gwyn and Chele's room had two twin-sized beds, a sewing machine, several bookcases, a desk, and a large chest. The carpet was a lime green but very soft. Gwyn didn't know why, but she felt extremely comfortable and fell asleep very quickly. The pale moonlight shone through her window onto her face, but she was in too deep a sleep to notice it.

The next morning, Gwyn woke up very early to the smell of bacon. She went to the kitchen and found everybody awake and sitting at the table. She sat and began spreading jelly on a piece of toast.

"Sleep well, Gwyn?" Delilah asked.

"Yes, ma'am, thank you," she replied.

"Gwyn, your first lesson will start today. Your teacher will be here in an hour," Franz told her.

"An hour?" she asked, then hurried through breakfast and went to get ready.

She wasn't sure what to expect, but before she knew it, an hour had passed, and she heard a knock on the door. "Hello, Mrs. Benadine!" a voice said from another room. She grabbed her harp and ran to join them.

"Oh, Kathrine, this is our niece, Gwyn," Franz said, gesturing to her.

"Nice to meet you," Gwyn said with a nervous smile.

"The pleasure's all mine, Miss Gwyn. Well, off we go. We'll be back in time for lunch," said Mrs. Benadine.

The harp teacher led Gwyn to the edge of the woods, where a stone path lay. She followed, and they made small talk about the grass and weather. They came to a dry stone fountain filled with leaves and sat on a stone bench near it. No one was around, and the atmosphere was genuinely peaceful. The weather itself was sunny and warm with a gentle breeze.

Distant waves could be heard rolling far off in the distance, but other than that and a few birds and insects, the place was fairly quiet.

Mrs. Benadine had her take out her harp and began showing her the basics of it: the pedestal, the tuning pins, the sound box, the pillar, how to hold it, and how to tune it were all part of her first lesson. She found it surprising that her harp hadn't fallen out of tune, and Mrs. Benadine told her how lovely the harp was.

"Consider this a precursor to class, Miss Gwyn," Mrs. Benadine told her.

After a couple of hours, Mrs. Benadine led her back to the stone house, ate a quick lunch, and left.

"How was it?" Jack asked.

"Good. There's a lot more to it than I thought, but I had fun."

"That's good," said Chele. "I hope you remember enough to show us."

"I will. I have to practice soon, though. It's a lot to learn."

She tried to practice the few scales Mrs. Benadine had shown her, but with Jack and Chele there, it was hard to focus. Mrs. Benadine instructed her to practice for at least a couple of hours a day so she could be prepared to learn more at the next lesson.

The day passed, and Gwyn found she had played more games than she had ever played in her life. She hadn't thought to pick up the harp for even a minute since she'd put it down that afternoon.

Nighttime fell, and they ate another delicious meal of honey-crisped chicken and rolls, then went to bed. Only tonight, Gwyn couldn't sleep.

Shining through her window were the indigo beams of the Electric Moon. She found herself staring at it through the window and thought of the owl. She looked at her harp case sitting on the bedside table, sat up, put on her cloak, grabbed the case and her bow, and tiptoed quietly out the back.

She made her way onto the trail going through the woods, past the dry fountain and up the trail—the pathway fading as it carved farther into the woods.

She could hear water crashing in the distance as she continued toward it. Soon, the trees opened up, and in front of her was an incline. She walked to the high point and found herself overlooking a spectacular view of an endless ocean.

The sound she'd heard came from rolling waves crashing into cliff walls all around. The ridge she was on, however, went much higher than the cliffs around her.

She knelt in the soft grass, her green cloak draping around her, unlatched the harp case, and pulled the instrument out. She closed her eyes and strummed the harp. The notes echoed and bounced off cavern walls from below. They kissed the ocean's surface and the edge of the forest, returning to Gwyn with a rich and beautiful sound.

She found herself staring up at the Electric Moon as she practiced, still comforted by it, the same as before.

As she finished playing, she looked down for the first time and saw curvy symbols in the wood had appeared. They glowed a silvery indigo color. Gwyn studied them and tried to read them, but they didn't spell anything she could understand.

She pried herself from examining the symbols, put her harp away, and made her way back to the stone house. Once there, she snuck back through the kitchen and into bed, where she could see Chele still fast asleep.

She stared at the harp case from her bed and drifted off to sleep.

In the morning, she took out her harp and examined it, but the symbols were gone. She couldn't figure out why they had appeared or what had happened to them. She thought maybe it was too bright to see them and took the harp into the closet, but still, no symbols appeared.

The day went on like the previous one, and Gwyn found herself flying kites, throwing Frisbees, and gathering food from the gardens but didn't find much time alone to practice.

She found she rather enjoyed sneaking out to practice but only did it every other day during the phase of the Electric Moon. She found she felt more awake and aware in the electric moonlight. Again, when she was done running through her scales, the symbols glowed on the harp. She couldn't figure out why, but she was very interested in them.

She hadn't told Chele or Jack about the symbols because she would have to admit that she was sneaking off to be alone. Gwyn actually kind of enjoyed the secrecy of it, and the privacy was helping her to improve greatly on her scales.

Her second lesson came, and Mrs. Benadine showed Gwyn how to properly play Twilight's Kiss. It was a fairly simple song, but when played with all the notes, it took a bit of practice before the timing and accuracy sounded right.

Gwyn snuck out again that night to practice in front of the Electric Moon. She felt a bit more careless in her sneaking, though, as her excitement about practicing a new song drove her to get to the high ridge's overlook quicker. She used leather straps to secure her cloak, preventing wind from blowing it into the harp while keeping her warm. She then knelt in the grass, laid her bow down next to her, and took out her harp.

She strummed and plucked away at the new fingerings, listening to the rich melody flow out and carry through the warm, salty air.

After several minutes of practice, Gwyn heard a noise from behind her. It was large and came from a bush on the lower part of the ridge's incline.

Gwyn knew there were several species of dangerous animals that lived in the woods and quickly grabbed her bow.

She drew an arrow from her quiver, nocked it, and pulled back the string. The second she had the arrow drawn, though, she felt something she'd never felt before. The end of the arrow was glowing and getting brighter. Her fingers tingled, and it felt as if cold air were dancing around them.

The odd sensation shocked her, and just as Jack emerged from the bush and said, "Don't shoot!" she let the arrow go.

The arrow soared in a beam of bright light, missing Jack by inches, leaving his left ear covered in frost, and flew off into the woods behind him. A flash, then a crack and shattering sound, came from the woods, followed by loud crackling noises.

"Are you alright?" Gwyn asked Jack.

Jack was holding his left ear and had a sincere look of fear on his face. "You... missed?"

Gwyn rolled her eyes, moved quickly past him, and headed into the forest in the direction the arrow had flown. A dozen yards in, she saw a shimmering view of a very large tree, large enough that it would take three or four Gwyns holding hands to wrap around it. As she came closer, she heard Jack behind her. "Whoa!"

She could tell why the tree was shimmering; it was completely covered in a layer of ice. The tree's limbs were making a creaking sound, and she could hear the ice crackling all over it.

"We'd probably better not step under it. The limbs might fall," Gwyn told Jack.

"Right," Jack said, still holding his left ear.

"Did it hit your ear?"

"No, I don't think so. But it got really cold—like it was burning, it was so cold."

Gwyn grabbed Jack's hand and moved it from his ear, finding it had suffered from frostbite.

"Gwyn... how did you do that?"

Gwyn opened her mouth to reply, but a large snap came from the tree, and a large limb hit the ground, sending frozen shards of ice in every direction. She pulled her cloak over Jack and herself just in time to take the sharp shards of ice to her back. Only a few were able to pierce through the cloak and didn't do much more than stab slightly into her back.

"Let's get out of here," Jack said, and they made their way back to the overlook.

"Gwyn, talk to me. Tell me what's going on here," Jack demanded, with a look of terror on his face.

She turned toward the ocean and stepped up to the edge of the overlook then down onto a ledge of stone. She watched the Electric Moon shining over the ocean, then peered straight down. The drop-off at the edge was at least a hundred feet to the water. She drew an arrow from her quiver and set it on her bow. She pointed it far off toward the ocean and slowly drew the string. As she pulled the string back, the arrow began to glow again, like before; only this time, Gwyn could see symbols on the bow itself, just like on her harp.

She pulled back fully and let the arrow whiz through the air like a shooting star. It flew fast and far over the ocean, and when it struck the water, there was a slight flash of silver where it splashed. They watched and listened as a round spot in the water froze over.

"Gwyn," a soft voice said from behind them. "Don't shoot, Gwyn, it's me, Chele."

Chele made her way up the overlook and stood next to Gwyn. Chele's face had a few small drops of blood on it.

"How'd you guys find me?" Gwyn asked.

"Jack said you'd been sneaking out. He watched where you were going. He tapped on the window and was going to meet me near the edge of the forest, but I guess you guys found each other first."

"Sorry, Chele," Jack said. "Tried to get too close and she busted me."

It took a minute of explaining to catch Chele up, and Gwyn demonstrated with another arrow into the ocean what had happened.

"What happened to your face, Chele?" asked Jack.

"I'm guessing she got too close to a certain tree," Gwyn replied.

"Ice shards did that?" Jack said. "But, Gwyn! Your back must be..."

"Don't worry, my cloak protected me."

Chele pulled back her thin, dark red hood and revealed a few more small cuts on her head. "It was so beautiful—that shimmering tree in the moonlight. I wanted to see it up close. Then a branch fell, and ice shot everywhere like pieces of glass... I protected my eyes with my hands." Chele held up her hands, revealing they had small cuts on them, too.

Gwyn let Chele and Jack shoot the bow, but nothing happened.

"We need to get Chele cleaned up," Gwyn said.

"There's a well behind the barn. Takes a bit of time to prime it, but it works," Jack said.

They cleaned Chele up behind the barn and snuck back inside.

Gwyn lay awake in bed with her hands behind her head, staring at the ceiling.

"Gwyn, are you awake?" Chele asked.

"Yeah," she said softly back to her.

"You know, I've never seen anything like that before."

"...Me either." Gwyn looked down toward the wall at the end of her bed, staring at dancing shadows from moonlight coming through a bush outside.

"Gwyn... You're really something great."

Gwyn thought about how to respond for a moment, then decided a simple "Thanks" was proper.

The next morning, Jack and Chele pulled her outside immediately after breakfast and had her shoot her bow. The arrow flew with intense accuracy but did not glow and did not freeze the tree trunk it struck.

"What the flip is going on!?" Jack asked, starting to get a little impatient.

"She doesn't know Jack," Chele said.

"Well, who does? This isn't freaking normal, is it!?"

"Lay off, Jack! She's just as confused as we are. Right, Gwyn?"

But Gwyn didn't answer. Instead, she shouldered her bow and went straight inside, where Franz was sitting, opening mail in the study next to the living room.

"Where are my parents?" Gwyn asked.

Franz stopped opening the letter halfway through and bit his lower lip as he looked at Gwyn. He took a deep breath and gestured for her to sit down as he ran a hand through his dark hair.

"Gwyn..." he took another long breath, now looking a little less composed. "What I'm going to tell you isn't going to be easy."

"I don't care anymore. I just want to know."

Franz gave a small shrug. "Okay, then." He took his pipe, struck a match, and lit it, puffing out gray plumes of smoke from the side of his mouth. The smell from it was sweet, like vanilla, and didn't make Gwyn cough like other smoke had. "Gwyn... your parents died a long time ago," her uncle said with a look of sadness in his eyes.

Gwyn's heart sank as he spoke the words she'd feared were true. She had known it was the likely answer, but thought facing it would be worth knowing; yet now, knowing was heavy and sad. A single tear rolled down Gwyn's cheek as she crossed her arms and stared at the floor.

"Gwyn, if you don't want to hear about it, just say so."

Part of Gwyn didn't want to now, but she was already here, so she would hear what she could. "No, I want to know," she said, still staring at the floor.

Franz nodded and took another puff from his pipe. "A decade ago, your mother, Selena, ruled over the Northern Kingdoms." Franz's eyes drifted upward as he recalled the memory. "She was beautiful, Gwyn. She looked a lot like you—the hair, the eyes, the nose." Franz looked down. "Something happened to her, Gwyn. She became, well, as your father put it, 'not well.'"

Gwyn looked up for the first time since Franz had started speaking and made eye contact. "'Not well'?"

"Yes. She was very powerful, and many people feared her. Of course, she also had some very powerful items." Franz drew another puff and watched as Gwyn processed what he was saying. "Gwyn, your mother..."

"My mother what?" Gwyn demanded.

Franz looked to the side, took another puff, then continued. "Your father asked that we watch over you from a distance."

Gwyn furrowed her brow. "What? Why? Why not raise me here?"

Franz shook his head and looked down. "He didn't want you here, Gwyn. He wanted you far away from... this."

"Far away from what? I don't get it."

Franz took a deep breath and made piercing eye contact with Gwyn. "Ok... Magic," he said softly, lifting a hand to explain while looking around.

Gwyn uncrossed her arms and sat up straight. "Then it is true—magic?"

"Well—Yes." Franz replied, puffing from his pipe again.

Gwyn fidgeted for a second, then took her bow from her shoulder. "This bow... is it?" Gwyn looked down at the marvelous bow.

Franz nodded. "It was your mother's."

"And the harp?"

Franz nodded again. "Also the cloak. All of them, items your father left you."

Gwyn looked at her cloak that she had always loved, and another tear rolled down her cheek as she realized that her parents' love had been wrapped tightly and securely around her for years.

"What happened to my father?" Gwyn asked.

Franz set his pipe down, then turned to Gwyn. "It's a sad and bizarre story—one that I only have theories to fully explain."

"Your father came here about twelve years ago. I had known your father for a very long time, even before he became king of the Western Kingdoms."

Franz looked to Delilah, who'd walked in for a moment, then back to Gwyn. "He overextended himself. I found him near the cliffs and brought him back here... where he passed shortly after."

Gwyn gave a confused look, then asked, "What? He overextended what?"

Franz sighed. "It's kind of complicated to explain."

Gwyn shrugged. "So?"

"Well, think of it this way: imagine working very hard, using every ounce of energy you had but kept going. Eventually, your body breaks. Now imagine if you were to extend and stretch your spirit's energy the same way."

Gwyn sat up, eager to hear what her uncle was explaining. "You can do that?"

"Yes. Well, your father could. He was a wizard of the light. He could absorb a physical blow by extending or projecting his qi and spirit into a shield. It's rare to do well. But if someone takes too much damage too fast from it..."

Gwyn listened closely, trying to follow along. To finally hear details about everything was exciting, but to hear about her father dying in a bizarre and mysterious way, doing things she'd never heard of, was a bit harder to process.

"Well, I guess you could say he overdid it... used too much energy too fast. Does that make sense?"

"Kind of. What did he do to overextend himself?"

Franz shook his head. "I don't know. Your father was extremely strong, so whatever—or whoever—it was must have been powerful."

"What do you think happened, then?"

Franz stared at the seat next to Gwyn for a minute, then shook his head. "I don't know. Besides, you've heard enough for one day."

"But I want to know. I'm fine. I can handle it."

Franz sat quietly for a moment, then gestured toward the door. "Enough. We'll finish talking it over at a different time." And he turned back to his letters.

Gwyn went outside and found Chele and Jack on the hill, talking and practicing their archery and knife-throwing at the range they'd set up near the hay barn. Gwyn avoided their attention as she headed for the trail in the woods. She found herself at the fountain of leaves and sat on a stone bench.

She peered down the path toward the ocean and imagined her father there, where she'd spent the last several nights practicing her harp.

CHAPTER 9
Silvania

Gwyn had wished for so long to learn more about her parents. The thing she feared might be true did indeed end up being true: her parents were no longer part of the world she lived in. What she hadn't expected was how deep the loss felt within her. It was much harder to accept than she had anticipated.

She spent the next several days walking through the woods in silent thought. She didn't practice her harp, nor shoot her bow. She did still go out at night under the Electric Moon to sit on the edge of the cliff, though she hardly snuck anymore, not caring to be as quiet.

After a week of mourning, she came into the study where Franz and Delilah were. "I want to visit them."

Franz and Delilah stopped mid-conversation and looked at Gwyn. Her aunt shook her head in confusion. "Who?"

"My parents. I would like to visit their graves—where they're buried."

Franz sat up in his chair and placed a hand on his chin. "Well, I suppose you could visit your father. It's a bit of a trip, but we could go tomorrow if you'd like."

"And what about my mother?"

Her uncle looked a bit stuck for words, then frowned and shook his head.

"No one knows where your mother's buried, honey," Delilah said. "It's rumored she was, well, taken by her enemies. The Northern Kingdoms have been unsafe for a decade now. Even if there were a place built in her honor there, we could be killed on the journey."

Gwyn looked down for a moment, then back up to her uncle. "Then my father it is." She got up and left. She couldn't explain why she felt the way she did, but it had taken her a week just to start talking to her friends again.

"You just need closure," Jack assured her. "You know, once you see 'em gone, it'll probably be just like before!"

But Gwyn wasn't certain she could ever feel as she did before. She was now carrying more than just a bow, cloak, and harp; the items that already meant so much to her were now heirlooms—the last physical remnants from her forgotten and hidden past.

Franz and Delilah woke Gwyn, Chele, and Jack very early for the trip to visit Gwyn's father. Once awake, Gwyn's heart raced at the thought of going to visit him. Chele and Jack fell asleep in the carriage, but Gwyn did not. Though she wasn't trying to, she paid close attention to the course they had taken to get there.

When they arrived at the city's border, the road widened, shifting from gravelly dirt to smooth gray stones. Large buildings began to pop up along the way. The farther they went, the nicer the buildings became. Then a large stone wall to their right started to emerge. It climbed higher and higher as they made their way deeper into the city until it was well over a dozen feet tall. They passed town squares bustling with crowds, fountains that shot water into the air, and a very large Xi crystal—much larger than the one they had seen before in Pantheon.

The wall to their right stretched alongside the road, with shops occasionally built into it. Ahead, they could make out a very large silhouette on the horizon that grew bigger as they got closer. Soon, it became clear; it was a castle—a very large castle with enormous flags flown from watchtowers. A large violet flag with a golden shield on it flew from the middle of three pointed towers at the top.

Gwyn stared in awe as the sight of the city was far more interesting than any she had seen before. "What is this place?"

"Silvania," Delilah said over her shoulder.

Jack and Chele had woken up and were both peering around.

"What about my father? What was his name?"

"King Cassius Sterling," Delilah told her.

"So my last name's Sterling?"

Delilah looked back at Gwyn, then at Franz, then back to her. "Well, yes."

Gwyn smiled, finding herself fond of the name. "It's nice. I like it!"

The road curved slightly left and came upon a large closed drawbridge behind a gate to the castle. Between the gate and the drawbridge was a very large stone structure, beautifully set for viewing in what appeared to be the entryway to the castle.

The carriage stopped, and Gwyn rushed out to the gate. She tried to open it, but it was locked. She tried to squeeze through the bars, but they were far too close together to fit. Finally, she stopped to read the sign on the gate:

Here Lies King Cassius Cato Charles Ed Sterling.
Finest and last Ruler of Silvania.
It is believed his rule was nearly for 1,000 Years.

"Is that possible?" Gwyn asked Franz. "A thousand years?"

Franz looked down and spoke softly, so only she could hear. "Very."

Gwyn held the gates and stared at her father's tomb. "I want to go in."

"Honey, we can't," Delilah said.

"Why not?"

"Because it's guarded. We could die just getting through the gate."

"But I don't see any guards," Chele said.

"No," Franz said, shaking his head. "No guards. Magic. King Sterling set up a protective barrier of magic around the entire kingdom, especially the east border where we are. If anyone crosses the wrong area, they die instantly. The castle has been vacant since he died because of it. It would take a powerful Auric to see it."

Gwyn let her gaze fall to the ancient stones that paved the road. She had hoped that seeing her father's tomb would bring closure to part of her, but it had left her wanting more instead. She wanted to touch the tomb, speak with her father closer, and tell him thank you and...

"Gwyn," said a small voice upon the wind. It was ghostly and calming, and Gwyn felt her mind slipping to its echoes. She closed her eyes and saw a white light appearing in the distance. The light grew stronger and stronger until she couldn't keep her eyes on it without tightly squinting. "Gwyn..." the voice said again.

"Yes?" Gwyn tried to say. But her jaw was heavy, and her voice was much harder to use than she had expected. Still, she tried again. "Who is it?" she managed to say hoarsely.

"Gwyn... You, must, take, it, back..." The words echoed and trembled within her mind.

"Take... what back?" Gwyn managed to ask, feeling her throat grow hoarser with every word. The light in the distance now had a face somewhere in it, but it was almost invisible, and the air itself seemed to be trying to remove it from the light.

"Take... what is yours... from the tomb."

Gwyn knew now what she must be hearing, what she was seeing. It was her father's voice. It was her father's face. Who else could it be? He had left her a message, and she was here to receive it. She tried to lift her arms to reach for him, but each arm felt as if it were made of lead. The effort alone was leaving her tired and breathless.

"I, will always, love you," the whisper echoed.

Gwyn felt warm rivulets stream down her cheeks as she fought with everything within her to get closer to her father. But the image was now fading back into the light, and the strange feeling of being between moments was passing.

She had wanted to tell her father thank you, that she loved him back, and most of all, to forgive him. But the light was fading, and in a flash, she was lying on her back on the floor of the carriage, crying uncontrollably. Delilah was grounding her and saying comforting things while Chele ran her fingers through her hair.

After a moment of realization, Gwyn stopped crying and let her breathing settle. She sat up and hugged Delilah, then fell asleep in her lap for the rest of the ride home.

Gwyn's sleep was restless that night once she was in bed. She had several dreams of what had happened, each one repeating the lack of control Gwyn had over the situation and the way she felt helpless about doing anything. She could hear the soft voice reaching out to her as it had, telling her to enter the tomb. She woke up to Chele shaking her.

"Gwyn! Gwyn, wake up! Are you alright?"

Gwyn sat up breathing heavily. "Yeah. I'm fine. Just bad dreams."

"You were making strange sounds. It sounded like you were..."

A knock on the bedroom door interrupted Chele. Delilah opened the door, and she and Franz entered the room. Franz sat on the end of Gwyn's bed, and Delilah sat next to Chele.

"Is everything okay?" asked Franz.

"Fine. I'm fine. Just a bad dream. What are you guys doing in here?" Gwyn said.

Franz sighed and combed his long, dark hair back with his hand. "Well, we were going to wait until you were older, but we don't think we can wait any longer."

"What are you talking about?" Gwyn asked, her gaze darting from one darkened silhouette to the other.

"We've decided it's time we took you to our guild," Franz said.

Gwyn sat up fully to listen closer. "Our what? What is that?"

Franz took a breath and placed his hand on his chin as if choosing his words carefully. "It is our home, our sanctuary, so to speak."

Gwyn looked at Chele to find the same look of confusion that she was feeling. "Sanctuary? So... who are 'we,' then?"

Delilah smiled. "We? We are the masters of the elements, the benders of space, the magi of great and old in books long forgotten. We are what the folklore and songs tell about."

Gwyn and Chele looked at each other, then back to Franz and Delilah. The room was barely lit by the light of the Electric Moon, but they could see the expression of amusement on each other's faces.

"So... how do we get there?" Jack's voice asked from the door.

"Jack!" Franz said. "That's very clever of you to sneak up on us. I didn't even hear him, did you, Delilah?"

"Not at all. You'll fit right in. Our guild is keen on stealth," Delilah replied.

"Thanks, I guess. So, um, yeah... how do we get there?"

Franz looked at Delilah, who spoke. "The gates to the guild are few and far between. One can always find them if they know how to read the signs."

Franz smiled and put his hand on his chin. "I suppose the quickest way would be through the old mines down in the Burrows, just south of here.

We could teleport there, but doing that with even one other person is extremely tiring."

"Teleport?" Jack asked.

" Teleport," said Delilah. "Like it sounds, you go from one place to another."

"Whoa!" Jack said. "Can I do that?"

Delilah and Franz both shrugged. "Can't say for sure. Almost anyone can learn at least some magic with enough time, dedication, and know-how. The problem is, I'm not sure what you're personally capable of. Anyway, grab your stuff; we're going for a walk."

Gwyn put on her cloak and placed her bow over her shoulder. She thought about bringing her harp but decided against it.

The group gathered outside the house and, instead of taking the carriage, walked the road toward the Burrows.

The sky was still dark as it was early in the night, and the Electric Moon had begun to rise over the horizon.

Franz and Delilah changed from farming clothes to robes and cloaks. Franz wore dark robes and a hood with dark blue wrappings around his ankles and wrists. A black wrapping covered his mouth, leaving his eyes and forehead visible. He didn't have any weapons on him that could be seen.

Delilah's robes were similar, though hers had a deep red and black theme. She carried no visible weapon with her either.

Franz threw a hand in the air, and for a moment, Gwyn thought her feet slightly shimmered. She felt as if they were traveling at least twice as fast as normal somehow, even faster than they had in the carriage.

They reached the Burrows in what should have taken hours, in only a few minutes.

They came upon the Burrows, and Gwyn looked around to see a large open field to her right and a very large hill to the left. The sign to the town was old and hanging from one chain, as the other had broken. It swung slightly in the breeze when it blew, clanging and rattling the old chain.

Franz bent over and caught his breath, and Delilah followed.

"We're here. Just up ahead and to the left. We'll pass through an old graveyard," Franz said, his voice now rich and baritone.

"It's been so long..." Delilah said with a sadness.

"Does anyone still live here?" Gwyn asked.

"A lot of ghosts," Delilah replied with a chuckle. "The ground is rich with the right stones for a portal to the guild. But it also feeds a lot of spirits, and when they grow strong enough, they can manifest."

"What happens when they do that?" Jack asked.

Delilah peered over at him. "They're just ghosts," she said, as calm as if it were passing news about the weather.

Jack swallowed hard and looked over at Chele. She had an eyebrow raised with a look of concern.

"Here," Franz said, stopping at a sloping entrance into the ground. The group had made it to the other side of the graveyard, now standing at a gravelly entrance to a mine. Inside, it was very dark, and looking at it gave Gwyn the creeps. "I will go first; Delilah will stay rear. No one fall out of line," Franz said, taking steps down the slope. "Something doesn't seem right."

The gravel was slippery, and Gwyn felt herself slide forward a couple of times but managed to stay in control of her descent.

Upon entering, darkness consumed their vision. Suddenly, a bright ribbon wove out, hovering in the air in front of them, making slight tearing and humming sounds. The silvery ribbon shot from the palm of Franz's hand and through the tunnel. It was fluorescent and lit the cave walls with a dim, pearly light.

The light slowly faded as they walked, but it kept the caverns lit enough to see. They descended deeper and farther into the caves, where old carts of stones lay abandoned, and Gwyn could tell certain drop-offs went very far down. Jack threw a rock down one, and they waited to hear the echo, but it never came.

Franz replenished the ribbon of light when it went out, and they followed him until coming upon an area that looked strangely like a giant rock door in the wall. Delilah stepped in front of the group and knelt before the door.

Franz held his finger to his lips and faced opposite the door in a defensive stance. Then, with a loud crack, the giant rock door split in two and started sliding open.

"Something is wrong," Franz said in a whisper.

Screeching howls came from somewhere in the distance behind them, the direction Franz now faced. He pulled two scimitars, one with green swirling energy and the other with purple. The blades seemed to come out of thin air.

Franz leapt into the air, spun twice, like a saw with his swords outstretched, and let a blade go. The scimitar shot across the shaft. A purple glowing figure suddenly came into sight at a bend just as Franz's blade struck it. The blade pierced the creature through the neck and stuck into the wall. Immediately, the screeching stopped, and the creature's head rolled down a shaft into an endless pit, its body fading to dust.

"What was that!" Gwyn asked.

"A ghost?" Chele added.

"That's no ghost," Franz replied while retrieving his sword. "Let's hurry."

The group went through the large stone door, which slammed behind them once they were all inside.

The room opened up into a very large cavern, the air damp and stale.

"Something's not right. What's going on?" asked Delilah. "Those creatures somehow crossed the seal... They're here!" she said before leaping into the air and, with a flash of lightning, pulled a wooden staff from the air. She landed in the center of the room, slamming the butt of her staff deep into the ground. As it landed, a large pulse of lightning burst out from around her. The wave hit several undead-looking creatures that appeared from the blast and flew back into the walls.

A few of the creatures faded into dust from the blast. Delilah stood and began whipping long ropes of lightning from her hands at the creatures who had not perished. She used the golden ribbons of energy to snap the heads off three of them, but they were closing in on her.

Franz had drawn his blades again and had entered the battle as well, quickly slicing through several of the creatures.

Gwyn tried to count how many were left, but it seemed like more kept coming. She'd counted at least eight, then another appeared, then another. "Chele, use your knife! Jack, my old bow!" Gwyn yelled.

Jack and Chele did, and to their surprise, they were both helpful. They managed to take down a creature by themselves.

"Gwyn, use your bow!" Jack yelled over the battle, but she did not want to use it. She was afraid of the power it might have. The last thing Gwyn wanted to do was hurt her family or friends.

Gwyn looked for anything in the area to use as a weapon. She found a good-sized rock, picked it up, and threw it. It hit a creature in the head, and the rock exploded into several small pieces. The creature didn't fall; it merely turned its gaze toward Gwyn, screeched, and rushed at her.

Gwyn stepped back into a wall, but it seized her by the wrist. The skeletal face had dark hollows where its eyes should be, and her whole left arm and hand felt instantly frozen and burned, as if she'd held it under ice water. Both the creature and Gwyn screamed. The creature raised its other bony hand and struck her across the temple. The blow was far harder than she expected, and Gwyn felt her knees buckle under her as her head bounced off the stone wall behind her.

Before the creature could land another blow, Chele's knife stuck into the side of its head, and it exploded into dust.

Gwyn was sitting on the cold stone floor when she looked up and saw a different creature burst through the stone wall. It was far larger than the other undead creatures. It wielded a jagged sword and had glowing orange eyes. The ghostly luminescence it gave off lit the cave around it.

"A LICH!" Franz yelled.

"Should I try to port the children out?" Delilah asked in a concerned tone.

"Not past the seal—it would be suicide," Franz responded, taking a fighting stance.

"Who dares enter?" the lich said in a deep, ominous voice, its bright orange eyes searching the cave like small spotlights.

Franz and Delilah wasted no time attacking it. Delilah lashed it several times with her whipping ropes of lightning, and Franz cast purple beams of magic that shot out of his swords like blades at the creature. The attacks landed, leaving deep scars in the armor and skin of the creature, but it didn't seem to slow it down.

Gwyn could see the lich had flesh and bone, unlike the previous skeletal undead creatures. She felt her stomach curl as the smell of rotting flesh filled the cave.

Delilah lanced her arms forward, and two bright ropes of lightning shot out of her hands and wrapped tightly around the lich. It screamed as it writhed and yanked Delilah around violently. She struggled to keep her footing as Franz began slicing into the creature at incredible speeds.

The creature suddenly used unbelievable force to lift its arms, breaking free from the tethers. As the binds broke, a bright flash burst through the cave, and Delilah fell to one knee, catching herself with her hands. She gasped in pain and held her side for a moment.

"Can you root it again?" Franz asked, stepping backward while blocking and dodging relentless and powerful attacks from the creature.

"I can try," Delilah said through bated breath while regaining her footing. "Try to shadow lance!" she said as she once again cast two bright ropes of lightning around the creature's upper body.

The creature seemed prepared for the attack and immediately began to break free from Delilah's restraints. Franz saw the creature break its sword-wielding arm free and advance a lancing attack toward him. Franz's sword glowed purple, and he swung his scimitar in the opposite direction of the lich. Just as the lich's attack was about to pierce Franz's back, Franz disappeared and reappeared behind it, his glowing purple sword landing perfectly into the creature's skull.

A loud crack echoed through the cave as Franz's scimitar came into contact with the skull of the lich. A green glow could be seen from within its head where the scimitar had chunked away a piece of skull, and the lich cried out in a booming voice that rattled the cave.

The lich suddenly spun around, snapping Delilah's ropes of lightning again with another flash, and quickly parried Franz's next attack. Franz was taken off guard by the powerful block and was knocked off balance. The lich then powerfully kicked Franz, sending him flying into a wall.

Delilah ran forward and fell to her knees, sliding to the side of the lich while barely dodging its sword as it swung at her. As they passed each other, she cast another rope of lightning that caught the creature across the face. She slid on her knees across the cave floor while yanking hard on the tether of lightning, tearing a gash into the creature's skeletal face. The sounds of electrical arcs echoed through the mines.

The lich yelled again but managed to loop the rope of lightning around its large, jagged sword and jerked, hurling Delilah violently across the cave. She landed on her side and rolled off into the darkness.

"Filthy magi!" it yelled loudly, causing rocks to fall from the ceiling. Jack and Chele moved quickly to dodge stones now crashing around them. They had just managed to kill the last of the other undead creatures.

The lich then turned and thunder-clapped toward a recovering Franz, launching him backward. Franz crashed through a stone column and into the wall. He then fell to his knees and onto his face, his scimitars leaving his hands and sliding across the stone cave floor.

Gwyn saw the battle play out at incredible speed and knew she had one choice left. She knew it was risky, and she didn't know if it would even work, but she drew an arrow and pulled back. To her relief, the arrow started to glow as it had before. It shone bright and silvery as ever, and she let it fly, praying that her dizziness would not affect her aim.

The arrow flew and pierced through the back of the creature's cracked skull. Instantly, the lich started to cover over in thick sheets of ice, and it was only a second before it was no longer moving.

"GWYN?" Franz yelled, still recovering from his fall.

"Delilah! Make sure she's okay!" Gwyn responded.

Jack and Chele ran over to find Delilah was shaken but seemed okay. She removed her headpiece and looked at Gwyn with confusion.

"Gwyn! How did you do that?" Delilah asked.

Gwyn looked to her left as if she might have an answer, then confessed, "I don't know."

"Gwyn..." Franz said. "Your mother's bow... You... USED it!" he said, scratching his head with a look of confusion.

Gwyn was still catching her breath, looking from Franz to Delilah. "Well, what do we do now? Don't we need to still kill this thing?" she asked with concern.

Franz stood to his feet and stretched, rubbing aches out of his muscles where he'd taken blows. "No. It looks like you've sealed him. At least, I think you did. Chances are he'll die from the shot in his skull anyway. If I had to guess, that ice won't melt for a thousand years, unless you remove that arrow."

Gwyn felt a bit confused but proud of herself, nonetheless. She hadn't really meant to seal the lich. In fact, she wasn't sure the arrow would even shoot magic. "Why did my arrow do that?"

"Good question," Delilah said, still catching her own breath.

"Regardless, we really need to go. Delilah and I have wounds we need healed," Franz said, ushering the group toward the other side of the room. They made their way through the rest of the mines quickly, using the holes in the wall the lich had made as a shortcut and finally coming to a small stone globe. "Everyone put a hand on it."

They all did as Franz instructed, and then he uttered an incantation. They felt the air around them suddenly change with a gust. They were now outside again, or somewhere that felt like it. It was dark, but they could not see the moon.

CHAPTER 10
The Shadow Guild

Gwyn could see what looked to be orange and red veins of magma in what she could only guess was a ceiling, hundreds, if not thousands of feet above them. There was a tree not far from them that had what looked like silvery-blue fluorescent lights running through its leaves. The ground was covered in a hazy pink glow that swept around tall yellow blades of grass.

She saw ahead that there was a large building that looked like a castle. She couldn't tell from her vantage point if the stalactite-like formations of the floating land on which the castle sat went all the way down to the ground or if the whole of it was truly floating.

A small, winding path through the air led up to the building. The path connected near where they were standing, and at the gate of the path stood two large, tall shadowy figures in shiny, dark spaulders and helmets. Gwyn couldn't make out their faces other than their eyes, which were shiny and white. Their skin, however, looked as if it were made of thick black smoke.

Franz and Delilah each took a turn standing in front of them and crossed their arms across their chests in a strange signal-like salute to them. The shadowy figures nodded, separated, and let them by. Jack and Chele followed and went through.

Gwyn had stopped for a few seconds to look at the guards and was the last to go through the entryway. As she started to walk through, both shadowy figures dropped very low to the ground. At first, she thought they were attacking her, but she quickly realized they were not. They were, in fact, bowing—deep, respectful bows.

Not knowing what to do, Gwyn made a quick bow back and hurried up the trail next to Franz, occasionally looking back at the tall shadowy figures. "What are those?" she asked.

"Shades," Franz said. "You should hide your bow under your cloak. I don't want them to think you're a threat."

Gwyn slipped the bow under her cloak and asked, "What do they do?"

"They guard the guild. They go well with why this is called the Shadow Guild," Franz replied, making his way up the long, winding trail.

Gwyn looked down off the narrow trail and could see a maelstrom stirring far beneath. It was dark and occasionally lit with lightning strikes within the clouds. "Oh... Where do shades come from?" Gwyn asked.

"They were once something like us, but very noble and fair. When truly noble people do something very wrong, and are honorable and accept their sins—yet do not allow themselves forgiveness—they can agree to be shaded here until their good deeds have paid for their sin. The ones here serve as guards for thousands of years."

"How sad," Chele said.

"Not really," Franz said. "It's better than the harsh punishments those who are truly noble wish upon themselves instead. I guess the only downside is they also lose their memories from when they were among the living, only remembering small things very important to them."

"Do they forget their loved ones?" Gwyn asked.

"Well, sometimes, but the spirit never forgets... And their loved ones are most likely long gone from the living by the time things are resolved. Even wizards don't live that long.

Gwyn felt a pulsating soreness on her left wrist and temple where the banshee had touched her. She looked down to find black lines on her wrist.

"Don't worry, we'll get them healed in the guild," Delilah said. "I have several as well. It's important we do it quickly."

"Where?" Chele said. "I never saw one touch you."

Delilah shook her head. "No, they didn't. I touched them with my Flits."

"Flits?" Chele wondered.

"Yes, those long strands of lightning you saw me using. They're kind of an extension of my qi—or magical energy, if you will. What I touch with them is almost as if I touched it with my own hands in a way. Especially a cursed creature like a banshee—they're so dark they rot just about anything living they touch." Delilah removed her gloves and held up her hands to reveal several blackened marks across her hands and arms.

"Qi? What is that?" Gwyn asked.

"It's your spirit energy—the energy of spirits and souls. It can be harvested and stored in the life force and used to power magic, like Flits," Delilah responded. "There are teachers that can explain it far better than I can, though."

"Can you not throw the lightning stuff, though? Kind of like you did with that shockwave thing at the start of the fight? Or is that attached to your qi, too?" Chele asked her.

"Well... actually, yes, I can. But I would lose energy very fast if I went throwing it like that. I personally can't blow my energy like that. Everyone's style and limits are different when it comes to qi and magic."

The group continued up the path to the castle steps. They passed more shades on the way in, but these guards did not bow to Gwyn this time—they merely stood still.

The entrance to the guild had a red carpet runner going through the hall. The ceilings were high, with candlelit chandeliers hanging from them. Gwyn could see stairways and archways leading to other rooms and large tapestries of beautiful scenes—battles, forests, mountains, and even space—hanging on the walls. Some of the scenes in the tapestries Gwyn did not recognize; places she'd never seen or heard of.

There were several shades in the large entrance hall. Some had similar shiny plates of armor on their heads and shoulders, others had larger, more colorful ones, and some were holding long shadowy blades that looked as if they were made from a similar thick, black, smoky substance as the shades themselves.

A tall, very skinny woman with dark hair wearing a green hooded dress approached the group. "Master Franz," she said with a slight bow. "The

Lady Arch Magia Delilah," with another small bow. "It is pertinent that the guild master speak with you at once."

Franz tilted his head to the side with a look of curiosity on his face. "Is it now?" Franz asked, then gave Delilah a knowing look.

Two shades swiftly glided up beside Franz and Delilah and placed long, black, shadowy fingers on their arms and shoulders. Franz and Delilah gave looks of shock, and three more shades stood behind Gwyn, Jack, and Chele.

"It has been requested that you have an escort. He is waiting; please follow me," the woman said, and took off walking toward the way she came.

"Belas, please, what is going on?" Franz asked the lady in green.

"Master Quidel will inform you. It would be best if you heard it from him."

The group made their way down a hall, taking a few turns along the way. Eventually, they took a right that led into a long hallway with several tall, armored shades lining the walls. Belas made it first to the other end, where there was a small archway with an open curtain in front of a door. Belas waved her arm in a quick half-circle, and a silver flash came from the door.

Delilah looked back and whispered to Gwyn, "That was a force field she just removed."

Gwyn thought about her father's tomb and castle in Silvania and wondered if similar magic was what protected it.

They entered a room that was quite large and had several people in it. The walls went up very high, and it was hard to see the ceiling—if there was one—as it seemed to fade into black. Giant red and green banners hung from the walls, and the back of the room seemed to fade into darkness.

Gwyn saw a couple of people wearing pointed hats here and there, and several people wearing hoods and robes. Several tables were set along the walls where people were sitting, locked in important-looking conversations with one another.

Gwyn's attention was drawn to a tall, muscular person in the center of the room. He was wearing black and gold armor and had an orange color of skin with black flames—either tattooed or burned—on his skin, going up his arms and neck.

The room was quietly buzzing with conversation, but as their group made their way to the center, the noise started to fade until it was completely silent.

"Guild Master Quidel," Belas said before bowing. "An audience with Master Franz and the Lady Arch Magia Delilah, as you requested."

Quidel was tall and muscular and didn't exactly look mean, but he didn't look nice either.

"Master Franz and Lady Delilah," he said in a deep voice, then nodded to them. "How is it you've made it here?"

The shades let go of Franz, and he gave a small bow. "Good evening, Guild Master. We came through the Burrows, sir."

Quidel squinted. "The Burrows, you say? The Burrows have been overrun with banshees and other demon foul far worse than the usual ghosts that reside there." Quidel took a step closer to Franz and peered into his eyes. "How is it... that you were able to make it through... alive?"

"We fought, sir," Delilah said, followed by a small bow. "We didn't know it was infected." She then held up her hands to reveal dark marks on her hands and wrists.

"I see." Quidel took a step, put his hands behind his back, and began slowly pacing back and forth. "So you... defeated a full-fledged lich..."

"Yes, sir, there was," Franz said, but Gwyn thought he'd started to look a bit unsure of himself. "One of Xess' creations?"

"Xess?" Gwyn whispered to herself. Chele and Jack looked at her and shrugged.

Quidel stepped closer and looked from Gwyn to Jack, to Chele, then to Delilah and Franz. "And how is it that you defeated the legendary creature? And with these children, nonetheless!?" Quidel took a deep breath and furrowed his brow. "Interesting creatures. They don't tire easily. Great wizards fall to less... No offense, but even much stronger than both of you combined."

Franz took a breath, looked a bit insulted, and stood up straight. "Sir, the children assisted us. It was a near miss... well, several, actually, but we managed. We even sealed the creature. There's a solid chance it may even be dead."

Quidel rubbed his chin as though he were thinking and started pacing slowly back and forth again. "It may be?"

Franz scratched his head nervously. "Well, we didn't stick around to find out."

"How exactly did you manage to seal an undead lich, Master Franz? Such magic seems on the verge of forbidden."

Franz shifted a bit nervously. Gwyn thought he would look at her, but he didn't. "Well, sir, if you wouldn't mind a private conversation over the matter, I'd be more than happy to explain it in full."

Gwyn looked around the room and found her group was at the center of attention. Everyone else around had backed themselves to the walls. It was quite uncomfortable, and Gwyn couldn't help but feel like they were on trial for something.

Her eyes suddenly locked onto two opal ones. They belonged to a woman wearing a black cloak. She also wore a shoulder piece of armor that tapered upward into a sharp point, as well as a diamond-shaped mask over her mouth and nose. Gwyn had the sudden sensation as if she were looking at someone very familiar. She nudged Chele, and when she saw the woman, she glanced back at Gwyn, giving her an odd look.

"Master Franz, I am afraid I have troubling news... We have been informed that there are similar bands of creatures gathered outside of all the hidden entrances to the guild," Quidel said. "Furthermore, the guild vault was breached."

"Impossible," Franz said in a low tone.

"Indeed, unless a Master Wizard allowed it—of which there are only a few."

Franz looked sincerely shocked. "You mean the..."

"Gone," Quidel said, cutting Franz off.

Several large shades moved closer toward their group. They didn't seem to have feet, and watching them float across the floor was rather eerie, Gwyn thought.

"Until we can be certain, we shall need to take proper precautionary measures. Due to your lack of attendance at the guild lately, and your unusual ability to pass through an undead-filled tunnel guarded by a full-fledged lich, we find it wise to detain you until we have more information. I'm sure you'll understand," Quidel said.

A large shade had placed smoky hands on Franz's shoulders, but he jerked away from its grasp. "You don't understand sir! I MUST speak with you!"

"SILENCE!" Quidel said in a booming voice. He took two steps closer to Franz and stared at him face to face. "There is something going on here, and your story does not add up, Master Franz. Someone's to blame for these security breaches, and the guild is likely to face an attack at any moment." Quidel stepped back a foot or so and began looking around. "Not to mention, we've also been missing vials of the forbidden wizard serum..."

Quidel paced a bit before continuing. "Consider it overly cautious of me, but it's a lot to swallow from you right now, Franz. And if you have taken the forbidden serum to increase your powers, I'd like to remind you that the penalty for such acts includes banishment and even death. I think I might know what you're planning on doing, and I'll have you know it's repulsive!"

"Sir, please!" pleaded Delilah.

"Delilah, I have my right to doubt such fantastic tales from the two of you, and you both know it," Quidel said.

"So that's it, then? Is that what this is about!? You think I'm a liar!? How dare you accuse me of such heresy!" Franz was now shouting. "I stand by my word then, and I'll stand by it now! You'd be wise to LISTEN!"

"Enough!" Quidel said.

A few seconds of silence stretched across the room, but to Gwyn, it felt like it lasted for minutes. The room buzzed with fear as Quidel's anger began to show. "I shall not allow such foolishness to go on!" Quidel waved his fingers without hardly lifting his hand, and a layer of skin grew over Franz's mouth. "After years of being absent... another fantastic tale... too good to be true. The Wizard Council has claimed for years now that you have lied to me about my dear friends, the Great King and Queen, and now you expect me to believe you bested a lich? Master Franz, I have every right to believe you've betrayed the Shadow Guild and the Wizard Council and now have disobeyed me openly!"

Two shades grabbed Franz by the arms. Quidel raised his palm, and a green bolt lit up the room with a flash as Franz moaned in pain through his sealed mouth. Delilah let out a scream, and two shades restrained her by the arms as well.

Smoke was coming from Franz's chest as he fell to his knees. He was trying to cough but having a hard time with his mouth sealed over.

Gwyn felt the cold, shadowy touch of a shade now restraining her as well and saw that Jack and Chele were also being detained by the strong creatures.

"Master Franz, you have claimed to have knowledge of the great King Cassius but have refused to share it. For too long, I have allowed you to keep things hidden from me and defile the sanctity of the guild. For well over a decade now, I've given you a pass, despite great scrutiny, and still, you leave me with nothing. Many have suspected you—leaking our secrets to Xess. You, who have been a traitor to the Shadow Guild... you, who stole the forbidden serum, and you, who somehow brought down the great King! And now you wish to test your powers on a greater evil this planet hasn't known for millennia!"

Quidel lifted his hand, and in it appeared a very long silver sword with a golden handle. "For too long, I have overlooked your sins. But tonight, your madness ends. I'd be a fool to swallow these thorny lies. It's obvious how you made it through the army of Xess's demons practically unscathed. This was the last straw, Master Franz."

Franz was breathing very hard and was now forced to lean his head down by the shades, his arms held tightly behind his back.

"Tonight, I undo the mistake of giving you time—time in which you've clearly used against myself, the guild, and the world." A few people in the room started to cheer, and a few started talking very quickly, sounding worried. Delilah was on her knees, crying and pleading, until Quidel covered her mouth with flesh as well.

Quidel lifted his long sword high into the air and took a step toward Franz. "Tonight, your sins shall be atoned, and you shall rest in peace... I hereby sentence you to de—"

Gwyn had been struggling to get free from the shade, but seeing that her uncle was about to have his head cut off had pushed her over the edge. Her mind had slipped.

With strength she hadn't known, she snapped the large shadowy hand with a loud crack and freed herself from the shade. The shade let out a wispy screech, and within no time, she had removed her cloak, armed herself with her bow, and had an arrow drawn, ready to fire straight into the heart of Quidel.

Something in the air changed the moment the arrow started to gleam with silvery light. The shades that were holding Franz and Delilah let go, and every shade in the room was now bowing a deep, low bow toward Gwyn—even the one whimpering softly in pain behind her.

Quidel had paused, staring directly at Gwyn, who had a shining arrow drawn and aimed directly at him. She could see fear in his eyes.

"Apollo..." he whispered, staring at the bow.

Quidel slowly put his hands in the air. The long sword vanished as he opened his palm. He looked at Franz and whispered, "I... I was wrong... I was so very wrong... I'm so sorry..."

Gwyn was kneeling with her head down, several strands of hair over her face. The whites and pupils of her eyes were lit with an indigo shine as she bared her teeth. She was clearly not her normal self at this moment, and although she was poised to kill Quidel, something deep down inside her told her not to.

It took everything in her to fight the urge to release the arrow and destroy the immediate threat to her uncle, but slowly the light faded from her eyes, as did the grimace from her face, and her composure slipped back to the beautiful young girl she was.

At this point, everyone in the room had stood up and was staring at Gwyn in awe.

Her fingers were getting frost-covered and were very cold as the cool magical air danced around them and the arrow. "Spare my aunt and uncle's lives and let us go!" she demanded, sounding more confident than she felt.

Quidel glanced at Franz and raised an eyebrow, both hands still raised in the air. He then turned his gaze toward Gwyn. "My dear lady, if you are who I think you are, your aunt and uncle are far more than free... And I have little doubt as to who you are. Please, consider lowering your weapon, and there shall be a mouthful of apologies and explaining for us all."

Franz looked back at Gwyn and nodded, and she slowly let the tension out of the string. To her surprise, no one rushed her or tried to take her bow or tell her to leave. Quidel waved his hand, and the skin over Franz and Delilah's mouths vanished, and the shades backed away from them.

Quidel raised them both to their feet by lifting his arms and said, "It has come to my sudden attention that I have made a terrible mistake. I have publicly shunned you, called you traitors—in front of your peers and superiors alike—and raised my fist in anger, giving credence to those who oppose us here in the guild..." Quidel's voice was now echoing throughout the chamber. It suddenly carried an undertone of sorrow.

"And worse yet, I meant to end an innocent life... I have succumbed to a weakness I have not known... fear... paranoia. I have allowed Xess a small victory here tonight in our home..." Quidel looked at the floor. His face was now contorted into a strong mixture of sorrow and anger. "It is clear now that I have been a fool—played through and through. Please, forgive me, my dear friends. I should have never lost faith."

Quidel turned his posture toward Gwyn before continuing. "Master Franz, for over a decade, you have claimed you knew secrets that you could not reveal because of a sacred promise—a magical oath sworn to the King. Of all the secrets you could have held, I would never have guessed you would bring the blood of King Sterling himself here—and with the Queen's bow, no doubt," Quidel said with an apologetic undertone.

Franz stood up, holding his blackened ribs. "Sir, I understand your doubts... All is forgiven. Can we just get something to eat now that the cat is out of the bag?"

CHAPTER 11

Healing Hands Before a Word

Quidel called for a feast. While it was being prepared, he held a private discussion with Franz and Delilah as healers addressed their wounds.

Belas took Gwyn, Jack, and Chele to a large bedroom lit with candles and oil lamp sconces mounted to the walls. She informed Gwyn that a healer would be coming by then left. A long moment of silence filled the room as the events of the night sank in.

"Gwyn, your aunt and uncle are nuts! What. Is. This. Place!?" Jack said, as if it were about to explode out of him.

For a moment, Gwyn sat silently before looking up at Jack. "I have no idea... I didn't even know this place existed," she said, placing her hands over her face. Her mind raced. She wanted to talk things over with Franz and Delilah.

Chele sat on the bed next to her. "Gwyn, this has been the craziest night of my life. I think we all nearly died a half dozen times!"

She looked at Chele and apologized. "I'm so sorry. I never meant to get you guys into this!"

Chele shook her head. "Honestly, it's also been the most exciting one I've ever had. I just hope the scary parts are over."

"Well, that guy did say the place could be attacked!" Jack said. "I don't know if these smoky things could hold off banshees, but they sure are creepy!"

"And the feeling when they touch you..." Chele added, shivering in disgust. "It's like being touched by ice water and... smoky bones!"

Gwyn took her bow off her shoulder and held it out in front of her to look at it. "I... I almost killed that madman tonight."

"But you didn't, Gwyn! That was brilliant!" Chele said.

She gave an unsure look. "But I... almost had no choice."

Jack got up from the bed. "What do you mean? You always have a choice."

Gwyn sank further into the comforter as she stared up at the ceiling. "I guess. But it scares me that one day it might happen, and I won't be able to control it," she said, silently recalling the events in her mind. "It's more powerful than I can explain."

Chele picked at the frill of a pillow on the bed beside her. "It's a gift, Gwyn. We've both seen you do amazing things. Maybe you should talk to your aunt and uncle and see if they can help you with it."

"Yeah, maybe," she replied.

A knock rapped on the door, and a lady wearing dark green, silky robes with white trim around the shoulders and other areas entered the room. As she got closer, it became apparent there was a thin golden symbol on her chest. Gwyn thought it looked familiar but couldn't place it.

The woman did not look old by any means, other than her solid white hair, which was pulled back into a ponytail. Her face, however, did look a bit older than most people Gwyn had seen in the Shadow Guild.

"Hello, everyone," the woman said with a smile. "My name is Kokolo. I am here to heal the scorch marks left from the banshees," she added with a slight accent.

Gwyn held out her left arm. "I believe you're here to see me, then."

Kokolo shook her hand, then knelt beside the bed where Gwyn sat. "I see. Does it hurt, my dear?"

"A little," she replied.

"I'll probably have to touch you a bit. Don't be shy, okay, Gwyn?"

She nodded shyly.

Kokolo's eyes moved up and down Gwyn from head to toe, looking at her as if she could see things they could not. She then rolled up Gwyn's sleeve, letting out a small gasp when she saw the white scars crisscrossing her arm. "Oh..."

She looked from her arm to Kokolo. "What is it?"

"Oh... you shoot a bow!" Kokolo stated.

It wasn't a question, but Gwyn answered, "Y-yes."

"But you learned it very quickly. With extreme determination, no doubt."

Gwyn looked off for a moment to recall learning to shoot with her grandfather. "Well, yes, I did."

Kokolo shook her head and pursed her lips slightly. "I haven't seen scars like that in a very long time. Scars of a stubborn but powerful mind! Just pray your wisdom can outpace your stubbornness."

"What about my hand, where the banshee touched me? And my face?" she asked, hoping she wouldn't have blackened scars on her arm or face for the rest of her life.

"Hmm. Those are not quite as bad as they look. I am gifted to see only a few levels deep into the aura, but it looks like the banshee didn't hold on to you long enough to burn any deeper than a couple of layers."

"Burn my aura?" Gwyn said with confusion.

"Oh, yes," Kokolo assured her. "This could have been much worse."

"But... how does that work?"

Kokolo looked up at Gwyn and smiled. "You must understand, my dear, you are so very pure and alive, and banshees are so very dead and rancid."

"Oh, well... If that is so, wouldn't it have hurt it to have touched me?" Gwyn asked.

"Well, I'm sure it did! Although, you must remember, the nature of a banshee comes from darkness, and darkness is like quicksand—once you are deep enough in it, the only way out is to find a significant source strong enough to remove you from it. Though touching something as wonderful and pure as you was likely very painful to it, pain is what it prefers. It has no choice."

"Hogwash," Jack spouted out. "People always have a choice."

Kokolo smiled and let out a laugh. "Perhaps. But you are from the living and have no experience making such choices."

Jack furrowed his brow and crossed his arms.

Gwyn cringed at the thought of her skin being touched by the wretched creature. An image of it grabbing her flashed through her mind, the cold skeletal fingers on her arm.

Kokolo took her hand and held it in the air between her own. "Now, I must ask that you give me a few moments of silence." She moved her hand around Gwyn's, focusing intently. She did not physically touch her while doing this but seemed to be working in the air inches from her hand. She then moved to her face and did the same.

Gwyn watched Kokolo work and felt sensations coursing through her arm and face. She found it very interesting, especially considering Kokolo was not even touching her.

Within minutes, the black marks from the banshee faded. Gwyn smiled, seeing the marks were not permanent, and the slight throbbing pain that had been there before quickly faded as well.

"That will do," Kokolo said, then rubbed an oil on the areas where the marks had been on her arm. It left a sweet floral fragrance that Gwyn could not identify.

"I scraped my knees up a bit in the mines. Any chance you could heal me too?" Jack asked.

Kokolo gave him a concerned look. "Oh, dear. I certainly could. But you wouldn't want me healing your knees."

Jack looked around in wonder. "Why not?"

Kokolo stood up and put her ointment away after wrapping a white bandage around Gwyn's arm. Then she looked at Jack with a very serious expression. "Because it would cost you a full year of your life, of course! What a waste of a year unless you plan to do something tremendous with your knees in the next few days!"

Jack's eyebrow lifted with curiosity. "Seriously!?"

Kokolo waited a moment, then smiled at Jack, "No. Only a very wicked person would charge such a thing. I charge in half years. Here, put some of this on it." She reached into her bag and handed him a small tincture of oil with a smile.

Jack gave her a smug look, then smiled a little before taking the tincture. "Thanks, but stay away from my life minutes or whatever."

Kokolo laughed before turning to walk away. "If you guys need me for anything else, just mix the colors white and gold," she said, then left the room.

A moment of silent confusion filled the room.

"That lady is freaking... nuts!" Jack said, breaking the silence.

Chele laughed.

"What do you think it means to mix colors?" Gwyn asked.

Jack shrugged and shook his head. "Maybe these vials of sand?" he said, lifting a small red vial from a shelf.

Jack mixed the red and green in a bowl. They swirled and looked like they melted into wispy smoke when Belas suddenly knocked on the door. "Please don't waste the binding sands. They're very expensive."

"Sorry... But, how did that just work?" Jack asked her.

"It's a complicated tech," she told him. "The bowls are bound together, and the sand activates a signal."

Jack shrugged, confused by her answer, as she left.

Gwyn felt exhausted and threw herself back onto the bed. "It is strange how things are here. Nothing like back at home in Pantheon." She closed her eyes and, for the first time, felt homesick. She thought of her grandparents before falling asleep.

Gwyn woke to Chele tapping her softly. "Feast time, sleepy head," she whispered.

Belas was standing in the room, waiting to escort the group. "After the feast, we have a better room prepared for you. Oh, and Gwyn, Master Quidel has requested to speak with you in private after dinner. Now, please follow me to the dining hall."

The three of them followed Belas through halls and stairways until they came into a beautiful, large dining area with several tables. The room was dimly lit as a nicely dressed band on a stage to their right played relaxing music. Candles flickered from tabletops and chandeliers, while a thick rope of Xi lighting ran around the top of the walls, giving the room a unique ambiance.

As they walked through the room, most of the tables were already filled, and Gwyn felt as if several people were observing her as she passed. It was a strange feeling that made her consider each step.

Belas led them to a table off in the corner where Franz and Delilah were already sitting. She hugged her aunt and uncle, then took a seat across from them, attempting to wait for the appropriate time to start asking questions.

"Well, what do you think so far?" Delilah asked first, throwing Gwyn off a bit.

"We, uh... I'm not sure... It's different," she replied.

"VERY different," Jack chimed in.

"Are we... am I... in trouble?" Gwyn asked.

Franz shook his head. "Far from it, Gwyn. We knew returning would be rough, but what you did tonight changed things. Delilah and I are thankful for it."

Gwyn looked at the table for a moment, following the grain that ran through the dark wood, then back to Delilah. "Can't you just tell Quidel who I am?"

Delilah shook her head slowly. "It's not that simple. We have to be careful with what we say as part of your father's dying wish."

Gwyn shook her head, a bit frustrated.

"Gwyn," Franz said with concern, "your parents wanted it this way."

She sat quietly for a moment before breaking the silence. "What for? I feel like all it's done is caused me confusion and grief."

Franz suddenly looked far more serious. "Believe me, your parents were working on some great things. They had their reasons, Gwyn. I would have waited longer to bring you here if I could, but your father underestimated some things."

She gave a sigh. "What is this place? I mean, why is it even here?"

Franz scratched the back of his head and gave her a puzzled look. "The Shadow Guild. It's been here for thousands of years. We haven't been here much lately, but we really enjoy it more than the others. Well, minus the hiccup tonight."

"Hiccup?" Gwyn asked, slightly offended. "That madman was going to kill you!"

Franz responded in a somber tone. "Gwyn, please understand. We were briefed tonight—there's been an effort to undermine Quidel's trust in us. He has a decent case against us. Not being here much, it appeared as if we're hiding. They nearly came looking for us. Even worse, at a different entrance, that lich killed two very close friends in a battle earlier today."

Her heart suddenly sank. "Oh," she said, remembering how close to death they had come. "How do you know it's the same one?"

"Let's just pray it's the only one," Franz said.

"Are you still in trouble?" she asked with concern.

"No, Gwyn. You cleared everything for us," Franz said with a smile. "We were bound to never say anything, so Quidel has never had a reason to understand us. But now, our trust has been restored."

Delilah added, "Quidel is typically a wonderful guild master and very level-headed."

"Did they ever clear the other entrance?" Chele asked.

"Seven wizards fought and ultimately retreated. Two died; almost all were injured. They need the entrances cleared for some dignitaries and council members to reach the guild," Franz replied.

"Quidel hopes we've prevented the attack he was anticipating, on our guild or others," Delilah added.

"Wait... There are more of these places?" Jack asked.

"Of course!" Franz replied.

"How many are there?" Chele asked.

Franz lifted his hand and started counting on his fingers. "Well, the Frost Guild, the Auric Guild, of course the Fire Guild—"

"Ahem," Delilah said with a knowing look toward Franz.

"Ah, yes. The Arcane Guild, which Delilah was from. They're an interesting bunch. Lots of electrical stuff there," Franz said.

"You can switch which guild you're in?" Gwyn asked.

"Of course!" answered Delilah.

"Can't you attend them all and learn everything?"

"Well, it would take thousands of years to learn everything. And even then, you wouldn't be that good at it all," Franz said. "And some people really can't learn certain things anyway. One of the greatest wizards in the past couldn't even light a candle with magic."

"Did you just say 'thousands of years'?" Jack asked, with a look of amazement on his face.

"Well, yeah. You don't learn anything magical overnight," Franz said. "Well, unless you're Gwyn, apparently. Don't get me wrong. Some people are born more magical than others."

Gwyn looked down where they had placed a plate with a giant bone-in steak, mashed potatoes slathered in butter and gravy, steamed veggies, and dinner rolls. "But, uh..." she said, trying to break her focus on her plate, "I'll be dead by the time I'm able to learn much."

Franz took a large bite of a roll, then washed it down with some red wine before speaking again. "No, Gwyn... You won't be dead."

Gwyn forked a carrot and watched steam rising from it. "What do you mean?"

Franz washed the steak down with another drink of red wine before answering. "Gwyn, you come from a wizard family—strong and early generation, at that. Using magic keeps you healthy and slows aging. Unless something happens, you should live to be as old as Delilah and me, if not older."

Jack stopped mid mouth full of steak and potatoes when he heard what Franz had said. "How ho'd harr hu?" he asked, shooting small pieces of food across the table.

Chele threw a dinner roll that bounced off Jack's head. "Don't speak with your mouth full, you savage!"

Franz laughed. "Well, I'm under a thousand, but getting close."

Jack spewed his drink across his plate when he heard the numbers.

"Delilah here's a few hundred years younger," Franz said, shaking his head at Jack with a crooked smile. "Not that old, in the grand scheme of things."

Gwyn took her first bite of steak. It was cooked perfectly and melted in her mouth. While she ate, she couldn't help but ponder the thought of living to be thousands of years old. All of her friends would be gone. By a thousand? Would the world even look the same?

"Can anyone learn magic?" Chele asked.

Franz had again stuffed his mouth and couldn't answer, so Delilah did for him. "Well, anyone can learn how. You might not be as good as someone from a wizard family, but you can certainly learn. There are schools that teach it. That's what we've been discussing with Quidel—whether all of you could attend a school together."

Jack's mouth dropped open. "Really? We can learn magic!?"

Franz smiled and chewed, letting Delilah answer again. "We think Gwyn just might have impressed Quidel enough to pull some strings. There are a couple of schools here in the Western Kingdoms."

"Which would we go to?" Gwyn asked.

Franz had finally finished chewing enough to answer. "The best one. The Academy in Silvania. Gwyn, you could probably teach them a thing or two about using a bow. It's a rare weapon for a wizard to use."

"It's a great school for the basics. They've got a book here we can look over later if you want," Delilah suggested.

After dinner, Belas came to escort them again. "Follow me, please."

She led them to a large staircase that intersected with several smaller ones from nearly every direction.

They came to a corridor with several arched doors then stopped at one on the left, and Belas took a golden key ring with three keys from her pocket and unlocked it. She handed the keyring to Gwyn. "These are your new quarters," she said, bowing with a hand out to let them enter.

Gwyn was amazed at how large the room was. The windows across were taller than her stone cottage house in Pantheon. The floor had steps going down to the right, where a large, round red sofa with fluffy cushions sat next to a large fireplace built into the wall. The fire felt nice, as it was chilly in the guild to Chele and Gwyn.

Straight across from the door was a dining and kitchen area where fresh fruit had been left in baskets. Behind it, a hallway led to individual bedrooms.

Gwyn thanked Belas and started to explore, but before she had gone far, Belas told her she would be seeing Quidel and beckoned her to follow.

She followed her out the door and straight down to the doors at the end of the hall. They were the largest doors there. Belas removed the barrier and Gwyn's heart raced as she led her inside.

The room was larger than her quarters, with paintings, shields, weapons, and relics on the walls. Straight ahead was Quidel, approaching Gwyn.

When he stood a few feet from her, he bowed. "Good evening, princess."

Gwyn was stricken by being called a princess. Not knowing exactly what to do, she mimicked his bow as best she could. "A princess... But, am I?" she asked shyly. "My parents... they died so long ago. I didn't think I could be."

"Thank you, Adept," Quidel said to Belas as he dismissed her. He motioned for Gwyn to sit on a round purple couch beside a table. "You are to me, even without a kingdom. To others, there may be some disagreements, especially given your age. Those announcements and discussions will be held another time."

Upon sitting down, a finely dressed waiter came and set a teapot and glasses on the table.

Quidel smiled. "It's jasmine mint. Please enjoy. I've had some sent to your friends as well."

She took a drink. The sensation it sent across her palate was amazing. The flavor was delightful—full, minty, refreshing, and sweet in the best ways.

She swallowed and asked, "You wanted to talk to me?"

Quidel laughed. "Straight to business? Alright. First, I wanted to thank you, Gwyn."

Her brow furrowed with confusion. "Thank me? For what?"

Quidel raised an eyebrow. "You saved many lives tonight and kept me from doing something terrible."

"You can say that again," Gwyn retorted.

"Please, hear me out. It's been a fairly rough day," he said with sincerity. "You weren't the only ones to battle a lich today."

"Yeah, I heard," she retorted, her voice still a little bitter.

Quidel nodded. "We did quite a bit of damage, but, alas, we weren't quite as lucky." He gestured to the black flame marks on his arms.

Looking closely, she wondered if the marks weren't the same as those she had from the banshee but even darker. "Those flame markings on your arms... Are they scars?"

Quidel nodded. "The lich used a special flame on us. I absorbed most of it, but I am saddened to admit it wasn't enough to protect everyone."

"You mean, you took the burns for your group?"

Quidel nodded.

"I thought they were tattoos. Can't Kokolo heal you?"

"Very observant. Kokolo has already done what she can," Quidel said. "Furthermore, my perspective before tonight was wrong, and I acknowledge and admit that. Had you not stopped me, I would have made a bad day much worse."

Gwyn nodded silently, her heart torn. She suddenly felt a sense of sadness for Quidel, surprised he would lead his men in battle.

"What I'm going to say next is confidential," Quidel said, sitting up straight before continuing. "Someone in the guild is giving away very sensitive information to our adversaries."

Gwyn listened as she sipped her tea.

Quidel looked to the side before continuing. "A wizard named Xess rules over the Eastern Kingdoms. We believe he is the one dabbling in forbidden magics."

"How could someone like that become a ruler?"

"The wizard council believed it would balance your mother and father's kingdoms. The people of their kingdoms desired they become rulers of those lands. Xess had little demand from the people but led efforts to restore the east. The council gave in to his pressure, bringing forth the age of wizards."

"Xess bullied his way to being a king?"

Quidel nodded. "Rumor is, now he's taking over your mother's kingdoms since she vanished. In past battles many believed she was a fool for not taking him out entirely, but she gave him a second chance and now..."

"How awful..."

"See, there was once a great city in our continent that connected the three kingdoms—Arcadia. Built nearly a thousand years ago after a violent feud between the north and east. It housed many relics and was guarded by the Atari Templar, but without them, no one is there to stop the east, and no one's been brave enough to stand up to Xess."

"What happened at Arcadia?" she asked.

"A fine question, but the history is blurry," Quidel said, taking a drink of tea before continuing. "Xess is getting bolder, encroaching on the west with undead armies. I believe he wants to take it over too. Sadly, I believe he's had help from within our guild. Thank God your father put strong safety measures to protect the Western Kingdoms. Even now, your father protects us."

She nodded, hoping Quidel would continue.

Quidel gritted his teeth. "Gwyn, for the longest time, I've had reasons to believe the traitors were Franz and Delilah."

She raised an eyebrow. "Why?"

"When Cassius passed, no one knew why or how, other than perhaps Franz. All I had to go on was Franz's vague word and that your father raised his rank to Master Wizard."

She tilted her head slightly while listening. "What do you mean, Master Wizard?"

"The highest wizard rank achievable—not something many wizards achieve. Furthermore, your father and Franz conducted a binding spell, so Franz and Delilah are spellbound to conceal you from this world of magic until a specific time. It seems they've found a minor loophole just in time."

"Couldn't he just write it down and show you?" she asked.

Quidel laughed softly. "Oh no. I thought it odd that Cassius would perform such a spell, but here you are before me. See, before tonight, you were a forgotten rumor. Even if Franz had found a way to tell me, I would have doubted him. Your parents masterfully hid you from the world."

Gwyn placed her teacup down and stood up to face away from Quidel. She took a few steps away from the table and took a deep breath as a tear rolled down her cheek.

"I forget how new this all must be for you."

"I'm fine," she said, trying to hide her emotions. She wiped the tear and returned to her seat. "What about my mother?"

Quidel nodded. "Your mother was very powerful. For years, I wondered if she wasn't still out there... I'm sorry, Gwyn, I lost that hope long ago. I fear forbidden magic was used on her. Some believe Franz somehow tricked and killed your parents—forcing your father to give him the rank of Master to avoid punishments and overthrow his rule."

The talk weighed heavier than she had anticipated. Hearing Quidel confess belief that her mother survived had brought her a glimmer of hope. She didn't like losing it so quickly.

"Your parents' relationship was somewhat taboo. The council likes to weigh in on such matters, especially since they were permitted royalty. They had ideas that were unpopular with the council, but the people often supported them. Your father even wanted to unite the Northern and Western Kingdoms. But I digress. When they passed, most looked at the only person who was near when it happened."

"My uncle..." she whispered.

"Yes, Gwyn... Franz," Quidel said, sipping some tea. "I have known Franz for a long time and did not want to believe that he could have done such terrible things. I suppose a decade of your closest advisors telling you that you're wrong and letting a guilty man walk free can do a lot to someone's mind."

She took a breath. "But now, my aunt and uncle are proven innocent."

Quidel sat silently for a moment, then nodded and smiled. It was a rather warm smile, Gwyn thought—a side he had not shown before. "I must say, you do look a lot like her."

Gwyn looked up with interest. "You knew my mother?"

"Oh yes. She even studied here. For a long time, this was her home."

"What drove her to leave?"

Quidel shrugged. "Some leave to look for something better. It doesn't mean we forget where we came from. When she volunteered to rebuild the north and later became Queen of the Northern Kingdoms, she kept Xess at bay. She helped to keep peace. I was thankful for that."

Silence crept into the conversation as both took the last sips of tea from their cups.

"Sir, why did the shades bow to me when I drew my bow?"

Quidel sat silently for a moment, and though it was brief, Gwyn saw a glimpse of nostalgia flash across his face. "They did that the last few times your mother came through the guild."

"Please, tell me more about my mother?"

Quidel smiled. "Some stories, even I have trouble believing. But those stories will come later. I do feel someone owes you a bit of explaining.

From what your uncle told me, you've been kept more in the dark than a blindfolded bat."

She looked down. "I... guess so. I haven't really heard much about my parents until now, and I've wondered..."

"We'll continue this soon, Gwyn. It would not be wise to put too much on your heart all at once."

"Sir." she said before he could get up.

"Yes?"

"I... could have killed you..."

Quidel smiled. "I'm sure you could have picked the very ribs you wanted to put that arrow between. I also have a feeling it took a lot of effort to resist. Don't be sorry, Gwyn—tonight happened for a reason, just the way it did."

"Sir," Gwyn said again before he could get up, "is the guild still going to be attacked?"

Quidel shook his head as he took another sip of tea. "Maybe not, after what you did to that lich. Your mother was the only wizard known to wield that power. When Xess finds out, he'll likely suspect someone has taken her place or that she's alive... Hopefully, he doesn't know about you. My spies should gather more information soon."

Quidel stood, helped her up, and walked her to the door. "By the way, it looks good on you," he said.

She stopped and turned. "What does?"

"Your mother's cloak."

Upon reaching the door, Quidel nodded and smiled with a slight bow. Gwyn returned the sentiment and left Quidel's quarters to join her friends and family.

CHAPTER 12

Shadows of the Stone Gardens

Gwyn's mind buzzed with thoughts as she wandered the hall, so lost in reflection that she nearly collided with a tall wizard striding toward her. His blue and black robes billowed, and his pale grayish-white eyes fixed on her beneath a strange tattoo etched below his right eye. Startled, she glanced up and stammered an apology. The man offered no reply, only a brief nod, before continuing toward Quidel's quarters.

Back in their room, Gwyn found Jack and Chele sprawled on the round red couch, a fire crackling warmly. She joined them, settling into the cushions.

"So?" Jack prompted, leaning forward.

"He greeted me as 'Princess,'" she began, her voice tinged with disbelief.

"Well, if your parents were royalty, that makes you a princess, right?" Chele asked.

Gwyn shrugged. "Quidel said he sees me that way, even without a kingdom." She recounted her conversation with Quidel, detailing his revelations about her heritage. Jack and Chele listened, wide-eyed and eager to learn more.

When she finished, Jack held up a book. "We've been reading about the Academy in Silvania. It looks pretty cool!"

Gwyn took the book and fanned through the pages while Jack and Chele told her about it: the several floors above and below ground, how it was once connected to the castle, and the barrier magic that sealed the passageways.

The three of them discussed ways they could somehow convince Chele's mother to let her go, but Chele was convinced she would not. "My mom would kill me if she knew what happened tonight!"

Jack, on the other hand, had spoken with Franz and Delilah about it and was confident they were willing to sign a waiver for it.

The three of them learned a lot about the magical world over the next few days. They found out that the guilds were actually located deep inside the planet. They also joined Franz and Delilah for the funeral of their fallen friends.

The funeral was similar to any other funeral but they were given a burial in a city Gwyn had never heard of. Franz and Delilah seemed quiet over the next few days.

Gwyn, Jack and Chele joined them at a meditation circle, which took place somewhere in an underworld forest outside the guild where it looked like stars twinkled far above them.

Gwyn thought the forest was strangely loud and full of life for being so far underground. The plants were beautifully exotic, with a luminescent glow sprouting from within the fibers of the leaves. There, they learned that wizards were generally born with far more magical ability, but some humans could actually learn it over long periods of time as well.

Overall, the Shadow Guild had proven to be quite fascinating on its own. Word somewhat caught on as to who she was and Gwyn had to get used to people randomly introducing themselves to her everywhere she went in the guild. She found it rather strange having people realize who she was but not know anything about them.

Franz and Delilah left on duty, stating they'd be back in a few days.

A few days went by, and late one afternoon, Quidel sent for Gwyn through Belas to meet her in a place called the Stone Gardens within an hour. Gwyn informed Belas that she didn't know where it was, so Belas offered to show her the way but informed her that they would have to leave at that moment, which would make them early as she was meeting someone in a small library café on the way.

Gwyn accepted the help, grabbed her things, and followed. Belas made small talk with her about the guild and pointed out a few key areas of interest along the way.

They reached the café, which was half café and mostly shelves upon shelves of books. Belas stepped inside to be greeted by a tall, thin man. He had long, wavy, auburn hair and a long beard that came to a point. He also wore black robes with red trim at the shoulders and an orange belt. "Gwyn, this is my boyfriend, Wesley."

She shook Wesley's hand. He had long, thin fingers that wrapped completely around Gwyn's hand. "Call me Wes."

The three of them proceeded to the Stone Gardens. Gwyn walked silently in step with them, while listening to them debate over what to have for dinner.

Wes had proven to be a bit foul-mouthed and made Gwyn blush several times during the walk, mentioning things from dirty undergarments to literally farting on a boy who was throwing a fit in the hall during his day job. She unsuccessfully fought off laughing at his stories, though she found Wes' sense of humor rather odd.

Belas smacked Wes for his misbehaviors, and several times reminded him that Sterling's daughter was with them.

They came upon the entrance to the Stone Gardens and bid Gwyn farewell. Wes had given her a bit of departing advice that sounded strange and dirty, and she was certain she wouldn't need it, even if she had understood it.

She made her way through the door and into the Stone Gardens. As the name hinted, the gardens were indeed filled and lined with very large and beautifully carved stones. Bizarre, exotic plants were everywhere. Tropical-looking plants with fluorescent lights, like deep-sea fish, seemed to be the theme of the place. Gwyn looked around in awe for some time, admiring how beautiful and colorful the large, glowing plants were. They reminded her of looking at the stars before the moon rose high enough to dull them.

The ceiling was dark with amber glowing in the cracks. Indigo light shone through random areas where she assumed Xi energy fed in a fluorescent manner.

Gwyn walked on the stone floor of the gardens, which had dry moss on it and thick patches of grass that grew in sandy areas. She made her way through the first part of the garden to find Quidel's waiter standing near a stone fire pit. There was a stone table and benches that sat between the trees next to the fire pit, which had a small fire in it. She decided to take a seat at the table.

The fire gave a warm, flickering glow to the surrounding plants and stones. Gwyn thought it to be nicely set up for an enjoyable evening.

Quidel's waiter brought her a tall glass of iced tea but told her Quidel had not arrived yet.

She couldn't help but think of her harp, wishing to play while she waited. It had been a while, and she wondered about Mrs. Benadine, who was supposed to be teaching her. *Was she also magic?*

She made a mental note to ask Franz and Delilah about it later. As she waited, a courting couple walked by holding hands in the distance. She did her best to ignore them, going over the fingerings of Twilight's Kiss in her head when Quidel emerged from the archway of trees leading to the fire pit.

Quidel was wearing maroon-colored clothes that seemed to go well with his orange tone of skin. "Good evening, Gwyn. I have brought a friend with me, if you don't mind."

Behind him was a man wearing red robes. He had a sharp face with gray hair pulled back into a ponytail and a long, pointed goatee. He also wore small, square glasses over his dark brown eyes.

"Gwyn, this is Professor Fox," Quidel said. "He is a professor at the Academy in Silvania and responsible for recruiting and enrollment to the school from the Shadow Guild."

Gwyn reached out to shake the tall man's hand, but he said, "My pleasure," bowed before her, and sat down across from her. Quidel sat next to Professor Fox, then smiled at Gwyn.

"Have you eaten yet, Gwyn?"

She shook her head, and Quidel beckoned to the waiter, who came and took his order of three roasted puffins with mushroom tea and coffee.

"Gwyn, Professor Fox and I have been talking, and he says he's excited to have you this semester at the Academy," Quidel told her. "In case your friends aren't able to make it, I thought it might be wise that you knew someone there before going."

Fox smiled and put his long hands together. "It will be a pleasure, I'm sure. I once had the honor of instructing your mother for a time, so I must be twice as lucky to have her daughter."

"My mother was there?" Gwyn asked.

Fox smiled. "Yes, shortly. She helped tutor there for a time as well. She was older than you are now when she went. The Academy has been around for a very long time and was built as a fundamental learning school for magic." Fox paused as the waiter brought coffee, and he took a sip from the steaming cup. "Once you feel confident in your basic abilities, you can learn more by joining a guild or, if you're lucky, apprenticing a more experienced wizard, like a Master Wizard such as Quidel."

"Right," Gwyn said, recalling what Quidel had told her before.

"Yes, well, Master Wizards are a bit high of rank to aim for even as a tutor, but there's an ancient system used to rank skill and authority," Fox told her. "It's a chart still used commonly. It all depends on your birthright talents and skill. Of course, the wizard council will want to weigh in, I'm sure. But there are several paths for real magicians. Many careers stem from within here in the guilds."

Gwyn tried to grasp the concept of ranks Fox had explained to her, but it seemed a bit much at the moment. "What rank would I be?"

"Most start off without rank, but say you do have a natural skill and can cast fire, for example, you might rank in the Magi system somewhere along the lines of a Mage, or Magius."

"Maggots?" Gwyn protested.

"Oh, no! No, not maggots," Fox defended. "Mag-us. It's for those who can perform more elemental-based magics or damage-inflicting magics, like your aunt and uncle, or your mom. Don't feel limited; some wizards can do a little of everything, although most wizards find they're good at only a few things and build on that."

"What about my father? Did he go to school at the Academy?"

Fox looked to Quidel for a moment, then back to Gwyn. "I... don't think so. But your father was much older. I suppose he could have before I was there."

Gwyn sat for a moment in silence. She had questions but hadn't expected Quidel to bring company and felt odd about asking them in front of a new acquaintance.

"Gwyn..." Fox said shyly.

"Yes?" she replied, her curiosity piqued.

"It has been brought to my attention that you're insisting on your friends going with you to the Academy. Is that correct?" Fox asked.

Gwyn hesitated for a moment, then answered. "Yes, of course I am," she replied, then sat up straight, ready to protest.

"May I interest you in an alternative to that?" Fox asked.

Gwyn gave a half grin. "...I suppose."

Fox looked over his glasses at Gwyn and lowered his voice a bit. "Gwyn, teaching un-magical folk is very hard and time-consuming. It's also quite frustrating for everyone involved. Not to mention, there are strict rules about it. It's against policy. Even having your friends here in the guild is somewhat looked down upon."

Gwyn looked off to the side, not at all prepared to argue the matter and hoping to devise a good retort.

"Consider instead having your friends return home and going to the Academy alone; then, on your breaks, you could teach them a thing or two?" Fox suggested with a wink and a smile.

Gwyn sat for a moment, trying to consider the proposition, but it didn't sit right with her. She shook her head and made an angry face. "Absolutely not. I'd rather not go if that's the case."

Fox breathed in, sighed, then looked at Quidel. "Okay then... I guess this will be an interesting semester."

Quidel smiled and nodded to Fox, who was getting up to leave. "I told you she wouldn't have it. Besides, from what I hear, you may be surprised."

Fox gave a quirk of a smile, then put a red, tall, pointy hat on and bid them farewell.

"Sorry, Gwyn. He insisted on meeting with you to change your mind about your friends. A bit of a coward when it comes to teaching magic to non-wizards, but don't let that fool you. He's a powerful Adept," Quidel told her.

Gwyn felt herself relax a bit now that it was just herself and Quidel. A slight smile crept onto her face as the waiter placed the puffin on the table in front of them. They both pulled a wing off, dipped it in a bowl of sauce, and ate.

Red wine was poured, and Gwyn enjoyed dinner in the Stone Gardens with Quidel.

"So, now that you've been here for a few days, tell me what you and your friends think of the guild?"

Gwyn tried to think of where to start. "I... We love it! It's so different down here. There are so many strange, new things to see and learn about."

Quidel took a drink of wine, then ordered a round of mint ice cream. "I'm glad you're enjoying it—all three of you. I do have a proposition myself to make to you," he said, raising a brow.

Gwyn sighed, hoping she was done with the propositions tonight, hoping she could talk more about her parents and more interesting things.

"Don't be that way," Quidel told her. "I just wanted to know if you felt safe here—and if not, would you prefer having a bodyguard escort you?"

For a moment, the security sounded kind of nice, but then Gwyn considered having someone she didn't know follow her around, and it sounded less fun. "I... feel safe. I don't need a bodyguard. Thank you, though."

Quidel nodded, smiled, and dropped the subject. "I suppose you've got questions for me?"

Gwyn smiled. "Perhaps a few, if you don't mind."

Quidel gave a shrug that suggested why not.

"Well, I'd like to know about my bow."

"Mm! You just missed out. Professor Fox is a weapons expert—probably could have answered your question better than me."

"Well, sometimes when I shoot, it's just a regular arrow. Other times, it's that shiny, magical arrow that freezes stuff. Why does it change?"

"You mean the Xeo arrow," Quidel told her flatly.

"Xeo arrow?" Gwyn asked.

Quidel nodded. "The bow, Apollo, is actually mentioned in ancient texts. It's what your mother called it. I believe she knew correctly, too. The names she used for her weapons always seemed accurate to me—and names are very important. Whether it's the same as the ones in the texts..." Quidel said before shrugging.

Gwyn nodded, mouthing the word "Xeo."

Quidel rubbed his chin and thought about it for a moment. "Hmm... I could certainly pose a theory or two on that, but I must warn you, they are only theories."

This time, it was Gwyn who shrugged.

"Okay, well... It's unlikely that you understand your magical energy well enough to fully control it... and even if you did, it doesn't make sense that you would know exactly how to channel it into the bow for such a powerful bit of magic."

Quidel looked at Gwyn for a moment, then asked, "Do you mind if I take a look at it?"

Gwyn removed her bow and handed it to Quidel. At first, he closed his eyes and held it. "Interesting."

"What is it?"

Quidel opened his eyes to look at Gwyn. "It has a strong aura of the Xi."

"You can feel the Xi?"

"Oh, yes," Quidel said, then looked closely at it, turning it over in his hands, examining every inch of it. "I daresay it has a secret function. Magic so encrypted that it is impossible to see into how it works for me. The design is there; I can feel it, but it's like reading a language I've never seen before."

Gwyn slouched a little, disappointed that Quidel didn't know. "So you don't know, then?"

Quidel lowered the bow and smiled. "No. But I must confess, it's a lovely bow."

Quidel handed Gwyn her bow back. "I sense there's a strong bond from that bow directly to the Electric Moon, or Xi Moon, as I call it."

Gwyn wondered how her mother could have come to own such a strange, powerful weapon. "Did you ever see my mother shoot it?"

Quidel took a deep breath, then crossed his hands on the table in front of himself. "Gwyn, I must warn you. There are some things you might rather not know, especially at such a young age."

Gwyn didn't want to hear that she was too young; she wanted to know the truth. "I don't care," she said, a bit hesitantly since the last time she insisted on hearing the truth, it had broken her heart to learn it. Even so, she persisted and gave Quidel a look that insisted on hearing it.

Quidel closed his eyes for a moment and sighed. "Very well. Do I have permission to show you something, then?"

Gwyn nervously nodded.

He held out his hands, and she reached out. He took her hands across the table. He asked Gwyn to relax, and within a few seconds, the area around them was suddenly filled with bright white fires and purple flames, and the Stone Gardens were gone completely.

Gwyn screamed and jumped up onto the stone bench that was there, but invisible.

"Do stay calm. It's just a memory I'm sharing with you," Quidel insisted. "This is the planet a thousand years ago."

Gwyn gave Quidel a look of terror. "What!?"

"This planet was once a very different place, Gwyn. It has been known by many names. It was once called Earth," Quidel said, raising his arm again, and suddenly they were launched high into the air where they could look at the planet from above.

Gwyn couldn't keep from screaming as the feeling of being jolted upward so fast was sickening.

"This feels so real!" she said loudly.

Quidel held her by the waist, the wind blowing violently behind them, whipping through Gwyn's hair. They were looking down on the Earth from far above and could see, to their left, the giant Electric Moon almost touching it.

Gwyn could make out the regular white moon far behind it. "What is happening!?" she screamed.

Quidel's deep voice cut through the loud wind with ease. "A thousand years ago, the Electric Moon came so close to Earth that it destroyed nearly everything on the surface and reshaped the world."

Nearly the entire planet looked like it was being engulfed with white and indigo-colored electric flames. Giant waves of water were kicking up, even going into space from the ocean. The planet let out what sounded like a scream of pain. Ice from the north and south poles was melting fast and poured into the oceans as chunks of land ripped from the planet and flew out into space.

Quidel pointed to a large continent. It stretched from the north to the south poles of the planet. Gwyn could see the faint glimmer of a force field in the mid-western part of the continent. It was stopping waves and fire from coming onto it. "That is where Silvania is now," Quidel said.

"Your father orchestrated that massive force field to protect it, while a group of highly skilled wizards worked to put the Electric Moon into a balanced orbit with the other moon. At first, it didn't work. We couldn't separate the Xi Moon from Earth, and after several long hours, we were exhausted and had nearly given up. Countless wizards died holding the force field over the continent with your father. They were taking too much damage too fast and overextended themselves to death. That was when your mother revealed the power of Apollo."

"What?" Gwyn yelled.

"Your bow—Apollo. I heard rumors of how she obtained it and where it came from, but I cannot say for sure. However, this was the first time I ever saw it used... Watch," Quidel said, pointing.

Gwyn saw a shining arrow of light come from somewhere on the continent. She recognized it as an arrow like her own. A Xeo arrow. It flew into space and hit the Electric Moon. Slowly, the Electric Moon froze over under a layer of ice. Electricity was still crawling under the thick sheet of ice as Gwyn had seen it so many times before. Within minutes of being shot with the arrow, the Electric Moon looked as if it had been tamed—covered in a glass ball made of ice.

"Your mother sealed the Electric Moon with the bow, stopping its destruction of the planet. It still took hundreds of wizards several days to get the orbits of the moons to where they worked, and it changed the tides of the oceans forever. Even to this day, few venture out to sea because of the unpredictable waves."

Gwyn didn't know why, but she was now freezing. She started to shiver. Quidel waved his arm, and they were back in the Stone Gardens. "I'm so sorry, Gwyn. You're in shock. Sit closer to the fire. It will help to warm you," Quidel said, then waved his arm, and the fire doubled in size.

"If you don't stop shivering soon, I'll send for Kokolo; she's rather fond of you."

Gwyn wrapped herself in her cloak and managed out a shaky question. "What about... all the people... in the world?"

Quidel shook his head. "The planet was almost destroyed. A lot of people didn't make it. Only around 1%. The guilds took in as many as they could, but a majority of the people on the planet died. Sadly, as it happens with those with short lives and short memories, most history has become little more than bedtime stories for regular humans. And the world as it was before, has mostly been forgotten, right down to the name. Only a handful of holidays, religions, and languages exist as they were before."

Gwyn remembered the building foundations she'd found in the forests back at home. "So... how different was it?"

Quidel thought back. "Quite different, and quite the same, altogether. There was still war, and people still bickered about nonsense. Wizards didn't play as big a role in the surface world back then."

Quidel paused and checked on Gwyn before continuing. "There was a unique power source back then they called 'electricity,' which no longer works correctly since the Xi Moon discharged itself on the Earth. The Xi crystals left behind by the event, however, do serve as a new type of energy source."

Gwyn looked up at Quidel, no longer shivering as badly. "Xi crystals are from the Electric Moon?"

Quidel nodded slowly. "Of course. They are far more spiritual in energy than electricity ever was, though."

Gwyn couldn't help but feel that her heart had successfully predicted the link somehow.

"I hope I've helped you with your questions. I do not think it would be wise to answer any more in your current state," Quidel told her.

Quidel helped Gwyn up. She was surprised to find her legs were heavy. "Why did that happen to me back there?" she asked him.

"Because the memory I shared with you is likely more vivid and real than your mind could handle, resulting in a sensory overload. Keep in mind, you not only were experiencing what I saw, but also what I felt. Your spirit is young and has a hard time processing the feelings of someone so much older, especially in a situation as complicated as that," Quidel said.

The explanation made sense to Gwyn. She had felt overwhelmingly distressed to see the planet going through what it did. She could still feel the helplessness breaking her heart as she had to watch everything she knew and loved be destroyed. She then realized how much Quidel really cared about the planet. It was as if she were seeing him in a new way. She hadn't thought he cared for much of anything, but she knew he would sacrifice himself in a heartbeat if it meant saving the planet and people he cared for.

Gwyn found her voice a bit hoarse but managed out a "Thank you."

Quidel stopped and looked down at Gwyn with a quizzical look.

"For doing what you did. You helped to save the planet," Gwyn said, looking up, revealing dark circles around her eyes.

Quidel could see the agony the memory had put her through and knelt down beside her. "Gwyn..." he paused for a moment, then shook his head, smiled, and walked Gwyn to her quarters.

CHAPTER 13

Determination

Gwyn returned to the quarters to find Jack slumped lazily over the couch, plumper than she'd ever seen him. Chele was flipping through a book while sipping on a chocolate iced nectar latte she'd discovered at a café called Hotes. Gwyn woke Jack quickly and beckoned the two of them to listen as she did her best to explain what Quidel had shown her.

Gwyn knew she couldn't justify the full experience to them with words, but she did so with a shaken voice that seemed to hold their attention intently.

"I think we should be training for the rest of the summer—as much as we can," Gwyn told them. They both looked at her as if she were crazy.

"Why, Gwyn? It's summer. There aren't any fish to catch... I think... and we're safe in the guild. Besides, it's fun exploring down here while your aunt and uncle are doing their business across the country," Jack retorted.

Gwyn stopped for a moment, counting the days since her aunt and uncle had left on a mission for the guild. She bit her lip as she realized it had been days since they'd left in a hurry.

"Because you'll need to make an impression on Professor Fox so he'll let you stay at the Academy with me," Gwyn retorted. "I got the feeling he's going to be hard on you guys if you even get to go with me."

"Well... crap!" Jack replied, reluctantly agreeing to train with Gwyn.

"Chele, we'll have to figure out a way to convince your mom to let you go. I think I'm going to really need you there."

Chele silently nodded, and they went to the nearest library. They spent several days poring through books on magic, energy, and discussing the bizarre and strange concepts of it.

Many books were in foreign languages or had unfamiliar words in them. Nothing they tried from the books worked, not even a little. It wasn't until Gwyn ran into Wes that they had a slight hint of a magical breakthrough.

"Please help us," Gwyn pleaded as he walked by with his head focused on something in the distance.

"Beat it, newbie. Get your basics at school. I don't have time," he retorted.

"Please, Mr. Wes! Nothing we do is working! We just want a good place to start," she replied with a slight look of desperation.

"Ugh. Fine! You owe me a drink, though."

Wes gave Gwyn the name of a book called Wizdough and told her to order a hidden menu item from the Hotes Café called poly juice.

"It's a tea made of polyphenols and some various roots. Just don't drink it all the time," he told her.

"Poly what?" Gwyn replied in confusion as Wes turned and left.

It wasn't long before Gwyn and her friends were sitting at a table in the corner of the café, staring down at their mugs of the poly juice with the Wizdough book in front of them. The book had very thick pages, detailing beginner techniques as well as a small ball in a glass tube attached to it. The book guided the reader in simple terms on how to use and manipulate shallow waves of energy to push the ball.

It was hardly magic but more than any of them knew.

"Bottom's up," Jack said as they all drank the frothy, dark green brew. The taste was chemically and had both bitter and sweet undertones. All of them coughed as it burned their throats.

Gwyn thought the taste was somewhat familiar but couldn't place it. As she sat there staring at the book, she began to feel a bit odd.

"Alright, Gwyn, if any of us are going to be able to move the ball, it's you," Jack said, holding his stomach in discomfort.

She sat up straight and worked to focus on the concepts the book gave. Her first attempts failed. After Jack and Chele tried, Gwyn went to try again. She felt eagerly determined. After strenuous focus, she let out a gasp of air.

For a moment, she thought she might have done it but wasn't sure if Jack hadn't just bumped the table. After a short debate, they decided to return to their quarters and sleep off the poly juice.

The next day, the three of them met up in the living room to discuss how they felt.

"What a waste of good taste buds," Jack said, projecting his feeling of utter disgust for the drink.

"I don't feel different. Not sure I want to do that again," Chele added as she finished writing a letter to her mother.

Gwyn nodded gently, considering if she could determine a difference in the way she felt. "I can't say if it made the difference, but I thought I felt a little stronger, myself."

"Maybe we got the placebo juice," Jack joked before shivering in disgust at the thought of drinking more.

"How many letters have you sent, Chele?" Gwyn asked.

"This is my fourth letter. My mother won't commit to letting me go. She still needs help around the homestead."

"Don't give up. We'll think of a way," Gwyn added.

Many of the books they had been reading suggested focusing on fighting and meditation techniques, so they gathered their weapons and walked around until they found the training area.

The area was a room with stone pillars that separated lanes where people were casting magic at targets. Others were sparring off against other wizards.

They stopped to watch a fascinating duel where wizards were throwing flits and beams of magic at each other. They both moved extremely fast, and watching the fight was entertaining.

"Geez! I hope you don't plan on us doing that today!" Jack said as they walked past.

Chele rolled her eyes. "I'm ready if you are," she said, holding up her knife and rope.

Jack swallowed, nearly choking on the hazelnut latte he had been sipping on.

"Easy, you two," Gwyn said. "We'll have to figure out what to do without actually hurting each other. It's just practice."

They made it to an area with fewer people around and set up in three empty lanes next to each other.

They had been practicing for some time when Gwyn looked across the lanes and saw the woman with opal eyes and black hair.

"Guys, stop..." Gwyn said, nodding in the direction of the woman to Jack and Chele. They both looked to see where she was looking.

"Who is that?" Jack asked.

"That's the woman from the grand hall where we first saw Quidel," Chele said. "I'd forgotten about her. She was giving you such an odd look that night."

Jack scratched the back of his head. "Wonder why?"

"The first night we were here, before I pulled my bow on Quidel, we locked eyes... I had a strange feeling about her," Gwyn confessed, a bit unsure about her feelings toward the woman.

The woman looked up and made eye contact with Gwyn from across the room. She then grabbed a dark bag and in a small flash vanished.

"Well... Guess she doesn't want to talk to you," Jack stated with a confused look.

"Don't worry. I'm sure Quidel will know who she is. Maybe he can tell you about her next time you meet up," Chele suggested with a smile.

The guild had proven itself to be very large, and though it offered several interesting places to visit, many required long walks. Gwyn was also surprised to see so many people walking the halls of the guild.

Some in the guild gave Gwyn shy and surprised looks as they passed, some nodding and giving curtsies or bows. Gwyn felt clueless as to what to do in such situations. She simply nodded and smiled in humble and bewildered gratitude.

While leaving the café one morning, a lady in worn-out black and dark blue robes bowed deeply before Gwyn at her feet. The woman looked very tired and slightly older than most there. "Please, my lady. If you are who

I hear you are, your people in the north need you," she said in a shaking voice as if she could begin crying. "Please, don't forget us," she pleaded to Gwyn.

Gwyn knelt and placed her hand on the woman's shoulder. The woman lifted her head to meet Gwyn's eyes. Gwyn could see fear and hopelessness had overtaken the woman's heart. She didn't know what to say, so she nodded.

"Tell me, what can I do?"

Her hands grasped Gwyn's free hand as she spoke, shaking slightly. "The people... Stop the suffering," the woman said quickly.

The woman then stood and dropped a large feather at Gwyn's feet, before walking off quickly. Gwyn stood still for a moment, processing the strange event.

She knelt down and picked up the large brown and white feather, then looked at it for a moment, admiring how it was speckled with tiny black dots.

She looked back up, peering around everywhere, but despite spending several minutes searching, she couldn't find the woman or anyone who had seen her.

Gwyn, Jack, and Chele continued practicing over the next few weeks. They even sparred with each other a few times. Chele was surprisingly vicious and managed to take down Jack several times, but Gwyn proved to be surprisingly stronger than both of them.

Only once did Jack anger Gwyn to the point where she lost it. She was having him insult her so she could prepare for mental attacks as well as physical attacks per the advice of a book. However, in all of his charming wit, he made a particularly cruel comment about her parents, and it set her off.

When he said it, he was trying to take her down from behind, but her mind slipped, and she slammed him over her shoulder before trying to slam a fist into his nose. Luckily for Jack, he had already begun rolling and made it out of the way just in time to avoid the powerful blow. However, Gwyn did manage to catch a fistful of his hair as he sat up and slammed her head into his.

Blood poured out of his forehead as Gwyn stumbled around, regretting what she'd done. She had a small mark on her head, but Jack was worse off. He wasn't thrilled to experience his own Auric healing from Kokolo.

Gwyn felt bad about what had happened and brought Jack hazelnut lattes to cheer him up.

"The worst part was having that crazy hag fix me up," he said seriously.

"I'm really sorry, Jack. But Kokolo's really not so bad!" Gwyn assured him. "She just likes to cheer you up with... weird, morbid jokes!"

Jack glared at her for a moment. "She told me that 'if I were a good boy, the stitches wouldn't come to life and eat my brain!'"

Chele fought back a snicker but eventually relented to laughing.

"Hey!" Jack said with a smile. "It's not funny! That lady is bat-soup crazy!"

It was near the end of summer, and Gwyn's fourteenth birthday was near. She had grown considerably since last year and was starting to take on more of the appearance of a young woman.

Franz and Delilah returned late one evening, both of them looking exhausted. Neither of them spoke much of their trip, only stating they were on a reconnaissance mission for the guild.

Gwyn eagerly asked them, "Do people visit from my mother's kingdom?"

"What kind of people?" Delilah asked, confused.

"Someone wearing blue, maybe?"

Delilah knelt before Gwyn with a tired and sorrowed look upon her face. "That sounds like someone in your mother's royal sect. I don't think they'd come here."

Gwyn shyly gritted her teeth. "Why not?"

Silence filled the room for a moment before Franz spoke up. "Pride... things ended badly for the north, but most say they're too proud to reach out," he said with humbling sincerity.

Delilah looked up at Franz with concern, as if he'd said something too harsh.

"Why did you ask about that color? Did you read about that somewhere?" Franz replied.

"I must have," she said, then silently nodded and held her questions.

Franz sighed before placing his hand on Gwyn's shoulder, continuing in a tired voice, "We'll be heading back to the house for your birthday, Gwyn. We don't really have anything picked out for you this year, so it's up to you. What do you want to do?" Franz asked.

Gwyn thought hard about what she might want to do. Of all the things she wanted, she felt visiting her new school, the Academy, would be interesting.

Franz insisted that they take the carriage. They rode into Silvania from the north, stopping at a busy town square. They parked the carriage and walked down a cobblestone sidewalk overlooked by balconies. The arched stone pillars holding them up were at least a couple of feet thick.

Franz and Delilah made their way to an alley where a staircase was cut into the wall. At the entrance of the stairs was a tall, wrought-iron gate. Franz looked around to make sure no one was watching them, then placed his hand on the center of the gate and said, "Awa tawksnet." The gate flashed lightly and opened. Shortly after they entered, the gate slammed closed behind them.

"You'll have to have someone let you in before you learn how to incantate," Franz told them.

"Before I can date?" Jack asked with a look of disappointment.

"Incantate, mister! You know, verbal magic?" Franz said.

"Oh," Jack said, a little confused.

"Make no mistake, children, words can be very powerful," Delilah added.

They made their way down the stairs and found the stairwell went further down than they had expected. The stairs turned and eventually came to a large wooden door. They knocked, with a large iron knocker ring fixed on the door.

A few moments passed, and it was answered by a very tall, pale, thin man in black robes with a dangerously stern look about him. Next to him was a small girl with bright ruby-red hair who looked slightly older than Gwyn, wearing a dark hooded robe. "Don't mind Guts here; he doesn't talk much, and he wouldn't hurt a fly."

"His name is Guts?" Jack asked.

"Well, I guess that's what we call him. He has a proper name, but I can't say I've ever heard it," the redheaded girl told them.

"Delighted to meet you, Guts," Franz said, putting his hand out in front of him.

Guts looked down and made a grunting noise at Franz's outstretched hand, then finally grabbed it. Guts' hand dwarfed Franz's long fingers when they shook hands.

The redheaded girl laughed. "I'm Sash! Principal Lyndsey is busy, so I'm giving tours for the day. Would you like to see around?"

Sash took the group through the main hall, which felt like the entrance to a castle with a hint of the smell of old books filling the air. Sash gave a surprising amount of detail about items throughout: what year things were made, the meanings of specific things in paintings on the walls, who owned certain weapons, and the battles they were used in.

"Here's a portrait of the late King Cassius," Sash said in passing.

Gwyn's heart stuttered when she found herself looking at the faintly familiar face of her father. He had blond hair and looked noble and strong in his golden armor and sword. His smile was gentle, and his eyes were kind, as she knew they would be.

Franz looked at Delilah and nodded before kneeling next to Gwyn. "This is all I have for you this year. Happy birthday, Gwyn," He handed her a heart-shaped locket on a golden chain. It had a star-shaped sapphire in the middle of its golden heart.

Gwyn opened it to find an old, worn-out note written inside.

Forever my love, remember this. Together we'll meet, in twilight's kiss.

"The lullaby..." Gwyn whispered to herself. "I love it!"

Gwyn hugged Franz and Delilah and they continued the tour.

They saw the weapons classroom, a laboratory for making strange things, and a room with Xi crystals in it labeled Symbology.

"What's Symbology?" Gwyn asked.

"It's the study of symbols and their use on physical objects. Xi crystals are the primary power source for the Academy," Sash noted.

"If I understand, little is known about them to this day. Is that still true, Sash?" Franz asked.

"Yes Sir Mr. Franz, you are correct, to a point. It's been advancing quite quickly lately. Just last semester, a kid stumbled on a symbol that bound Xi energy to a geode that caused it to strobe and glow different shades of colors." Sash informed him.

"Wow. That sounds awesome. We could use that for parties!" Jack said.

Sash chuckled. "Party on, Mr. Jack! I will also tell you this: some have spent untold hours tinkering with Symbology, and it's believed that some discoveries have not been shared with the rest of the world for safety concerns, supposedly from right here in the Academy."

"Interesting," Franz said, rubbing his chin.

Sash then led them briefly past Principal Lyndsey's office upstairs, who appeared to look very young and thin and had blond, spiked hair and small, rectangular-framed glasses. He had two other wizards in his office and looked to be locked in an important conversation.

She then led them deeper underground to the bunking rooms. The girls' hall of rooms was split from the boys', and Jack had to go in with Franz while Gwyn went into the girls' side with Chele, Delilah, and Sash. The rooms were sectioned off of hallways like dorms, and they were informed that Chele and Gwyn would likely be sharing a room together.

There were no windows, as they were told first-grade bunks were the deepest level and most abundant bunks, and that they would not have windows until they advanced.

"Doesn't seem like there are many rooms here?" Chele pointed out.

Sash shook her head. "Nope. We don't really have that many wizards per year. Maybe a dozen or two per grade per semester, and it's unlikely they'll all pass their first grade. Usually less than half do. And half of the next grade. Fail rates are expectedly high."

The rooms were simple: two beds, a bathroom, and a couch. There was also a strange wooden box Gwyn had never seen before. She opened it as a plume of cold frost came out of it. She placed her hand inside to find it very cold. "Is this a cellar?"

"That's the cooler. It's powered from Xi crystals. Someone found a symbol to change the energy to cold a couple of years ago. Well, it actually pulls heat out to be more technical. But the insides of it are wired to a Xi crystal that sucks the heat out and keeps things cool," Sash said.

"Wow," Delilah said with a surprised look on her face. "I wonder why they haven't sold any of these yet. Beats an underground food cellar."

"Not sure!" Sash said with a chuckle, then shrugged. "I think they're trying to get them into the guilds first."

Sash led the group back to Franz and Jack, and together they made their way back up toward the top.

They thanked Sash, waved goodbye to Guts, and left the Academy.

Gwyn suggested ice cream, and Franz informed them that a park was nearby. They bought bowls of homemade ice cream and sat and ate them at the park.

Gwyn ran and jumped into a swing and was joined by her friends shortly after. Franz and Delilah sat at the table, talking and finishing off their ice cream.

Gwyn looked down the road as she swung and could see her father's tomb sitting off in the distance in front of the castle behind the tall iron gates. Upon seeing it, she remembered the trance it sent her into. She recalled the voice whispering to her to reclaim something from the tomb. Gwyn was convinced that she'd heard her father speaking to her, telling her that he loved her and sending her a message after his death.

Part of her wanted to visit the tomb, but she did not, as she did not want to cry on her birthday. Instead, she blew a kiss toward it and wished her father well with the freshly painted vision of him in her mind.

CHAPTER 14
Ready Set Magic

Early the next morning, Gwyn was walking along the trellises of the vineyards at her aunt and uncle's. They were neatly aligned rows of grapevines, covered in the morning's dew. The hill she walked on gently sloped down toward the homestead that was nestled in a light fog.

Beyond the vineyard and fields, the woods encircled the farm, providing a sense of privacy and seclusion that she had forgotten how much she loved. Behind the tall and majestic trees, of which the leaves were rustling gently in a light breeze, the sun began peeking through the morning sky.

She was happy to see the sunshine again and breathe fresh, cool air after spending weeks in the underground corridors of the Shadow Guild.

Gwyn woke Jack and Chele and had them wait in the crisp morning air while she gathered Franz and Delilah outside to help her train one morning. The sky was sunny, and there was a nice crisp breeze in the morning air hinting that fall would arrive soon.

"Okay, we're here. What do you guys want?" Franz asked, rubbing the sleep from his eyes. Gwyn thought they might be a little run down after their long mission.

"We need to learn some real magic. The books in the guild were, uh, confusing," Gwyn told them.

Franz furrowed his sleep brow and gave Gwyn a crooked smile. "What's the rush, little one?"

Gwyn was considering how to answer when Chele chimed in. "Mr. Franz, we've been stuck at square one for weeks. We've read books, tried the moves, the meditations... it just doesn't feel like we're doing anything magical."

Franz shook his head. "Why? That's what school's for. They'll show you all the fundamentals and then teach you right."

Gwyn shook her head back at Franz. "No. Professor Fox doesn't seem to want Chele and Jack there. I know if they don't make an impression, things won't go well," Gwyn said.

"What gives you that idea? How do you even know who Fox is?" Delilah asked.

"Quidel introduced me. He asked me to change my mind about bringing non-magical people into the Academy."

"Err! That slimy little..." Franz said, then cut himself off before he said a bad word. He looked at Gwyn and told her, "Fox, not Quidel." He then scratched his head and thought for a second, "Okay, I was worried about Fox. He's not a bad guy or anything, just a bit wizard-bias."

"Well, regardless, can you teach us something?" Gwyn asked, not trying to hide a hint of desperation in her voice.

"Hmm." Franz rubbed his chin, thinking to himself for a moment. He started pacing back and forth.

"I suppose we could teach you to throw your qi," Delilah suggested. "It's a good basis and the fundamental base used for a lot of magic. Plus, you already know a few steps to gathering and storing energy," she suggested.

"That would be a good place to start!" agreed Franz, then led them to the barn. There, he hung four cans on fishing line from the rafters. "Okay, watch me." He then stood a dozen feet from the cans, pushed out his arm palm first, and a small wave of energy shot out, swirled through the air, and hit a can, causing it to slam up into the barn ceiling before spinning and swinging back and forth.

"Yyyyeaaahhh... think we could actually do that?" Jack asked in disbelief.

"That's the plan. It takes practice, and you'll have to keep exercising and gathering your energy. Even if you don't move a can, you will eventually drain yourself trying to use it," Franz told them. "Many forms of magic start with this practice. Even flits."

"And flits are qi?" Chele asked.

"Eh, not exactly," Franz replied. They're streams of elements infused through your energy. Like the ones Delilah uses are synergized with lightning. Lightning magic is rare, though," Franz replied.

"There are several types of flits. Or every magic spell, really. It's sort of unique to the caster. Often times, spells depend on what type of element suits your personality best," Delilah said with a smile.

"Well, regardless of flits, practice projecting your energy. If one of you moves a can, come get us. We'd love to see it," Franz told them before leaving to attend chores.

The three practiced throwing qi for several days. They would gather it using specific brocades, performing the careful movements in meditation. The steps were difficult to do at first, particularly while trying to meditate.

The practice proved to be far more exhausting than any of them expected, at first.

Gwyn woke early one morning, her mind weary and drained. She made her way into the kitchen and sat at a bar stool. She let her cloak's hood drape over her head and closed her burning eyes. She then put her hand on her cheek and rested.

As she sat there, she drifted for a moment and saw a great tower in the distance. It had a dark energy around it and it radiated through her. It felt familiar but wrong, as if someone had hurt someone she had loved. She took a deep breath and moved towards the tower.

She felt her head nod, catching herself from falling asleep; she pulled her mind away from the vision

Again, she closed her burning eyes and tried to let her mind wander back into the vision. It wasn't long before her mind slipped into a dream of fishing in the creeks in Pantheon. Suddenly, a loud clink snapped her out of the dream, and she opened her eyes. Laid before her was a speckled mug of coffee that her uncle had set down.

"Thank you," she uttered softly, before taking a sip from the steaming mug. The coffee warmed her tired spirit from inside, and she embraced it in the crisp morning air.

"Come," Franz said, nodding toward the fireplace in the living room. He placed a few logs neatly in the fireplace and used a flickering dark purple colored spell to light them quickly. "Sit, and meditate here for a bit in front of the fire. You've been working hard. You need to let your spirit recover."

Gwyn thought about taking the opportunity to ask more about her parents, but something inside told her to wait. So she nodded and spent nearly an hour meditating before returning to her practice.

After several more days, they all agreed that they could feel the difference between having energy and being without it. The difference was minor but noticeable.

Franz came down one day to watch and mentor them. "Alright, you guys. I'm going to share a little secret with you."

Gwyn, Chele, and Jack gathered around and listened closely.

"All energy has two sides. A negative side and a positive side. It is our life force given from the creator. When you meditate, it's impossible not to gather both. But here's the secret, the negative and positive can be controlled inside of you. Like magnets, they can balance each other, or oppose each other, even wind each other up. The power can be increased just by how you control it; a skilled wizard will use this secret to exponentially project the best forms of magic."

The three of them were giving Franz bizarre but interested looks as he explained theories like this behind magic to them.

"Guys... I'm losing you... Listen, you must let go of your disbeliefs."

Franz did his best to show them where the separate energies are stored and how to identify them. "If you can bring your positive and negative energies together, you'll create a stronger magic, and it'll be easier to manipulate and more than twice as powerful."

Franz saw the looks on their faces and realized he was probably just making a fool of himself. "Well, anyway. Give it a try. Good luck."

"Wait," Chele said. "How do you do it?"

"Oh. Right," Franz said, followed by some detailed guidance. Afterward, he went back to doing work around the property.

They all focused on bringing their negative and positive energy together, hoping to increase their powers. The first day, nothing noticeably different happened. But the next morning, after their meditation, Gwyn managed to project a visible ball of qi. It hit a can, making it swing back and forth.

"Whoa! Gwyn! You did it!" Jack and Chele cheered for her.

They brought Franz down, and she was able to repeat the show of magic. It actually hit the can harder the second time, and it almost hit the ceiling of the barn. Gwyn did it again and was confident that now she could always do it.

They celebrated with a hot cider to warm them up as the fall air was now getting colder by the day.

Gwyn pulled Franz aside, and asked him, "Why is it so easy for me to do bow magic with Apollo, but this magic took months to get anywhere?"

Franz laughed, "Gwyn, you don't know how special you are; some people spend years and even decades trying to do what you just did. If I'm being honest, there's something very special about you. As for the bow magic, some people are born with special abilities. Maybe that's one that runs in your family."

A couple more days went by, and Gwyn could easily make the can hit the ceiling with magic. She felt proud of her accomplishment. Her heart was lighter than it had been in a long time until she remembered her uncle's words, that it could take some people decades to do.

To her and everyone's surprise, Chele managed to project her energy just a few days later.

"I felt it. I felt it all come together! It was so easy to control once I felt it! Like it wanted to be used, and I just had to direct it!" she exclaimed, and another celebration of hot cider was held. Franz and Delilah were in sincere, happy disbelief.

Time passed, and there was only one day from their trip to the Academy. Jack had still not managed to project energy. "I give. I just don't feel like I can do it," he said with a sour look on his face. Jack then turned and kicked the barn wall. "Why do I have to be the one who sucks at everything!?"

"You don't suck, Jack! This is hard! You just can't give up!" Gwyn told him, feeling his frustration as well as her own fears nagging at her.

Jack didn't say anything and went over and sat on a bucket. He stared at the ground and rubbed his sore foot while Chele and Gwyn practiced.

Nightfall came, and Gwyn couldn't sleep. Her heart was heavy again. She looked out her bedroom window and saw the Electric Moon in the sky.

She decided she'd take her harp out to play on the ridge one last time before school started. She put on her cloak, grabbed her things, and snuck out the back.

When she reached the moonlit ridge, she could see a figure already sitting near the edge of it. She quietly snuck behind the bush at the bottom of the ridge and looked up to see if she could tell who it was.

It quickly became apparent to her that it was Jack. He had his head down and had a hood pulled over it, but Gwyn could tell who it was.

"You okay?" Gwyn asked softly as she made her way up the ridge.

"Yeah, I'm fine," he sighed. "Just frustrated, that's all. You and Chele do so well at everything. It seems like I'm just not cut out for this." She could tell in his nasally voice that he'd likely been crying.

"Jack, we haven't been doing anything easy for years. We've had to do such hard things since we were so young, we've forgotten that we're still kids. We're still growing up and figuring things out. Don't count yourself short on this. Last summer, we didn't even know magic existed."

Gwyn knelt down beside him and placed a hand on his back. "You probably just haven't found your technique yet. I know it was strange when I found mine. Almost like I'd always known it was there, but forgot how to reach it."

Jack didn't say anything and continued to look down.

"Jack, I need you and Chele with me. I feel it in my heart of hearts. There's something bigger on the horizon for us."

Jack sat silently still, staring at the rolling waves in the indigo-lit moonlight.

Gwyn didn't think her talking was doing much good, so she opened her harp case and took it out. She began plucking out the only song she knew well enough to play through all the way by memory.

The symbols were glowing around the harp as she played, but she paid no mind to it and performed Twilight's Kiss the best she could.

Something happened in Jack while she played. It was as if the notes mended his heart. If he could explain it, he would tell you that the notes themselves became needles that stitched his heartstrings back together the way they were meant to be.

When Gwyn finished, the air itself felt warmer and more comfortable around them. And though she didn't mention it, the sad vibes Jack was putting off before had all but vanished.

"They adopted me," Jack said with a crooked smile. "I don't deserve it, not one bit, but they did."

"Wait, what?" Gwyn said with true and stunned interest.

"Your aunt and uncle. The orphanage director told them they had to after withdrawing me for so long, or that I had to go back immediately. So they just... adopted me."

"Jack... That's excellent news!" Gwyn said in amazement.

Jack looked up. He had an excited look in his eyes. "Gwyn... I think... I think I can do it. You're right, I just can't give up." Jack got to his feet and started collecting his energy. She watched as he performed the movements of the brocades they had learned. In the electric moonlight, there was something magical itself about the meditation; slightly tribal, yet graceful. His arms moved smoothly from one stance to another.

After a few minutes, Jack walked over to the bush he had hid behind to listen to her play harp at the beginning of summer. He focused for a moment, then threw his arm forward, palm out. A small, but tangible distortion flew through the air and hit the bushes, causing them to rustle slightly.

His breath was heavy as he whispered, "I did it!" He then yelled it, "I did it!" And although they didn't have cider to celebrate, Gwyn shot a Xeo arrow over the water and watched as an explosive burst flashed, and a large circle of ice formed where it had landed in the ocean. They then took turns laughing and playing the harp that night on the ridge.

CHAPTER 15
The Academy: Semester 1

Travel to Silvania was filled with laughter and talk about Jack's adoption by Franz and Delilah, who had prepared steins of hot chocolate to celebrate.

They arrived late in the morning. Franz was unloading the carriage when Jack went around to the back. He found Jack there, his face etched with anxiety as he nervously bounced a coin in his hand.

Franz took his hand off a trunk from the carriage and walked up to Jack. "What's on your mind?"

Jack looked at his newly adoptive father and shrugged.

Franz caught the coin he was bouncing, snagging it out of the air with incredible speed. "There's no reason to beat around the bush about it!"

Jack dropped his head, seemingly embarrassed. "I keep wondering... what if... I fail? I don't want to let you down..."

Franz was listening intently. He looked to the side, took a breath, then turned back to Jack and gave a fleeting gesture, waving off the comment. "So what if you do?" He placed a hand on Jack's shoulder while he placed the coin back in his hand and knelt down. "Believe it or not, failures can be a blessing, so don't worry about that."

"They can?" Jack asked.

"Indeed, if you learn from them, they can teach you lessons that success never will."

Jack looked up to meet Franz in the eyes. He was somewhat taken aback to see him smiling. His eyes had gentle lines of crow's feet, giving them a warmth that comforted him. Jack smiled back, feeling more confident, and helped unload the carriage.

There were only a few other parents, a couple of adults, and a few younger people at the door of the Academy when Guts pulled it open.

Several kids screamed when they saw his large, pasty face impassively staring down at them; but Gwyn, Jack and Chele merely laughed when it happened.

They hugged and bid farewell to Franz and Delilah, promising to behave and be careful as they entered the large stone building of the Academy.

They split up to settle their things in their dorm rooms. Chele and Gwyn's room was windowless and small and had two modest beds and a tiny sofa. Chele chose the bed on the right, and Gwyn the left.

"Hey, Gwyn?"

She looked over at Chele to find her smiling slyly. "Yeah?"

"Wanna give the beds a quick endurance check?"

She felt confused at first, but then her face broke into a wide smile when she realized what Chele meant. They both kicked off their boots across the room before they began jumping on the beds.

She felt her nerves melt away as she enjoyed a moment of being a kid again.

After several minutes of the ruckus, they met up with Jack in the hall for dinner. It was not like the feasts of the Shadow Temple, but had plenty of fresh and delicious meats and fruits to choose from.

The next day, they met up before their first class, which was Magical Essence, Alignment, and Defense. They called it MEAD for short.

"So how did you get your mother to let you come?" Gwyn asked Chele.

"Well..." Chele said, hesitating, then lowered her voice to a whisper and leaned in close. "My family had wizard blood some generations back."

"Why are you whispering? Why be ashamed of that? Hold your head high! It might help you here!" Gwyn said with enthusiasm.

But Chele shook her head with a slight frown, then continued softly. "No, you don't understand. I've known about it for a while. I'm like one-eighth wizard blood. But it's enchantress blood."

Gwyn listened, waited, then shrugged. "Oh well. So what? Magic is magic. One-eighth has got to be better than nothing!"

Chele gave a half smile across her face. "I guess you're right about that part. But being an enchantress is looked down upon, from what my grandmother told me. She said it was 'dirty magic.' It's why I've never told you, but that's how I knew how they dressed. I knew because I've seen pictures of my great-grandmother. I'm sorry I kept it from you guys. I'm just a bit embarrassed about it."

"You mean you knew about magic?" Jack asked.

Chele shook her head. "I had no idea it was anything like this."

Gwyn bit her bottom lip, trying to think of something to cheer Chele up, but drew a blank. Jack unfortunately beat her to it. "Looks like you'll just have to show her up, show ol' Grammy how real magic is done."

Chele glared at him for a moment but then relinquished a smile as the door to their class opened. They gathered inside, and as Gwyn expected, Professor Fox was standing in the middle of the room. The air smelled stale, like a basement with a smoky hint to it. The floor had a fancy, thick, bright red carpet strewn across it and a lengthy dark mat on top of that. The walls were gray stone with oil lamps on them, dimly casting light around the room, and there were no windows to let the sunlight in.

"Good morning, class," Professor Fox began. He was wearing his red robes and pointy wizard hat, like the evening Gwyn had met him in the Stone Gardens. He ran his fingers over his pointy gray beard as the class piled in. "This morning, we are going to benchmark where your skills are. It helps me to teach you. Do not get upset if you do not advance to the next grade in your first year. Or even second or third. Most students will take years to advance."

Jack gave Chele a concerned look and swallowed hard.

"I've brought in a fifth-grade student to help us out this morning. If you are brave enough, you may duel him."

The low voice of a teenage boy then spoke from the front row. "Why doncha get ol' Queen Selena back here to fight him," the voice said from the front, invoking a few laughs around the room. Gwyn couldn't make out exactly who said it, as she was near the back, but knew it was about her.

Professor Fox, however, looked directly at the boy and said, "I assume you're talking about Miss Gwyn." Fox walked up to the boy and gave him a severe look. "I assure you, Mr. Parker, she is not one to be trifled with."

The crowd parted slightly, and Parker glared back at her. She met his gaze, unsure if she'd even seen him before, but he didn't look friendly. He reminded her of Matthew, being much taller, larger, and louder than most there.

"Let's talk about weapons," Fox said, breaking the tense stare Gwyn held with Parker. "At some point in your lives, you're likely to encounter something unfriendly. It's wise to make sure you have your weapon on you. If you don't have one, you can check a staff out here. In a more advanced grade, we'll work on teaching you how to store weapons and items in the nether. You can carry and draw it at will."

Jack nudged Gwyn and whispered, "Remember Quidel's sword?"

She thought back to Quidel, when he pulled the large sword from the air. Her mind hovered on the memory, only to be broken by Fox addressing the boy again.

"Now, Mr. Parker, if you wouldn't mind stepping over to one side of the mat across from Dirk, my fifth-grade student, and we'll begin our duels."

Dirk was much taller than most of the kids in the class. He was bald, thin, and very muscular. He wore strange red ninja-like robes.

"Dirk is going to weakly attack you. If you can fend him off with magic, please do so. If you cannot, use physical force. Remember, magic first, but try not to wound."

Dirk and Parker squared off with each other. Parker was slightly taller than Dirk, but Dirk looked more fit. Fox gave the signal, and Dirk attacked. Within seconds, he'd flipped Parker onto his back, then managed to get him onto his belly where he flailed his arms. Fox called the duel over and then had others take a turn dueling Dirk.

A few managed to project qi at Dirk, but they did it from so far away that he easily dodged it, except for a small girl named Kat with a dark complexion and dark hair. She knocked Dirk back a foot with a blast of energy, and Professor Fox pulled her aside and spoke to her for a moment with a smile.

Jack was called, but he'd forgotten to meditate and felt a pang in his gut when he tried to bring his negative and positive energies together. He did, however, throw a small amount of energy at Dirk before he was knocked to the ground. Fox didn't seem to notice that Jack had done magic at all.

Chele had been meditating through the duels, and she was called next. She took a common fighting stance she had seen Dirk take and Fox started the duel. Dirk rushed her and threw a wave of energy at her. Chele ducked it, her blonde hair whipping in the air behind her as the energy brushed through it. She managed a counterattack, and though she didn't mean to, her blast of energy hit Dirk in the crotch, bringing him to his knees.

Chele clasped her hands to her mouth as she watched Dirk writhe in pain on the mat. "Oh! I'm so sorry!"

Fox ran up to Dirk to check on him. He spoke with him for a few moments, then Dirk nodded. Fox then went up to Chele and put his hand on her shoulder. "You are... Gwyn's friend, correct?" Chele nodded. "Despite the fact that you just took away my top fifth-grade student's ability to reproduce, did I just see you project qi?"

Chele felt her face go bright red as she slowly remembered to nod. "Yes, sir. I'm so sorry, sir. I didn't mean..."

Fox shook his head. "Accidents happen. To see you do what you just did—That took me by surprise! Very well done!"

Chele felt herself relax a bit, and her face flushed from the compliment. Soon, she was beaming as she returned to the crowd.

"Excellent job!" Gwyn told her.

Fox helped Dirk to his feet where they waited a moment for him to regain his wits. He then called Gwyn up, and she took her place on the mat across from Dirk. From this angle, she could see how much taller he was than her. It was strange to have the class looking at her.

She attempted to focus. She had watched the other students go before her and had seen them release energy too quickly, watching Dirk dodge it easily. Her plan was to wait until he was closer to her to project it. She just had to time it right.

Fox started the duel. Dirk, who had attacked first for every student before, did not. Instead, he struck a strange pose with his feet spread evenly, one arm in the air and the other down, fists clenched tightly. The second he struck it, a flash of light ran through Gwyn, pulling her downward and slamming her face-first into the mat. The class began making a variety of sounds.

She crawled back slowly to her feet, looking up at the several pairs of eyes watching her, and took her fighting stance again. She was hoping now he would rush her, but instead, he projected qi at her. She dodged most of it, but it barely grazed her shoulder, giving her quite a jolt.

He threw three more blasts of energy. She dodged the first, but the second struck her shin, knocking her leg out from under her, and the third struck her in the stomach, pushing her back several feet off the mat onto the carpet near the wall. Several gasped when she landed.

She got up, removed her bow, and set it next to the mat, feeling herself getting heated. Once again, she took her stance, this time smiling slyly and waving Dirk on. "Come on, wouldn't want a little girl to show you up now, would ya?"

Dirk's expression was confused for a moment, then darkened. He looked at Fox with a glare and then lunged toward Gwyn.

She expected a blast of energy when he rushed her, but instead, he threw a bright yellow flit that flew within an inch of her head. She felt the heat of it on her skin as it hummed by. She dropped to her knee and brought her negative and positive energies together and let every drop of magic she could muster within her out.

It hit Dirk in the chest, and he hunched over. She took a swing at him, but he caught her with an elbow in the chest, knocking her a few steps back. Dirk then threw another blast of energy. It hit her in the face and knocked her back several feet.

She tasted the metallic tang of blood in her mouth. Dirk threw another flit, and Gwyn felt her mind slip. She dodged the flit by an inch, and before Dirk could withdraw his arm, she grabbed his wrist and pulled herself to him. With incredible force, she landed her fist into Dirk's nose. A loud crack echoed through the room. He instantly fell back, screaming and holding his nose as blood streamed down his face.

She stood still as her mind returned. She watched Dirk writhing in pain as Fox handed him a cloth. She then looked around the room to find everyone staring at her with a mix of responses between awe and concern.

"And that, is why you don't want to be messing with Miss Gwyn here," Professor Fox told his students.

She saw Parker leave the room well ahead of everyone else as Fox dismissed the class. She was nursing her lip with ice and gauze that Fox had handed out when Chele and Jack met up with her in the hall.

"Oh, Gwyn! That was my fault!" Chele told her, looking extremely upset. "I made him mad, and he took it out on you!"

Gwyn was holding her head down as she walked, afraid of what people were going to think or say now. "No, Chele, it's not your fault. Fox didn't call the duel off, even after Dirk knocked me down. I should have been out after the first strike."

"Why did he let Dirk use flits against you? He didn't use them against anyone else," Jack stated. "It was unfair."

She shrugged. "I think he wanted me to do that." To Gwyn's surprise, several people introduced themselves and complimented her.

"Hi, my name's Kat. You kicked that fifth-grader's butt!" said the brown-haired girl with a dark complexion.

A few others complimented her before walking off.

Gwyn was starting to get mixed feelings about what had happened.

Jack placed a hand on her shoulder and sighed. "Well, Gwyn, it's the first day, and everyone's both impressed and terrified of you."

Gwyn chuckled, giving Jack a sarcastic glance. "Thanks for the pick-me-up, Jack."

Their second class, Magic Lore, went smoothly considering how MEAD went. It was an entry lecture over magical history. Professor Plumb preferred being called Mrs. Plumb. She was energetic and quite good at explaining smaller details when people had questions.

They had a meditation hour afterward, learning what was called diaphragmatic breathing and brocades. They worked on being centered and stilling the mind. The teacher would silently correct them when they moved incorrectly in the dim, misty classroom. The strict rule in meditation was absolutely no talking.

There were several types of meditation used for different reasons: some for replenishing, others to clear the mind, or to lower heart rate and even reduce pain.

The more they practiced, the more they understood their positive and negative energy internally.

Next was lunch. They'd learned that food itself could affect their abilities. Certain foods reduced it a bit while others let it flow more easily. This hardly stopped them from enjoying hearty meals.

Gwyn discovered that there were many in her grade who had gone through it more than once. It was common for students to not make it through a grade on their first attempt. The professors explained that it wasn't as important to make it through a grade as it was to advance in knowledge and skill.

At lunch, they had the choice to eat out in the courtyard where some students would stay in a meditative state while they ate. They did eat outside but sat far enough away so as not to bother anyone meditating while they talked.

"So what's the point of meditating through lunch again?" Jack asked.

"Didn't you listen to Mrs. Plumb? Several things!" Chele stated, listing them off on her fingers. "It helps aid digestion, allows for better production of magic, better control over mind and body. Not to mention, if we're ever going to master any of this, we probably need all the meditation we can get."

Gwyn looked around at the courtyard. There were topiaries, statues, a large fountain, fancy benches, exotic trees, flowers, and tall hedges. Some hedges made maze-like designs through the yard, and others blocked the large courtyard from the outside view. She took a moment and admired her father's castle visible from the courtyard. It had been several days, and she hadn't taken time to enjoy the beauty of the place. A warm breeze mixed with autumn's chill in the air made the courtyard lunch blissful.

Their next class was Magic Lore. They weren't sure what to expect the first day and found a table to sit at together in stadium seating. The professor arrived several minutes late, a short, skinny wizard with spiky white hair. He placed several things on his desk and addressed the class.

"Hello. Sorry I'm late. Name's Professor Spike," he said as he shuffled through a mess of clutter on his desk.

"This class is introductory to many things," he said, holding up a rounded device with a red rune on it. "This is a summoner. They're expensive. If you ever do work that requires one, include it in the bill. About anyone can use one. Takes two wizards, just focus on the person you want to summon, and utter the words 'summon so and so.' If they're not there to summon, you'll know, it'll jolt you. Just make sure you don't summon someone above your level of magic; the combined powers of the summoners need to exceed the wizard you're summoning." He then went through a few other magical basics.

He then pulled a silver helmet with brown straps from his bag and set it on his desk.

"What is that?" asked a student.

"A piece of history and a great reminder that being a wizard comes with great risks. This particular headpiece was worn by the leader of the peacekeepers known as the Atari Templar. A powerful, neutral army in the center lands of Arcadia who kept the North, South, and Eastern armies from invading each other."

"What happened to them?"

"They were all slain in one night by the queen of the north."

Gwyn swallowed hard.

"History tells us they all fell in one swift battle before she invaded the Eastern Kingdoms."

Was this why some of the students were slighting me? she wondered. Perhaps they had heard this, and this was her legacy.

The last class of the day was Symbology. They often arrived early. Examples of projects from other students sat out for viewing and the classroom had several large, circular glass cases with Xi crystals in them connected to workbenches. Many projects had lights or fountains that sputtered water. One had a spinning fan that oscillated with glowing blades.

They observed a project that had a carved wooden wizard holding a staff above his head. It was hinged in the middle of its torso, repeatedly bending over to whack a creature that looked a lot like a fat goblin with its staff.

Many thought the professor of Symbology, Warren, was the least interesting. He was nasally, slow, and joked a lot, but the jokes came off to her as odd and confusing.

Jack, however, found it very interesting and completed the first project—connecting a basic light-emitting crystal to a Xi crystal to generate a warm tone of light—before anyone else. Chele and Gwyn, and several others in the class, had to turn theirs in unfinished, and this was how most days in Symbology went.

MEAD class had a different feel to it now for Gwyn. Some people weren't making eye contact with her. Others smiled, said hi, and waved. It seemed some classmates had already left or dropped out.

Still, Fox mentioned the class being rather large compared to others. He had several tables set up throughout his class one day. Each was a station, equipped with some sort of element or energy source.

"The point over the next several days is to find an element that you jive with. We call this a synergy alignment test. Each station has fundamentals for its element on it. Take, for example, the braziers at the fire station," Fox said near a brazier and lifted a hand slightly. The unlit wick ignited into a bright flame. He then put his hands around the flame. "You don't need to touch it; just let its aura interact with yours. The trick is to learn the aura—its feel, texture, and essence in your mind and soul. Synergize and connect with it.

"Many of you will find they align best with only one element type, and sometimes two, but have trouble connecting with any others," Fox continued as he ran his hands along the outside of the flame as he spoke.

Kat raised her hand and asked, "What happens when you have synergy with an element?"

"Good question!" Fox lifted his hand, and the flame grew several feet into the air, almost touching the stone ceiling.

Gwyn could feel the heat of the flame on her face from several feet away as it grew.

Fox then made the flame twirl in dizzying spirals. He started doing it faster and faster, then placed the spiral around himself until he was surrounded with ropes of flames.

The class applauded, and Gwyn noticed that Jack's mouth was open as he too joined in applause.

Then, as if he'd flipped a switch, Fox pointed at the wick in the brazier, and the flames all shot back into the small flame it started as. "Do not think it will be that easy at first. Or in a few years," Fox said as he walked to a station set up with plants. "Be sure to focus on the aura of the plants and the buckets of different types of earth. If you have any positive interaction at all, even a hint, let me know. Meditate, and focus.

"I will benchmark success so that you learn who you are spiritually, physically, and magically. The point is to help you improve, not compete. So please, remember to disregard jealous or envious thoughts, as it can interfere with your ability to synergize, especially in these early stages."

Gwyn, Chele, and Jack went to a station that had water and ice set up. Gwyn thought she might have luck with it, given her ability to shoot ice arrows from Apollo. She found, however, that she could detect little interaction with it, if any at all. Jack and Chele got nothing from it either, and after several minutes of trying, they moved on.

The fire station was packed with nearly the whole class at first, but as time went on, only a couple of people stayed.

She tried the plants and the dirt and ore but had no luck there either. Next to her, she watched a strange, nervous boy named Buddy eating mint leaves off one of the plants. He turned and pulled a half-chewed sprig from inside his pudgy cheek and offered it to her. She shook her head and quickly left the station.

Fox suggested taking frequent breaks to meditate because they were going to exhaust themselves just attempting to find synergy.

Gwyn walked to another station and found Parker standing at it. She found he avoided being at the same station at all costs, and several times she caught him looking away from her quickly when she made eye contact. She managed to sneak up beside him while he was attempting to synergize with a plant. As he was waving his hands around it, he quickly stopped and looked at her. He grunted and quickly walked off.

Jack, who was watching from a station just a few yards away, snickered.

She found herself smiling slyly, surprised Jack had somehow slipped past her to spy on her experiment. "What?" she whispered to him with a slight chuckle. "I haven't done anything!"

Jack shook his head. "He's just a bully, you know. Tried to make a name for himself by picking on you—now he gets a tummy ache when he sees you."

She shot Jack a look, half blushing from the odd compliment, half embarrassed that Jack had managed to sneak up on her so well. "So, I'm that unpleasant to look at, you sneaky little prat?"

Jack fumbled his words a bit, caught a bit off guard by Gwyn's retort. "Uh, well, no. You know... uh, now I'm getting a tummy ache!" he said quickly.

She chuckled almost too loudly at him.

Jack huffed with a grin and a shrug.

The three of them grouped up and found an empty station with a bright yellow beam of electrical energy arcing across from two metal points. The sign at the station read Plasma. Warning, DO NOT TOUCH! WILL CUT OFF FINGERS! but that didn't tell them much about what it was.

Fox saw them looking at the station and walked over to it. "Whatever you do, do not touch the beam. The aura of plasma is rather large, and it's rare that anyone can synergize with it."

Jack stepped up and felt around the beam, giving it a wide berth with his hands. "Is this too far, Professor?"

Fox shook his head. "No, that's perfect. Your auras can definitely interact from there. Do your best to meditate and relax while you try. When you feel it, you'll have a strange sensation. It'll feel familiar and yet completely foreign."

After a few minutes with no success, Jack gave up and moved to the fire station. Gwyn let Chele have a turn next.

Chele also kept her hands nearly a foot away from the plasma beam. She was careful so that she didn't touch it by accident when she closed her eyes.

Gwyn was watching Fox, who was occasionally watching Chele and Jack. It seemed that he did keep a closer watch on them than others. She walked over next to him so that he was in close earshot. "Professor?"

Fox stood, rubbing his pointy beard, then nodded.

"Why did you let Dirk fight me for so long?"

Fox took a deep breath. He had his hands crossed in front of himself and rolled on the back of his heels while he contemplated his words. "I needed to benchmark your abilities... and your limits."

She cocked her head slightly, waiting for more. "My ability to dodge a flit!?"

Fox was silent for a moment, then looked down at Gwyn from the corners of his eyes. "Dirk can split the wings of a fly with his flits. You were never in any danger... Furthermore, I sense the same abilities in you that your mother had."

She felt confused by the response; she wasn't exactly sure what Fox meant. "You said my mother was much older when she came here."

"She was. She came here while building her kingdom in the north," Fox told her.

"What? Why would she do that? Why not go to a guild to learn?"

Fox shook his head. "She had gone to guilds. She believed she needed something more fundamental. Many wizards come back to the base-level academies at some point. She was interested in acute, deep studies of the mind, particularly aura-based studies."

Gwyn gave the professor a look of confusion. "What? Why?"

Fox gave a half smile, half grin as he thought of a better way to explain what he'd said when Chele called from the plasma station.

"I've got it! Look! I feel it!"

Fox and Gwyn went over to the station, and sure enough, they found that Chele could make small tethers of plasma bend out from the primary beam.

Fox gasped and bent down. "Very good, Chele! Very good! I'm impressed!"

Gwyn waited while the professor helped Chele, and after several moments when he had turned back and looked at her, he said, "Oh yes. I was saying. Your mother was doing Auric research. Oh, and if you haven't noticed, I did you a favor with Dirk." He then smiled at her and walked over to help another student before she could reply.

Gwyn took her turn with the plasma beam, and after several minutes, she thought she could see hairs of plasma interacting with her, but her mind shifted back to what Fox had said. Had he actually helped me? She thought about how Parker was now treating her, avoiding her. He hadn't tried to pick on her again since the duel. She didn't tell Fox about the plasma and moved on to a table with Xi crystals.

She had to wait behind some other students, so she meditated.

She saw Jack, going down a line of different hanging metals and materials to see if he synergized with any of them.

Gwyn's turn came, and she stepped up to a table with Xi crystals on it. She waved her hand around a stack and instantly felt her energy interacting with it. A few minutes later, and she felt connected with the aura. In a way, it felt like being reunited with a lost friend. It was strange because she felt her energy leaving to connect with the Xi's energy, but she also felt it returning, as if she were part of a circuit.

She pulled, and felt the ebb and flow within the aura, like invisible tethers connecting them. It took a few tries, but she pulled the top crystal off a stack using just the synergy. She pulled two more off, then went to move the ones on the table and found she could move them. The longer she played around, the stronger the connection felt, like she was getting to know it better. She wanted to attempt lifting one, but didn't know if it would break the connection if she failed.

Gwyn decided after a few minutes to risk it. She did her best to stiffen the connection and went to lift a crystal. To her surprise, the crystal lifted straight into the air at least a foot off the table. She could feel her energy quickly draining from holding it in the air.

Several voices made awed sounds and chatter around Gwyn as she fought to maintain her focus on the connection.

"Very impressive, Gwyn," Fox said, with a hint of astonishment in his tone.

Her focus broke, and she looked up at Fox. The crystal fell back to the table with a loud thud. "Thank you," she said shyly and slightly out of breath.

"You'll find that's another rare connection to make: Xi crystals. Very rare. Which is strange, considering how close the energy is to our own human energy."

Fox walked around to stand by Gwyn. "Most people who synergize well with Xi can also connect with at least one other element. Do keep that in mind."

Gwyn looked down at the Xi crystal. She had a desire to synergize with it again. It had left her qi feeling somewhat recharged.

"Gwyn," Fox said, looking down at her through rectangle glasses. "if you do find another element, let me know. Amazing things can be done by blending elements."

"Like what?"

"Well, for example, someone who synergizes well with electrical auras, water, and wind might one day be able to conjure up an entire storm."

"Oh!" She responded, trying to imagine herself controlling an entire storm.

"Now, of course, I'm using an example that would take an extremely powerful person. It's good that you know there are times when an idea is simply too big and fantastic, and if any wizard were to attempt them, he'd probably damage himself in the process."

She looked up at Fox. "Is that what overextending is?"

Fox looked at Gwyn and tilted his head. "Could lead to it."

"Should I be careful with my energy, then?"

Fox nodded. "Yes. Always. But don't worry, I don't think you're powerful enough to overextend yourself quite yet. It's best if you practiced hard now; it'll extend your abilities and make them far more powerful," Fox told her while bouncing a Xi crystal around in his hand.

CHAPTER 16

Finals and Fine Things

When Gwyn left MEAD, she saw Dirk walking by. His nose had a white bandage over it with tape holding it on, and his eyes had dark purple circles around them. He locked eyes with her for a moment, then quickly turned and walked away. She wanted to speak with him, but didn't pursue him.

She found herself occasionally searching through the library for more information about her mother's kingdom. She found but a few books. The first one flattered her mother, noted her beauty and passion for all creatures, and even mentioned her noble work restoring the north. Another was the opposite, with stories of how power corrupted her or how having wizard rulers in the world was a bad thing.

She wasn't sure what to believe, as the truth seemed elusive. She did find multiple sources claiming her mother had something to do with the fall of the Atari Templar. Jack found some pictures of the Templar; they wore a red cross on white tabards. The leader wore a red cross with four dots on it—a dot in each corner of the cross. The pictures were drawn by hand but done with incredible detail.

For MEAD homework, they were supposed to research the element they synergized with best and find methods to improve synergy.

Magic Lore was becoming surprisingly fun as they learned more about foods, qi, and auras. They briefly talked about something called 'shadow magic', which was the ability to draw energy from a different dimension or realm, and they called it synergizing with the nether.

Professor Spike was usually late and scatterbrained most days. They learned the basics of incantations and how a minor slip in a syllable could sour them. It was equally important that the proper mixture of positive and negative qi be used when drawing on the power of words.

According to Spike, words were one of the most powerful and underused forms of magic. "Every word—every syllable—could be used in a positive, negative, or even neutral way. Words can shake foundations or ignite a flame powerful enough to change the world!" he told them. "Use their power carefully. Some of the best wizards are only mediocre in their abilities to conjure elements but have a way with words that would make you lay down your weapons or life."

Symbology was Gwyn's least favorite class. She had a hard time carving out the bizarre symbols for the connections running to the crystals. She messed several up and had Chele show her how to hold her hand to make certain slashes or designs.

Jack was, surprisingly, on the third project by the time Chele reached her second. Gwyn was still finishing up the first.

It was a great surprise when Chele was drafted into a special class to start working on plasma and flit magic. Apparently, Professor Fox was so impressed with her ability to align with the plasma beam and project qi that he recommended her.

Over the next few weeks, Gwyn tried synergizing with every element. Though she could eventually move a little fire, pull a hair of plasma, and shuffle some dirt, she found herself drawn to the Xi crystals. When connected to them, she felt energized. She felt powerful, and it became easier to move the other elements. She didn't mention her ability to synergize with the other elements to Fox, though she suspected he already knew.

Days passed, and they came to a weekend with no homework. The weather was surprisingly decent, so they decided on spending a few of their hard-earned coins from Pantheon on ice cream then went to the park.

Again, Gwyn saw her father's tomb down the street from the park, but she did not visit. Instead, she resigned to blowing another kiss to it and spent the weekend hanging out with Jack and Chele. It was surreal to believe it could be her father there.

They window-shopped in the town square for a bit but realized they had no way of making money if they spent what they had. There were no ponds to fish or woods to hunt, no garden to grow a crop in, and Gwyn wasn't sure where the nearest forest was to fletch arrows. Jack suggested that they put on a street show and move things with their qi, but magic was a bit more common in the heart of Silvania, and it wasn't likely to impress anyone.

"That's also strictly forbidden, according to Mrs. Plumb," Chele reminded Jack.

"Yeah, I remember. Stupid guild decree not to show off, or, what was that big word they used? Vaunt?"

Chele nodded with a half smile. "They just don't want us flaunting. It sounds like there are good reasons they made that law. Seems a lot of good wizards have died from superstitions."

Jack then suggested that Gwyn and Chele work as barmaids serving beer at the pub to earn some real coin—a suggestion that earned him two sore arms.

"Go work at the stinky pub yourself, mister!" Gwyn retorted.

She had never intentionally hit Jack before, but she felt he'd earned it. Jack bit his tongue a bit more for the rest of the day, now that his arms felt tingly and sore.

The coming weeks were similar, only more in-depth, and Jack had still not found an element that he could synergize with. Though, he wasn't the only one. There were several others who couldn't, but they also could not throw qi like Jack could, though Fox had still not seen it.

As the weeks passed, Fox told Jack and the others who hadn't synergized with elements to stay and continue learning, but they would likely need to retake the grade. He then pulled Gwyn aside after class. "May I speak with you for a moment, please?"

She nodded, and they stepped into his office, a small room at the edge of his classroom.

"Gwyn, as you've likely noticed, I have been watching your friends closely."

She nodded again, a bit annoyed. "Yeah. I noticed."

"Well, I am pleasantly surprised by Chele. She's at the top of the class in several areas and a pleasant pupil to have. Not to mention... surprisingly magical!"

She smiled, feeling proud of her friend.

"However, I am afraid the opposite is true for Jack."

She felt her smile fade away. She knew Jack wasn't doing well, but had hoped he wouldn't be judged quite so quickly.

"Gwyn... I pride myself on being able to teach fundamentals of the very complex craft that is magic. But your friend Jack... He is an enigma to me."

She gave Professor Fox a strange look of confusion. "Ee—what?"

"I apologize, it's a strange old word. What I mean is, he is a mystery."

"Oh," She said in relief. "I thought he might have a disease or something."

Fox's expression went blank for a moment, and then he chuckled. "You're funny," he said. "However, I'm having trouble with Jack. I've never had a student that could throw qi and not synergize with an element."

She waited, not sure where Fox was going and surprised he knew Jack could project qi.

"Gwyn, help me. Is there anything the boy is good at?"

She thought about Jack's abilities and started listing them off. "Well, he's a decent shot with a bow... He's great at tying knots..." She suddenly felt embarrassed and was having trouble coming up with anything on the spot.

"Hmm..." Fox stroked his pointy beard and then took off his pointy wizard hat and hung it on a hook.

Then, she did think of something he'd done well at. "He is rather good at Symbology. He's more than a week ahead in projects. Professor Warren says he'll be able to wire an entire house with Xi crystal energy before long if he wants to, and the efficiency of it; he's good at that part too."

But Professor Fox didn't respond. He waved the thought off passively with a hand. "That's more of an elective... Is there anything else?"

She tried thinking again. She thought of his cooking—"definitely not that." She was having trouble finding anything else that Jack was good at off the top of her head. "No," she finally said. "Not right now. I'm probably just not thinking of it."

Fox nodded, staring off toward the wall in thought. "Well, let me know if you do."

She nodded and headed out the door.

"And Gwyn..."

"Yes, Professor?"

"Have you had any luck with any of the other elements?" Fox asked her. "Some other students thought they saw you at several other stations with some success."

"No," She lied. "Well... Some, yes, but nothing like the Xi crystals."

Fox nodded slowly. "Hmph, I see. Next week, we'll be focusing more on weapons and how to apply synergized elements to them. I might have a fifth-grade student come by and work on reviewing how to multi-class elements if you'd like?"

The idea sounded fun to her. "Of course!"

"Good. Make sure you pick two elements you feel the strongest about then."

She left the room with a smile. She walked out of the professor's classroom and started making her way toward the stairs to her next class when, from nowhere, Jack said, "Boo!"

He was now suddenly walking beside her and she let out a slight scream as she jumped back.

"Goodness, Jack! How do you creep up on me like that? It's freaky!" She told him, her heart still beating fast. Then, an idea clicked. She told Jack to head to tell Mrs. Plumb that she'd be late, and ran back to Fox's office.

"Mr. Fox, I just remembered something."

Fox looked at her, "Go on?"

"He's sneaky," Gwyn said, a little upset with herself for using the word sneaky.

Fox raised an eyebrow and looked at her funny. "Sneaky?"

"You know... He sneaks up on ya. Does it really well too."

"Oh. Like that. He's stealthy," Fox said.

"Yeah, stealthy. He's done it several times to me and Chele."

"Now that is interesting," He said with curiosity. "That might be a lead to go on. Thank you, Gwyn."

She took off for her next lesson. Mrs. Plumb didn't mention her being late. They found their homework involved going to the library and researching things that were often fun to learn about. Chele even took a little time to look into what enchantresses really were and why the wizard community looked down on the craft.

It seemed they used magic of a trickier kind. Many sources mentioned mind control, emotional manipulation, and deceiving victims. Chele did find one source that mentioned enchantress magic being used to gather resources from an evil king long ago, leaving room in her mind that perhaps they weren't all using their power to do bad things.

It seemed everyone had a unique twist in their magic. One person might throw a fire flit curly, another may throw it spiky or straight, and another as entire waves of fire but not maintain a flit at all. It was interesting to see how unique magic was.

The next week, a fifth-grade student named Josh came to Fox's class for a day. He was the only one in the Academy known to be able to multi-class. He had a strange ability to take water and run it through metals. It seemed like a useless ability to Gwyn, but she did her best to learn from him.

Josh said that she needed to learn the feeling of each aura first. She'd chosen the Xi and fire as her elements.

Josh told her to practice feeling the auras with her eyes closed. Surprisingly, she could easily tell the Xi aura. To her, it was smooth and flowed easily, and it was easy to make it respond to her. The fire, however, felt more foreign. It was reluctant to respond to her in comparison. She had to focus more to know it was fire, but she could tell it had its own feeling.

"It's like making a new friend," Josh told her. "Once you know them both well enough as individuals, you can introduce them to each other, and because you're the friend they trust, they work together. Does that make sense?"

"Kind of," she told him.

Josh assured her once she did it, it would all make more sense.

Fox also brought in a Nethermancer to work with Jack. He was a very tall man with dark skin and wore armor with skulls on it. His name was Toski, which apparently meant 'to squash bugs.'

Toski used to be a Necromancer, but Necromancy is forbidden. He no longer actively practiced the craft and had been cleared by the Wizard Council to help create the similar one known as Nethermancy. Toski worked with Jack in a backroom, and they didn't come out until the end of class.

"He told me that I synergize with shadow magic. That I draw my energy from the nether," Jack exclaimed to Gwyn and Chele. "He said a lot of healers synergize with that source."

"Where is the nether?" Gwyn asked Jack.

"Well, he said it was like, a... another dimension that was lateral to the one we're in now, whatever that means."

Chele gave Jack a funny look. "That sounds really advanced!"

Jack shook his head. "Yeah. It is," he said, disappointedly. "Toski told me I'd learn a lot more in a guild. He suggested the Shadow Guild, but said I'd have to go through the Academy first."

"Well, that is cool in a way. I didn't see any of the others that couldn't synergize with anything get a special mentor in class," Gwyn told Jack, hoping to cheer him up.

"Yeah. It is nice in a way. Especially since Necromancy is so forbidden, and Nethermancy is so close to it! There are some other cool things it can lead to as well, like cloaking."

"Cloaking?" Chele asked. "What's that?"

"It's where you slip your body into a place called the Hollow. It's between the nether and this dimension. Toski said as long as you don't go fully into the nether, you'll be okay. But it's crazy advanced stuff."

"What happens if you go fully into the nether?" Gwyn asked.

"Well, I asked that too. Toski didn't really answer; he just told me I wouldn't want to do that."

"Are you going to be able to synergize it with your weapon like Professor Fox is teaching us to?"

"Yeah, Toski's teaching me how to sense the aura of the nether. He said it's a great source to draw from because it's so powerful, but it can take a while to learn to discern where and what it is."

Sure enough, within a few weeks, Jack had learned to use the energy from the nether with his weapon. The energy from the nether came out a greenish color with a mix of shadowy black. At first, when Jack struck an object with his staff, it looked like a slight green flash took place at the same time, but after a while, a discernible green hue could be seen, making it far more powerful.

Gwyn had been experimenting with multi-classing. She had gotten to where she could pull fire and Xi together with her weapon, which caused a bluish-purple and orange glow when it struck. She even once had a flame at the end of her arrow after it stuck in a target, which seemed to impress Professor Fox.

Chele was learning how to cast a flit in her advanced class. There were several types of flits that could be used for several reasons. Some for lighting, some shot out as ribbons of lightning, some could be used to restrain or grab something, some were whipping tongues of flame, and several others.

Chele hadn't produced a full flit yet, but her advanced class professor was impressed by her small ribbon of sparks from her hand.

One day, when Chele and Gwyn were walking up the stairs behind Jack, Chele held out her hand and shot a ribbon of sparking plasma into Jack's rear.

"YEEEOW! What the heck was that!?" he yelled while jumping and holding his bottom.

Chele blushed, as she didn't expect it to hurt him as badly as it did. Jack, of course, claimed that it hurt to sit down for the next several days, making sure to milk it for all it was worth.

Halloween came, but the three of them were so exhausted that they didn't do much. They ate dinner, then did some walking around the town square. Seeing the trick-or-treaters run from door to door left them feeling slightly nostalgic for their home village in Pantheon.

They lit a fire in a park where Chele managed to roast some pumpkin seeds. They spat out the shells while swinging.

In the coming weeks, Jack continued private lessons with Toski, and Chele continued her advanced classes, learning about flit magic.

Gwyn found herself increasingly capable of affecting multiple elements as she grew stronger in her magic. She felt oddly ashamed of her unique abilities, as if others knew, she'd have to defend them from more bullies, so she mostly hid them.

Fox mentioned dueling to her at the end of the semester.

She took a Xi crystal to the practice target range. Taking several minutes to meditate and synergize with it, she bound the energy to her bow, attempting to conjure an arrow made of Xi energy. She fired—a faint indigo-colored bolt of energy flew into the target dummy.

When she examined the dummy closer, she realized she'd left a small burn mark on it. She looked carefully over Apollo, and although she didn't see any sign of damage, using the bolt of Xi energy on it made her nervous. She then used ice, which was harder for her to conjure, but found she could shoot small bolts of it.

Through practice she discovered she could control the shape and density of the bolt.

Fox saw her doing this and told her it was impressive.

Thanksgiving break came, and Franz and Delilah took them to Pantheon for the holiday. They were all excited to show off what they'd learned.

Gwyn embraced her grandparents before helping them catch up with chores. Chele's family came to her cottage where Delilah, Chele, and her mom prepared a tremendous spread of food. They filled themselves far more than they ever should have.

The break was well-needed, and they agreed that the holiday weekend went by far too fast.

End-of-season testing was approaching at the Academy, where each class had its unique method of assessment. Gwyn felt confident in Chele's abilities to pass but was less sure about Jack. Despite his improvement, Jack's focus in class was often lacking.

Their first final was in MEAD. Fox was teaching them to store objects in the nether. He demonstrated by pulling his staff from thin air, explaining that it must be bound to the user's energy or be lost forever. The students practiced with toothpicks, where Jack managed to vanish one into the nether, though he couldn't retrieve it. Fox mentioned that only a 'Hollow

Walker', someone who could slip in and out of the nether, could fetch it back.

Fox told them the final required successfully synergizing an element with their chosen weapon while striking a willow board. The element had to be synergized strongly enough to leave its magical residue on the wood, proving a connection with the element.

Kokolo was brought in to examine the willow for residue. Jack and Chele completed the final successfully.

Kokolo told Jack his magic was "icky" and recommended that he have his aura examined for wizard diseases as soon as possible. Gwyn and a few students snickered quietly as Jack turned red, crossed his arms, and rolled his eyes. "I hate that woman," he muttered to himself.

When Gwyn was not offered a turn at the final, she gave Professor Fox a slighted look and asked him about it.

Fox looked confused for a moment, then let out a snicker. "Sorry, I thought I told you."

"Told me what?"

"First-grade students who successfully synergize with two or more elements are considered Magius rank and do not need to pass a final in this class. Multicasting elements is more advanced than the test. I'd like to see that improve, but regardless, you're already approved to the next grade."

"But Professor, I thought each grade was a year long?"

Fox looked at her with curiosity on his face. "What made you think that?"

She thought about it for a moment, then shrugged. "I guess that's just how it is in normal school."

Fox let out a small laugh. "Well, Gwyn, this is not a normal school. Grades typically advance with semesters, although, as you know, some grades can take years to complete—especially core classes. After those, you'll mostly be in specialty classes."

"Professor, can you fail a grade in one class and advance in another?"

"In later grades, yes. Not in the first and second grades, though. Each grade becomes a little more unique after that, and Principal Lyndsay often has the final say on such matters."

Several students were unable to synergize an element strongly enough to leave residue on the broken pieces, Parker being one of them. They were told they would have to retake the grade next semester. Some of them had already been through the grade at least once before.

Mrs. Plumb's test was an in-class essay and exam. The essay had to be written within an hour and delivered in front of the class. Gwyn did hers on a good use for magic, choosing self-defense as her example and citing the bandit attack.

Meditation was mandatory still, one Gwyn had grown to enjoy. It was a chance to recharge mid-day, and she'd even opted to meditate through lunch a few times. Her favorite place to meditate was in the sauna. She enjoyed her privacy and tried to find time to bathe and enjoy the sauna alone when possible, finding it refreshing to her spirit.

Professor Spike handed out a written test, which quizzed about various relics, auras and lore they'd learned in his class.

He then had a visual test over things like what a summoner was and some relics he had in the class.

Gwyn didn't expect to pass Symbology. She despised the class and had fallen behind on her projects. Professor Warren didn't have any advice for her but to keep practicing. Jack was the star student, and Chele was just above average in the class.

The final project was to create a working water fountain pump. The number of symbols used on it was crazy, in Gwyn's opinion. They learned that symbols have parent symbols that could be used in place of them, that certain symbols could cancel a symbol out in certain areas, act as a container for energy between two symbols, or direct or multiply it.

She knew Xi energy in a different way; she felt Symbology was a form of math and madness, but she kept her opinion to herself.

She found the class confusing and complicated, and though her fountain sputtered a few drops of water, it was hardly a fountain.

Jack's fountain wasn't perfect either by any means, but it was by far the best in the class. It would effectively pump water for at least fifteen seconds, then stop for roughly five, and pump again.

Chele's pump wasn't much better than Gwyn's, but it managed a small stream here and there.

To her utter surprise, they all passed Symbology.

Fox had told Gwyn to consider dueling by the end of the semester. She was unsure but agreed to try. The rules were: no biting, no stabbing, no pulling hair, no jabbing eyes, no arrows, no spears, no deadly spells or deadly use of magic, no puncturing of any kind, and absolutely no deadly force in any way. For fun and practice only.

The duels were held in a back room of Fox's classroom, one at a time in the early evenings. She showed up to it by herself. Chele was busy with a flit lesson, and Jack was taking advantage of one last tutoring session with Toski.

The dueling room was not what Gwyn expected. It looked like a place where people would go to watch a real fight. The contending ring was in a circular room with stone walls, tiered seating carved from stone, and windows that overlooked the battle area. Glass had been put up for people to watch safely from behind it. Some of the glass had eerie stains—marks left by powerful magic.

She stood against the wall, waiting for her duel, watching two that took place before hers. First, a third-grade duel, though the participants looked much older. She watched in awe as a girl blasted her opponent with a beam of ice, leaving a thin layer of frost over his neck and chest. When they left the ring, his neck had red streaks where the blast had frosted his skin.

He smiled and nodded at Gwyn as she stood against the wall, fighting what felt like butterflies swimming in her stomach.

The next duel was two fifth-grade students. They were much older than the previous duelers. Fox warned that they would be using more powerful magic.

Watching it was even more suspenseful, especially when one of them blasted his opponent with a jolting flash of energy to knock him out of the circle.

Fox raised the winner's hand, signaling a victory.

As everyone applauded, Gwyn wondered why she hadn't come to watch the duels before. When she realized her turn was up, her heart began pounding in her chest.

As they exited the dueling ring, both were out of breath. She saw a tear in the robes of the one who lost. She could see the material around a wound was wet and bloody as he passed by her. It was unnerving to see before her duel, so she did her best to put it out of her mind.

She entered the dueling ring and saw her opponent standing across from her. It was Kat, the tiny, dark-haired, and dark-skinned girl from her class. Professor Fox told them both, "Keep it clean, no advanced magic, no stabbing or anything that will permanently injure."

Gwyn buckled leather straps around her cloak to keep it close to her torso then Fox called the duel to start. They both took fighting stances across from each other.

They started by slowly circling the dueling ring. Gwyn kept her bow on her shoulder, and Kat had a long wooden staff on her back.

Finally, Kat threw a blast of energy at her. Gwyn knelt to her right and felt the breeze of the energy as it flew over her left shoulder.

Kat drew her staff, rushing at her. She planted the staff into the ground and used it to leverage a drop kick at Gwyn. She connected her feet and Gwyn shifted the energy into a reverse somersault, proud her practice with Jack and Chele had prepared her a bit—though she felt her movements were a bit sloppy from nerves.

Kat's face looked surprised as she led with another blast of energy, then gracefully twirled and swung the long wooden staff at her. Gwyn dodged the blast again and removed her bow just in time to use it to defend against the attack. She knew she wasn't great at defending against staff attacks, and after a few blocks, Gwyn took a sharp blow to the ribs.

The strike stung but provided an opening to counter. Gwyn moderated the amount of energy she used, but the blast was enough to trip Kat up, knocking her several feet back to the ground near the edge of the circle. Kat was quick to return to her feet but looked slightly less composed, her hair falling from the wrap it was in.

Gwyn's tactic now was to keep Kat far enough away to wear her out while avoiding Kat's staff attacks.

Kat threw a blast of qi at her, which she ducked, but she felt the force of it pull her hair as it flew by. Gwyn returned fire with a blast of her own energy, this time conjuring a small hollow orb of ice to blast with it. It was thin but hit Kat in the forehead and shattered, leaving a small wet spot on Kat's forehead and leaving her slightly confused.

Gwyn used Kat's tactic against her, planting Apollo in the ground to support a drop kick. The force pushed and knocked her out of the dueling ring. She landed on her side on a mat and sat back up as Gwyn made her way over to her.

She reached down, smiled, and helped Kat to her feet. The two shook hands and hugged as the audience applauded.

"Great fight, Gwyn! I really tried hard!"

Gwyn was surprised at how alive she felt in that moment. The duel had been exciting and left her wanting more. As she went to leave, she saw Jack standing in the crowd. As she left the ring to head to him, she felt a hand on her shoulder. She turned to see Professor Fox standing behind her.

"Congratulations, Gwyn," he said, smiling. "I hope you consider coming back."

She smiled back and thanked him. "Of course! It was a blast!"

Fox looked up for a moment, then back to her. "Good. Just do me a favor and don't go telling everyone you know about these duels... Don't get me wrong, they're allowed—it's just some students are better off not dueling."

She nodded, then took her things and made her way around the stone halls. She came to the stone benches where people watched and made her way to where Jack was sitting. He immediately stood up and congratulated her. "You were amazing, Gwyn! I could watch you fight all day! Great job!"

"Thanks! I can't believe I've never watched the duels before. They're awesome!"

"We didn't even know they existed before Fox invited you," Jack reminded her.

"You should have seen the first two,"

"Gwyn, I need to tell you something," Jack said, then suggested that they go outside for a walk. "Gwyn, I did it! Toski showed me some things, and I actually figured out one! I can't believe it!" Jack said as they walked outside.

"What are you talking about?"

"Gwyn, I can slip into the Hollow... between this dimension and the nether."

She stared at Jack for a moment, not sure what to say.

"I can't do it for long because it takes a lot of energy, but it's so awesome!"

"Really? You've got to show me," she said excitedly.

"Okay, I will. But let's go somewhere people won't see," Jack suggested. As they walked, he began explaining his training with Toski and how strange it had been. "I can see how necromancy is forbidden! Nethermancy technically isn't, but it's definitely darker magic!"

"What do you mean?" She asked with sincere curiosity in her voice.

"I think it would be easy to convert from one to the other. It all uses similar energy. The spells for necromancy are just harder to find, is all."

"Well, that's a bit scary."

"I know. It's like Toski said—it's mostly about how you use it."

On their way outside, they passed Professor Spike. He was standing near a stone statue with a wooden dinner bowl in one hand. He raised his free hand when they came near.

"Where are you two going at this late hour?" he asked them with a stern voice.

"For a walk," Gwyn said sternly back to him, looking up to find his eyes were a pale gray. She paused for a moment when she saw his eye color, never having noticed it before. "It's not past curfew yet."

Spike 'hmphed' and waved them by.

As they neared the door, Jack leaned over and whispered to Gwyn, "What's gotten into him? The semester's over anyway."

"Probably sick of all the nonsense you say during his lessons," She retorted while opening the door.

The two walked down the street, waiting for the occasional passerby to move out of sight. It was twilight, and they had nearly walked to the castle where her father's tomb was. They stopped to look around to make sure there weren't any people around.

"Alright, no one's here in the square tonight," she said.

"Okay, I'm going to do it," Jack finally told her. It took a minute, and he did make some noise on the first attempt that might have attracted attention. Suddenly, he turned and vanished completely into thin air.

Gwyn let out a gasp and felt around for Jack, but it was as if he were truly gone.

Jack appeared a few seconds later, breathing heavily and staring at Gwyn's father's tomb. "Gwyn!" he said between heavy pants. "There's something strange about your father's tomb..."

CHAPTER 17
The Tomb's Secrets

Gwyn stared at Jack, waiting for him to elaborate, but his gaze remained fixed on her father's tomb, standing there in silence. Still, she waited patiently, studying the entranced look that seemed to have captured his expression as he stared.

Finally, with an attempt to swallow the growing lump in her throat, she broke the bloated silence. "What is it?" she began modestly, trying to ease into it with a bit of grace and subtlety. "Please, Jack, what are you talking about? Is it my father? Is he alive?"

For a few seconds, Jack remained silent, staring as if afraid of something he'd seen. "I..." he said in a panicked tone, then shook his head. "Hold on, I have to explain some things first," he added, finally breaking his stare on the tomb to meet Gwyn's eyes. "I'm not really supposed to tell anyone... but... well, I tell you everything anyway." He sighed and turned his thin frame toward her. "In the Hollow, everything looks different. I can see things you can't see here—it's usually dull and subtle. It's like I see a mix of things that are here and in the nether."

"Your father's tomb... It's covered in a bright glow. And, well, it has a weird blue flame at the bottom, glowing inside or something. It's really weird. I actually thought it was on fire at first, it was so bright." Jack turned his eyes back to the tomb for a moment. "Like seeing a sun in the night or something. It's completely out of place."

Gwyn listened eagerly to Jack.

"Another strange thing, though, is... well... there's this weird glowing writing on it."

She pondered carefully for a moment, then shook her head. She hadn't known what to expect—not a strange flame that couldn't even be seen. "What about barriers? Franz said there were barriers around everything—the castle, the tomb. Can you see anything like that?"

Jack thought about it. "No. Well, I don't remember seeing any." He scratched his head, looking unsure. "Let me check again. I'll look closer this time." They walked up close to the gate, waiting for a couple to walk by before Jack slipped into the Hollow again. The couple laughed and slowly meandered through the square.

Jack took a deep breath and, just as before, vanished as if he'd slipped behind a wall of nothing, only to emerge several seconds later. This time, he was out of breath and panting when he returned. "You know what?" he said between heavy breaths.

"What's wrong with you?" She asked the panting Jack.

"Hollow walking's hard! But there does look like there might be an invisible barrier around the tomb. It's kind of hard to see—like... well, I guess a soap bubble. Almost too invisible to notice. And there's a weird glow around this whole area right in front of this fence. It's all subtle, really, but the barrier is everywhere now that I looked for it."

Gwyn grabbed the iron bars and looked at her father's tomb. She'd been avoiding coming here the entire semester, and now that she was here, she didn't want to leave.

The sky had greatly darkened over the last few minutes as thick dark thunderheads crept eerily across the evening sky. Jack pointed out that it looked like it was going to rain soon as a bright flash of lightning flickered through the sky, but she told him that she didn't want to leave. Not yet, and not now. Now that she was finally here, facing an issue that burned deep within her. Deeper than Jack could possibly know.

"I had a vision here last year," she confessed in a deep moment of silence. "A vision of my father."

A cold chill swept through the air with a hint of rain as Jack pondered the confession.

"What?" Jack asked, unable to hide the surprise in his voice.

"I couldn't see his face, but he was calling to me from far away in a low whisper."

Light pattering sounds of raindrops began hitting the ground around them, growing increasingly louder as the sky began to sprinkle on them. Though Jack was eager to get back to the Academy, the story of her vision was too intriguing for him to leave. "What else did he say in the vision? Did he want something?"

She stared at the tomb from behind the iron gate for some time before she answered. The rain wasted no time before it came down hard and thick. With every passing moment of silence, it intensified. "No..." she lied, afraid of opening her heart fully to the matter. But why am I lying? she thought to herself.

It wasn't long before she reconsidered. It wasn't like her to lie to Jack, and it left a sour feeling in her stomach. In her mind, she thought she really just didn't feel like giving away the secret yet. But Jack had always told her everything, hadn't he? Didn't she owe him at least the truth about this? "Well, yes, actually," she said. "He told me to take back what was mine from the tomb, or something like that. But I have no idea what it means." She thought about the words for a moment as rain dripped and splashed off the brim of the hood of her cloak. "Think it might have been metaphorical?"

"Maybe," Jack replied, now soaked through his thin cloak. His wet hair draped over his eyes down to his freckles. "I suppose it could mean something like... maybe about taking back your place in the magic world. Or... well, something like that."

She was happy for the rain now pouring down on them. The thoughts of her father had been hard for her to process—knowing, but not knowing how much he cared or loved her. Seeing her father only through actions and stories, never through his own words, though she wished dearly that she could hear them.

She wanted more than ever for her father to see her—to watch her win the duel, to see her skills advance in the craft that he was so brilliant at. How different would it be with his powerful hand on her shoulder? The rain was an easy mask that she conveniently wore. It covered those difficult emotions she'd held back all semester, now uncontrollably boiling to the surface, leaving salty rivulets to mix with raindrops, trickling down her pale cheeks.

Truth be told, she had never cared much for the rain. It had always left her cold and wet, keeping her from doing things she enjoyed. But in this moment, she had a newfound appreciation for it. It was another cloak to protect her, and she embraced its welcome.

"Gwyn," Jack said after a long silence. "What if it wasn't a metaphor?" he asked softly, only to be forced to wait patiently for a response. Yet again, Gwyn's hood faced the tomb and didn't move. After several moments of silence, he tried a new approach. "What if your father left you something in the tomb?"

Again, he waited, but received silence, so he closed his eyes and placed his wet head against an iron bar. It wasn't until then that she finally looked away from the tomb and over at Jack. He tilted his head to meet her eyes. Her bloodshot eyes immediately gave her crying away, but he didn't say anything. "So, what if? He forgot to tell me how to get it if he did. He also forgot—Hollow walking doesn't seem to run in the family... Besides, I don't want to wreck my father's tomb to go looking for it."

Jack looked around. "Maybe he did leave you something. Maybe he left you a sign or a clue."

She shrugged. "Look around. I can't see any clues—can you?"

Jack looked around, his feet splashing in puddles of water as he turned and looked from one place to the next. "Well, maybe those weird symbols I can see in the Hollow are clues? They look extremely out of place."

She shrugged again. "Why would he do something I can't see?" She pondered it for a moment, perplexed by the idea, then shook her head. "Alright, draw one out—maybe one of us will recognize it if we can look at it."

Jack ran over to a place where a bush was planted across the square and sketched the symbol into the mud, where they both stared and looked at it for a moment.

"Jack... that's a musical note! It's a C note! Jack... that must be a song written on the tomb." She turned to Jack. "Let me get my harp. Regain your qi—I'll be back with Chele. She'll be done with her class and wonder where we are by now anyway."

Before Jack could protest, he was watching Gwyn's dark green cloak trailing off behind her as she ran through the dark rain toward the Academy. He found a dry place on the sidewalk under a balcony overhang and began performing a brocade to gather as much energy as he could.

A few minutes later, Gwyn was back with Chele, carrying her harp under her cloak.

"Does she know what we're doing?" Jack asked Gwyn, nodding toward Chele.

"Kinda. I explained it on the way here," she replied, pulling her harp out from under the balcony. "Jack, I need the rest of the notes."

Jack nodded and ran over to the gate, vanishing into the Hollow.

"Whoa, what the? What just happened? Where'd he go?" Chele asked in surprise.

Gwyn had forgotten to tell Chele about Jack's new ability to slip into the Hollow. She quickly tried to give her the gist of it, and within a few seconds, Jack reappeared and ran over to the mud to carve out the rest of the notes.

Gwyn practiced them several times. There were only eleven notes, and the song was simple but sounded peacefully harmonic when plucked out on her harp. Though there wasn't any indication as to what the timing should be, she felt a natural rhythm to the flow of the notes, playing it the way it felt right.

"I'm guessing you need to play it over there in front of the gate," Jack said.

She tucked her harp under her cloak and made her way to the front of the gate. She sat down, rain still pouring on her, and did her best to pluck out the notes on her harp while keeping it concealed under her cloak. She could see symbols on the harp glowing from under the cloak, and for the first time, she realized she could feel the unmistakable sensation of the harp's aura as it sang out the song her fingers requested. It was a warm and gentle aura that grew and developed as she played. It filled her with happiness and hope as she began to feel a dull vibrating sensation throughout her mind.

The instant the last note was played, the gate came to life and slowly retracted open. Mindlessly, Gwyn stood up and stepped forward onto the other side of it.

"Gwyn, stop! The barrier—remember!" Jack yelled to her.

But she didn't listen. Her eyes were locked on her father's tomb.

"Jack, check for barriers! Quick!" Chele demanded.

Jack reluctantly slipped into the Hollow again, coming back even more out of breath than before. He panted for a minute, hunched over while he spoke. "It's still there, but it looks a little weird—like it kind of became loose and dull-looking. She must have walked right through it. I mean, do we have to do this now? Come on, Gwyn!"

Gwyn continued to walk toward the tomb. "We're leaving tomorrow," she said to Jack in a somewhat distant tone. When she looked back, he could see her eyes slightly glowing with a greenish-indigo hue. "We do this now."

Chele and Jack stood outside the gate, staring at her. They watched as she slowly knelt down in front of the tomb.

Gwyn heard a grinding noise coming from the bottom part of the tomb. She looked down to see a sheet of stone slowly retracting, revealing a recessed rectangle that appeared to have been carved into the stone base of the tomb. The inlay of the rectangle now exposed revealed two indentations that appeared to be small handprints, about the size of a child's hands.

She felt as if her mind were slipping, but she was still in control. She knew what she was doing—or at least, until now she had—as she suddenly felt an urge to do something that logic told her was insane. It was only for a moment that she could resist the urge burning within her, and within that moment, she spoke from her heart. "Sorry, father," she whispered, a mere moment before driving both of her fists through the stone handprints.

Her hands tingled, and she could feel something running up her arms and through her for a moment. It was as if, for a moment, she had remembered something wonderful. She closed her eyes and saw flashes of images of herself putting her hand into gray, cold clay. It then occurred to her that someone was holding her hand, placing it into the clay for her.

The stone rectangle had collapsed into several small pieces, and behind it was a new, deeper recess. She closed her eyes again as the memory began fading like a good dream does after breakfast, but she didn't want it to end. She was certain she must have broken her hands on the stone, and pain would soon surge through her. To her surprise, she found both of her hands were perfectly fine, aside from a few scratches and some slightly lifted skin on her knuckles.

"Gwyn! Look!" Jack told her.

She looked down into the stone recess behind the broken stone to find a long, brown leather apparatus with a strap. It was somewhat elegant but rugged at the same time.

"What is it?" She asked.

"Well, it's not a quiver," Jack pointed out. "Get it and get out!"

"I think it's a sheath," Chele said. "A really big knife or small sword sheath."

Gwyn picked it up, turned it over a few times, and then wrapped the strap around her body.

"We need to return things to normal here," Gwyn said, but the second she stood up, the stone sheet slid back into place, covering the recess completely. She walked out of the gate, and within a few seconds of standing outside of it, it quickly closed.

"Well, that was easy," Jack said with a shrug.

"'Bout time," a low, dark voice said from the shadows.

The rain was still pouring, and they couldn't see anyone until a flash of lightning revealed the form of a hooded person in the street, walking slowly toward them.

"Who are you!?" Gwyn yelled through the rain.

The silhouette stepped closer and let out a few low, raspy laughs. "Sig," the raspy voice said in a deep hiss.

Another flash of lightning revealed the man's face. He had pale skin, pale gray eyes, and a thick, dark scar that stretched diagonally across his entire face, running right between his eyes and down his cheek.

Chele and Jack both gasped when they saw him.

"What do you want?" Gwyn asked, taking a step in front of her friends.

"Brave, are you!? ... What an honor it is to finally meet you. You know, I was starting to think you were dead after all." The dark figure lifted a small orange light to his mouth. The light glared brighter as he took a deep puff from it. He smiled, then blew a cloud of smoke into the rain. He then flicked the cigarette from his fingers toward them. It landed a couple of inches from Gwyn's feet, only to hiss as the rain from the cold stone street doused the life from its tiny ember. "What I want is the sheath. Hand it to me, and we'll go our separate ways."

Gwyn was holding the sheath under her cloak, but she also still had her harp tucked in it. She wasn't sure who the strange person was, but he was much taller and larger than she was. "Why should I? It's not yours."

Sig laughed, the dark, raspy laugh of a longtime smoker with a deep voice. "How very wrong you are. Xess will laugh hard at that." The man held up his arm in a familiar clawing stance, fingers ridged and pointed at Gwyn. It was a clear sign that he most likely was about to perform or cast magic. "It's taken a lot of work to rig your father's spells to go off prematurely. I'm rather proud of myself."

"Spells?" Gwyn asked, unsure of what they were.

"Yes, the old fool had several trigger spells. It took some work to change them around, but it looks like it was worth it. Now, I'd rather not take it by force, but I really don't feel like waiting around for you to make up your mind."

She wrapped her hand around the sheath, wondering for a moment what importance it could possibly have, then nodded. "...Okay... You can have it. Just leave us alone!"

Jack gasped and looked at her. "What?" he whispered.

Sig lowered his arm and stepped forward. As he walked, he chuckled to himself and mumbled, "You're doing the world a favor."

Gwyn carefully took the sheath from around herself and started to hand it to Sig, but as he leaned down to take it, there was a bright flash of lightning. She braced her harp tightly and swung it upward swiftly, slamming the bottom corner of it into his face. The harp rang out loudly as it connected with the sharp blow.

Perhaps it was because it was so dark, or the blinding flash of lightning, but Sig didn't try to dodge the blow. The harp cut a deep gash into his forehead just above his eye. He jerked back, screaming and holding the spot as blood ran down his face. He stumbled backward in the rain.

Chele cast a burst of blinding sparks at his face, hoping to blind or stun him, and the three of them took off running.

Jack made it to the gate of the school first, placed his hand on it, and yelled, "Awatawksnet." The gate opened, and he ran inside, followed by Chele. They both waited a moment before closing the door.

"Wait! Where's Gwyn?" Jack asked.

Chele shrugged. "I thought she was in front?"

Gwyn had run the other way to get her harp case from under the archway. By then, Sig had gotten up and was firing green bolts of magic at her. The blood covering one of his eyes seemed to affect his aim and the blasts blew off chunks of stone when they hit the walls, narrowly missing Gwyn.

She ran fast, following the sidewalk that wrapped around to the back of the school. It was fenced off with a tall, stone-walled fence preventing her from getting in. To her right, across the street, was the park. She thought briefly about running there, then quickly decided against it, and instead ran straight, crossing the street into a dark alleyway. She quickly put her harp into its case, and pulled her bow into a firing position. She reached for an arrow but realized she hadn't put her quiver on for the duel, so she focused her qi to make the sharpest ice dart she could in the moment.

Sig came around the corner into the alley, and she launched the ice dart. It flew quickly through the dark alley and stuck Sig in the shoulder. He screamed and grabbed it, yanking it out and throwing it onto the wet street.

"You prat!" he yelled, his raspy voice echoing down the alley. He sent a blast wave of energy out, sending the shards down the alleyway.

Gwyn grabbed her harp and turned a corner, the shards flying by just after. She ran through the alley and found a thin stone ramp going up against a building and managed to scale it to the roof.

Not sure where to go, she took a running start and jumped across the alley to another roof, slipping slightly as she landed on the wet stone. She hid behind a large structure on the roof and tried to catch her breath. As she listened, she heard Sig on the other roof.

"Come out, girl! You're making ol' Sig reeeally mad."

Gwyn didn't know what to do. She could see the school straight ahead but didn't have a way down off the roof without showing herself to Sig.

A door slowly crept open to her left, nearly causing her to scream. She managed not to and a small girl stuck her head out, looking around. She made eye contact with Gwyn and quickly waved her inside.

Gwyn followed her in, and the small girl bolted the door behind them. The girl removed her hood, revealing bright tomato-red hair as she greeted her. "Hey! How are you!?"

"Sash?" Gwyn said with sincere surprise.

"I heard screams in the alleyway. I looked through the window and saw that creepy guy chasing you."

Gwyn tilted her head, a bit curious to know more. "You saved me... Thank you."

Sash nodded. "I saw you shoot him and go up the guttering. After I saw you jump, I came to get you. I don't think he knows you jumped."

"I see. Thank you!" Gwyn said again, with sincere relief. "Sash, my friends are expecting me back at the school right now. Is there a way I can get back there safely? If I don't get there soon, I'm afraid they'll go out looking for me."

Sash smiled. "Of course! There's an old passageway underground." Sash turned and led Gwyn through her house, to the cupboard, and into a trapdoor in the floor. They crawled down a dark ladder, and Sash shot out a flit. A smooth, pearly ribbon revealed a long, dark corridor made of stone. She got the feeling that the passageway was very old, smelling of stagnant air and dust.

"I didn't know you could throw flits," Gwyn said.

Sash looked back and smiled without a word, then ran through the underground passage.

After running through the passageway, they came to what looked like a wooden door. Sash grabbed it, pulled sideways, and it retracted like a sliding door. It came out in the back of the library in the school. Gwyn looked back and saw that the door was really the back of a bookcase.

"Brilliant! Thanks, Sash!"

She made a quick goodbye, then took off running, trying to make it to the front of the school in hopes of keeping Jack and Chele from going back outside. Her heart raced, and her stomach churned with worry as she replayed thoughts of them running straight into Sig.

She finally made it to the front of the school to find Jack trying to go back outside. Luckily, Jack's shirt was being stretched and held by Guts. He was kicking and screaming to be let go when Gwyn spoke.

"Hey, guys!" Gwyn said, a bit out of breath.

Jack stopped flailing and kicking as they both looked back with awed expressions on their faces. "Where'd you come from?"

CHAPTER 18

The Dive

"Sorry, Gwyn," a restrained Jack told her, "would have come back out, but Guts..."

"It's fine," Gwyn quickly interrupted. "It's better that you didn't! I don't have to go looking for you now."

"Wait, but—"

"Thanks, Guts. You probably saved his life," Gwyn said, nodding to the tall, slender man holding Jack's shirt.

Guts grumbled, nodded, and released Jack.

The three of them moved away from the door where Guts stood. When they'd gotten far enough away, Gwyn told Chele and Jack what had happened: how Sig had thrown magic at her and chased her through an alley, and how Sash found her on the roof.

"How could Sash throw a flit? She doesn't look old enough!" Jack asked in disbelief.

"She's never been to my class." Chele said with a shrug.

"I've never seen her in any class," Gwyn said. "She certainly looks young enough to be in school, though."

Gwyn took them to the library to see the bookshelf that led to Sash's place. When they got there, she looked down a long row of bookshelves against the wall and realized, in her haste, that she'd forgotten which one she'd come out of.

They tried pushing several bookshelves to move them, but they were all heavy and wouldn't budge. Frustrated, they found a quiet study room in the library and sat to examine the sheath.

"Are we sure it's even a sheath?" Jack asked.

" It just looks like a sheath to me" said Chele.

"Yeah," Jack admitted, "just looked so weird in the nether, thought it might be something else."

"Gwyn," Chele asked shyly, "do you think maybe Cassius didn't want you to have this?"

Gwyn sat silently for a moment, considering Chele's words, then a brief expression of anger flashed across her face. "I certainly hope he did. Why else would the song be on his tomb?"

Chele contemplated the retort for a moment before replying, "But Gwyn, you couldn't even see those notes without help."

"Yeah... I suppose."

"Maybe he knew that Gwyn would find them if she had help?" Jack suggested.

Chele shrugged. "I guess anything is possible. I just think it's odd that he managed to get her everything else through her aunt and uncle."

Gwyn started to reply but realized she couldn't. She looked at the sheath, then asked herself, 'Is Chele right? Does my father not want me to have this?'

It was somewhat thicker than most sheaths and was sort of oval in diameter; whatever blade went in it must have been slightly curved, like a claw.

"What about Sig?" Chele asked.

Gwyn shook her head. "I don't know."

"I don't think he can get in here," Jack stated.

"Well, even if he did, he'd probably get caught by a professor," Chele stated. "Besides, this place is pretty big; I doubt he'd be able to find us."

"Why did he want me to find this?" Gwyn said, holding the sheath up to look at it.

Suddenly, there was a deep boom from somewhere, causing the warm lighting in the room to flicker. It shook the table slightly, causing the sheath to rattle on it.

"What was that?" Jack asked in concern.

"I don't know," Gwyn replied, while grabbing the sheath and running into the other room. But before she could, there was another boom, much quieter and muffled.

They looked around but didn't find or see anything that could have made the noise.

"Maybe it was an earthquake," Jack suggested, as they moved on.

They believed Sig was unlikely to make it into the Academy unless he knew the password or secret passageway but still spent a couple of hours discussing what had happened.

"Should we tell someone?" Jack asked.

Chele shook her head and shot a serious look at Jack.

"What?"

"Are you crazy? We just broke into the tomb of one of the most legendary wizards ever!" Chele told him with a sense of urgency.

Gwyn nodded. "That and Franz and Delilah would flip. You saw how serious they got when I wanted to touch it for my birthday. Those barriers are probably dangerous... or deadly."

Jack scratched the inside of his ear while staring at the wall. "Well, I guess you're right. I wonder how you made it through."

Gwyn hadn't thought much about walking through the barriers. "I don't know—it just happened."

Chele and Jack let out a sigh, nerves growing as they considered there could be someone looking for them.

"It's not just anyone," Jack pointed out. "He mentioned Xess."

Gwyn nodded. "Yeah, don't think my mother and Xess got along too well."

"No telling. It's anyone's guess where he went now," Chele said.

"Maybe we should tell Franz," Gwyn pondered aloud.

"Gwyn, please!" Chele pleaded with compassionate ocean-blue eyes. "If he tells my mom, I'll never get to come back here."

Gwyn glanced at Chele with concern, then sighed. "You really think so?"

Chele nodded. "Mom makes me write every week to let her know I'm safe. If she found out we were attacked by a madman..."

"Wait a minute, we weren't attacked," Jack stated with a slightly defensive tone.

"What are you talking about? Gwyn was!" Chele replied.

"No, she attacked him!"

Chele looked at the table while she thought about it. "Well, I guess you're right. But we were about to be mugged!"

"Yeah, but that's not an attack!" Jack stated.

"Actually, it is," Gwyn said with finality in her voice. Her eyes were fixed on a spot on the wooden table they were sitting at.

"Well, not physically," Jack said.

"She freaking saved us, and you're arguing with her about it!?" Chele asked, staring intently at Jack.

Jack's mouth opened slightly as he stared back. "I..."

"I felt threatened. I'm not going to justify it any more than that," Gwyn stated firmly. She then let out a brief sigh before speaking again. "I guess we won't tell anyone. But we need to figure out who Sig is and why he wants this sheath."

The three of them, tired and exhausted, decided to leave the library and go to bed. On their way out, Gwyn felt someone looking at her from near a bookshelf a few yards away. She turned to look and saw Parker, the kid who embarrassed himself after making fun of her. She nonchalantly walked out, ignoring him. She could almost feel his anger rise as she left.

In their dorm, Gwyn sat nervously, holding her bow and staring at the door.

"I don't think he'd even know where we are, Gwyn, even if he did make it in," Chele told her. After a couple of hours, Gwyn decided it was best to get some rest, but she slept facing the door with her bow ready in her hand.

It was hard for Gwyn to sleep that night. She tossed and turned and kept waking up to look at the door. When she did fall into a deeper sleep, her dreams were filled with images of Sig and of busting her hands on her father's tomb. She suddenly woke with a strong desire to keep the sheath close to her. She tossed and turned, doing her best to ignore the desire, but eventually gave in. She got up, took it from her cloak, and slid it under her pillow.

The stressful dreams did not stop, but the nagging desire to have the sheath close to her did.

In the morning, she woke up with her hand under the pillow holding the sheath. She didn't think much of it and decided to enjoy one of the school's breakfasts before leaving. She met up with Chele to eat a bacon, scrambled egg, melon, and waffle breakfast in the cafeteria.

It wasn't much longer after they'd finished packing that Franz and Delilah arrived. While carrying their luggage through the main hall, Gwyn thought she saw a redheaded girl in burnt robes at the opposite end. She was hunched and limping as she stopped to observe her. Jack, unaware of Gwyn stopping, ran right into the back of her, knocking her violently forward.

"Geez! Watch it, Jack!"

"Sorry, Gwyn. Didn't see you stop."

She looked back to where the girl was, but she was no longer there.

"What are you looking at anyway?" Jack asked.

Gwyn shook her head, unsure if she had seen anything worth mentioning.

When they stepped into the crisp morning air, all three of them looked around for a sign of Sig but didn't find one. Gwyn saw a small group of people down the way, standing near a wall that had been blasted by him after she'd run. An old man in the group pointed at the sky while he talked, and Gwyn wondered if they'd chalked the damage up to the lightning storm.

The morning ride was hazy when they took off. There was a slight mist in the air as random blankets of fog rolled across the road, as well as the grassy plains and hills around them.

Gwyn, Chele, and Jack decided not to tell Franz and Delilah about the incident from the night before, unsure of what would happen. They knew they had disobeyed and feared they might stop them from returning to the Academy. Gwyn especially feared for Chele, given her mother was worried about her safety. She'd just learned that Chele's mother was having her write so frequently.

When they arrived back at Franz and Delilah's, they unpacked and helped with chores. The ground outside had patches of snow on it, and the air was crisp with winter's chill. Franz and Delilah had built rows for extending the vineyard on the hill behind the house for grapes and berries.

They already had several established fruit trees on the forest edges, including apple trees, orange trees, pear trees, and peach trees scattered around their farm. Gwyn, Jack, and Chele were tasked with insulating the trees with mulch and blankets.

Franz explained that the Academy was too far south to get much snow. He then told them about warming crystals that came from deep within the planet. They were rare and required a master symbologist to make one work right by wiring them up to Xi crystals. When done right, it could keep fruit trees warm in colder climates.

Franz and Delilah insisted that they continue training and meditating several times every day. The next semester of school would begin in February.

Chele's ability to produce a plasma flit had only slightly improved, though it still took a lot of energy to produce what looked like a hint of a flit.

Jack's ability to slip into the Hollow didn't noticeably improve much, but his ability to synergize with the nether had.

Gwyn continued to work with all the elements she knew well enough to synergize with. She knew she was improving, but it felt slow. Franz assured her she was far ahead for her age.

They had built dummies out of old scrap wood and barrels to use. It was fun beating them to pieces with magic and seemed to help pass the time quicker as they trained.

Christmas was only days away, and they had finally experienced a bit of a warm front. The weather had been so crisp and cold it was hard to avoid catching a head cold or at least getting a runny nose.

As Jack was getting over a cold, Chele caught it and slept most of the day. Franz and Delilah wanted to make arrangements to have Kokolo visit for healing and left to the Shadow Guild.

"I'll need Delilah's help," he told Gwyn before leaving. "There's plenty of food; just do the chores and don't go anywhere! You're in charge!"

Delilah had also alluded to doing some holiday shopping and expected the trip to take at least a couple of days.

After Franz and Delilah left, Gwyn found herself doing most of the cooking and cleaning. She was feeling a bit better than Jack and Chele, and often found herself awake at night.

Being slightly warmer, she decided to sleep with the window open, hoping to enjoy an occasional breeze. She opened her eyes to the sound of leaves rustling and sat up on the edge of her bed. She stared out the window while rolling a coin across her fingers. The Electric Moon was beaming down on her, comforting as always and pulling at her like a magnet.

A day later, she got a letter from her aunt and uncle. It read, Called to duty. Emergency. Will return ASAP. Stay at the cabin. Will be back shortly.

Gwyn, frustrated by the letter, decided that the air was warm enough to be outside and thought it to be a good chance to play her harp. She had somewhat abandoned it as of late. She was so busy with chores and magic that she didn't have much time to spare for it. Furthermore, she was having to care for Jack and Chele as they fought off winter colds.

She grabbed her bow and harp and had already been wearing the sheath under her cloak, as she'd done daily since she'd obtained it. She wasn't sure why she wore it, but she told herself that 'because it was her father's' was the likely reason, and it didn't need more justification than that.

Her nightmares, however, had not stopped but gotten worse. She had often found herself waking up at night, looking at a concerned Chele, who would wake her to make sure she was alright.

Gwyn snuck out that night as quietly as she could, making her way across the field to the pathway in the woods and past the old fountain of leaves.

When she reached it, she thought she heard a noise in the woods. She stopped, set her harp down, and armed herself with Apollo. She didn't draw the arrow back as she waited for another noise, knowing that the arrow would glow under the Electric Moon and give her away. Several moments of silence passed, and she spotted Jack running up the pathway far behind her.

She hid behind the fountain of leaves, and as he ran past her, she said, "Boo!" causing him to spin and lose his balance in a fit of terror.

Jack ended up tripping over himself while quickly turning to see a laughing Gwyn sitting behind the fountain.

"Aw man! I can't believe you caught me!" Jack said, sitting up to look at his scraped hands.

"Serves you right. You're always sneaking up on me! About time I paid you back!"

The two of them walked to the ridge and sat down next to each other. The air was still a bit chilly coming off the ocean, but it was still warmer than it had been all winter.

"Think Sig's still out looking for us?" Jack asked.

Gwyn shook her head with a slight shrug, replying, "Could be. Who knows? I don't see what the big deal with this sheath is anyway." Gwyn lifted the sheath from beneath her cloak, running her hands over it.

"You... brought it here?" Jack asked.

Gwyn looked at him for a moment but didn't respond to his question. "Suppose it's a great night to play music, isn't it?"

Jack looked at the harp case, still expecting an answer to his question, then back to Gwyn. He let out a short sigh and said, "Yeah."

She started to unlatch her harp case, but before she did, she felt something strange had happened. Her mind had slipped, as it had done several times before, and she slowly stood up.

"Gwyn?" She heard Jack distantly ask in concern as he watched her, her eyes glowing brightly with a pink-indigo hue in the whites of them.

Gwyn faced the ocean, then took off in a dead sprint toward the edge of the cliff. She then saw her vision drop from the navy-blue sky, then turn down to the ocean as she dove from what must have been over a hundred feet.

Like an arrow, she saw herself diving straight toward the water. She cut the surface of the water sharply and shot deep into the icy coldness. Dark images of bubbles rushed past her, tickling her cheeks as they went by. She was soaring deeper and deeper into the depths of the darkening waters, her speed never letting up.

Suddenly, her body hit the sandy ocean floor, and her hand grasped something she could not see. For a moment, she thought it was a stick, but whatever it was, its aura was very powerful.

Gwyn started to become aware of the cold water on her skin as her mind slipped back to its normal state. Her long hair was whipping around her face in the undertow as she looked in every direction for light; but light was nowhere—it was as dark here as dark could be down there.

The reality of things became sickeningly clear as her lungs began burning and screaming with a need to fill with air. She tried to calm herself, but they burned like fire, and she slowly began giving in and released what little air she had in them. It was terrifying, knowing she was but a breath of saltwater away from drowning.

As her heart beat throbbed in her ears, a hand grabbed the back of her cloak and began pulling her upward. She clasped her tongue to the roof of her mouth as she did everything she could to avoid breathing in. She began to attempt to distract her now-dizzying, suffocating mind with thoughts. Did he come... but how? Am I not too deep? she thought, assuming Jack had somehow found her in the depths of the ocean.

Gwyn felt water rushing around her as she was quickly pulled backward through the depths. She then saw a pearly ribbon of light trailing off behind her. Its silvery glow didn't light up much in the murky water, but for a moment, she admired the beauty of the strange sight. As dizzy as she was, the realization that someone had cast a flit occurred to her. Gwyn knew Jack could not cast a flit of light and expected to see Franz or Delilah upon breaking the surface.

Her head finally broke the ocean's surface, and she took deep gasps of cold air, coughing up the acrid saltwater from her lungs between breaths.

She was still being dragged backward, relieved when she felt shells and sand beneath her. The hand let go and left her to a fit of coughing. Gwyn slowly stood, still coughing and wheezing. She was standing waist-deep in water, trying to ignore an impending headache. Her teeth began to chatter in the cold water. The breeze was now a violent, stinging force upon her wet skin and clothes.

Gwyn finally turned to face who had saved her. She expected Franz or Delilah to be standing there with crossed arms, ready to scold her for her stupidity. But what she saw shocked her even more. It was not Franz or Delilah, and it was most certainly not Jack. It was the dark-haired woman from the Shadow Guild—the lady Gwyn had locked eyes with several times.

She had long, black hair like Gwyn's, and a similar pretty face and build.

Gwyn stared for a moment, caught between shivering and stunned disbelief at why and how this strange woman would save her from such a dire situation.

The woman stood there silently, her hair flowing gracefully in the wind behind her as two brightly lit opal eyes peered into Gwyn's.

Gwyn finally broke the silence, asking in a weak, shivering voice, "Who are you!"

The waves and wind overpowered her words, so she asked again—louder this time—though hoarse after choking on saltwater.

A thought popped into Gwyn's tired mind, Could it be? Is this… my mother?

The woman was not shivering. She stood there impassively, majestic in the wind, standing a few feet from Gwyn. Her piercing stare lasted for several lengthy moments before she spoke. "You're a fool… like your mother."

Gwyn didn't know why, but the words that the mysterious woman said stung, more painfully than she'd thought possible. It was so painful that she wasn't sure how to respond. She quickly decided on a misdirecting approach, hoping to yield an explanation and avoid more painful words. "What is your name!?"

The woman turned her head and was silent for a bit.

"Jade," the woman finally answered. She then turned her gaze back toward her. "It's true then? You have the sheath?" she asked. Her eyes pierced into Gwyn's like burning opals of blue flame, gleaming in the Electric Moonlight that illuminated her figure.

The cold ocean waves beat on Gwyn's back as she gritted her teeth in an effort to keep them from chattering as she nodded.

Jade looked back toward the ocean for a moment, then her face grew angry. She then reached over and slapped Gwyn hard across the face. "You don't know what you're doing!"

Gwyn added a ringing in her ear to the list of uncomfortable things she was experiencing at that moment. She lifted her head back up to see Jade's shining, angry opal eyes still peering into hers. It felt as if they were cutting into her soul, and she had to fight to maintain eye contact.

"Where is it?" Jade demanded, but for some reason, Gwyn did not reach for the sheath. She realized she still held the thing she had grabbed in the depths of the ocean, her hand just under the water with it.

Gwyn stood in silent thought when she felt Jade's quick hand strike her face again. Her hand was so fast Gwyn didn't even react until it had slapped her cheek. "Answer!"

Gwyn felt her mind starting to slip. She raised her hand out of the water, revealing a long, blue dagger. The blade itself was slightly curved and looked a little thick for a dagger. Even so, she somehow knew it was very sharp and powerful. She stared at it for a moment, admiring how it looked, as if it had been carved from a deep blue sapphire.

Jade's eyes flew open wide, and she immediately backed several feet away from Gwyn. "You have it? Put that evil blade away!"

Gwyn felt her mind return and looked from Jade, who now looked concerned, to the dagger in her hand. It was beautiful in the Electric Moonlight. But is that what she was holding? Something evil? She pondered on it for a moment, then dismissed it.

"Why should I?" Gwyn asked her. "You've given me no reason to trust you! You struck me!"

Jade looked slighted at the words, and her expression went from shock to angry. "I saved your life..." she reminded her.

Gwyn suddenly remembered that the last few minutes did involve being pulled from a dark, watery grave and thought that perhaps Jade could have a point.

Jade's expression drifted back to impassive as she gazed off toward the distant ocean. "When Xess finds out that you have the blade..."

Gwyn looked down at the dagger again, then back up to Jade. "Why? What is it?"

Jade stared at the blade, her appearance now slightly daunting through her blazing opal eyes. "The Xi Blade," she said.

"Does Xess want the Xi Blade, then?"

Jade waited a moment before answering, "He wants it destroyed." After another moment, she locked her gaze on Gwyn and slightly shook her head as if in disbelief. "Sig's looking for you. Keep your eyes open."

Jade turned her back on her, but Gwyn wanted the conversation to continue, although she was freezing and uncomfortable. "Wait, I'm not done!" she yelled through a chatter. "I want to speak with you!"

Jade shook her head. "No... you don't. Besides, you'd better help your friend. He jumped in after you." And as quickly as that, she vanished.

"Jack..." Gwyn whispered, then turned to look out over the ocean. Her eyes darted around, searching for movement. Finally, she spotted a dot far off in the distance. She quickly sheathed the dagger, surprised at how perfectly it fit, and went back into the water. "JACK?" she yelled. "I'm coming!"

She swam as fast as she could, the waves throwing her around like a ragdoll. She fought desperately to make it to the deeper ocean where she saw a figure flailing. She was close enough now to tell it was a person without doubt; it had to be Jack.

She broke past the white caps, the waves now rolling under the surface. Some waves climbed several feet above their head and pushed them both under. The struggle back to the surface was immensely tiring.

Gwyn was a decent swimmer, but her muscles now burned, and the cold water was starting to do something strange to her body, making it stiff and hard to move.

She finally reached Jack, he was barely able to tread water anymore. Gwyn tried to tell him to stop flailing around, but she took a gulp of water in the process. He then grabbed her, and she felt her head being forced underwater. She began to realize that trying to save Jack could mean drowning herself.

She managed to pull away from his panicked grip and swam a few feet away. She knew she needed a plan and fast, or the situation was dire.

She looked around for land, but it was difficult to see the shore from where they were. She feared that now she might not even be able to swim that far back anyway. Hope was quickly fading as she turned to see that Jack was struggling hard to stay above water.

"Hang on, Jack!" she yelled.

In desperation, she pulled her bow off and prayed that her quiver had held onto at least one arrow through the night. She had to stop treading water to do it, but she found her arrows had tangled in the hood of her cloak. This was a mixed blessing, as getting one out while trying to stay afloat was difficult.

Gwyn felt herself sinking as she worked a tangled arrow from her quiver. She felt it pull free, and she kicked herself back up to the surface. She was surprised at how deep she'd sunk and gasped for air when she reached the surface again, her head reminding her of her recent oxygen deprivation.

She pointed the arrow straight up and shot it. It glowed like a shooting star as it soared into the air and came back down into the ocean a few yards from them. A giant patch of ice formed on the surface where it landed, pushing them both back several feet.

Gwyn swam to it and threw her arms onto it. Her legs felt like lead, trying to lift them onto the ice. She grabbed the dagger and stuck it into the ice, using it to pull herself up.

Jack was dipping under water frequently, and she barely caught him by the scruff of his shirt to pull him up before he sank too deep. His body was rigid and like dead weight and she struggled for some time before getting him onto the floating platform of ice.

He was coughing and shivering, half-conscious, as Gwyn lay close to him, shivering as well.

The wind was once again a painful threat. She knew she needed to get both of them warm and fast.

Gwyn slowly stood and moved to the center of the ice, her legs buckling as she shivered, and performed a technique to gather qi. Her moves were rigid, and she stumbled, losing focus. She then fell to her knees, depleted.

She stayed kneeling for a moment to catch her breath, then took a deep breath and pulled off her fingerless glove, before trying to bind fire to light it. But there was no energy to fuel it.

Still, Gwyn tried. She had to try. She stood up and tried so hard that she reached the border of overextending herself and became physically sick.

It was a terrible feeling, like breaking a bone in her stomach. She fell to her knees and vomited over the edge of the sheet of ice, holding her now-aching stomach. She stayed there bent down for a few minutes, staring dizzily into the dark ocean waters.

When her wits had somewhat returned, she slowly stood up to find herself feeling somehow worse than she did before.

She looked out in every direction, but her vision was too blurred to make out how far they were from land. She felt around in her pockets, hoping to find something useful. Her hands moved from pocket to pocket before landing on the handle of the dagger—the blade Jade called the Xi Blade. She then drew the blue crystal blade from its sheath. The power that radiated through its aura was strong, and she felt as if her energy was recharging.

She closed her eyes and let herself absorb the feeling. Still, quite exhausted, she decided not to burn her glove but instead decided to try binding heat directly into the frozen Jack. She knelt down next to him, put her hands on his chest, drew her negative and positive qi together, and attempted to send a small amount of heat into Jack's body.

Gwyn used what little energy she had left to mold the ice up a little around them, making a slight wind block. It wasn't even a foot high, but it helped tremendously.

She was unable to keep her eyes open and laid close to Jack, then threw her cloak over both of them and fell asleep.

CHAPTER 19
The Glade Goblins

Gwyn woke on her side with a pounding headache. Waves splashed and tickled the side of her face, covering her ear and cheek. The air was slightly warmer, as was the water, and the sun shone brightly in a hazy sky. She felt near Jack's mouth to check his breathing and was relieved to know he'd survived the night.

She lifted her head and found her left ear had been underwater. She shook her head, but her ear was heavily waterlogged, making it almost impossible to hear out of it.

She looked around and saw they were on a long sandbar. She'd never seen one before. It was a stretch of beach mixed with rocks and sand, with no sign of life other than birds and clams. To the north, the snowcapped mountains looked closer than she'd ever seen them, and she could see land and trees a ways away.

Gwyn used her tired arms to drag Jack up onto the beach, as high as she could, knowing the tides could randomly cast a rogue wave onto shore and swallow them both.

She was chilled and wanted to start a fire, but she lacked the will to gather qi and didn't have the energy to do it the old-fashioned way. After a few minutes, she realized she had to wake Jack and get them both dry and fed. She shook him several times before his eyes finally opened. He looked around, his face pale, and sat up. His eyes looked sunken, with dark circles around them. Gwyn felt his forehead and, sure enough, he felt slightly feverish.

"Are you okay?" she asked concerned.

Jack shook his head.

"Are you hurt? Please, tell me where."

"My... everything hurts," he croaked with a hoarse voice.

Gwyn knew she had no choice, so she stood and began meditating. She attempted to sink into a deep meditation as gracefully as she could.

At first, her muscles ached, and she was miserable, but with every passing minute, she felt slightly better.

Near the end, she had a desire to perform the moves while holding the Xi Blade. It was a strange addition to the movements but seemed to speed up the process of gathering energy.

When she had finished, she gathered what driftwood she could find and built a fire using magic.

Gwyn felt proud of herself. For some reason, magic was much easier today than she'd expected. She found more driftwood and hung their wet clothes behind them, which served as a wind block while drying them at the same time. She sat next to Jack, and within a few minutes, their clothes were dry.

Jack was lying on his back, looking pitiful.

"Is your ear full of water?" Gwyn asked.

"No," Jack answered. "I feel like Professor Warren sat on my ribs, though. Why, is yours?"

Gwyn chuckled. After a few minutes, she got up to look for food. She found some clams near the shore and brought them to Jack.

"I've never eaten clams before. Have you?" she asked him.

Jack shook his head.

Gwyn set the clams in the base of the fire and, after several minutes, pulled them back out. She pried one open with her fingernails and handed it to Jack. She then pried one open for herself and slurped its fishy contents.

"Aw yuck!" she said, almost spitting it out.

"It wasn't bad," Jack said softly.

Gwyn tried to hide the disgust on her face as she looked at Jack and told him he must've broken his taste buds.

She made a disgusted noise, then stared at the shiny clam shell before throwing it back into the fire in protest of the taste.

Jack chuckled, but it was obvious he didn't feel well.

"I threw up all my food last night and swallowed loads of saltwater. I've got to eat something," Gwyn said, trying to convince herself to eat more clams.

She saw gulls flying around and felt to see if she had any arrows left. She was surprised to find that the hood of her cloak had tangled around several, keeping them in the quiver. Removing them was easier outside the water, and she readied her aim at a gull. When Gwyn drew back her arrow, it shone with silvery magic.

She had never seen her arrow glow in the day before, only during the night when the Xi Moon was up. The shock of it made her prematurely release the arrow, and to her surprise, it struck a gull. The gull turned into a block of ice and fell to the sand.

Gwyn ran up to it and removed the arrow. As she grabbed it, it glowed and seemed to slide out, melting the ice where it had been. When the arrow was fully removed, the ice quickly melted away around the gull.

"Jack!" she yelled. "Jack, I just shot a magic arrow!"

Jack opened his eyes and grumbled, "Okay, thanks."

"No, I mean a magic ice arrow—the kind that seals things! A Xeo arrow!"

Jack opened his tired eyes again with a look of confusion. "How? I thought you could only shoot those at night, with the Xi Moon out?"

Gwyn shrugged. "I'm not sure. But it'd be nice if I could control when it happened, so I didn't freeze everything I shot." She then started plucking the feathers from the cold, wet bird, stuck it on a stick, and turned it slowly to rotisserie it over the fire.

"Gwyn, how do you have so much energy today?" Jack asked.

"I'm not sure," she said, and began counting on her fingers. "My head hurts, my muscles are sore, I can hardly hear out of one ear, I'm dehydrated, I think I almost died several times last night, and haven't eaten anything but a nasty clam all day, but I actually feel pretty good. It's like my energy feels really good."

Jack gave a tired shrug, and before long, they ate the gull.

Gwyn knew they needed fresh water, so she helped Jack walk inland and found that it opened up to grassy flat. A stretch of tall, dying grass separated the beach from the flats. There were tall trees across the prairie.

To the north, they could easily see the giant, snowcapped mountains far beyond the trees in the distance. She could tell they were still far from the mountains.

White, puffy clouds covered the sky as they walked, and a light snow began falling. The flakes found their way to the ground but refused to stay long. Had the wind been blowing more, the frigid air would have been painfully cold.

Gwyn decided to head deep into the forests to the north, hoping to find fresh water to quench her growing thirst. They walked for hours before coming upon a creek. They stood at its edge, where a sandy drop-off led down to where the creek had cut a deep ravine through the earth. Gwyn jumped several feet down to the sand, then helped Jack, who clutched his ribs as he slid down.

"We can't just drink it," Jack told her. "We have to purify it. You know, boil it or something."

"If we get desperate enough, Jack, we'll have to just drink it."

Jack grunted, opposed to the idea, but Gwyn didn't know if she had the ability to boil water or not. She had never thought of herself as being very good at fire magic but decided to try. She walked upstream where the water was running over a large rock. She placed her hands on the rock and focused. She felt herself fill with a growing warmth and guided that heat quickly down into the water. She had to pour quite a bit of energy into it, but she did it. The water bubbled, and the stone quickly became too hot to touch.

"Great!" Jack yelled, sounding more excited than he'd been all morning.

"That actually took less energy than I thought it would," Gwyn confessed in surprise.

"Yeah, but now it's just too hot to drink," Jack pointed out.

Gwyn took Apollo and fired a Xeo arrow slightly downstream from the boiling point. It hit the water with a jolting splash, creating a large frozen point that started just past where the water was boiling. The water now flowed over the rock and onto the ice to quickly boil then cool. It resulted in loud crackling sounds, as large plumes of steam puffed into the air.

Gwyn tried using the dagger's sheath to drink from but spewed the water out saying it tasted leathery and putrid. After some gagging, they used their hands instead, taking large gulps. "Thanks, Gwyn. You're pretty much a genius!"

Jack found a few small fish and a crawdad that had boiled in the water. She had Jack gut them because she still didn't like doing it, and they ate a small meal while resting near the creek. The ravine served as a nice block from the cool air.

Gwyn started a small fire and filled Jack in about what had happened with Jade, now that he seemed to be feeling a bit better.

"She sounds bat crazy. Who does she think she is?" Jack boasted, sounding better than he had all morning.

"She saved my life," Gwyn retorted.

"Yeah, but she still sounds crazy! Why didn't she save mine?"

Gwyn shrugged. "I don't know. I don't think she wanted me to have this dagger, though." Gwyn held the Xi Blade in the light in front of Jack. His eyes locked on the carved-sapphire design.

For some time, they debated Jade's intentions. Their conversation eventually led to recapping the incident with Sig, pointing out how strange it was that Jade mentioned him. They pondered the possible connection for some time. While thinking of the night she found the sheath, Gwyn recalled that if it hadn't been for Sash taking her in, she might have been killed.

Their conversation ended abruptly when Gwyn heard a faint sound coming from the woods. She crawled up the sandy wall of the ravine and peeked her head just above ground level. In the distance, she saw a small gray object. After a moment of watching, it became clear that it was a person hunched down into a small ball. She realized the small person was crying.

Gwyn climbed back down and told Jack to put out the fire. He threw sand on it, covering it completely, and went up to the ledge where Gwyn had peeked over to look at the small, crying figure deep off in the distance.

"We should help them," Gwyn insisted.

"What, Gwyn? Why? What even is that?"

She shrugged, then crawled out of the ravine, and slowly walked up to the small, crying creature. When she neared it, it heard her footsteps and lifted its head. She could tell now that it wasn't just a gray blob—it was a small, thin, gray goblin with long, uniquely pointy ears and a long, pointy nose. Its skin was smooth and youthful with a slight purple hue to it.

Gwyn was struck by the creature's ears, the rim of them following a long, elegant curve that started wide at the base and tapered sharply toward the tips.

She had never seen a goblin, unaware they existed, but she thought its face looked feminine and slightly feline in shape. It stopped crying and got to its feet, only to stand a little more than a couple of feet tall. Its stature resembled that of a little human girl.

"Hi!" Gwyn said to the little creature, but it only stared up at her with a look of surprise, slowly taking steps backward. Its heel caught on a root, and it fell back onto its bottom. It looked up from the ground in awe and asked, "Are you angels?"

Gwyn tilted her head to the side in slight bewilderment as she thought about what the small creature meant. "Angels? No, I don't think so."

"We're just... lost," Jack told her.

"Lost?" the girl asked in sudden excitement. "I'm Jasmine! I never knew one Lost; now I know two."

Gwyn slightly furrowed her brow and gave Jack a knowing look before shaking her head. "No. We're not Lost... I mean, I guess we are, but it's not what we go by."

The creature chewed on a fingernail as her large eyes filled with tears again. "Please don't lie! It is a bad day for it!"

Gwyn knelt down in front of Jasmine. "Why? What's wrong?"

"My sissy! I know the bad guys are heres to take her!"

"Bad guys? Who are the bad guys?" Gwyn asked kindly.

"The bad guys! The ugs in the shiny armor!" Jasmine replied, pointing off in a direction behind her.

"Well, they're not going to hurt her, are they?"

Jasmine put her head in her arms and cried loudly. "They already took Father! Now, he is no more alive!" she screamed through her now-pouring tears.

"What?" Gwyn replied in shock.

"They want to end us! Stupid ugs! I just know it!" Jasmine said, tears streaming down her tiny face.

"Let us help you!" Gwyn told her.

Jasmine stopped crying as hard and lifted her soggy face from her arms. "The Lost will help us? You mean it?"

Gwyn nodded, though she felt bad about letting the girl remain confused about their names.

"I will take you to my village, Myrrh, but I must stay hidden. It was my mother's orders!" Jasmine said before getting to her feet.

Jasmine led them through to the other side of the woods, going under branches and limbs that Gwyn and Jack had to find ways around. They emerged from a tree line that opened up into a large valley with large boulders scattered about it. Jasmine stopped at a boulder and whispered to Gwyn and Jack, "It's over there across the field. They are here to hurt us! Stupid Ugs! I can't watch!" Jasmine said, then got up and headed back to the woods. "Be careful, Losts!"

Gwyn and Jack stood for a moment while peering around. The sky had begun to darken, and they heard screams and clashes coming from across the field to the north east. They both looked eastward through the light snowfall and were surprised to make out a battle taking place not too far in the distance.

Gwyn saw soldiers wearing shining suits of metal armor with wicked horns and sharp points protruding from the metal. There were only about a dozen of them, all wielding weapons like swords, maces, and spears.

She could see smaller robed figures as they stepped closer to the battle. The robed figures were wielding swords and bows, attempting to fend off the knights in spiked metal armor.

□

Gwyn got up to move closer.

"Gwyn, wait! We don't want to get too close! They might see us," Jack pleaded.

But Gwyn ignored him and ran up to hide behind a large gray boulder that was closer in the field. She looked around and saw that there were several large stones and boulders in the field big enough to hide behind.

She then found another large boulder much closer to the battle and again another, going from boulder to boulder until she was close enough to hear voices.

There was a melee of fighting taking place not far from where she was. At least four of the knights in spiky armor were fighting what appeared to be dozens of short greenish-gray people in brown and gray robes.

She could see that the creatures had long pointy ears, like Jasmine.

Jack startled her as he joined her behind the boulder. "Are you crazy? What if they see us?" he asked, clutching his ribs.

Gwyn shushed him and continued watching the battle. After a minute, a large robed soldier wearing black robes riding a large horse ran into the scene of the battle. Gwyn thought that the creature resembled the lich she'd frozen deep beneath the Burrows, only this one was smaller.

The robed soldier stopped to speak and did so in a wicked, booming voice. "Denounce your queen and bow, King Patel!"

There was a hill of boulders and bushes to the north. From the top of the hill, Gwyn saw one of the gray creatures emerge from a high burrow. She thought it might be the king. He was portly, wore a red robe, and had a few guards shooting arrows off a stone balcony at the knights below. Gwyn thought it looked like he might be wearing a crown as well, but in the dim light, it was hard to tell.

She heard the portly little figure yell back at the creature in a nasally voice. "Never, you foul beast!"

The robed soldier then ran north toward the hill and then toward a large boulder that was embedded into the hillside. He performed some sort of powerful magic that blew the boulder apart in a loud explosion, causing tiny rocks and shards to shoot everywhere. Gwyn had ducked down to avoid the spray of debris, even as far as they were, only to look up in time to see the soldier ride into the hole where the giant boulder had been.

Gwyn looked at Jack with concern. "These must be Xess' men attacking these poor people," she whispered.

Jack looked back at her with his own concerned look. "I don't like being this close, Gwyn! We could get killed!"

Bloodcurdling screams came from within the hill, and a few moments later, the soldier emerged from the hole carrying a small figure over his shoulder. He stopped a few yards away from where Gwyn and Jack were hiding, so close that they were able to see several arrows sticking out of the soldier's body. He dropped the small goblin girl roughly onto the ground.

The goblin girl was wearing a yellow dress, staining it as she hit the ground and rolled roughly across the frosty grass and rocks.

The goblin girl's dress was a golden yellow, and Gwyn noticed she was dressed much fancier than the others.

Suddenly, a flash of magic filled the sky with an electric zipping sound crawling through the air. Strangely, the entire place became eerily silent. The colors of everything faded into a dark pink and purple tint, and a different kind of chill filled the crisp air.

Gwyn looked to where the flash happened and saw a new person in dark hooded robes had appeared next to the black-robed soldier. This new person seemed almost transparent, as if they were not quite all there.

"Zarep..." the thin person said in a strange tone, as if many voices had spoken at once.

"Yes, my Lord?" the knight's voice replied.

"Where is she? ... I sense a royal nearby." For a moment, the hooded figure turned its gaze in the direction of Gwyn. Gwyn's skin crawled as she felt an icy wave blow over her.

"Perhaps it is the goblin princess, my Lord?" Zarep said.

The hooded figure turned to face the pointy-eared girl and ran a slender gloved hand over her pale greenish-gray cheek. "I see," the voice said. "Well done. You already have her ... Zarep? The prophets said it was to be a human princess. ... Could the goblins have hidden the real writings all along?"

"This is my theory, my Lord."

Gwyn could see that the pointy-eared girl was shaking with fear as the dark figure ran its fingertips slowly across her face. As she did, Gwyn thought she could see tears running down the pale, gray cheek of the goblin princess.

Zarep laughed. "These creatures ... They are weak but feisty."

"Shame to waste it on what's necessary," the hooded figure said with a voice not quite human.

Gwyn could feel her heart beating in her ears for a moment as the voice reverberated unnaturally through her mind.

"Sincerely, I believe our time is near. This princess is as pure and powerful as dragon's blood."

They laughed together, and for a moment, the two laughs harmonized in a strange tone of a wicked melody, echoing across the land and into the distant forests and mountains. Gwyn felt that no creature who could hear it could possibly feel safe right now.

"Let your knights have some fun. These annexed creatures who will never meet their potential anyway ... But do not kill them all—and do not harm the crops. As for the princess, take her to the tower," the ominous voice said.

Jack leaned over and whispered to Gwyn, "I wonder if that's Xess?"

Gwyn shook her head, unsure. "Surely not?" she whispered back. "It sounded like a woman."

Jack's face revealed how nervous he was. The energy in the air was electric and dark—palpable in a way he'd never felt before. He shrugged before turning back to watch.

Zarep stopped laughing as the hooded figure vanished in another flash. The atmosphere instantly became lighter, and the dark purple tint that had filled everything faded back to normal. Flames were now scattered across the field.

Zarep then took off riding towards the east with the goblin princess over his shoulder. They heard his booming deep voice call back as he rode off, "Enjoy yourselves for awhile."

Gwyn looked at Jack and could tell that he knew what she was thinking. "Don't do it, Gwyn!" he pleaded, shaking his head.

Gwyn shook her head back. "I have to, Jack." She took her bow and quiver off, handed them to Jack, and got to her feet. "Don't shoot unless you have to. Stay down."

She pulled the Xi Blade from its sheath and ran quickly toward the closest armored knight, who was swinging a jagged halberd at several goblins, laughing manically. She saw his armor was covered in arrows.

The knight saw Gwyn coming and turned his halberd toward her. As she ran toward him, she shot a blast of energy ahead of her that knocked the knight sideways and off balance. She leapt and kicked the knight, knocking him over onto his side. He was immediately overrun with gray, pointy-eared people who began hacking at him. She heard guttural screams come from the armored knight as she turned to look for her next target.

Not far away, another knight was swinging a sword at more goblins. She quickly made her way toward him, but he was much faster than the first knight. He swung his sword at her, and she had to slide to a stop and lean back, lifting her arms to narrowly avoid being sliced in half. The sword tip barely grazed her stomach, leaving a small slash through her shirt and a small line of blood where the tip nicked her.

She blasted him with qi, knocking him off balance, but he quickly recovered and swung at her. Gwyn was forced to take large leaps backward to avoid the fast swings of the sharp blade. She could hear the buzzing sounds it made as it cut the air within inches of her. He leapt forward, taking a huge slice through the air, narrowly missing her. The swing hit the boulder Jack was hiding behind and sent bright sparks flying into the air. She quickly realized which boulder he hit and felt a flame of anger rising inside her.

Gwyn felt her mind slipping and welcomed it. On the knight's next strike, she swung her dagger and parried the long sword extraordinarily hard, throwing his arms into the air. She felt herself release a blast of energy at him as she took several strong slashes at his armor, parrying his sword and throwing him off balance as he tried desperately to recover. Loud smashing clangs echoed through the battlefield with every strike, the power of Gwyn's blows forcing the knight to stumble backward awkwardly.

The knight howled out guttural cries of pain as she left several, deep, sharp indentions in his breastplate and armor. She had now backed him onto a large boulder when she suddenly felt the sense of danger behind her. She quickly leapt aside without looking as a knight came swinging a mace from behind her. The mace slammed into ground where she had been a mere second before, kicking up chunks of dirt onto the wounded knight, now leaning against the rock, holding his chest.

Gwyn reached out her hand and cast another blast of energy, hitting the mace wielding knight, nearly knocking him over. The blast left him staggering as she quickly ran and jumped up onto the wounded knight, slammed her blade across his helm, and sprang from his breast plate, diving directly into the knight with a mace. She grabbed him and immediately began binding heat to his armor.

She quickly stood up as smoke poured from the suit of armor, now glowing hot. Muffled screams spilled out of the smoking heap of metal. Wooden arrows in his armor burst into flame as the goblin creatures moved in to attack.

Gwyn got up and turned to see several pointy-eared-people were now attacking the wounded knight against the boulder as well.

She looked eastward and saw another knight who was swinging a sword at a group of the pointy-eared-people. She ran up from behind him, attempting to stay in his blind spot, her mind shifted and she jumped and spun, twirling through the air with her blade outstretched as she gained a tremendous momentum. Her spinning stopped as the sapphire blade connected with the back of the knight's head, slashing a giant dent into his horned helm. The knight collapsed instantly to his knees and then onto his stomach. As he landed, several arrows protruding from his armor broke creating several snaps.

Gwyn looked up and around while holding the sapphire Xi Blade upside down. She crouched down like a cat ready to pounce on her next victim. The blade was a new element to her fighting but it had felt as natural as breathing to use it. Readied, as she was, standing fiercely in the dim light, it became evident that there were no more knights left standing in the field.

She felt her mind begin to slip back to normal. As it did, she noticed she could feel the mist and cool air hitting her face again. After a moment, she heard a loud voice from atop where the portly King Patel was.

"Stop! Do not move! Stay right there, strange warrior! Why have you interfered with our battle?" the nasally voice asked.

Gwyn was standing a few yards from the boulder where Jack was hiding. Expecting she might be receiving some form of gratitude for her assistance she turned toward the voice, sheathed the dagger, swung it around her side and gave a bow before replying.

"It appeared you were being unfairly attacked!" Gwyn yelled sincerely. "I only wanted to help!"

The King made a few puckering sounds "Help us? The Glade Goblins have not had help from your kind in years!" The King made a few more puckering sounds "Who are you, girl? Why do you help us?"

"I am Gwyn! I helped because..." Gwyn paused for a moment, suddenly realizing several bows and spears were pointed directly at her from nearly every angle from the pointy eared goblins. The realization of her situation suddenly made it a bit harder to think. "I... I couldn't stand by and watch Xess' men do what they were doing to you. I wanted to help!"

The King spoke to a few guards atop of the stone balcony then looked back at Gwyn "Xess!?"

Gwyn suddenly felt iron shackles clamp around her feet and wrists. Something felt strange in her as she felt her dagger being removed in its sheath. Chains ran between each of them, limiting her movements. "What are you doing? I helped you!"

Suddenly, the goblin holding the Xi Blade in its sheath screamed. Gwyn, surprised by the scream, turned to look. The goblin was furious and threw the dagger into the field in protest.

"Stupid magic blade! It's cursed!" yelled the goblin.

"I'm sorry," Gwyn started, unsure of what to tell him as she wasn't quite sure what happened.

King Patel made a few puckering noises. "Someone like you must be dealt with carefully. We will have this worked out in our courts tomorrow after we clean up from battle."

Gwyn didn't know if it was because she was at least a foot taller than the goblins or because they'd seen what she'd done to the knights. Or, perhaps, because they seemed to pick up on the fact that she was magical, but the goblins were more forceful with her than she felt necessary. Several of them pulled and led her into the hole in the hill and through a maze of finely carved out tunnels within it.

Fancy glass lamps were dimly lit on the walls. Even with the evident destruction Zarep had left while barging through the place, Gwyn was able to admire the finely crafted wood designs within it; the coffee-bean-colored hand railings trailing alongside elaborately carved stairways and corridors, planters and terrariums that were embedded into the walls growing herbs and even trees that seemed to grow up through the floors and through the ceiling.

There were several areas that were still smoldering and missing large chunks of the finely carved wood. Gwyn assumed it was from the battle that took place while she was outside. The dark wooden floor, which looked shiny and waxed, had several horseshoe-shaped-scratches running down the middle of it and ominous deep scars had been cut into some areas of the walls.

The goblins led Gwyn downstairs into a leaky basement dungeon with dirt walls and dirt floors that had worn out rugs on them. Several large wooden support beams had been installed in the room, running the length of the ceiling. The ceiling itself was mostly wood, but the feeling here was dark, damp and dirty and Gwyn was no fan of it.

They put her in an iron-bar cell with a small bed and a small nightstand then locked the gate.

The ceilings, however, were at least a few feet higher than her head, unlike some areas of the tunnels. Her cell also had a small window at the top near the ceiling that she could reach if she stood on her nightstand. Through it she could see the window was at the ground level outside. Although she thought she might be able to fit through it, there were iron bars on it.

Gwyn sat on her bed, suddenly feeling more tired and exhausted than she had since she'd woken up on the beach. It felt as if all of the day's exhaustion had hit her at once, so she laid down and hoped that Jack would think of something to help her. She remembered that he hadn't been feeling well and hoped that he wouldn't relapse in the cold now that she needed him more than ever.

As she sat there she started to feel dizzy. She wanted to feel a sense of pride for defending the goblins but a stark sadness crept into her spirit as she remembered her greatest loss, allowing the goblin princess to be captured. She laid down and immediately fell asleep in the bed. Her mind was ruthless to her and made her relive each fight from the battle that day over and over until she woke up.

CHAPTER 20

The Chilling Truth

Gwyn was gritting her teeth and groaning when she woke to Jack's whispers: "Psst! Gwyn! Wake up!"

Her heavy eyes burned when she opened them. She leaned her head back and realized Jack was at the bars of the small window, and wondered how long he had been trying to get her attention, given she was still having trouble hearing out of one ear. Then she wondered how long she'd been asleep, as it seemed late into the night.

She stood up, a bit dizzy, and noticed her palms were clammy and sweaty. She carefully climbed onto the nightstand to speak with Jack.

"Jack! How'd you find me?" she whispered through the bars, fighting to keep her eyes open.

"Took a little sneaking, but I managed with Jasmine's help."

She let out a sigh of relief. "Thank God. Sorry if it took a while to wake me. My ear's still clogged," she said with a weak voice.

"It's fine," Jack replied.

"Are you okay?" she asked him with a worried tone.

"I'm fine, thanks to Jasmine. She showed me some places to hide."

"That's good to hear. Do you have my weapons?"

Jack shook his head.

Her eyes focused on her hands, wrapped around the rusty iron bars of the window. "I need my dagger!" she told him with urgency.

Jack nodded. "I'll go get it. Might take a while, though. Used up my energy looking for you. Had to slip into the Hollow a couple of times to avoid trouble. They've had patrols out guarding and collecting their wounded all evening!"

Just then, the door at the top of the stairway creaked open, and footsteps could be heard coming down. "Jack, go! Someone's coming!" she whispered.

She quickly jumped off the nightstand and sat on the bed as an old, long, gray-haired goblin walked into the faintly lit chamber. He began looking around under saddle blankets and other odd items lying around the room.

"Where is it? Where oh where oh where in the blue goblin glades is it?" the old goblin mumbled to himself.

"Where is what?" Gwyn asked.

The old goblin looked over at her, a bit surprised, and tilted his head sideways, "The uhh... rapppsberry jelly, of course!"

Gwyn stared at the old goblin for a moment, wondering if he was serious. He was a snaggle-toothed creature with kind, sharp, graying eyes. "Oh, I see..." she said, looking around the room. It wasn't a large room, lit dimly by a lantern hanging on the dirty stone wall.

Flickering shadows danced on a stack of crates and assorted items across from her cell, as well as a smaller empty cell. She wondered if this was the kind of place a goblin might even keep jelly.

"Mr. Goblin," Gwyn said politely, "where am I?"

The old goblin paused his search through a pile of things to tell Gwyn, "In the cellar, of course. Where all good jellies and criminals should be kept."

It wasn't quite the answer Gwyn had hoped for, but she was actually kind of happy to have some company now that Jack was gone. "Well, I can't say I've ever put jelly in a cellar like this. Are you sure this is the right place?"

The old goblin turned back toward her, pursed his lips, and closed one eye. "No. No, I'm not!" He fidgeted with his hands for a moment, looking off to the side. "Okay..." he paused dramatically, "fine! You got me! I'm looking for the port!"

"Oh. Well, I can't say I'm an expert there either, but perhaps there might be some in that barrel over there!" Gwyn pointed to a large barrel sitting on a tall crate across the room. It had a tap sticking out of it, ready to pour with a twist. The goblin ran up to it and turned the tap, causing dark purple liquid to run out.

"Ooo! Young lady! You have found it!" The goblin quickly ran upstairs laughing in a giddy sort of way, then shut the door.

Gwyn sat patiently, hoping he would return soon, but he didn't. It had been at least an hour, and she assumed he had left for the night. She knew Jack was tired and not feeling well, which made it less likely he would return anytime soon either. He gathered qi much slower than she did, making it even less probable.

She ran her finger up and down an iron bar, enjoying the sensations it made as it ran over her skin. She began picking a flake of rust off the bar when the old goblin burst through the door at the top of the stairs, the noise sending a wave of shock through Gwyn as he came running down. He ran up to the barrel of port and filled two large wooden mugs to the brim. He then handed one of the mugs to Gwyn through the bars of her cell with a large smile on his face.

"A-hoy! Sorry it took so long. Had to wait for the kitchens to clear to sneak some mugs!" the old goblin said. He then began chugging his mug full of port before letting out a loud sigh. He sank back into a gunny sack full of corn and grunted in relief. "Ahhh! Good stuff!"

Gwyn had been very thirsty and was excited to finally drink something. She took a sip from her cup and immediately let the bitter liquid dribble back out of her mouth. She looked down at the drink with a look of great sadness. "Blech," she muttered to herself in disgust.

She was a bit unhappy with the drink but closed her eyes and forced another sip. She forced a swallow, and the drink warmed her from within. She then forced a larger drink, despite a burning sensation in her throat, and set the cup on the nightstand. "Thank you!" she choked out.

The old goblin was smiling and frequently taking sips from his mug. "My pleasure! Not quite right without my port! Keep tellin' 'em it's what makes me tick, but he just keeps hiding it from me!"

Gwyn shuffled her chains around, trying to make the wear on her wrists more comfortable. It hadn't been very long, but the iron was already chafing her something awful. "Tell me, Mr. Goblin, what is this place?"

The old goblin looked more lucid now that he was relaxed and full of port. "Oh, please lass," he said, putting his free hand up, "the name is Chili. That's what you should call me!" He then smiled at her before taking another swig from his mug.

"Nice to meet you, Chili," she said, smiling back, feeling strangely weak. "My name's Gwyn."

The goblin lowered his mug slowly from his lips, looking at her for a moment. "Is it now…" he said softly. The goblin stared at Gwyn in silence, then took another large gulp of port. "This is one of the few Glade Goblin settlements left. Of course, this village was never meant to be our primary kingdom; 'tis just what happened when the Glades were sealed from us. I'm sure villages in the Glades still thrive, though."

Gwyn felt a bit dizzy and sank to her knees, finding the cold dirt rather comfortable on them. She was already starting to feel a tad tipsy from the port and found the sensation odd. "What happened?" she asked, a little winded.

Chili's wrinkled lips slowly broke into a wide smile. He let out a couple of small laughs and took a deep breath. "I suppose it all began over a decade ago. We had been living peacefully in the Xi Glades just behind the village, between us and Mount Scott, that giant ice-capped mountain over there." Chili pointed off behind Gwyn toward the north.

The old goblin took another sip of port and continued, "To be honest, we never saw it coming. We had built several trails up the icy mountain and were looking to start living there… when…" Chili's eyes grew grim, and he shook his head slightly as if to clear it. "We were… cut off. Those outside of the Glades then were unable to return to them. The entire area was sealed off with strong magic. We've been forced to live in our villages outside the Glades ever since."

Gwyn looked at Chili with sincere sadness for him. "That sounds awful! Hic!" Gwyn's head had become much lighter. She continued drinking her port with Chili, each sip burning less than the one before.

Chili sat on his sack of corn, looking content. "Ahh! What I'd give to have it back. The Glades are a sight, I tell ya, the only place on the surface of the planet where the Xi crystals seemed to have bonded with the plant life like that."

Gwyn thought about the plants in the stone gardens deep underground in the Shadow Guild and wondered if the plants there were similar. "What kind of person would Hic evict you from such a beautiful place?"

"Well..." Chili started to look uneasy. "It's not right, ya know? Just blamin' her—you gotta have context first!" Chili took another gulp, then refilled his mug. His eyes looked a bit watery as he stared off toward a wall while pouring. "A lot of bad things started happening in the world then, about a dozen years ago." Chili sat for several moments in silence, thinking to himself.

It was difficult to tell for sure, but she sensed the old goblin wasn't telling her everything. "It's alright if it's too hard to talk about."

Chili shook his head, and she thought she could see a tear roll down his wrinkled cheek. "It's not alright, Miss Gwyn. I dealt with her on several occasions. She was kind to our people—a hero! More so than anyone here now gives her credit for! ... You see, something wrong happened. Something very terribly wrong! She was different when she came here. Completely different!"

Gwyn put her hands on the iron bars and leaned against them, watching the sad goblin. "Who?"

Chili now had a very sad look on his old face. "Oh, Gwyn, I knew the second ya told me your name." The old goblin said as if he'd admitted to a terrible sin. He then shook his head as if to clear it. "You look a lot like her, really. And the way you fought... Who else could you be?"

Her heart began racing as she listened closely to the goblin. "You mean... my mother?"

Chili swallowed hard, nodding, no longer looking at her. "Many thought you were just a rumor. Or long dead. Your father's untimely death and all..." The goblin wiped another tear from his eye. "Good people, they were! Treated the goblins fair 'til your father vanished and then turned up dead..." Chili sniffled and took another drink. "Patel don't understand. Blames the queen, but some know better."

For a moment, she forgot that her mother was a queen. "Chili, what are you saying? Please, tell me what happened!"

The goblin sighed. "I'm going to be honest with you, Gwyn. Your mother came here right about the same time your father died. She was practically in death's arms already… covered in blood, weak, pale, clutching tightly to her ribs… She couldn't stop coughing… It were as if she were holding onto life by a thread, as if she would collapse at any second… I'd never seen anything like it… Nothing like the woman I knew."

Chills ran down her spine with a gasp. "Oh…"

Chili sobbed for a moment before continuing. "Ah, but before, she was so noble and strong… So brave, so charismatic, so majestic and full of life… Seeing her reduced to that state was… crushing."

She suddenly felt a wave of sadness sweep through her.

Chili nodded. "I'm sorry, Gwyn, but it's true! She went north; everyone knew she'd die. Next thing we knew, the Glades were sealed with strong magic. Incredibly strong. Rumor has it she went up to Mount Scott to die and sealed something important with her." Chili shook his head. "I'd be surprised if she even made it to the base of the mountain."

Gwyn suddenly felt her stomach turn. Hearing about her mother was as unsettling as it was intriguing. She wiped a tear from her eye and asked, "Chili, why did my father die?"

Chili's face lit up for a second. "Oh, Gwyn, that is a huge mystery! He was so powerful! He was believed to be about to unite the Northern and Western Kingdoms, a thing unheard of at the time!" Chili sat thinking and shook his head. "I've heard 'em all: rumors about curses and dark magic… Rumors about his closest allies betraying him… Strangest thing is… His magical barriers still exist, even after all these years."

"Why is that strange?" she asked.

Chili shook his head. "Magical barriers are rare to begin with; sustaining one is even more impressive… Sustaining one after death?" he said with a pause.

"So…" Gwyn said with a hopeful tone. "Do you believe my father could still be alive?"

"Well…" Chili said with a lump in his throat. He then shook his head. "I regret to say… More than likely not… See, your father's body was recovered and…"

"Then how? How do the barriers exist?"

Chili looked sad for a moment. "My uncle says he knew how to balance them so perfectly while creating them that they don't have a way to decay.

A skill so finely tuned it would be like slicing a grain of salt in two while blindfolded."

"Wow," Gwyn replied in surprise, leaving a moment of silence to fill the air before speaking again. "Could it have been Xess?"

Chili frowned and shook his head, making his pointy ears flop a bit. "Unlikely. Xess is strong but not compared to your father or mother. I believe Xess is a victim as well."

After thinking for a moment, Gwyn sat up tall on her knees, looking at Chili. He'd gone quiet for quite some time, and she didn't want him to lose interest in the conversation. "You know, don't you?" she asked, thinking he surely wasn't spilling all he knew yet. "Please tell me what happened!"

Chili frowned deeply, then let out another sigh. "Gwyn, I'm afraid I only have secondhand information."

She frowned. "I'll take it! Besides, it's better than no information."

"Yes, but this is not a happy tale. If you want the full story, you'll have to find my uncle. He's one of the only known goblin wizards alive. He's an Auric-Healer and can see deep into a person's aura."

Gwyn suddenly thought of Kokolo—how she talked about seeing the different depths and layers of auras before healing her banshee wounds.

"My uncle is one of the best when it comes to healing and seeing auras. He sees deeper than the wizard textbooks say is possible. He was commissioned by your mother, you know..." Chili said, taking another giant gulp of port.

"What?" Gwyn asked, pulling her face close enough to the iron bars that she could smell the rust.

"To... eh, assist in parturition, and to..." The goblin slowly closed his eyes, then looked down when he opened them. "He told me he was looking at you..."

She grew curious but donned a leery expression. "Me? But... Why? What was wrong with me?"

"Well, he said she wanted to know if you were... cursed."

"Cursed?"

"Yyrup. Said you did have something, but he wasn't sure what he meant."

"Could he... Did he heal me?"

"Uh, no, I think not. Said it was too woven in. Said it was unlike any curse he'd ever seen. Was hard for even him to detect."

Gwyn felt odd, suddenly. Thinking that she had something deeply cursed inside her felt unclean.

"I'm not a gambling man, Gwyn, but I think the whole matter had to have something to do with your parents' demise. I guess it's really hard to say exactly what happened, but I'd like to think she had her reasons, the way she treated us and all for so many years. It's completely backwards from the way Zarep treats the goblins. He took the princess today, Princess Lily. I'm sure he figures we'll leave the only homes we have left on the surface and let him have our few precious ancient herbs, gardens, and recipes. Can't imagine the awful things they'll do with Princess Lily."

"Why would he want your herbs?"

Chili almost looked offended for a moment before answering Gwyn's question. "No greater artisan for herbs exists in the world than the Glade Goblins. Adventurers from every corner of the continent come to us in search of cures for themselves or their beloved. Our recipes for potions and cultivation are ancient and sacred to my people, dating back to even before the queen saved us to the surface."

"Saved you to the surface?"

Chili nodded. "Yes. There was once a time my people lived in peace deep below ground, using secret gardening techniques to create our recipes. But dark times came nearly a thousand years ago to many of our underground villages. Your mother saved countless lives from the chaos, bringing them to the surface and building them appropriate homes to thrive as we did so long ago. Without her, we would have never had the Glades or mountains to begin with."

"So, by taking the princess, Zarep thinks Patel will give his village over?"

Chili shook his head. "Zarep doesn't need Patel to surrender. He's just breaking the goblins' spirits. Princess Lily isn't even Patel's real daughter. And Patel is not true royal blood, just the highest in command left when the Glades were sealed off. Lily, on the other hand, is royal blood but too young to legally rule. She is destined to become queen of the Glade Goblins someday. What really irks me is that Zarep entered our village because someone let him in."

"What?" Gwyn asked, surprised.

"Zarep never could have entered the sealed entrance to our village without someone telling him our secret incantation set in place by your parents."

"But... Why?"

Chili shook his head. "I assume someone made a deal with him." He let out a long sigh before continuing. "Now, it's just a matter of time, given that he knows how."

She felt a growing concern for the goblins as she sat listening. "What will happen?"

"As the realization spreads, many will begin to head back to what few underground villages remain. Those who are most loyal will stay and endure whatever comes. I fear many will be doomed to slavery under Zarep, forced to share our secrets with him. A life of pain and torture."

"That's awful," she whispered. "What about the princess?"

Chili sighed again, deeper than before. "Our last royal connection to the Glades... I'm sure he'll keep her alive for control and negotiation purposes, but I fear she'll lose a terrible amount of her royal blood for dark rituals."

Gwyn frowned, then sat on her bed. She thought for a few long moments in silence. "Chili, I'm going to get her back if I can."

Chili shook his head. "That's not an easy thing to do. I'm sure you fight well, but they are a lot stronger than you are at your age. They'll probably do terrible things to you too, if they can, just in spite of your parents."

"I don't care. I can't stand hearing these stories about people ravaging through my mother's land in terror. I can't stand seeing these evil people tormenting innocent villages like yours! No one's standing up to them!" she said, standing to her feet.

The goblin sat on the gunny sack of corn, looking off to the side for a moment, then looked back at Gwyn. "You know, you've got that same flare in your eyes that your mother had. She hated evil just as much as you." A tear rolled down Chili's cheek before he continued, "That's what I liked about her—always standing up for her people, even the little guys, like us. She was a natural leader. It's rare to find someone who actually stands up for the little guys. Some people talk about it, but to actually see it..."

"I'd like to know where your uncle is. I have some questions for him. And I need to know where they took Princess Lily."

"Uncle's name is Galanga. They called him Galanga the Great. Last I heard, he was in Clove. It's a small section our people built in the giant city of Sterlington. Sterlington is the largest city your mother presided over. The west side of it is in rough shape, though. Clove is one of the places left in the west city that wasn't damaged much, last I'd heard. I wish I could see Sterlington from Mount Scott again in all its glory. It was a beautiful stone city, buzzing with townsfolk and communities from all over the world. Walking through it was pretty amazing, but seeing it from Mount Scott was breathtaking."

"How do I get there?"

"Well, pretty much straight east of here you'll find it in about a day's journey or so on horse. Sterlington, that is. Lots of things between here and there, but once you find Sterlington, look for signs pointing you to Clove. The Glade Goblin village is mostly underground there. Just keep an eye out for those signs."

Gwyn nodded before speaking, letting the directions sink into her tired mind. "Thank you, Chili. I appreciate everything."

Chili shook his head and sat up straight. "Thank you, Gwyn. It's nice to feel like there might be hope again."

She nodded, unsure if she could do much, but something compelled her to try.

"Gwyn, are you going to be needing anything?" Chili asked as he stood from the gunny sack, now deflated as much of the corn had spilled out from it.

She placed a finger on her chin and thought for a moment. "Are there any horses in the village I could borrow?"

Chili stroked his gray, pointy beard, then smiled. "Ah yes, I believe I can provide you with a pony. I'll leave it in the patch of trees to the southeast, just past the boulders, and no one will know if you go in there."

"Can I get two?"

Chili nodded, then stood and bid Gwyn farewell. It wasn't long after that she started feeling lonely again. Her mind was spinning as she lay down and rested her eyes.

After a restless wait, Gwyn had fallen asleep and again woke to Jack's whispers. "Pst! PSST! Gwyn, wake up!"

She opened her eyes and felt her head throbbing. She felt weak as she put her hand to her head, her chains dragging across it. "Oh... Crud! ... I think I'm hungover!"

Jack cocked his head and gave her a curious look through the bars. "I don't think I heard you right."

Gwyn climbed to her feet and stood on the nightstand to reach the window. "Don't worry about it. What took you so long?"

"Almost got caught."

"What about Jasmine? Didn't she help you?"

Jack shook his head. "She and her mom are trying to escape. They plan to leave on horseback soon."

"How long have I been in here?" she asked, concerned.

Jack shrugged. "I dunno. It wasn't that late when they put you in here last night. I'd guess it's about morning now."

Gwyn was surprised. "Wow. It took you a long time to gather qi, mister!"

"Hey! They searched the woods while I was gathering energy, Gwyn! I mean, I almost got caught! Had to slip into the Hollow, then gather my energy again." Jack shook his head in frustration. "Anyway, I think they saw my footprints in the light snow cover and started chasing me and all. It was stupid."

She looked past Jack and saw the sky glowing with pink and orange light from the waking sun. "You have my dagger?"

Jack slowly slid the dagger through the bars, holding it by the sheath. "I can't touch the stupid handle of the thing. It did something terrible to me."

"What?" she asked, confused. "How did it do something to you?"

"It shocked me. I really didn't like it. My whole body seized up, like a sneeze but a hundred times worse."

Gwyn took it by the handle and immediately felt herself re-energizing. Her headache began fading, and the dizziness started to subside. "Alright!"

she said, suddenly feeling better than she had since being locked up. "I'm going to try to melt the iron on the window. I might be able to fit through without the bars."

Jack nodded and scooted back while she focused her magic. She grabbed the iron bars and tried binding heat to them. Almost instantly, she jerked back and fell to her knees in pain. The iron bars glowed red where she'd held her hands.

"What happened!?" Jack asked.

Gwyn held her breath for a few seconds as she bit her lip to avoid screaming in pain. After a moment, she held her wrists up to the bars so Jack could see. The iron clasps around them were smoking, and Jack could smell burning flesh. "I'm not sure," she choked out while wincing.

"I think the shackles are keeping me from using magic. It felt like it went into these cuffs."

"There aren't any guards outside right now. Seems to be a shift change or something. We've gotta hurry!" Jack got up and looked around outside for a moment, then came over to the window with a thick rope he'd found. He tied it to the window and pulled hard on it. The rope went taut, but he slipped and fell to the ground. "Ugh... It's no use. They're really on there!"

"Jack, I've got an idea. Go to the patch of trees behind the barn. There are two horses there waiting for us. Hurry before people start waking up!"

Jack left and came back a few minutes later with a large pony that was saddled with two saddle bags attached to it. He tied the rope around the horse's neck, mounted it and gave it a kick. The horse took off quickly pulling the rope taught as the bars ripped from the cell.

He rode back and helped pull Gwyn out, handed her Apollo and her quiver and they mounted the brown pony and rode to retrieve the other one.

As they retrieved the second horse Gwyn looked in the saddle bag and saw a small sack with a drawstring on it. She pulled a note out that said: I think you need this more than I do. Take this summoner. My uncle left it years ago. Maybe you could use it to bring a helper. -Your friend, Chili.

She smiled, excited to have the rare relic, and put it in her pocket.

They both mounted and started to go east, but through the dim morning light she saw what appeared to be a couple of people standing by the treeline of the forest.

"Stop. Jack, look over there!" she said, pointing in the direction of the trees.

"Ah, come on, Gwyn. It's probably that search party looking for me from last night. Let's hurry and get out of here."

"No, dummy! I don't think it is," she replied, feeling a desire to ride toward the figures in the distance.

"And why do you think that?" he asked starkly.

"I think it might be Jasmine. Let's ride toward them."

"But she went home?" Jack said, as he sharply turned and rode toward the woods. As they got closer, it became clear that it was indeed Jasmine and her mother.

They dismounted and Jasmine excitedly embraced Gwyn.

Jasmine proudly exclaimed to her mother, "Mommy, meet the Lost! The Lost, meet my Mommy, Rosemary!"

"Thank you," Rosemary said, breaking her silence while looking a bit surprised. "I saw what you did for our people."

Gwyn swallowed a sudden lump that filled her throat. "I... I'm sorry. I didn't act sooner," she said earnestly, knowing she had failed to protect Princess Lily. "And I'm sorry, Jasmine. I didn't save your sister. But I promise I'm going to try again."

Rosemary put her hand over her heart. "Sweet child, you mustn't. See, Jazzy and the princess are not blood sisters, but Princess Lily has helped to raise her since... well, since her father passed. He died in a battle against those... Those..." she said, her words trembling with anger.

"Ugs, Mommy!" Jasmine cut in. "Those stupid ugs!"

"Yes. Those stupid ugs," Rosemary affirmed.

"Man..." Jack said, looking at the goblins. "You guys helped me out a lot last night. Thank you!"

Rosemary nodded.

"Jasmine," Gwyn started.

"Yes, Lost?" Jasmine replied.

Gwyn smiled at the reminder of the previous day's conversation rushing back to her. "How did you know your sister was in trouble?"

"Oh!" Rosemary said in excitement. "She's—she's like you!"

"What do you mean, like me?" Gwyn asked.

"She sees the future. She's magic, like you!"

"What?" Gwyn replied with interest. "Did you warn the king?"

Rosemary shook her head. "No... No! No! No. That would be a very poor decision. He does not take kindly to magics ever since... Sel..."

"Sel...?" Gwyn asked as Rosemary stared oddly at her.

"I'm... sorry. It's just, humans sometimes look a lot alike to me. I couldn't help but think you look like her."

"Who?" Jack asked earnestly, but Gwyn already knew.

"My mother," Gwyn said.

Rosemary stood for a moment in silence before Gwyn's response hit her. "Ooh!?" She gasped loudly. "How... how wonderful! How... How..." she said before taking a moment to pause. "How... strange," she said, her last word ringing both sobering and somber.

Gwyn listened in the dim morning light, nodding her head slightly.

"Sometimes, our friends and family end up leaving us far too soon," Rosemary said after a long silence. "That's why we must love them while we can."

The words brought Chele and Jack to Gwyn's mind. "Hold on!" Gwyn said with sudden excitement, pulling the summoner from her cloak.

"Whoa," Jack said with interest. "Gwyn, where did you score a summoner?"

"A friend on the inside," she joked.

"Should we summon Franz?" Jack suggested.

"They said at the Academy that could kill us."

He nodded, remembering the warning.

Gwyn then asked Jack to help summon Chele. They both grabbed the summoner and whispered Chele's name, focusing on her in their minds. They both did their best to let the magic bind to the summoner, but it felt empty at first.

After a moment of silence, Gwyn and Jack felt a sudden jolt, then a pulsing draw from within their abdomens.

A slight electrical wisping sound fluttered about the air. Where the noise happened, a blonde-haired girl appeared, wearing a brown hooded jacket over a long white nightdress.

"Chele?" Gwyn asked.

Chele looked at her, and they quickly fell into a hug.

"Gwyn, where have you guys been?" Chele asked with shock and worry.

"It's so good to see you! How are you?"

Chele was clearly confused, standing next to Jasmine and her mother, Rosemary. "I woke up a couple of nights ago, and Gwyn was gone. My fever had broken, and I thought I'd join Gwyn on the ridge since that's where she usually goes, but no one was there. Just her harp," Chele said with a concerned look in her eyes. "I called to the woods, the vineyards, beyond the roads... no one answered... I've been alone, worried sick about you guys, Gwyn. What happened?"

Jack looked at Gwyn. "Yeah... The whole thing's a bit blurry to me now, but I remember... We were on the ridge, then out of nowhere Gwyn's eyes began glowing bright green and pink. She stood up, and then jumped right off the ridge... So... I jumped in after her and don't remember much after that."

Chele looked confused. Jack sighed and shrugged. "What can I say? It's Gwyn!"

Gwyn laughed, then explained how she saved Jack to Chele and how they drifted throughout the night. "Welcome to the Northern Kingdoms!" she told Chele.

"I'm so happy you guys are alive!" Chele exclaimed with excitement.

Gwyn turned back to Rosemary. "Sorry. We kind of had to do that," she said. "Rosemary, look, we want to save the princess. Is there anything we can do for Jasmine?"

Rosemary shook her head.

"Yes, Mummy!" Jasmine chimed in.

Rosemary sighed. "Well, she needs to see Galanga. He's an Auric and the only one in our race that King Patel seems to be okay with being magic."

"Well, we're heading to find Galanga ourselves. You guys want to come with us?" Gwyn asked.

Rosemary's face suddenly went pale. "Oh... I... I..." She then looked down again at Jasmine.

"It's okay, Mommy. I told you this day was coming! Remember, I'm eleven, and the Lost will get me there safe! I know it," Jasmine said to her fearful mother, as if she already knew what she was thinking before her mother said a word.

Rosemary slowly turned her head up toward Gwyn, tears rolling down her face. "Watch over my baby... Please...! I cannot go. But she knows she must."

Gwyn shook her head, slightly confused. "Where are you going?" she asked.

"My family lives in the old world below. My parents are very sick and need our herbs from the surface to help them. I have to go there."

"Oh..." Gwyn said, realizing the dilemma. "In that case, be safe. We'll see that Jasmine makes it safely to Galanga."

"Gwyyyn!" Jack mumbled in a whiny tone, invoking a slight elbow to his ribs to silence him.

Rosemary's eyes filled with tears as she knelt down next to Jasmine. "Jazzy, listen. You do whatever Gwyn says and make sure you use your power to help her out, okay?"

"Of course, Mommy," Jasmine said softly. The two goblins hugged each other tightly before Jasmine kissed her mother's salty cheek goodbye.

"Hop on," Gwyn told Chele. Jasmine then hopped on Jack's horse behind him, and they began heading east.

A light snow still covered the ground in patches as scattered clouds stretched across the early morning sky. To their advantage, the snow had stopped falling for the time as they rode on.

CHAPTER 21
A Moonless Forest

wyn took deep breaths of fresh morning air as they began their travels. The dampness of her cell had been pungent and starkly contrasted the cool, crisp morning air. She was thankful to be there.

Jack and Gwyn both took turns explaining to Chele what had happened over the last couple of days as Jasmine slept.

Chele was thankful to be back with her friends, still a bit surprised to be there.

"Gwyn, how was it in there?" Jack asked her, referring to her time in the goblin cell.

"Not too bad. I'm sure if I'd stayed any longer, it would have gotten much worse."

"Well, now that you're out, is there anything you wanna do?"

Gwyn thought for a moment. "Yeah. Sleep. I think I drank too much port last night."

"What!?" Jack retorted.

Gwyn explained her visit from Chili and how he shared a port with her.

"That doesn't sound bad at all!" he said with surprise in his voice.

Gwyn then told them about everything Chili had told her.

"I'm actually jealous! I stayed up all night sneaking around, gathering qi, risking my neck, and you got to drink with some cool old dude?"

Gwyn shrugged, unsure of what to say. "Well, anyway. What should we name the horses?"

Jack pondered in silence for a moment. "I know! I'm naming mine Guts!"

"Guts!" Chele asked. "Why would you name anything that?"

"Hey, I like Guts! He saved my life by keeping me from going out and looking for Gwyn, remember?"

"Huh," Chele said in true surprise. "Well, he wouldn't have had to if you'd just listened to me in the first place!" she replied.

Jack shrugged. "Whatever. I'm calling him Guts."

Jack's horse snorted and shook its head but didn't protest the name further.

They followed a creek east for some ways, hoping to keep it near as a supply of food and water. As the miles passed, they passed several roads leading off toward stone and wood cottages or what might have been the outskirts of villages. Occasional faraway lights and chimney smoke in the distant mountains gave the impression that people lived in the lands, though they seemed scarce.

As the hours passed, the ground became sandy in some places, with thicker patches of grass and weeds growing in others. Eventually, they stopped at a large gathering of tall trees where the creek narrowed and deepened.

Gwyn dismounted and walked up to the edge of the water. She placed her hands in the water and tried to conjure heat to boil it again. She used less energy this time and found the iron clasps on her wrists burned her the instant she tried to use magic. Jasmine screamed, "No!" just before she did, causing Jack and Chele to jump and turn their heads.

Gwyn gasped loudly, her eyes watering slightly from the intense pain. She bound ice to the water, and again, the iron seemed to soak up the magic and became freezing cold. The cold felt soothing on her raw burns, though it was already cold outside, and made the rest of her body shiver. She left her wrists in the water for a minute to relieve some pain, hoping they wouldn't get infected.

"Let me see your wrists," Chele said, kneeling next to her.

Gwyn slid back a cuff as far as she could. The skin under the cuff was raw, bloodied, and badly blistered.

"Geez, Gwyn! Why didn't you say something?" Jack asked.

Gwyn looked down at her wrists, disappointed with herself. "Take my dagger. Try to at least break the chain," she ordered before laying the chain that connected her clasps over a large rock. She sat there waiting patiently as Jack slowly moved to pick up the Xi Blade. He lifted it only an inch, then quickly dropped it, falling to his knees.

"Ahh!" he screamed. "I told you, I don't like that thing!"

"Sorry, Jack. I'm not sure why," Gwyn said.

"It ... It shocks me!"

"Just use a rock," Chele suggested.

Jack picked up a large stone and slammed it into the chain. It took several attempts, and Gwyn endured several pieces of shattered stone hitting her face, but the chain finally broke.

Gwyn spread her arms as wide as she could, enjoying the feeling of freedom.

"Should I try magic again?"

"No!" Jasmine yelled again, her pointy goblin ears drawn back in fear.

Jack shook his head. "No! Are you crazy? We need to get those shackles off!"

"Jack's right," Chele said. "Someone in my flit class said something about iron grounding magic. This must be what they meant."

Gwyn reached out for her dagger, then laid her left hand on the stone.

"Ohhhh! Gwyn, I don't know about that!" Jack protested. He flinched and closed his eyes as she took her first swing. He could hardly watch as she took another. Several swings later, he felt relief as half of the cuff broke, and she was able to slide her hand free.

The group cringed to find her wrist had become a bloody, chafed bracelet. "Jack, my wrists look awful. I don't even think I can shoot. Take Apollo, just in case."

Jack took the bow and quiver and watched as Gwyn hacked away at the cuff on her right hand.

Every time Gwyn slammed the dagger into the cuff, it caused the iron to chafe against her already blistered skin.

She took her time chopping away carefully at the cuffs on her other wrist and then her ankles. They, too, were slightly chafed but not nearly as badly as her wrists.

Once free, she held her wrists in the water and imbued cold into it. She tried to regulate it so she wouldn't freeze her hands into a block of ice, though the thought sounded nice. She managed to make a nice slushy area to soak her wrists in. "Jack, I need a bandage."

Jack glanced around, unsure of what to do.

"Look in the saddlebags. Chili left us something," Jasmine said with certainty.

Jack went to the saddlebags and dug through them. He was surprised to pull out several woven sheets of green-looking cloth, a small pot, and a metal tankard. "This cloth stuff might work."

"That's herb paper!" Jasmine told them. "Wrap it around; it'll help save her wrists from the rot!"

Gwyn had Chele wrap her wrists with the herb paper. It was a similar consistency to a thick layer of cloth. Within a few short moments, she began feeling a soothing relief from the pain. "Ahhh! It's like this stuff has medicine in it."

"Maybe there is," Chele suggested, then sniffed the green cloth material. "Mmm! Smells like fresh herbs and spices!"

Gwyn placed the remaining sheets of herb paper in her cloak and managed to carefully boil some water from the creek. Chele shared the herbs she'd gathered with Jasmine throughout the day and made hot teas and small snacks that warmed them in the chilled air. The herbs, however, refused to fill their hungry stomachs.

Chele gathered pawpaws, and they managed to catch some fish to roast.

"These pawpaws are sweet," Chele noted. "It must be a cold-resistant strain. I didn't know it grew in cold areas. We can eat them, but don't eat the seeds."

"Why not?" Gwyn asked.

"Because they're poisonous!" Jasmine chimed in.

They ate several pawpaw fruits and saved a pocketful of the small black seeds at Jasmine's request. Unfortunately, their taste for pawpaw quickly wore out. It was then that Gwyn suggested they move on. So they filled the tankard with fresh water and did just that.

The four of them rode eastward. The creek had become hard to follow due to thickets of trees and brush growing close to it. As they walked, a beautiful sight broke on the horizon. They could see the majestic waving branches of a forest of tall, thick pines and oaks ahead. As they rode closer, the large forest further revealed itself in their path. The closer they came to it, the more a purple and silver haze-like fog could be seen swirling slowly between the trees. Many of the trees themselves were tall pines, thin and bare near the bottom, growing hundreds of feet tall and stretching their tops high into the cold winter sky.

They found what looked to be a faint pine needle-covered trail leading into the woods and decided to follow it in. Mere moments after entering the forest, the sky seemed to darken as if someone had dimmed the lights. They could still tell it was daytime, but the misty silver and purple haze seemed to swirl and filter the light from the sky, leaving a dark purple hue on the forest that occasionally let in spots of true, wintry sunlight.

"Where is this place?" Jack asked.

Chele pointed to a small, old, worn wooden sign a few yards away and read, "The Moonless Forest."

"I've never heard of it," Gwyn confessed. "We'll just keep pressing through. No telling what's ahead."

They cautiously stepped forward, unable to see more than a few dozen yards ahead due to the trees and misty, purple haze. The floor of the forest was blanketed in a layer of dead pine needles, making the path difficult to follow. Still, they trekked through what appeared to be a trail for a while until they came upon a fork in the road.

They discussed the dilemma of which direction to go for a minute, then agreed to choose paths that stayed closest to the creek. Knowing they were near the creek was difficult due to the brush and terrain around it. The creek itself seemed to have a knack for getting lost as it wound and bent through the forest. Walking down by it would be difficult and somewhat dangerous, so they continued on the path through the woods.

The path wound around, taking several turns through the woods. It wasn't long before it passed over an old stone bridge. At first, they thought the creek had wound around, but it was difficult to know if it was the same creek as before or a new one that fed into the one they'd followed.

They continued to follow the path for some time and found it forked again. There was a signpost at the fork this time, but they could not read the words. They had what looked like strange, curvy symbols written on them. They continued to take the path that they felt stayed closest to the creek, but without the sun to reassure them that they were heading east, they began to question their sense of direction, and each passing minute made them feel more unsure of their decision.

"Gwyn, why don't we just go back? We've already been through hell," Jack said with a hint of nerves in his voice. "It's already hard to see in here, and it just keeps getting darker."

"I made a promise, Jack. Do you think there'll be time to save the princess if we go back?" Gwyn replied.

"Why on earth did you make that promise? You don't have to be a hero, you know! What do you owe these people?"

Gwyn bit down on her tongue. She knew she had been secretly ignoring that very feeling. She couldn't ignore that inside her burned a desire to help and make things right again.

She had seen what was happening to the Glade Goblins and what Zarep's evil men were doing to them. Was it right to leave them to burn and die at the hands of a madman? Now that Jack had called her on it, she could see her desires a little more clearly, and it bothered her for a bit. Was it not my mother who left these people to fend for themselves? she wondered. Do I not owe it to them, to make things right? To defend them?

Gwyn was about to reply to Jack, but Chele spoke up first. "Don't you get it, Jack?" she said. "This is her mother's land. It's her mother's quest! She can't just ignore it!"

"Eyahhh ... Oh," Jack said with a hint of embarrassment. "I ... guess I can see that."

Gwyn enjoyed a moment of silence, digesting what Chele had just done for her. It was nice to hear her stand up for her in that moment, surprised that Chele was able to interpret the internal confusion she was having with the issue.

"Jack," Gwyn eventually said, breaking the silence, "you saw the fear in Jasmine's eyes when we first met her? That's the same look I saw in Chili's eyes. These people are losing hope. Maybe I'm crazy, but I think I can help," she said with sobering sincerity. "If I'm wrong, I'm sorry, but my heart's telling me to do this."

Jack was silent for a moment as he processed what Gwyn was saying. "Well, I hope you're right about this one."

Gwyn thought about it for a moment, about to tell Jack he didn't have to go with her if he'd rather turn back, when Chele spoke up.

"Jack ..." Chele said, waiting for him to look back at her. "Al-ways ..." she said with a knowing look and tone.

Gwyn looked from Jack to Chele and saw that they both had a look on their faces. It was as if they were discussing something they both knew about but she didn't. She waited for them to continue, but neither of them did. "What?" she finally asked.

Jack sighed and looked forward. "Don't worry about it. You're right, Gwyn. I'm sorry about before. I am with you."

Gwyn looked back at Chele, hoping for an answer.

Chele gave Gwyn a warm smile and said, "WE are with you."

Gwyn thought about pushing the matter but, for some reason, didn't. She made a mental note to ask about it again in the future as another split in the road came upon their path.

"Gwyn must take this journey," Jasmine said confidently. No one objected to her statement but pondered the meaning behind her words.

They had agreed to take the path that they thought stayed closest to the creek, but the path was unwelcoming and somewhat downhill.

"I... d... don't... like this," Jack stammered nervously, having to lean back to keep on the horse. "Is this even a path?"

The forest had gotten much darker as the sun seemed to be setting.

Gwyn and Chele were forced to lean back as well as they descended the steep path.

Jack slipped a little, and Gwyn leaned down quickly from her horse to grab him and pull him back up.

"Thanks, Gwyn, but I really don't think this is a path!" he said.

Gwyn tried to keep from crushing Chele as she leaned back. "I think it is. Relax. We're going ..."

"HEY!" a small voice cried from below, interrupting Gwyn.

They pulled their reins to a stammering stop and looked around. They quickly discovered what appeared to be several rows of very large mushrooms with dim, glowing lights on them near the path. They looked back to see that some had been completely knocked over, out of which had spilled what looked to be a bunch of small, colorful items.

"Who's here?" Gwyn asked, trying to focus her vision in the misty, dim light.

"US!" the tiny voice yelled.

As they looked around, a bright flash flew by Gwyn's head, causing Jack to let out a faint scream and fall off Guts. Gwyn, Jasmine, and Chele jumped down as well as another bright flash flew by, making a sound like a hummingbird as it bolted through the air.

"What do you want?" Gwyn yelled, trying to dodge the humming creature as it flew back and forth.

Two more suddenly buzzed by, and Gwyn felt a sharp prick in her cheek.

"OW!" she yelled, plucking a small pine needle from her cheek. As she held it to her face to look at it, she realized it wasn't just a pine needle but had been carved into a small arrow or spear. "I think one of them attacked me!"

"What?" Jack said just moments before screaming at his own pain. He reached up and pulled two needle arrows from the back of his neck. "The heck is this? What's going on?"

Several more times, the creatures buzzed past them, leaving sharp needles in their skin, each one feeling like a sharp prick. Chele threw what she could of a small, crackling flit into the air, which caused them to scatter for a moment, but they quickly returned with even more of them buzzing around.

Within seconds, they were surrounded by a swarm of what sounded like thousands of bees flying right next to their ears.

"What do you want?" Gwyn screamed.

"Leave!" she heard a faint voice scream from within the humming. "Leave! Go away!" came from all around them.

"Okay!" Gwyn replied, trying to dodge the countless spears, but as she tried to make her way to the horses, they reared up and took off running.

"Dang it! They scared the horses!" Chele said.

"Come to me!" Gwyn yelled. Jack, Jasmine and Chele crouched down near Gwyn as hundreds of the creatures swarmed around them. Gwyn draped her cloak over them the best she could, which seemed to provide surprising protection from the small pine needle arrows.

"We can't stay in here forever!" Jack pointed out.

Gwyn knew he was right as she began feeling small pricks jabbing through her cloak and into her back.

After a few seconds of trying to think of a solution, Gwyn felt a rapid fire of several sharp pricks across her back. "THAT'S IT!" she yelled, drawing the Xi Blade from its sheath, then stood and revealed herself from the cloak. As she stood, her eyes were glowing with a deep green surrounded by an indigo hue as her mind began slipping.

Within a couple of seconds, the swarming and buzzing stopped completely. Gwyn looked down and saw on the ground before her what appeared to be rows upon rows of tiny winged people now staring up at her in reverent awe.

CHAPTER 22
A Spirited Encounter

Gwyn let her mind slip back to normal and took a step closer to the winged people. As she moved toward them, she realized that their eyes seemed focused on the Xi Blade she held in front of her.

To be sure, she moved it slightly from side to side. She could see awed expressions on their tiny faces as they followed the blade's movement.

"Who are you people?" she asked with sincere curiosity.

"You have the blade..." a small, winged girl with green hair said, standing near the front.

Gwyn looked at the Xi Blade. "Yes, it was my mother's."

"So, you are... the new queens?" the winged girl asked.

"Err, about that," Gwyn said. "I think I have a ways to go before—"

"She is!" a male winged creature yelled. "She looks just like Queen Selena! Look!" He then turned and made clicking noises.

Suddenly, all the winged creatures bowed down before her. Gwyn stared for a moment, unsure how to react. She thought about curtsying back but decided against it. The truth was, she wasn't sure at all how to respond to such treatment or whether she even deserved it. She decided to keep a straight face and respect their decision to bow.

"Who are you?" she asked, hoping to end the bowing.

The plan worked, and the winged creatures returned to their full height, which was only about seven inches.

"Sprites!" the green-haired girl said. She took a few steps forward. "Wood Sprites. What are your names?"

"I'm Gwyn," she said, and Jack, Jasmine, and Chele followed suit.

"Why did you attack us?" Gwyn asked, tilting her head slightly to the side.

The green-haired sprite tilted her head as well, looking at Gwyn with intense curiosity. "Why did you knocks our houses down?"

Gwyn looked over at the large mushrooms and saw several they'd knocked down. She then realized that the mushrooms had spilled out remnants of small sprite homes.

"Oh!" Gwyn said in embarrassment, putting her hand to her mouth. "Oh, crud! We're so sorry! We really didn't mean to."

The female sprite flew up next to Gwyn's face. "What happened to the queens? She sees us no more!"

Gwyn looked away for a moment, then back at the wood sprite. "She's gone. No one sees her anymore," she told her, hoping the sprites wouldn't get upset at the news. But they didn't. Only a few reacted with concerned faces.

"What's your name?" Gwyn asked.

The wood sprite flew close to Gwyn. "Spirit!" she said.

"Nice to meet you, Spirit," Gwyn said, then offered to help set the houses back up.

The wood sprites accepted and they all helped with the effort. It took a few minutes, and they certainly weren't perfect, but only a couple were damaged.

Spirit then graciously thanked them

"Spirit," Gwyn said, "it's gotten very dark. Is there somewhere safe we could stay for the night nearby?"

Spirit flew and landed on Gwyn's shoulder. "Queen Gwyn stays here!"

"Oh! Well, thank you, but I'm afraid I'm not quite the queen, and we're not small enough to fit in your homes," Gwyn replied.

"I'm tired enough to try," Jack said.

Spirit flew up to his face. "Nots there! Oh no! A bigger house!" Spirit then turned toward the large group of sprites watching and spoke in a wispy, clicking, chirp-like noise. A cheer rose among the wood sprites, and several of them took off into the trees.

Spirit flew back over to Jack's face. "We builds for you!" she told him. With that, several wood sprites returned with vines, leaves, and twigs from the forest. Hundreds of them quickly tied the materials together and wove them into a small tent. The whole process looked magically in sync and took only minutes. When they were done, Gwyn, Chele, Jasmine, and Jack were ushered in.

The inside was tall enough to stand up without hunching, and the atmosphere was noticeably warmer than the chilly outside air. They stood in the tent talking for a few minutes, and Gwyn decided she felt warm enough to remove her cloak. Upon removing it, she found hundreds of tiny spears and arrows sticking out of it.

"Good lord!" she said in honest surprise.

"Uh, yeah. You took the brunt of it," Jack told her.

"We's so sorry, Queen Gwyn! We did not know!" Spirit said.

Gwyn nodded. "'Tis fine. None of us knew. You can have them back if you want."

Spirit nodded, then spoke again in the wispy clicks, and several dozen sprites gathered around Gwyn's cloak to remove the needles.

Gwyn thanked the sprites, and as she stepped back outside, she saw a dim group of sprites walking with the horses toward them.

"We has the beasts!" Spirit said to Gwyn.

"Thank you!" Chele said.

Spirit introduced two other female wood sprites and one male wood sprite to them. "Kyla and Feist are my sisters."

Kyla had bright red hair, and Feist had jet-black hair, like Gwyn's.

"Nice to meet you," Gwyn told them.

"Kyla speaks human, but nots as much for Feist," Spirit said. "This is my kindred, Xeros."

Jack began snickering behind Gwyn, and she could hear him mumble to himself, "Kindred-Spirit."

Gwyn rolled her eyes and tried to ignore him. "Thank you, Spirit. It's very nice to meet you all. Would you mind if we started a fire?" Gwyn asked.

Spirit's face lit up. "Like a camp fires?"

Gwyn thought about it for a moment, then nodded. "Yeah, like a campfire!"

Spirit's face lit up even more. "We loves campfires! Yes! Yes, please! But please don't makes it dangerous!"

It didn't take long for Jack, Gwyn, Jasmine and Chele to gather logs for a fire. They built a small firepit with stone circles and stacked the wood into a tepee shape.

"How will you light?" Kyla asked.

"Don't worry, Gwyn can handle it," Jack said.

"Thanks, Jack," she replied sarcastically. She then placed her hands on two logs and closed her eyes while focusing on binding fire into the logs. A large flame burst suddenly from the logs, causing several wood sprites, Chele, and Jack to jump slightly. Gwyn smiled as she looked upon the roaring flames in the firepit.

"Whoa!" several sprites said as they gathered around to enjoy the warmth of the fire. Gwyn heard whispers saying, "She is the queen," as they came closer.

They sat around the fire, talking with the wood sprites, answering questions about the world and what had happened since years ago when Gwyn's mother had last visited.

Spirit explained how the wood sprites had come from the underworld forests long ago to live on the surface. She refused to say exactly what, but it was clear that awful things had happened to them in the underworld, and they were thankful to come to the surface.

"We are so thankfuls to Queen Selena," Spirit said. "She has saved us from the darkness in the underworlds and made us a place in the Moonless Forest."

"Spirit, do you know the way to Sterlington?" Gwyn asked.

Spirit nodded. "Thats is just straight that way," she said, pointing in a direction similar to the way they were headed before walking over the large mushrooms. "You must make it through the forest first!" Spirit then flew up to Gwyn. "I will show you!"

Gwyn smiled, and Xeros flew up next to her. "No!" he said in a demanding voice. "We cannot to having you go! I will go!"

"Nos!" Spirit replied. "I must shows the new Queen Gwyn! She needs us!"

Kyla and Feist then flew up next to Xeros. "We could goes!" Kyla said. Feist nodded eagerly with a smile.

Spirit looked at them for a moment, a nail resting on her long canine tooth. "Wells... I suppose it's good that ways." She then looked at Xeros. "Not yous! You stay! Feist and Kyla can show!"

Xeros looked slightly disappointed at Spirit, then nodded and flew back down to the fire.

"Tomorrow, Kyla and Feist will take you out!" Spirit told Gwyn.

Gwyn looked at the wood sprites and smiled. "Excellent! Thank you!"

"But we's wishes you'd return soon!" Spirit told Gwyn sincerely.

"I certainly hope to!" Gwyn replied.

They continued resting around the campfire, eating berries and smoked fish that the wood sprites provided. They had a surprising amount of food ready to share, and all four of them enjoyed several helpings.

The forest grew very dark once the sun had fully set. The only things coming through the thick ceiling of fog were occasional flakes of snow that melted as they touched a surface.

When the fire died down, they stepped into the tent the wood sprites had built for them. They stood in the tent talking for a few minutes with Spirit, Kyla, and Feist. Gwyn decided to remove her cloak so she could use it as a cover for her, Chele and Jasmine.

"Goodness, Gwyn. Wish I had some of that warmth," Jack complained.

Spirit flew up to Gwyn's face. "This is your mother's cloak!"

Gwyn smiled and nodded at the wood sprite. "Indeed it is!"

"We shall fixes it! Like when we mades it new!" Spirit told her. "We will mend it backs to new for you!"

Gwyn's expression changed to a curious look. "What do you mean? You made this cloak?"

Spirit nodded enthusiastically. "Queen Selena dids request it! She knew we could make the best!"

Gwyn began to get excited. "Could you make more for my friends?"

Spirit's expression grew excited as well, but then she placed her fingernail back on her canine tooth. "Well, we do not has much materials left."

"What do you mean?" Gwyn asked.

"Queen Selena brought special threads and herbs to makes it!"

"Oh," Gwyn said, disappointed. "Well, if we ever get some, we'd love to have three more!"

Spirit nodded, and several wood sprites flew in and started repairing the cloak. Within minutes, the cloak looked less worn and patchy than it had in years. Her grandmother had always done a great job repairing it, but now the stitching seemed nearly back to new and better than Gwyn had ever remembered seeing it. They also let some of the hemmed material out a bit so that it fit her better.

"Good night, Spirit. Thank you all so much for your hospitality!" Gwyn told the wood sprites as she closed the stick-made door to the tent.

"Gwyn?" Chele asked from the dark tent floor.

"Yes?" she replied.

"Thanks for thinking of us back there."

"Oh," Gwyn replied, realizing she was thinking about the cloaks. "Of course!"

The four of them lay in the tent, listening to distant owls and crickets in the forest. It was easy to enjoy the comfortable bedding of pine needles that the wood sprites had woven into a mattress for them. To say the bedding was uncomfortable would be a lie. In fact, the four of them slept comfortably and calmly through the night and well into the morning.

After a quick breakfast of berries and smoked fish, the four of them climbed onto their horses and rode east. Kyla and Feist sat on Guts' head between his ears. Guts didn't seem bothered by the wood sprites as they traveled.

Things were rather uneventful and quiet for some ways. It wasn't until Kyla stood up and whispered, "Stops the horse!"

Jack pulled the horse to a stop as Kyla and Feist both took off. They zoomed far ahead on the trail, then came right back.

"Wolves!" Feist said. "Hides! Quick!"

They pulled the horses to the right off the road, and they quickly went downhill. They were forced to lean back to avoid falling off as the terrain steepened sharply. Unfortunately, Guts' foot caught a tree root and stumbled into Gwyn's horse.

All four of them fell off, sliding and rolling uncontrollably down the hill.

Gwyn was the first to catch a tree by the base, stopping her descent but still hanging on the steep hill. Chele and Jack managed to grab saplings and slid to a stop as well, but Jasmine slid all the way to the bottom, landing in a bush.

They could hear howling and footsteps back up the hill where they had fallen from.

Gwyn looked up and saw an abnormally giant wolf wearing spiky metal armor. It was sniffing around quickly, as if it could smell them. Two more wolves appeared by its side, and she saw them both sniffing around frantically.

She looked down at Jack and Chele and saw them both hanging onto thin saplings to keep from sliding. She also saw Kyla and Feist at the bottom of the hill with the horses. Their saddles were turned upside down, but they seemed to have survived tumbling down the steep hill, as far as Gwyn could tell.

Gwyn motioned for Jack and Chele to be silent just as Jack's limb broke, and he fell backward, rolling down the hill. The noise sounded like a thunderstorm despite their attempts to remain quiet, and Gwyn looked up to see the giant wolves staring directly at her. Their eyes reflected what looked to be a blood-red light as they licked their giant teeth.

"LET GO!" Gwyn yelled.

Chele let go of the sapling and skidded down the rest of the hill to land near Jack as gracefully as she could. She quickly removed Apollo from the saddle and handed it to Jack, then bent down and removed a knife that was strapped to her ankle.

The wolves had been considering a path down, but after a few moments, they leapt from the top of the hill down toward them.

Gwyn, still hanging from the branch, saw the wolves as they bolted down the hill, heading straight for her. Chele's knife went into the eye of the one on the right, followed by an arrow into the chest of the one on the left, both with loud yelps.

The one with a knife in its eye flew downhill to the side of Gwyn, and the one with an arrow in its chest to her other side, but the third was still headed straight for her. She let go of the branch and allowed herself to stand up for a moment while falling backward. In that brief time, she felt her mind slip.

The giant, snarling wolf was bearing down on her as she removed the Xi Blade and held it firmly in front of herself. The wolf's chest landed directly onto the blade as she fell skidding backward down the hill. She felt and smelled the creature's foul breath, its teeth only inches from her, as she rolled backward and powerfully kicked it with both feet, causing the giant wolf to free fall down the hill.

Her sight twirled in violent circles of foggy pines as she felt her body crash through some thick bushes and onto a pine-needle-covered ground.

Her vision spun violently for a moment before it returned, she saw Jack shooting arrows into one of the wolves as it growled and struggled to get back to its feet. Kyla and Feist were also zooming around the wolf, firing pine-needle arrows into it as fast as they could.

Gwyn looked to her side and saw Chele removing her knife from the eye of one of the fallen beasts. She then watched her turn and throw the knife into the neck of the wounded one.

Jack was holding his side again, as he and Chele went over to Gwyn, helping her remove the pine needles and leaves from her hair and cloak as she felt a piercing pain suddenly coming from her right wrist. She looked down and saw pine needles sticking out of the herbal wrapping on her wrist.

She painfully worked the needles from her herbal paper bandages, tearing the wrappings in several areas.

"These don't look like normal animals," Gwyn noted.

"Those were nots a normal wolfs!" Kyla said. "Those are nots from in heres!"

Chele helped Gwyn redress her wrist as Gwyn thought about what Kyla said. "Where are they from?"

Kyla shook her head. "We's just not know! It's dark like the underworld with them! Please, human! We must goes back to warns Spirit!"

Gwyn nodded to Kyla. "Of course! Go!"

With a hum, the two wood sprites blasted off through the forest.

"Should we go back?" Jack asked.

"No," Chele said. "Gwyn needs help. I don't think she should try to climb back up. Her wrists are not good."

Gwyn felt her heart sink. She wanted to go back to the sprite village, but they'd fallen so far downhill.

"We've fallen too far," Gwyn finally said. "Honestly, I can't say I even remember the way now, anyway."

Gwyn knew that even if she managed to climb back up the hill, getting Jack, Chele, Jasmine, and the horses back up it was nearly impossible.

"I think we should head for Sterlington," Chele said.

Gwyn nodded, a bit reluctant to give in to the reality of things. "Yes. Hopefully, the wolves won't find Spirit's village."

They fixed the saddles, climbed back on the horses, and headed in the direction they believed to be east. There was no clear trail, but after only an hour or so of fighting through thick brush, the lighting in the forest brightened a bit as the swirling, misty silver-and-purple haze thinned. The trees thinned as well as they walked into a valley where the ground became slightly sandier, with patches of grass spread about.

It wasn't long before they had left the forest far behind and were now walking through large hills with only a few trees scattered about them.

It was a surprise to find a creek running in the lower part of the valley, and they kept it as near to them as they could as they traveled.

They followed the creek for what seemed like several hours, stopping occasionally where they could access it to fill drinking vessels Chili had left in the saddles, let the horses drink and eat, or find small fish for food. The afternoon sun felt nice in the chilly air when it occasionally broke through the clouds.

The topography of the land eventually flattened out to the east. Gwyn still couldn't use her bow because of her wrists, but Jack and Chele were skilled enough hunters, and Jasmine a skilled gatherer, to help them all survive the journey.

Staring at her wrists and thinking quietly to herself, Gwyn wondered how terrible they would look once they'd healed. Ripping her from her thoughts, Jasmine told her, "He can make you better, you know."

"What do you mean?" Gwyn asked.

"He'll do it using magic. Real magic!"

Gwyn shook her head. "You mean Galanga?"

Jasmine nodded, leaving Gwyn with a hopeful feeling.

They ventured on for a long while. Gwyn's mind reflected on her experience with the Wood Sprites as she rolled her neck to refresh her focus. She lifted her arms behind her head for a quick stretch, her muscles relieved for the temporary change of position. Her mind now freshly focused on the horizon. As she looked, she saw what looked like dark gray clouds rising into the eastern sky.

"Looks like we've got a storm coming, guys." Jack stated.

"Maybe we should make camp," Gwyn said, glancing around for a patch of trees to hunker down in.

"That's not a cloud," Chele insisted.

Gwyn took another look on the horizon. "Chele's right," she said in a moment of stunned realization. "That's a city..."

CHAPTER 23

As they traveled, it became clear that the stretch of gray was indeed the walls of a large city. They were in awe, seeing its tall, majestic towers peeking in the distance around the enormous city as it came closer into view.

"That must be Sterlington," Jack said. "Gwyn, I think that city was named after your last name."

Gwyn sat in reverence for a moment before responding, "Don't get me thinking about that. It doesn't seem real."

Even though they could see the city from afar, its vast size made it seem to take forever to arrive. They passed several farms on the outskirts—some with tall, withered cornfield crops, others with lavender or cotton. An old cobblestone road, almost too pristine to be outside a city, led them several miles toward the city's tall walls.

The buildings were made of round gray stone, with moss and vines growing on some. A brief observation revealed the area they were in had been largely deserted. Several buildings showed severe damage, with large chunks blown off into the streets, fountains blown in half, and occasional craters in the road. Pieces of Xi crystal littered one street corner where it had once stood majestically.

Gwyn pocketed a few shards of the crystals, enjoying the sense of power they lent her.

It was hard not to admire the ghostly image of the once-bustling city. A light dusting of snow began to fall onto the streets, and the wind swept over the road's surface, preventing the snow from sticking as it slithered across the cold stones.

Some districts looked as though they could still be inhabited, but they saw no people. Merchandise remained in shop windows, with "open" signs still hanging. They peered inside but it was dark.

They decided to enter a store to warm up and look for food. Inside, they found bags of jerky and jars of pickles. They ate as much of the pickles as they could, but the jerky smelled funny. Jack, unable to swallow the bite he took, ungracefully spat a chunk of half-chewed jerky onto the floor in front of a disgusted Chele.

"Ow, my nose!" he yelled as she jammed a small pickle into it.

Jasmine went into a giggle fit when a half-stunned Jack launched the pickle across the room with a violent sneeze.

"Again! Again!" Jasmine demanded.

"Heck, no! I feel like that pickle hit my brain!" Jack retorted, holding his sore nose.

"Come on," Gwyn said, trying not to laugh. "We need to keep going."

The four of them walked down the lonely streets of Sterlington, knowing they hadn't seen a fraction of it—toward the center where tallest and most majestic towers stood. Even from far away, they resembled a castle.

"Do you think your mother lived there?" Jack asked.

Gwyn shrugged, though she felt confident her mother had. "Hard to say since it's so far away."

"This place is huge, and the sun's going down," Chele pointed out. "Maybe we should look for a place to stay the night?"

Gwyn sighed, feeling a bit defeated after coming so far without finding Clove yet. "Jasmine," she said, kneeling on one knee.

"Lost?" Jasmine replied.

"Well... kind of. Can you see where to go?"

Jasmine shook her head.

Gwyn stood back up and conceded. "You're right, Chele. It's getting dark and cold. We should find a warm place for the night."

The part of the city they had reached was far less damaged. The area didn't seem to have many shops, though, as if it were a long alleyway for traveling. The nearby doors all appeared locked or jammed shut as they searched for a place to sleep. Finally, one door opened to them, allowing them to slip inside a dark, quiet room.

"This place is a creep fest," Jack said.

"Suck it up, pickle nose!" Chele jokingly told him.

"Hey!" he retorted, a bit hurt.

"She's right. It's the best we've got," Gwyn chimed in.

They walked in to find the room was very small but had a door just inside that was locked. They felt around until Chele grabbed a puffy handful of silky material. "What is this place?"

"I think it's the front of a shop," Gwyn replied.

"I think these are curtains," Chele pointed out. "Or blankets. Either way, we can use them."

After huddling the materials into a bed just large enough to fit them all, they fell into a quick but deep winter's sleep.

Gwyn woke to a shaking door. The wind howled outside, and small, poorly sealed creases around the door let chilled spurts of wind creep in. She got up first and pulled back the curtain to a window. The darkness outside was thick as she strained her eyes to see the blowing snow in the alley.

"Lost?" Jasmine said, tugging at her cloak.

Gwyn gasped at the unknown thing pulling at her robe but then sighed in relief to find it was Jasmine. "What is it?" she whispered back.

"I just want you to know, when it's over, that it's not your fault."

Gwyn felt uneasy about Jasmine talking in such a way. "What do you mean? What's not my fault?"

"None of it. You were caught in destiny—like the great wizard Eos prophesied—that another age of wizards would come but would be faced with a great darkness."

She shook her head, not quite frustrated but confused by the small goblin girl. She opened her mouth to speak, but Jasmine beat her to it.

"Don't worry, you'll get it soon. You're just tired. You've been through a lot."

She took a deep breath and let Jasmine's words sink in a bit. "You know what? You're right. It's been quite the adventure."

Gwyn lay down in a silky bed on the floor close to Chele and fell into a deep sleep. The cold chill on her cheeks began to thaw the next morning as a small sliver of sunlight pierced through a tiny slit in the curtains and landed on her face. She smiled, knowing the sun would be out to melt some of the snow.

Jack got up to check on the horses. They had placed them between alleyways that blocked the wind, and they seemed to be fine. He found some patches of grass growing in a nearby garden and let them graze there.

The room they had stayed in was apparently a tailor shop with giant, puffy comforters and curtains. The bed they had crafted in the dark was a mixture of the two.

They found a door to the back that led to a kitchen. The place looked untouched and felt as if it had been quickly abandoned. Nuts, fresh jerky, and pickles were a feast of a breakfast for them.

"Let's get moving," Gwyn commanded.

As they traveled, the city took on a different feel. More of the walls were intact, and things appeared cleaner and tended to.

Before long, they came upon an alleyway with an overhead archway guards could patrol on. They passed through and for the first time saw another person. It was a young woman dressed in modest clothes. She ran, grabbed a small child sitting next to a barrel, rang a triangle, and ran into a building.

"That was weird," Jack said.

A group of men carrying pitchforks, spears, and axes soon rushed upon them. The man in front was a strong-statured blond man with kind blue eyes.

"What do you want?" he insisted with seriousness.

"We seek Clove," Gwyn replied, looking around to see several men now surrounding them.

The blond man grunted and remained defensive.

"Come on, they're just kids, Stan," a dark-haired man said, standing next to the blond man.

"Jason, you can't be too sure these days," Stan replied.

Gwyn sat passively for a moment. She caught the eyes of several of the men, each gaze leaving a unique fingerprint on her heart. It was as if she felt their innocence and then their suffering.

After peering into the eyes of the people in front of her, she began to wonder what had brought them to feel so much fear. Even though they pointed sharp weapons at her, her heart broke for them.

"We do not wish you harm," Gwyn said firmly. She sensed there was no threat of magic from them, despite their sharp weapons pointing directly at her. She then looked at her wrists, and the thought of using magic herself seemed extremely uncomfortable if forced to defend herself—yet her confidence somehow remained high.

"Fine. Just make your trip through here quick. This sector is closed," the man named Jason told them.

"Sector?" Gwyn asked.

"Yeah. You're looking for sector 707. This is 705. And like I said, we're not accepting visitors right now."

She gave a nod. "Very well. We'll be quick then. But, if you don't mind..."

"Young lady, we do mind," Jason cut her off. "You get your friends and go."

"Jason, you're being mean!" Stan protested, pushing him aside.

"Shut up, fool!" Jason retorted. "I'm doing what's best for the sector—what's best for the city! You've seen what's happened! How do we know these kids aren't more of them in disguise?"

Stan's face became vexed as he looked at Gwyn. He stepped forward and handed her a scroll. "Here, it's my own map." The map was made of fine leather and rolled nicely. "Forgive us. We've... just been through a lot. Jason here lost his brother to those demons out there. There's not a one of us who hasn't lost family and friends; it's just... dark times... is all."

A warm wind suddenly blew through Gwyn's hair and an overwhelming sadness swept over her as she looked at the people's faces. She glanced past them and found the eyes of their families peeking through windows. Some appeared angry, but she looked deeper and saw that they all battled one of the worst burdens of all: hopelessness.

Compassion began to grow within her as she looked upon countless eyes bearing puffy dark circles from sleepless nights, weeping, and terror.

Above that, a great sense of responsibility weighed on her to offer them something.

"Listen!" Gwyn said firmly. Her voice carried a slight echo in the sector. It seemed to pique great interest, causing the men's stirring to quickly fall into silence as she continued, "I see your fear... it fills your hearts." Her voice echoed louder. "You have a right to embrace it, but it will only weaken you. So, I beg of you to encourage one another instead and do NOT lose hope." She spoke in a manner so bold that the men were shaken still, now frozen in her presence. Most had lowered their defenses stood instead in reverence, eager to hear more—like starved dogs waiting for another scrap of food at the table.

"My lady," said a man from the crowd, "we have not heard such words in so long. How can you speak these things with such conviction in times like these?"

"Maybe she's too young to understand," Jason uttered.

"Let her speak," others demanded.

Gwyn looked at Jack and then at Chele. Both wore a mixture of fear and anticipation on their faces as they stared at her. Chele eventually nodded, as if to say, ' Go on.'

She took a deep breath and held her head high as she spoke, slowly at first, then boldly, "Citizens of sector Seven O Five, you have not been forgotten. Count yourselves among the bravest heroes of history. When darkness came and others ran, you stayed to defend your home at all costs. Let your passion burn on to victory, and may your bravery and love for this land one day be reconciled with the peace and prosperity you so deserve."

The entire sector fell silent, staring at Gwyn. Not a single one of them questioned her any longer.

"My lady..." the man with kind eyes said hesitantly, "you don't speak like a child... Who are you?"

Gwyn looked directly at the man and replied softly as she dismounted the horse, "I, myself, am a lost native of Sterlington, and my mission is becoming clear..." she boldly added, "Whether I succeed or fail, you'll know who I am soon enough." She looked out to a now-subdued crowd.

Jason finally lowered his weapon and knelt before Gwyn. Then two others followed. She felt a wave of sincere shock wash over her.

Soon, nearly every man and woman was kneeling before her, as if she were royalty.

Gwyn wasn't sure what to do next, so she remounted the horse, sat speechless for a moment, then rode through.

When they had gone out of earshot of the people, Jack asked Gwyn, "How did you do that?"

"Do what?"

"Make your eyes glow like green fire?"

"My eyes were glowing?" she asked in true surprise.

"When you said that thing at the end—that they'd soon know who you are—they were as bright as the Electric Moon."

"I..." she started. "I only meant to inspire them..."

"You did," Chele said without hesitation.

Gwyn sat silently in her thoughts. Her heart was overwhelmed with emotions. Half of her wanted to cry, but the other half wanted to free the people of her mother's city—or perhaps, someday, her city.

They went through another tunnel and found themselves outside the main part of town and in another alley. Gwyn opened the map and saw that the city was far bigger than they had assumed.

"There must be hundreds of sectors!" Gwyn said, looking the map over. It was a view of the city from above, showing four giant watchtowers at what could be called the corners. The tower in the southeast was recently marked with red.

The map also showed sectors 1 through 100 to be part of the castle in the center. The castle centerpiece had its own walls and towers surrounding it as well. Just north of the castle appeared to be a forest right inside the city.

An odd thing about the map, Chele pointed out, was that there were missing sector numbers—300 to 500 seemed to be missing.

They realized they were between the large northwest perimeter tower and the castle because they could see them towering over the city. Clove was due south from where they were, but thankfully, not very far.

It still took the better part of the afternoon to find a sign that read "Clove". It was an arrow-shaped sign that looked as if it had nearly been blown down, so they went in the direction they felt it was likely pointing.

Before long, more signs pointing to Clove appeared, and eventually, they came upon a tall, light-brown mound of hard dirt with patchy grass on it. It almost looked like a termite mound, only much larger. There was a round door on one side, much like the door in the Glade Goblin village, so they knocked. Standing there in silence, no one answered. They knocked again, much louder this time, but still, no one answered.

"Wait," Jasmine said.

After a few moments, they heard a loud click on the other side of the door. It sounded like someone unlatched a deadbolt, but the door did not open.

Jasmine suddenly opened the door and quickly ran down a hall made of nicely polished wood.

"Jasmine, wait!" Gwyn pleaded, but Jasmine didn't stop, so she went in after her.

Jack tied off the horses and climbed in after Chele.

The tunnel was between three and four feet high, forcing her to crawl. She had to use her elbows to avoid putting pressure on her wrists. It took a minute for her eyes to adjust to the lighting. Everything was dimly lit with Xi lighting that ran near the handrails and corners of the floors. She came to a door at the end with a ladder just inside.

She climbed down the ladder, thankful to stretch out after the awkward crawl, finding herself on a platform at the bottom. She easily stood now as Jack and Chele joined her on the platform. They looked over the rope railing to a deep, wide hole cut into the earth below them. Different levels below were lit up brightly with golden Xi light—an odd sight. They followed the platform around and walked into a round room with ropes and handle cranks attached to the wooden flooring. A spool of ropes and a few chains hung above their heads.

Jasmine, who was standing at one of the cranks, smiled as they all entered the room.

"What are you doing?" Jack asked her.

"Waiting for you, silly!" Jasmine replied and pulled back on one of the levers.

Gwyn felt her stomach rise as they descended. She could see the pulleys and chains all come to life as they dropped.

As quickly as their descent started, it came to a stop when Jasmine pulled another lever. The group shuffled for a moment before telling Jasmine not to do that again.

"Let me off this puke-coaster!" Jack said, holding his stomach.

"This is it!" Jasmine said, running off toward a curved hall.

Gwyn started to call for her but heard a voice from the tunnel. "What a pleasant surprise! Welcome, all of you!"

She followed Jasmine and saw a goblin in gray robes who looked a bit like Chili, only slightly thinner and wearing glasses. "Are you Galanga?"

The goblin smiled and nodded while hugging Jasmine. "Indeed, I am he! How are you, Gwyn?"

She paused and looked at Jack and Chele for a moment. "How did you know my name?"

Galanga smiled. "My dear child, I rarely forget an aura—especially one like yours. That's why I unlocked the door. It took me a minute to place it, but in my defense, it really has been a while."

Gwyn gave Galanga a half-smile, unsure how to reply. "So do I blush or run?"

Galanga smiled. "I suppose blushing would be appropriate, my dear."

"I ran into your nephew, Chili."

The old goblin chuckled. "Ah, Chili. And he sent you my way, then?"

"Yes," Gwyn replied. "Princess Lily was captured—I thought it was by some of Xess's men. I'd like to help get her back, and I also have some questions for you."

Galanga rubbed his bearded chin and frowned for a moment. "I see, child. Interesting you should bring up Xess," he said, then waved them to follow him down the tunnel while carrying Jasmine in one arm. "Come. We can discuss things over tea. I sense horses; I'll tend to them in a bit."

They followed Galanga through the tunnel and into a large round room that opened up with a domed ceiling, and with a fan that had long wooden blades. A round couch sat in the center, and a pipe organ rested against the wall next to a desk. Gwyn could see two hallways leading out of the main living area and a kitchen and dining area straight across from the door where Galanga went to make tea.

"Please, make yourselves at home," Galanga told them.

They sat on the couch and looked at several abstract pictures and paintings hanging on the walls. Some of them seemed to depict layers of auras around people. Gwyn went up to one and noticed it showed several energy vortexes.

Galanga came into the room with a teapot and five teacups. "I call this 'The Weary Traveler.' I made it when I traveled the whole continent searching for new herbs and remedies. I find it helps restore qi more quickly and relaxes the heart and mind."

He poured each of them tea and handed them cups. When Gwyn reached up to receive hers, her cloak sleeve slid down her arm, revealing her green, worn-out bandages.

"Oh my!" Galanga gasped loudly. "You are injured! I knew your aura looked flustered in that area, but I didn't realize how badly."

"You can tell how bad it is through the bandages?"

"Of course! The aura tells me far more than the surface. This is bad—very bad. It was done by magic! Who did this?"

"Well, to be perfectly honest, the Glade Goblins put me in iron shackles. I was burned when I tried to use magic."

Galanga rubbed his beard while he listened. "Hmm! Well! As terrible as that is, I'm actually quite impressed. Most magicians your age can't light a match with magic. And please forgive my people—they are rather hasty in casting judgment these days, with all that's been going on, especially regarding wizards. But I must know, where are you studying?"

"Silvania," Chele told him, while Gwyn winced as she attempted to remove her bandages.

"Ooo! I bet Professor Fox is dying to show you off! Last I heard, Lyndsey is still serving as head there too."

Gwyn nodded.

"Good thing. Lyndsey will keep a lot of nonsense out. Fox is a great teacher but wants the notch on his belt for it. Now, if you don't mind, I need to see your wrists. It's not good to wait and let injuries like these set in."

Galanga took Gwyn's wrists and began unwrapping the green sheets. "I take it Jasmine knew to use the herb paper?"

"She sure did. Smart kid," she confessed.

Galanga smiled. "Well, you couldn't have chosen a better wrap. It's a medical herb paper, a secret recipe woven by the Glade Goblins. You could use it for writing, eating, bandages, or even starting a fire—though I feel that would be a waste, given your skill with fire magic."

"You can see my magical skills?"

Galanga laughed. "I can see the damage you did to yourself, and that's enough. You see, if you touch iron while casting a spell, it will ground most of the spell to it. Iron is toxic to magic users. If you wore it for too long, you'd become extremely weak and even sick, as it would siphon your magic."

"But why?" Jack chimed in.

"Once you begin using magic, your qi becomes much stronger. More importantly, it slowly bonds with your life force in a powerful way, extending your life and changing you from the inside out. That magic is part of you now. Iron is the most ferrous and crude of metals. It grounds magical energy and life force, sucking it out of you like a magnet."

"That sounds awful," Chele said.

"It is! It's even worse for creatures born magical, like us Glade Goblins."

Galanga had both wraps off and was observing things Gwyn couldn't see with her eyes. Like Kokolo, he ran his hands over the area of the wounds, not actually touching her.

Gwyn felt the same tingling she had felt when Kokolo healed her; however, Galanga seemed to have stronger magic, and his healing was faster. She sighed in relief as the burns healed and became less painful by the second.

The process took a few minutes, all of which Gwyn found enjoyable, and she nearly passed out from the relief. When Galanga was done, she once again had her pale skin instead of bloodied blisters around her wrists. She could still tell the skin was new and slightly different-looking, but overall, the appearance and feel had greatly improved.

"Thank you so much, Galanga. That feels tremendously better!"

Galanga nodded, then lifted the bottom of Gwyn's cloak. She jerked in confusion. "What are you doing?"

"I'm sorry, I thought you'd want your ankles healed, too."

Jack snickered but held it back when Chele threatened to elbow him.

She had forgotten about her ankles even having burns due to the pain her wrists had caused, but now that her wrists were healed, the pain in her ankles had room to exist. "Oh, yes, sorry. Of course, please do!"

Galanga smiled and nodded. "Just be glad you hadn't tried something more foolish or dark. There are some forms of magic that cannot be healed so easily. Your wrists, for example—a few more degrees, and they would have burned beyond aesthetic repair. Not to brag, but not many Aurics could've done so well with them in the condition they were in."

Gwyn suddenly felt tired, as if her mind hadn't realized how much stress it had been under while she was in pain.

Galanga turned to Jack. "Young man, your ribs are bruised! What in the world did you do?"

"Uh, jumped off a cliff," Jack said before shrugging.

Galanga gave Jack a healing as well, and Jack fell asleep on the couch before it was even completed.

"You may feel free to stay here. I have spare beds, and the sofa's fair game if you wish to try waking Jack for it," Galanga said, as if he could read Gwyn's mind and knew how tired she had become. "I'm planning on making some herbal chicken stew in a bit. There'll be enough for all of us several times over if you wish to have some."

Jasmine went up to Galanga and said something in a quiet tone. Galanga's expression was very attentive to her. "Excuse me, I must show Jasmine my herb lab." The two of them got up and walked into a hallway to the side of the dining area.

Gwyn thanked Galanga before he left the room. She stood up, walked toward a darkened hallway, and found a room with a bed in it. She didn't remember hitting the pillow before she fell asleep.

Gwyn slept in a comfortable, dark room containing lava lamps and dimly lit aquariums. Her sleep was restless but deep. She had several dreams that mirrored the events of the last few days, especially the Moonless Forest, where giant wolves attacked them. In the dream, she saw Spirit crying, with Feist and Kyla comforting her.

She slipped into a dream where she stood in a prairie of yellow wildflowers and wheat. It was a perfect place to meditate—warm and peaceful. She took a deep breath of fresh air.

She started counting her breaths to the ticks of her heartbeat, as her teachers had instructed at the Academy, but after only a moment of quiet, something caught her attention, and she opened her eyes. In the distance, she saw the dark, shadowy silhouette of a woman. She couldn't make out any details, but she had the instant feeling that it might be her mother. The woman disappeared into a path that cut through a forest.

Gwyn saw flashes of strange images.

Suddenly, she was back in the prairie. She had fallen asleep. 'But wasn't I dreaming? Am I still asleep?' she wondered as she stood up and saw the silhouette of the woman again in the distance.

It wasn't her mother. She believed this. She longed for her mother. The dark figure was evil, and the air around Gwyn shifted to a cold staleness. The hue of everything turned pink and indigo, as if the Xi Moon were lighting it through a dark, swirling mist.

She didn't want to look at the woman. Suddenly, a strong wind caused Gwyn's hair to whip violently in the air. She looked up toward the woman to see a vortex spinning down from the clouds. She could barely open her eyes as dirt and rocks blasted her skin.

As Gwyn went to scream, her eyes opened, and she was back in Galanga's bedroom.

She found herself breathing heavily and feeling homesick. She thought it an unfair feeling, though, considering it wasn't for her grandparents or Franz and Delilah, but rather for a place she had almost no memory of, with people she couldn't even say she knew.

She suddenly recalled the memory of her little hands being placed in gray mortar to make the mold on her father's tomb. It wasn't the image itself that was comforting, but the memory of the feelings she had at the time.

She bathed in it for a moment before her mind shifted across thoughts so quickly that she grew frustrated with her mind tormenting her with all of it at once as it tried to process it.

Gwyn heard a knock on the door that shook her from her thoughts, and Galanga came in with a bowl of soup. He flipped on a dim Xi-powered light and walked over to her bed. "Here you go, might want to blow on it first—'tis very hot," he said, setting the soup down on a table next to the bed.

Gwyn sat up and ate a few spoonfuls. It was good and well-seasoned, with a fine balance of fresh herbs, spices, and chicken.

Galanga shut the door and pulled up a chair to Gwyn's bed. "Unless I'm terribly mistaken, I'm guessing you have quite a bundle of questions for me," he said while taking a seat next to the bed.

Gwyn put her soup down and rubbed her sleepy eyes. "Actually, yes, I do. But I'm not sure where to begin!"

Galanga smiled, then shrugged. "I suppose that means we should start at the most logical place, then."

"Where is that?"

"The beginning." He smoothed his long white hair back as he thought, then rubbed his pointy white beard. "I suppose for you, that goes back hundreds and hundreds of years—over a thousand years ago now. The world was a very different place back then.

"Before humans lost their power source, which was somewhat like the Xi power we use today, called electricity, they actually detected the Xi Moon coming to Earth—a collision course of almost certain doom. The world was very divided then, and several places on the planet started doing drastic things to save themselves. Unfortunately, the Xi Moon threw flares of Xi power through space that reached Earth far sooner than the moon itself, destroying the sensitive systems here.

"Humans relied so heavily on those systems that many of them went crazy within days of losing electricity. Soon, chaos broke out across all of the world. Within only a few weeks, the world's population began to dwindle in the chaos. It was a very sad time. But it brought forth the second age of wizards. The age of humans was coming to an end."

"The age of wizards..." Gwyn whispered. "Is that where we are now?"

Galanga gave a slight nod before continuing. "A few decades later, the Xi Moon reached the planet. It was more chaos. The brilliant magician Cassius, your father, who later became King of Silvania, orchestrated a powerful team of wizards to channel energy into a collective shield to protect against the chaotic energy of the Xi Moon. Your father opened the barrier and taught others how to add to it. You may find it interesting that Academy Head, Lyndsey, was part of that team. We managed to protect the whole of Silvania and parts of the mainlands, but the moon still changed the world completely.

"It took many days, and many wizards died. The Xi Moon was a force that wanted to destroy," Galanga told Gwyn. "That's when your mother sealed it, and the strongest wizards of the world placed the docile Xi Moon into orbit... Strange calling the Xi Moon docile, isn't it? Considering how active it appears in the sky. The only alternative was to cast it away again, but there were several risks in doing so. It could collide with another planet or sun, sending unknown amounts of energy hurtling back toward us."

Gwyn listened, though she had heard most of what Galanga said before. It was interesting hearing it from someone else's perspective. "What happened after that?"

"Well, shortly after, a rebuilding effort led to the formation of the three great Kingdoms of the continent. Guilds had taken in hundreds of humans to shelter them from the Xi Moon's destruction, but humans are forgetful. If you don't show their children magic, they stop believing it exists. So, within a few generations, only those humans living close to wizards know about magic. But most consider it folklore.

"Your mother took rule over the north by popular demand. She built this wonderous city we're in and named it after your father, of course—Sterlington."

Gwyn had heard most of this before, and Galanga seemed to pick up on it.

"Perhaps I should tell you something you don't know?" he asked.

Gwyn looked surprised. "How'd you know?"

Galanga smiled and shook his head. "It's in your aura. I suppose you've learned more than I first suspected. Here, let me show you something new.

"Xess did not get along with your mother, but after you were born, things became even more serious. Some of Xess's men bombed the southeast towers of her kingdom just after she'd signed a peace treaty with him that your father had arranged. This was a very dark time. In retaliation, she took her best warriors, who held great respect for her, and clawed a path of destruction through the southeast toward Xess's kingdom. The great dividing lands of Arcadia were supposed to uphold peace between the three kingdoms. They attempted to stop your mother, but it did not end well."

Galanga ran his hand over his pointy white beard and nodded. "I was at the castle when she came back."

Galanga took Gwyn's hand, and a tremendously comfortable feeling took over her. The room slowly changed into what appeared to be a castle bedroom with high ceilings and tall windows. He stood next to a bed, painting one of the pictures Gwyn had seen in his living room. Gwyn looked around and noticed odd, colorful halos on almost everything around her. She guessed they had to be auras, assuming she was seeing inside one of Galanga's memories.

"Can I see auras in your memory?" Gwyn asked.

"I'd imagine you could, but it's unlikely you have the ability to process them quite like I do, so I've done my best to tone them down for you."

A feeling suddenly changed, as noticeable as a cold snap in the middle of summer, and Gwyn knew someone was coming. The past Galanga set down his paintbrush and stood facing the hall that led to a door.

A few moments later, a tall, thin, beautiful woman with black hair, pale skin, and green eyes, wearing Gwyn's long, dark green cloak, entered the room. She looked very serious but very beautiful nonetheless. Gwyn instantly knew she was looking at her mother, and her heart skipped a beat.

"My quarters—immediately," Gwyn's mother, Selena, told the past Galanga.

A bright flash occurred, and Gwyn saw the entire area change from Galanga's room to what appeared to be the royal quarters. Tall stone tower walls surrounded the wide room. Beautiful indigo tapestries hung on the walls, while red carpets lined the floors. Gwyn saw a fancy crib with a very small, black-haired baby girl dressed in a green outfit inside it. She looked to be about a year old. Gwyn walked over to the crib and looked at the small version of herself. The tiny Gwyn stood wobbling against the bars of the crib, staring at her mother with a near-toothless smile and jet-black, wispy curls.

Selena walked over to the crib with Galanga, then looked at him. "I had the sprites and druids give her one of their ancient remedies. It was quite an undertaking for them. Please, check her again."

The past Galanga looked at Selena, then at the infant Gwyn, and frowned slightly. "I'm sorry, my lady, it is as I've seen before—the curse is still there."

Selena's face didn't change much, just enough for Gwyn to tell she was disappointed. The hue of her aura, which stretched a few inches out from her body, shifted from reddish gold and silver to a shade of blue. "How is the cure coming?"

The past Galanga shook his head. "I've been charting it out and have traveled across the entire Glades gathering medicines, but these things take time. Even then, remember what I told you: this curse is far different from any I've ever seen. It runs deeper than the inner aura. It looks as if it's almost a part of her very being. It might be genetic now."

Selena frowned slightly and looked down at the small Gwyn. Her aura turned pink and nearly disappeared from Gwyn's view.

"It's not good enough," Selena said softly. "Help her, Galanga! Please!" she pleaded.

The past Galanga shook his head. "Your Majesty, you're asking me to change water into honey. It will take some time... if it's even something I'm capable of."

"But do we have time?" Selena asked Galanga.

He swallowed hard, as if he knew something more.

The atmosphere suddenly changed again as a loud crash came from the ceiling. Shards of shattered glass rained down from one of the high tower windows, scattering across the un-carpeted part of the tile floor. Gwyn looked up as a shadowy figure leapt down from the high window, landing on the stone floor of the room. The figure wore tight black robes with a large, shiny, wet spot covering the area around the heart. The figure stood about Selena's height and had a similar build but wore a half-mask and hood with dark hair flowing behind it.

Gwyn looked at the figure's feet and saw large speckles of blood on the floor. The figure's aura was lined with a deep, bright red, its ridges appearing angry to Gwyn.

A familiar voice spoke through the mask, and she suddenly noticed Jade's gleaming opal eyes shining angrily through the black hood. Her voice was violent, dark, and shaken. "You..." she said in a low, dark tone.

Selena stared at the dark figure. Gwyn felt a tremendous sense of energy rising in the room, making the hairs on her neck and arms stand on end.

Jade spoke again, her aura pulsing and swirling between black and red. "Do you realize what you've done!?"

Chills ran down Gwyn's spine. She felt Galanga must have felt this memory so strongly that it still gave him chills.

Again, Selena said nothing as the energy levels surged.

"You've undone everything I've been working for!" Jade said in an angry, steady tone.

Selena looked almost indifferent, her aura steadily holding a light gold. "He has broken the treaty," she said calmly.

Jade stood for a moment, breathing heavily. "He had a troop go rogue! It does not justify what you have done." Jade turned her gaze toward the past Galanga, then to the crib. She looked from the crib to Selena a couple of times. "Without Arcadia, the age of wizards is no better than the age of humans..." Jade looked at the crib again, staring at the small Gwyn. "And you've passed the curse onto the child?"

Selena's face flashed a hint of anger, her aura slightly lining with red. "That's none of your business."

Jade's opal eyes grew angry. "Like hell it's not!" She then pulled two blades from the nether. "You've lost control. This will grow stronger and doom us all! This cannot go on!"

Selena stood for a moment, staring blankly into the void before she turned and drew the Xi Blade from under her robes. Instantly, the energy in the room felt as if a thick blanket of static buried Gwyn. She felt as if the air were sucked out of the room as she looked at her mother's aura, which now looked very strong and had a thick golden and red hue. The

Xi Blade's aura was stranger than any other; it swirled violently with black, red, and indigo colors. Gwyn watched as it intertwined with her mother's. She observed the powerful aura of the Xi Blade creeping into Selena's aura as strong vortexes in her absorbed and directed the energy throughout it.

Gwyn was fascinated by what she saw but couldn't help wondering if the same thing happened when she wielded the Xi Blade.

"Take one step toward her, and it will be your last," Selena said in a tone that left no room for misunderstanding. Gwyn had no doubt Selena was serious and ready to cut Jade down, her heartbeat drumming in the tense silence that followed.

Jade stared at Selena for a few heated seconds. Her opal eyes seethed with anger as the speed of her breathing increased. "DID YOU SEE WHAT YOU DID TO HIM?" she screamed, the sound of her voice echoing throughout the castle tower. A tear rolled down Jade's cheek. "You nearly killed him! He was on your side!"

Selena's face shifted from angry to almost sad. She breathed out and looked down. Several seconds of quiet passed, but it felt much longer in the moment.

Jade placed her blades back into the nether and stood tall, staring defiantly at Selena. "You can't undo this... but you can make it better."

Selena looked at the infant Gwyn with sadness filling her eyes. "I'm working on a cure," she said with a calm voice.

Jade put her hand on the wet spot of her black robe over her heart and flicked blood-covered fingers toward Selena. Specks of blood landed at Selena's feet, appearing as darker red spots on the already red carpet. "There's far more than my blood on your hands tonight. I'll spare you the regret."

Selena looked hurt as she stared at the floor, then back up at Jade. "He's alive?"

"Barely," Jade said, another tear falling from her cheek. "But not many are..." she added, her voice finally sounding slightly shaken. "Including yours."

Gwyn suddenly felt something in her stomach turn sharply, as if Jade's words meant something awful to Galanga.

"You know, she's getting stronger, and you're getting weaker. Where does this end, Selena? How many ancient magi will you kill before it's enough?"

Jade's question left a stale silence in the air.

"You're doing her bidding, and the world does not deserve this. And you know what will happen if Nok returns... She'll use you...both of you..."

Selena placed the Xi Blade back in its sheath, took a deep breath, and turned away from Jade. Gwyn suddenly felt as if the air returned, becoming comfortable to breathe again.

She felt overwhelming concern and sadness, as if something awful had happened and she had just received the bad news.

The room slowly dissolved to a different location. It was night now, and the past Galanga was walking down a cobblestone road through Sterlington toward the castle. Gwyn and the present Galanga followed him.

"Why are we out here?" Gwyn asked.

"I had just returned from my herb lab, making every concoction of a cure I could think of from every known source I could find on the queen's urgent orders. I was still doubtful that anything would work because I don't believe it's a curse, but I was coming to administer it to you upon the queen's orders anyway. Sadly, I never saw you again, my little friend—not until today."

The past Galanga suddenly stopped and looked up. A loud crashing sound came from the castle towers ahead, followed by another, then the cry of a child and another crash. The past Galanga bolted toward the castle, suddenly stopping to look up. Gwyn could see what looked like her mother jump from the tower of the royal quarters onto the top of a castle wall. She ran very fast and jumped off the other side. A tall man, who was carrying something, followed not too far behind, jumping from the same window and pursuing Gwyn's mother. Gwyn then saw a dark figure appear behind him. The dark figure had flowing black hair. She recognized the silhouette as Jade's as she leapt behind the wall after them.

"Why is she here? What's happening? Where did they go?" Gwyn asked.

"I do not know. I cannot teleport here in Sterlington. Only your mother and father could. They had it set up that way. If I tried, it would send me somewhere randomly outside of town. It's a fun trick to play on wizards who don't know any better, though most know now."

"You can't teleport anywhere in Sterlington?" Gwyn asked.

Galanga shook his head. "No. A rare type of magic your father knew about."

They followed the past Galanga into the castle, up several sets of stairs, passing several guards, and finally to the royal quarters. Galanga had special access to enter and did so. He found the room had been trashed. The curtains looked torn, the crib was tipped over, and several windows had been shattered.

"What happened?" Gwyn asked.

Galanga shrugged. "This was the last night anyone here saw your parents—or you."

The scene dissolved back to Galanga's room with the fish tanks and lava lamps. Gwyn was surprised to find herself shivering and in shock. She attempted to swallow the lump in her throat—the same lump Galanga must have felt in the vision.

Galanga laid her down and covered her up as the emotional backlog poured into her heart. "Please rest for a bit. I should have asked before mind-melding you."

Gwyn gave Galanga a strange look. "Gala-a-anga?" she said through chattering teeth.

"Yes?"

"Was it... J-J-Jade?"

Galanga took a deep breath and gave Gwyn a knowing look. "You know what I know."

Gwyn fought the feeling of her stomach turning as she shivered. "Wh-wh-who was the man cha-a-a-sing my m-m-mother?"

Galanga looked a bit confused at Gwyn. "Your father, of course. He was carrying you!"

Gwyn tried to ask who Nok was, but without trying, she closed her eyes and fell asleep.

CHAPTER 24

Breakfast Over Ancient History

Gwyn woke early the next morning. She had relived Galanga's memories a dozen times throughout her dreams. She got up and crept into the living area to find Jack asleep on the couch. Looking around, she didn't see Chele in the room. She walked through the room quietly and sat down on the couch across from Jack. The room was dimly lit with the soft glow of crystal Xi light.

Gwyn gazed around at the numerous paintings hanging on the walls. Her gaze suddenly stopped when she found the one Galanga had been painting in his memory. She quietly got up and walked over to examine it more closely. As her eyes wandered across the canvas, she couldn't help but find a new appreciation for what she saw. It was obvious that the figure in the painting was small, like a baby or toddler. She could make out several layers of halos of flowing energy around it; she knew this because they were similar to the auras in Galanga's vision.

She ran her fingers softly over the elevated paint where there was a complex network of lines that tied into her aura. These things hadn't been shown to her in Galanga's vision. She wondered if he had withheld them or if she simply hadn't been able to see them. What stood out to her were strands of red, indigo, and pink, similar to those of the Xi Blade. They looked slightly out of place to her. Several vortexes ran throughout the aura, intertwining with them. She wondered if this was the curse.

After looking at the painting for several minutes, Gwyn walked back to the couch and sat down across from a sleeping Jack. She did some meditation in the silence, but it didn't last long because Jack said her name.

"Gwyn?"

Gwyn gasped and shook out of her tranquil state. "You scared me. I was meditating."

Jack chuckled, then sat up with a yawn. "So jumpy. What happened last night with you and the old guy?"

Before Gwyn could explain, Chele walked into the room, rubbing her eyes. She grabbed a blanket and cuddled up next to Gwyn. "Merry Christmas," she said softly.

"Oh... crap. I totally forgot!" Jack confessed.

"Sorry, guys. It's my fault we're not back at Franz and Delilah's, opening gifts."

Chele patted Gwyn on the back. "Don't worry, Gwyn. You haven't done anything wrong."

Gwyn explained the previous night's events to Jack and Chele, sharing every detail she could remember about Galanga's memory.

"Hmm. Sounds like Jade has it out for you," Jack said.

"That doesn't make sense, though. She saved her life," Chele reminded them.

"Yeah... She did save my life," Gwyn said in whispered frustration. "But why?"

Jack scratched his head. "Did she want something?"

"Well, actually, she asked if I had the sheath. And she backed away from me when she saw the dagger."

Chele pulled the blanket up higher on herself. "Sounds to me like she might be scared of that blade, and I don't blame her. It buzzed the heck outta Jack when he touched it! Maybe if you didn't have it, she would've done something."

Gwyn shrugged. "No telling now."

She set her chin on her knees for a moment, staring off to the side of the room, before remembering a name. "Nok... She mentioned someone returning named Nok..."

Jack and Chele looked at each other, confused. "We've never heard that name," Jack confessed.

They heard a door creak open from the back rooms, and a few moments later, a yawning Galanga and Jasmine came in. "Good morning, everyone.

I suppose it would be presumptuous of me to think you guys would want a nice breakfast for Christmas, wouldn't it?"

The spirit of the room lifted at the thought as Galanga and Chele whipped up bacon, eggs, croissants, fruits, and even a Christmas tea.

As they ate, Galanga asked them all to sit and talk with him in the living room.

Gwyn savored the Christmas tea as he spoke. "I must tell you, attempting to rescue the princess is not only not your job, but it is also incredibly dangerous. It's not something I could dare advise any of you to do, especially without help."

"Well, then help us!" Jack said with a mouthful of croissant.

Galanga sighed, as if he knew he'd never get anywhere with his lecture. "I'll do my best... Jack, Chele, if my guess is worth much, I'd say you two are probably far above where you thought you'd be in magic, no?"

Chele looked at Jack, then back to Galanga. "Well, yes, actually. Nowhere near Gwyn, but how did you know that?"

Galanga smiled and took a deep breath. "Simple, really. Gwyn is an incredibly powerful magician. She can perform magic most wizards could only dream of, and yet she's not even a year into her craft."

"Yeah... but that's Gwyn. How does that affect us?" Jack asked.

"Well, I'm sure you've noticed, young sir, that people always follow those who are powerful and great, hoping some of that greatness will rub off on them." Galanga cracked his knuckles and sat back. "It so happens there's a reason for that. Energy can actually learn traits from the auras interacting with each other, especially those you hang around the most. In other words, being around Gwyn has helped you to come to where you are."

Jack's face was in awe. "How... how do you know all of this?"

"I can see the evidence in your auras. Her fingerprints, so to speak, are on both of you."

Chele and Jack stared in great interest, listening to Galanga.

"Always be careful about who you hang around the most. You don't want your energy being drawn down by the wrong influence. Of course, at times, we have no choice. There are so many negative people out there. The hardest thing to do is to blend in without becoming one of them."

Gwyn felt a bit proud for a moment but then refocused. "Is that all you wanted to tell us?"

"No, Gwyn. I wanted to tell you not to go. It's a fool's mission, and I can't imagine how you could pull it off."

Gwyn sat up straight and shot Galanga a disgusted look. "It's not a matter of negotiation. I've given my word. I'm doing this."

Galanga looked Gwyn straight in the eyes for a moment, then nodded. "Well… then I'm certain there's a bit more to the story behind your wrists you might not be telling me," he said, then sat up straight and looked a tad less friendly. "Though surely there was good reason behind it."

Gwyn fidgeted with a piece of the blanket Chele was using for a moment and bit her lower lip, trying to decide what to tell Galanga. She had a feeling he could see if she was lying in her aura, so she decided on the truth. "Well…" she started, "we stumbled onto the goblin village by accident. When we arrived, there were these people in spiky steel suits of armor."

Galanga nodded as Gwyn carefully wove her sentences together.

"This dark figure was on a large horse and rode into the battle. His name was Zarep, and then everything went dark, and a thin, hooded person in dark robes appeared next to him."

"Oooh?" Galanga said with interest. "What was their name?"

"Well… I don't know. I didn't hear it… But whoever it was felt powerful to me… Powerful and dark, similar to how it felt when my mother drew the Xi Blade in your vision."

Galanga's interest intensified as Gwyn spoke.

"Zarep ended up breaking into the goblin village and took the princess, leaving a few soldiers behind to harass the village. That's when I couldn't stop myself. I had to help. Jack didn't do anything because I told him not to… but I did…" Gwyn's stomach suddenly turned as she tried to confess to what she'd done.

As if Galanga knew, his eyes veered off to the side for a moment, and his face suddenly looked concerned.

Gwyn saw his concern and asked, "What's the matter?"

He continued to stare off for a moment, then looked at her. "Tell me, Gwyn, did you kill those men?"

Gwyn's heart saddened as she thought about it for a moment. She was almost certain she had. "I don't... I don't know." She then thought about the knight she'd hit in the back of the head—the crushing sound, the almost certain death. Was the dent deep enough to kill him? Even if it wasn't, hadn't the goblins immediately attacked and killed them as they fell?

"Gwyn, it is okay if you did. Those are not humans. They are not even from this world. They are evil creations not meant for this world."

"What are they, then?"

Galanga shook his head. "They are reanimated dead, running on some form of dark energy..."

"Afterward, I was captured by Patel's men and thrown into a cell. I tried to melt the cell window bars with those shackles on... I was trying to escape. Then Chili helped me with Jack, and we met with Jasmine and her mother, Rosemary."

Galanga nodded, sitting in cold silence. It was a good minute before he responded. "I see. Thank you all for bringing Jasmine to me. She has prepared something for you." Reaching into his robes, Galanga pulled out a small sack with a drawstring. "Inside this is a potion Jasmine made for you. If you make it to Princess Lily, she'll likely have anathema—a poison made to rot her mind and spirit but leave her alive."

"What?" Chele asked. "That's sick! How is that even possible?"

Galanga shook his head. "It's a form of necromancy. He's been doing it to people in the city for some time, growing an army of mindless creatures—although he wants the princess for a more terrible purpose."

"Mr. Galanga," Gwyn said softly, ready to change the topic, "who was Jade talking about in your vision."

Galanga's face gave way to disappointment. "I have no idea. That was the first and only time I had heard that name."

"Uncle!" Jasmine said excitedly. "Check the books!"

Galanga looked at Jasmine with confusion for a moment, then a look of interest crossed his face. "Now there's an idea!"

Galanga stood up and went over to a finely crafted wooden desk that looked to be hand-carved and stained to perfectly match the area it was in.

Galanga fiddled with an area near a top corner of the desk, and a hidden shelf rolled open from the lower part of the desk.

"A hidden library?" Jack asked, fascinated with the craftsmanship.

Galanga chuckled. "Just a shelf. But I'd appreciate it if you didn't tell anyone." Galanga grabbed one of the tomes sitting on the hidden shelf and laid it on the coffee table in the center of the living room. It had a unique, handwoven embroidery on the spine of the book in the shape of a circle with spokes coming out of it.

"What design is that? I remember it from somewhere," Jack asked.

"'Tis the Auric's symbol. This is one of the few remaining books from Les Cavernes des Anciens," Galanga said, a bit of sadness flashing across his face.

"The what?" Jack muttered in confusion.

"We called it the Hall of the Ancients. Before it was destroyed, it was the most renowned place for ancient history," Galanga said, clearly saddened by the memory. "This tome here is from that library and is believed to be one of the most ancient, written by Eos the Great himself."

"Maybe it was on that crazy lady's robes. I think she had that symbol on them," Jack said to himself.

Gwyn and Chele chuckled lightly to themselves. "No wonder you remember it," Chele mumbled.

Galanga opened the tome. Gwyn was surprised to see the letters looked much different from normal ones, but many still resembled the ones she knew.

They slowly flipped through the book, Gwyn finding it difficult to read. They were surprised when Jasmine placed her finger on a page and pointed to a word. "This one?" she asked.

Three faded symbols were written near where she pointed.

"H... circle with a spear in it... and maybe a K?" Jack said, reading the letters.

"It says Nok," Galanga said firmly, his eyes staring at the page. "N, O, K—it's just written in ancient symbols, not letters," he explained, rubbing his chin. "I've never noticed it before; it's so faded."

They looked at each other for a moment, unsure of what to think and surprised that Jasmine's ability allowed her to sense the name out of the ancient tome.

"It's the next words I'm unsure of," Galanga admitted, lifting the tome to his face to see more closely. "They're even more faded, but I believe it's something related to lightning, or maybe fire."

"What's that section of the book about?" Gwyn asked.

Galanga looked up at Gwyn with a bit of an anxious look on his goblin face. "Demons..." he confessed, almost as if he didn't want to. "Otherworldly things."

Gwyn felt an uncomfortable twinge in her stomach when Galanga said it.

Galanga suddenly sat straight up and set the tome down on the coffee table. "Hold on," he said as he got up and ran to the kitchen. He moved so fast it was surprising.

"What's going on?" Gwyn asked in concern.

"We've got company. They're searching the city for you—I'm sure of it. I can sense them." Galanga pulled a scope down from the ceiling that was attached through a pipe and looked through it. "They aren't at the mound yet, but they may invade if they followed your tracks in some way."

Gwyn jumped to her feet. "Chele, Jack, get ready. We might need to fight."

"No, no, no," Galanga told them. "They'll have an army out for you if Zarep caught wind of what you did to his men."

Gwyn looked around, gathering her things together quickly. "What do we do, then?"

Galanga shut the eyepieces on the scope and pushed it back into the ceiling. "There's a secret way out. I'll show you." He then stopped suddenly while running from the kitchen to the living room. "Oh my..."

Gwyn looked at him with concern. "What now?"

Galanga looked at Gwyn, a bit saddened. "They've found the horses."

"Oh no! Not Guts!" Jack yelled.

Galanga tilted his head slightly, giving a quizzical look. "Guts?" he asked sincerely.

Chele shook her head as Jack explained that it was the horse's name.

Galanga's face shifted to acceptance as he nodded. "Hmph. Guts! I kind of like it."

As they headed out the door, Galanga grabbed Gwyn by the shoulder and whispered to her, "Your friends admire you a lot. They think of you as a leader."

"I'm lucky to have them," Gwyn replied.

"Indeed. It is impressive to see how much your power has rubbed off on them. It is truly a powerful relationship."

Gwyn smiled as they prepared to leave.

The group followed Galanga, who was carrying Jasmine, out to the elevator. Gwyn grabbed her bow and followed behind Jack and Chele. Galanga pulled the handle, and they felt their stomachs drop as they descended what must have been several stories underground.

Galanga stepped out onto a ledge made of stone, leading from the elevator into a carved tunnel in the wall. The tunnel was taller than the others, and Gwyn found that she could comfortably stand up while walking.

"I must advise you to leave the Northern Kingdoms as soon as you can. If Zarep finds you, there's no telling what he'll do. He's as cruel as they come!" Galanga yelled while running through the tunnel. They all felt a little faster, as if he had shared his aura with them.

The tunnel appeared to be hand-carved and dimly lit with a running line of Xi energy on the sides, glowing a deep blue.

"How'd you get the deep blue rope of light out of the Xi energy?" Jack asked, trying not to lose his breath.

"Oh, you like that?" Galanga asked excitedly. "That's a relatively new addition I added myself. I was one of the first Xi Symbologists."

They ran for what must have been at least a mile, with Galanga carrying Jasmine, until they stopped at a fork in the tunnel. "Here," Galanga said, pointing them toward a pitch-black shaft. "It leads out to the northeast side of the city. It's not a great place, but Zarep will be expecting to search my quarters, and I must go back and distract him, or I'm sure he will suspect an escape and find us."

Gwyn looked down into the darkness, then back at Galanga. "Where are we supposed to go?"

"There are some underground caverns and cave-housing where you'll come out. Stay there, and I'll come get you when the coast is clear. And please, keep Jasmine with you. She'll be safer with you."

Galanga turned to leave when something occurred to him. "Gwyn, I think it just came to me! Remind me to tell you about the Azerael."

Chele gasped loudly as Gwyn nodded to Galanga. He then turned and took off, much faster than he had been running before, disappearing into the glowing blue distance.

"Gwyn," Chele said, "my grandmother used to talk about the Azerael."

Gwyn, still breathing heavily, looked into Chele's concerned blue eyes. "Any good news?"

Chele shook her head. "It's been so long. It was more the way she talked about it. It always felt strange and dark. I think the name stuck with me because it scared me as a kid."

Gwyn nodded at Chele as the four of them stood for a moment, catching their breath.

"Do we have to keep going?" Jack asked.

Gwyn nodded. "It'd be a nice time to be able to cast a flit of light."

Chele tried, and although she could almost produce a flit, the ribbon faded shortly after it was cast, costing her a lot of energy and providing little light. "Sorry, guys."

They stood at the entrance to the black tunnel for a moment, too proud to admit their fear of it. Then Gwyn picked up Jasmine and took the first step into the shadows. After three steps, Chele and Jack could not see them. "Come on, I'll lead. Chele, take my cloak. Jack, hold her jacket. No one let go."

They slowly made their way through the darkness, occasionally tripping as stairs carved into the stone seemed to come out of nowhere, often winding down, up, or curving slightly one way or the other.

After what seemed like an hour, they saw a faint light ahead. As they got closer, they saw that the tunnel split and went around a large pillar. Light gleamed down through deep, small cracks in the ceiling.

"Gwyn, this looks like that place in the burrows," Chele said. "You know, the entrance to the Shadow Guild?"

"You're right. Maybe it's a guild entrance. But how do we get in?"

Jack knocked on the large, round pillar. “Bet there’s an incantation.”

They tried several things in an attempt to find a secret opening but gave up and went around the large pillar and through the dark tunnel on the other side. It wasn’t long after that they saw more light.

They turned a corner, and bright light from outside crept through, forcing them to squint their now-sensitive eyes.

The path circled, and there was a large opening where light came through in the ceiling high above. Stone pillars had been carved into the walls around the open, circular area.

Jack dragged his shoe across the dusty stone floor, which was cut to resemble tiles, before noting how the place felt very old.

Beams of sunlight shimmered off pottery sitting in carved windows and shelves throughout the stone walls, as well as old, dusty cave paintings of strange creatures and symbols—things that caught their attention as they crept by.

Gwyn pointed at a particularly intriguing painting that appeared to depict a group of robed people moving the Xi Moon with magic.

“I wonder if an old tribe lived here a long time ago,” Chele pondered, staring at a long leather tapestry.

“No doubt. It feels ancient,” Gwyn said, her voice echoing slightly.

“It’s the music people!” Jasmine said in excitement.

“Huh? What do you mean?” Gwyn replied.

“It’s the music people. Can’t you see?”

A few cobwebs shimmered from Gwyn’s hair as she shook her head.

“Listen!” Jasmine demanded excitedly. Then, in the cute voice of a child singing, she sang, “Haaaa raaaay!” As she sang, her voice echoed back to her off the walls in a strange, dazzling way.

“Oorrrh may vuuuu!” she followed her first line with, as they all stood listening to Jasmine’s captivating song bounce around the stone walls of the cavern.

Gwyn repeated Jasmine’s notes once, timing the lyrics to match her. The echoes of them both returned in a hauntingly beautiful, cathedral-like fashion.

“That gave me chills,” Chele confessed.

Jasmine and Gwyn smiled at each other, then continued to walk, finding several small rooms that had been carved into the walls, some with dusty furniture.

After exploring for a bit, they decided to leave the caverns through a winding staircase that went up around the circular room. The outside appeared to be mostly sandy flats with patches of grass.

Gwyn stood in the wind and looked outside to what she believed to be the west, where she could see the long stretches of Sterlington filling the horizon not far in the distance.

"Should we wait for Galanga?" Jack asked.

"Of course we're waiting for him," Gwyn told him.

"What if he doesn't come?" Chele asked.

Gwyn set Jasmine down, then looked down for a moment. She thought about how long it had been since they had departed from Galanga. "It is strange how long it's taken him to come back, considering how fast he ran on his own."

"And how long it took us to get through that dark tunnel," Jack noted.

Gwyn nodded. "Okay, we'll meditate. Give him fair time to smooth things over. No telling what kind of story he'll have to give for having the horses near his place."

"And the dishes for visitors," Chele noted.

And with that, they did their best to meditate.

CHAPTER 25

The Plan

An hour passed as they traced the now familiar steps of gathering qi and meditation. Gwyn explained the odd things she'd seen again with Chele and Jack in Galanga's memories, this time with Jasmine listening. They discussed the likelihood that Jade was involved with her parents' deaths, but Jasmine kept saying "Might not" at each guess.

Jack still defended the fact that Jade saved Gwyn's life, but Chele and Gwyn felt it was more for the sheath than for Gwyn's sake.

"Leave it to Jack to take the side of a beautiful woman," Chele said.

Jack glared at her for a moment, then admitted she had a point.

"Gwyn?" Chele asked. "Can you really shoot Xeo arrows anytime you want to now?"

Gwyn thought about it for a moment, then drew her bow and shot an arrow into a pot. The arrow lit up with silvery, swirling magic. When she released it and it hit the pot, shards of broken pottery and ice shattered across the floor.

"Wow!" Chele exclaimed. "How is it you can do that now?"

"Ever since I've had the Xi Blade, my energy feels like it's stronger, and I have more of it, kind of like it's always charging... It's like when the Xi Moon is out, but even more than that."

Chele put her fist under her chin for a minute and thought. "What if you don't have the Xi Blade then? Can you shoot a Xeo arrow without it?"

Gwyn took the Xi Blade off and handed it to Chele. Chele screamed and dropped it on the floor. "Ouch, Gwyn! That thing's dangerous!" she said, her eyes wide.

"What?" Gwyn replied anxiously.

"Jack was right! Your dagger shocked me!" Chele told her.

Gwyn looked at the Xi Blade in wonder for a moment. She pictured the auras that were swirling around it when her mother wielded it. She sensed a connection with it and wondered why it allowed her to wield it, but not others.

"Sorry," she said, then refocused, turned, and drew an arrow back. At first, it glowed bright with silvery magic, but she felt the strong boost the blade was giving her fade quickly as it drained her, almost painfully fast. After holding the arrow drawn for only a few seconds, the silvery magic faded from the arrow.

"That settles it," Gwyn let out. "It is the Xi Blade."

"Well, it makes some sense when you think about it," Chele said, sitting on a pot she'd flipped over. "You synergized perfectly with the Xi crystals and under the Xi Moon."

"Right... I've always been fond of it... I used to climb trees and stare at it in the wee hours of the night as a child," Gwyn confessed, suddenly thinking of the giant owl. She had rarely thought of him, but in that moment, she remembered—or was it a dream? She could see his giant eyes staring deep into her soul. She thought of what he told her, how he knew she had magic in her eyes. Gwyn smiled at the thought. It surely was a dream.

As time passed, they felt their hope of Galanga returning dwindling.

"Maybe he gave up on us," Jack said.

Gwyn shrugged, staring at the ground. "Or... maybe they killed him too."

"Well... that's not dark!" Jack sarcastically protested.

"Sorry. I'm trying to cope with the possibility. I can't think of how he could have persuaded them to believe he didn't help us, considering they found the horses we had from the goblin village. The more I think about it, the less I think we should expect him to come."

Chele frowned slightly. "Gwyn, don't talk like that! We've got to stay positive!"

Gwyn stared at a dusty vase for a moment, considering Chele's words, then lifted her head and nodded. "You're right, Chele. Sorry about that. But we're going to have to move on our own."

Still, they waited for nearly another hour before walking outside into the sun. They occasionally covered their footprints behind them this time in the thin layers of snow and sand. The wind was blowing heavily, which also helped to cover their tracks.

They could see Sterlington to the west. As they went to the southeast of the city, they found a stone path and followed it. Not far from the city, they found an abandoned house in a small patch of trees and went in. Inside were dishes, a few jars of water, knives, a cabinet of various ingredients, and a bow with several arrows.

"Are the arrows still good, Gwyn?" Jack asked.

Gwyn tested their flexibility and sharpness. "They seem to be. Take the bow, Jack. We'll split the arrows, I'm running low."

Gwyn found a vial in a cabinet with some oils. Jasmine taught her how to make a poison for the wolves. She crushed the papaya seeds into a paste and mixed it with mugwort and a few other oils, then filled the vial. "Just in case," Jasmine told her.

"Gwyn, we need to discuss signals. In case we get separated or need to communicate without talking," Chele told her.

Gwyn nodded. "Okay, but first, this can be our meeting point if we get split up. We only have about an hour before dark, so let's work this out." She then went over a few basic gestures to signal each other.

"Jasmine, can you fight?" Gwyn asked her.

Jasmine looked at Gwyn with fear in her eyes. "I... I can try, Lost!"

Gwyn gave her a half smile and nodded. "That's all I could ask of you. Though, if we do have trouble, it'll be best if you hide."

"Where are we entering the city then, Gwyn?" Jack asked.

Gwyn pulled the map out and pointed toward a mid-eastern entrance.

"No, Lost! Not there! Here!" Jasmine told her, pointing toward the collapsed tower in the southeast.

Gwyn thought about it for a moment, then nodded. "Okay, then we'll go in there. It's not much further."

The sun had settled early into the Christmas sky, and the moon hadn't quite risen high enough to give them away yet, giving them a stealthy advantage to enter the city.

"Remember, we're just trying to get Princess Lily out. I don't think we have enough to fight Zarep's army. So let's keep it stealthy."

The walls of the city were very tall, much like on the western side, but severely damaged in several places. Gwyn made it through the initial wall and hunched down. The city loomed silent, its ruins casting jagged shadows in the fading light

Gwyn navigated around more rubble and found a staircase that went up to the high point of the walls. Once she saw the coast was clear, she waved the rest of the group to come up to her position.

The path wound around a small, damaged watchtower that went high into the night's sky. They all climbed a winding staircase that went up to the top of it to find that it peered down over the rubble of the collapsed tower. The area of the tower was large and round. Some walls of the tower were still standing tall, though most of it had become large stone piles of boulders.

One tall tower sat in the center of the rubble, connecting to nearby buildings left standing.

"That's it!" Gwyn said. "He's built a base camp in that tower."

"Looks like he might be using buildings in the area," Jack noted.

"Look over there. What is that?" Chele asked, while pointing at two tall gray stones with faint glowing indigo circles near the pathway to the tower.

"Binding stones," Jack said. "Professor Warren told me about those. If you get close to them, they'll pull you into them, and you won't be able to move. They work by binding anything within the living frequency to their energy field."

Gwyn chuckled, glad to have Jack with her in that moment.

"It's just a byproduct from the high ionic waves output from a fusion process. It's hard to get started, and Warren said they're usually used for insect traps," Jack explained. "These are massive."

Gwyn raised her eyebrow and looked at Jack for a moment. "Okay, Professor Warren... Can you turn it off?"

Jack nodded. "Yes, but I'll have to find the source of energy."

"Okay then, it looks like we can slip in from the south once you turn it off."

"Look!" Chele said, pointing at a pair of giant wolves in spiked armor.

"I bet they're guarding the power source," Jack said. "I would imagine it runs through to somewhere back there."

"Ugh!" Gwyn replied. "I hate those things!"

Gwyn reached into her robe and pulled the vial of poisoned pawpaw seed juice out. "Jack, do you have any jerky?"

Jack sighed. "I wish."

Gwyn returned the sigh. "Okay then, you're going to have to do this the hard way then."

Jack gave her an anxious look, waiting for the order. "Uh... O... Okay?"

She handed him the vial. "You're going to have to find their food and put this in it after you turn off the binding stones."

Jack's face went pale as he swallowed hard. "Okay... I'm on it."

As he left the overlook to attempt his task, Gwyn looked over at Jasmine, who was sitting patiently on her knees. "You need to stay here and point out where bad guys are for me, okay?"

Jasmine looked at her and nodded with a smile.

"Once I'm inside, head back to the old house, okay? Do you remember the way?"

Jasmine nodded again, this time with a sad look on her face.

"Don't give me that look. It's going to be alright," Gwyn said as the wind whipped her hair around her face.

Jasmine didn't reply but again gave the same nod.

Gwyn stood, slow to break eye contact with Jasmine, and looked at Chele. "Ready? As soon as the binding stones are off and those wolves are down, we have to get in and find the princess."

Chele gave a half smile and nodded at Gwyn. "You lead—I'll follow."

"Chele," Gwyn paused suddenly, "If I give you a three-fingered wave like this, come back and get Jasmine."

Chele nodded as she and Gwyn ran down the twisting stairs of the damaged watchtower. Gwyn's cloak billowed through the air behind her. As she ran, she felt an electrified excitement brewing within her.

She quickly scaled the walls nearby leading into the camp. Dusk was setting in as Chele and Gwyn snuck toward the building sitting on top of the rubble.

The hill on which the building sat was much higher than it had looked from the overlook. Gwyn and Chele looked around until they found a rough stone stairway carved up the stone wall. They carefully ascended it and made it to a level where they could see the binding stones shortly ahead.

Past the binding stones was a stone ramp that went up a few more tiers and then on to what appeared to be the entrance to the tower. Outside the tower, surrounding the area, were several old stone buildings.

"The binding stones—it looks like Jack got them shut off," Gwyn pointed out. Darkness now where the stones were.

"We could be seen here," a concerned Chele pointed out.

Around the binding stones sat large boulders, likely rubble from the destruction. They moved closer and used the large boulders as shelter to hide behind while plotting their next move.

Gwyn looked up at the stone overlook to barely see Jasmine in the shadows to their south. She was signaling up toward their north past the binding stones, raising one finger.

Gwyn pressed a finger to her lips, indicating silence to Chele, then removed Apollo from her shoulder, and slowly drew an arrow from her quiver. She hid comfortably behind the boulder, waiting for a guard to patrol by.

She was careful not to pull the arrow back so that it wouldn't shine brightly. She felt her heart beat increasing, knowing that an untold number of guards might hear the shot and run to the sound.

The guard finally appeared around the corner, and Gwyn sent a Xeo arrow into his armor. The arrow pierced it, causing the guard to become encased in ice as he fell to the ground. The wind was howling through the area, covering the loud clash as the armored guard slammed into the ground. Gwyn and Chele quickly ran up to him and both pulled as hard as they could to drag him behind a large boulder to conceal his body from others.

"Thank God for the wind tonight, Gwyn! That would have been too loud!" Chele said, thinking out loud.

"Someone still may have heard it," Gwyn told her as she looked to Jasmine to see her pointing again. This time, she was signaling that a pair of guards were coming.

"Crap. I hope this isn't the wolves Jack was supposed to take care of," Gwyn said as they ducked and ran behind the binding stones.

Gwyn peeked her head around the corner of the binding stone, but the patrol had already started their way toward them and were moving quickly. She signaled to Chele to let her know that they were going to have to fight. "I'll take the left one," Gwyn whispered.

She nocked another arrow, and Chele pulled her roped knife from her boot.

The guards rounded the corner, one receiving a knife in the chest with an immediate yellow flash of electric plasma that ran through the rope from Chele's hand. Gwyn also released her arrow at the same time, and it struck and froze the guard on the left. Both fell at the same time, one to his knees and the other backward.

This fall was louder as the clashes overtook the sound of the wind. They ran up to the fallen soldiers and began dragging the guards one at a time behind the large boulders. "Killer shot, Chele! Are you doing okay?"

Chele's face turned red as she examined her slightly scorched rope. "I didn't want to... But Galanga said it was okay. They're not human... Right?"

Gwyn knew inside that she didn't want to kill anyone either, but mustered up the courage to nod and smile at Chele, hoping Galanga was right. She then peered up at Jasmine to find her giving the okay sign.

As they reached the top tier, Jack appeared next to them.

"It's done!" he said, proudly and out of breath.

"Goodness, Jack! Okay... good job!" Gwyn told him, surprised to see him.

"I think we can use a hole the wolves were digging to get inside. It's better than the front. Far fewer guards."

They followed Jack around the tall building made of wood and stone. The wolves were still in the cage in the back but looked to be sleeping or dead.

"We got lucky. They were feeding them as I got here. I poured the poison right into their food. I stayed and watched as they seemed to fall over. I… I think it killed them," Jack said with sadness in his voice.

Nervous to get close, Gwyn slowly crept over to the edge of the thick wooden fence and made clicking noises near the wolf, arrow readied on Apollo just in case. She poked them. Seeing the wolves were unresponsive, she waved Chele and Jack over and saw a steeply sloping hill to the west of the tower.

"If we need a different way down, this could be a quicker one. I'm pretty sure we can slide down this without getting hurt."

"Good idea, Gwyn," Chele said. "It might be a longer way back to the house, but I bet it loops back around if you go west first, then south."

Gwyn agreed and recommended it as a quicker way to escape if needed. "Of course, one of us will need to get Jasmine up in the overlook."

Gwyn then led them to the hole that Jack had mentioned near the wall. The hole was just big enough for them to slide into one at a time under the wall, so one-by-one, they did.

CHAPTER 26

The Tower

wyn moved some stones and had to forcefully push aside a large block to squeeze through. Jack and Chele followed closely behind her.

As Gwyn stood up, steam billowed in the air around her. The smell was acrid and stale, like rust and mildew. She looked down and saw large metal grates in the floor nearby. She could also see some type of swirling liquid in a river far below, its odd pink and green glow suggesting it might be dangerous.

She softly cleared her throat and looked up. In the dim light before her towered a giant war machine. The device appeared to be a catapult, made of large cut logs fastened together with iron bolts.

"Whoa," Jack whispered, gawking at the technology as he stood. "This thing is crazy!"

"Mind the spikes," Gwyn said, referring to several sharp, pointed cones protruding from the device.

"What is that smell?" Chele whispered, covering her nose as she stood up last.

"It looks like a water source running below us," Gwyn said. She opened the map and found her location on it. "Yeah, look. There was a creek that ran through here next to my mother's tower. They built over it."

Jack leaned in close to study the map with Gwyn. "I bet they're using it as a power source."

"Or to poison the people in the city," Chele chimed in.

Gwyn nodded. "Right, either of those could be true. I know I wouldn't drink that water down there."

Occasional large plumes of steam burst from the vent in the floor. The steam burned, and the smell made breathing difficult, causing them to want to cough.

Gwyn covered her face and moved away from the vent. "We need to find the princess," she said as she snuck around the catapult to peer into the large hall that opened beyond the shaded area under the staircase overhang.

The room held smaller structures and crates, with lit braziers billowing plumes of smoke into the tower's heights. Gwyn ran to a storage crate and knelt beside it, certain she remained in the shadows. From this angle, she saw that most of the tower was an open hall, with the southern main entry staircase to her right. Staircases on each side of the main entry ascended along the walls, leading to small rooms high up in the tower.

Gwyn moved slightly further into the open hall and, to her amazement, spotted a giant Xi crystal suspended near the ceiling. Intricately wound chains and wires traced from it to the walls and various parts of the tower.

"I think we're under a staircase," Chele pointed out.

They looked up to see the ceiling tapering higher on one side, suggesting a staircase above them.

"Alright, we need to find the princess. I think she's in one of those rooms upstairs," Gwyn said as she moved forward for a better look.

A plume of steam shot up through another vent beneath her, making her cough slightly. She managed to do it quietly but was unhappy about it.

"Look down there," Chele said, pointing into the vent below them.

Gwyn saw a stone wall below with shackles and chains hanging from it. "She's underground," she said. "I bet she's in one of these vents."

They tried to lift the metal grate, but it wouldn't budge.

Gwyn went to melt it but realized it was iron. "Don't touch this metal. It's iron," she warned them. "We need to find another way down there."

They searched for another way down, carefully peering around the hall.

Suddenly, a large group of guards walked by, moving urgently toward the tower's entry.

"Maybe they found the soldiers we hid," Chele mentioned to Gwyn.

"Maybe... We need to get higher," Gwyn whispered.

Gwyn noticed a few chains running from a hoist and pulley in the middle of the room.

"The wooden door in the middle of the room floor. I bet that's it. That screams dungeon!" Gwyn said.

Jack looked around and spotted a crank up the stairs that seemed to operate the hoist. "Look, Gwyn. I think that's the crank to open it."

Gwyn nodded at Jack. "I think you're right. Do you think you can make it up there to crank it?"

"I'll head up there now," and with that, Jack turned and vanished into the Hollow.

Gwyn waited, giving him time to reach the crank, but he suddenly returned, breathing heavily. "Sorry, Gwyn. On my way up, I saw through the main entry and overheard some guards talking. They're headed toward Jasmine's overlook right now."

Gwyn's stomach sank.

"Jack, go! Use the Hollow to get Jasmine and get her back to safety."

Jack nodded and slipped back through the hole in the wall.

Gwyn bit her lip, worried about Jasmine.

"It's alright, Gwyn. Jack's got this," Chele reassured her.

Gwyn nodded and asked, "Can you make it to the crank?"

Chele peeked into the opening and saw no soldiers around. "Now?"

Gwyn hesitated for a moment, then decided. "Yes. Let's go. It might not be clear again if they find the soldiers outside."

Chele stood and raced up the stairs as fast as she could. Gwyn waited a moment, watching Chele ascend, and pulled Apollo out with an arrow gently nocked to protect her if needed. When Chele neared the crank, Gwyn stood and ran to the middle of the room where the wooden door lay in the floor. Sliding to a stop, she dropped Apollo by the door and looked up at Chele, giving her a go signal to open it.

Chele struggled to move the crank, but eventually, it began rolling the chain up as the wooden door slowly opened. The loud rattles of the hoist, pulley, and chains echoed throughout the large tower, louder than Gwyn had anticipated.

Gwyn looked around, expecting someone to investigate, but no one came.

She turned and knelt as a plume of steam burst up through the opening. The steam burned her eyes and face as she closed them tightly and rubbed them clean with her cloak before taking another look. Below, she saw Lily through the billowing steam, chained to a stone wall.

"Lily!" she called down to her.

Lily rolled her head but looked somewhat unconscious.

Gwyn knew jumping down would trap her, forcing her to find another way up. She examined the large wooden door and found a thick metal pin to lock it open. She lifted the heavy pin and slid it through iron rings on the door's side, then ran to the back where the chain connected to a metal ring.

She grabbed the Xi Blade and sliced into the chain. The cut marked the chain but didn't break it, so she struck again several times until the link snapped. She grabbed the chain and signaled Chele to crank it down. Gripping it, she jumped into the pit where Lily was, using the chain's tension to glide smoothly to the bottom.

Her feet touched down on damp, old gray cobbles between pools of water as more plumes of steam burst, threatening to burn her skin. She used her cloak to shield her face as much as possible. The water looked and smelled awful as it boiled randomly.

She approached Lily, who looked barely alive. Her clothes were tattered, her appearance suggesting torments Gwyn could only imagine.

Jasmine's potion, Gwyn suddenly remembered, recalling the poison Galanga and Jasmine had warned about. She pulled the drawbag from her cloak, removed the vial, and opened it. She lifted it to Lily's mouth, hoping the liquid would reach her throat.

The vial began to glow a bright gold in Gwyn's hand and grew very warm. Gwyn almost dropped it before resealing the vial and placing it back.

Lily's appearance became far more aware as she looked around. "Where... where am I?" she asked Gwyn. "Who are you?"

She glanced around before answering. "I'm Gwyn. You've been kidnapped by Zarep. Try to hold still while I break your chains."

Lily's expression turned terrified, as if she'd just realized she was in a nightmare.

Gwyn drew the Xi Blade and began slicing the chains woven through iron loops holding Lily. A sudden burst of steam under her foot shifted a cobble she stood on, causing her to slip while swinging, and she accidentally busted her knuckle on an iron loop, slicing it open.

Her mind slipped, and she saw herself drive the Xi Blade through a chain loop next to Lily, the blade sinking deep into the stone behind it. In a flash of sparks, the loop burst into pieces, leaving carbon trails on the surface. Gwyn pulled the Xi Blade free, her mind returning as the sound of the broken chain loop echoed in the distance.

Gwyn looked at Lily, who stared at her in terror.

"Who did you say you were, again?" Lily asked, as if she might recognize her.

Gwyn noticed blood pooling next to the water where her knuckle bled. It sizzled when it hit the strange liquid, swirling into bizarre black, red, and indigo colors.

Gwyn freed the chains from the cuffs on Lily's wrists and ankles. She took the princess by the hand, now free, and ran to the hanging chain she'd used to descend. She quickly wrapped it around both of them, looping the slack over itself several times. She gave the chain a whipping jerk to signal Chele, hoping she'd understand, then held it tight, praying Chele had the strength to crank them up.

After a moment, the chain began rising and tightened around Gwyn and Lily. Gwyn felt it dig into her hips as it lifted them. She endured the pain, trying to spare Lily by shifting her weight onto the loop.

Finally, Gwyn rose above ground and anchored her boot on it as soon as she could. She pulled them both onto the surface, unwrapped the chains, and picked up Apollo before waving to Chele to begin exiting.

Chele quickly ran down the stairs when a group of soldiers entered the hall.

Gwyn saw three soldiers charge up the stairs toward Chele. She drew an arrow and fired it into the wall behind them. The arrow struck, instantly covering the stairs with thick ice. The soldiers slipped and fell, one sliding off the stairway to the ground far below.

"Hurry!" Gwyn yelled after the loud clanging echoed through the room.

Gwyn watched as Chele threw her knife into one soldier, then boldly leaped over the iced stairs. She barely landed on a clear step, using the rope lodged in the soldier to balance, then jerked the knife back to her hand and continued down.

Lily screamed, and Gwyn looked up just in time to see a soldier in front of her. Her mind slipped instantly; she drew the Xi Blade and parried an attack from a battle axe. As he regained his balance, she sliced into the soldier's armor, knocking him back just as another soldier appeared behind her.

Gwyn barely dodged the flanking attack, letting his sword strike the stone floor beside her. She spun with the Xi Blade, slashing the soldier's metal chest plate. She alternated between them, maintaining the offensive. The battle came easily as she parried and countered their attacks swiftly.

She ended the fight with both soldiers lying side by side, their armor bearing brutal gashes. Her mind returned, and she noticed a stinging in her arm. A wet red spot had appeared through her sleeve near her bicep.

I got hit? she wondered. She realized a dart was sticking out of her arm. She looked up at the main entry and saw a soldier with a crossbow being electrified by Chele's knife and rope. Her rope burst into flames and exploded from the plasma's energy, so Chele performed a jump kick, knocking the soldier down before bending down and retrieving the knife.

Gwyn's vision blurred as she glanced up the stairs, seeing Chele had finished another soldier, who lay on the lower steps. She took a deep breath and pulled a barbed dart from her arm. It was small but left a large blood patch on her bicep and a bizarre, pulsing ache running through it.

"I remember now!" Princess Lily told Gwyn with concern. "That's what they did to me. They poked me with one of those darts."

Gwyn suddenly realized she was poisoned as she felt it creeping through her body.

"Hurry, Lily, over here," she said, moving her to the wall with a hole in it.

Chele soon joined them, turning to throw her knife at a soldier following her. Gwyn heard the soldier fall as Chele stopped beside them near the hole, looking exhausted and breathing heavily.

Gwyn found it difficult to think as she knelt and pulled the drawbag with Jasmine's vial, taking a sip with shaking hands. The vial glowed a bright gold again and grew hotter than before. It burned so badly that Gwyn laid it on the ground before knocking it back into the drawbag.

She felt instant relief, as the poison consuming her body began to fade. She still felt the wound in her arm, and her hands were still a bit shaky, but the creeping poison had stopped spreading.

"Go with Lily first. No matter what, get back to the house," Gwyn told Chele.

Lily moved slowly, so Chele helped her through the hole, then quickly crawled in behind her.

Gwyn knelt to crawl after them but felt a searing pain through her scalp as the hole in the wall seemed to fly away from her.

As she flew through the air, her mind slipped, and for a brief moment, she caught Zarep's dark eyes. He had grabbed her by the hair and slung her across the room, followed by throwing a javelin at her.

Gwyn arched her back and caught the ground with her hands, turning the attack into a backward somersault, gracefully kicking the javelin out of the air just before it hit her. She slid to a stop, fighting the momentum as she repositioned herself and drew Apollo with an arrow ready to fire at Zarep from across the room.

Zarep stared and smiled at Gwyn. Several soldiers entered the doorway, but he ordered them to go. "Go find Lily and check the siphon," he said to them, then turned back to Gwyn. "I've searched the entire world for you, just for you to turn up at my doorstep."

Gwyn's mind returned as she held the readied Xeo arrow, the glow lighting the room around her with silvery swirls of light.

"Go ahead. I'm sure you're pretty confident after hitting my lich."

Gwyn sensed Zarep was too fast to hit from that distance, so she waited. She saw him holding a small device and turning slightly to throw it into the hole after Chele and Lily.

Gwyn sent the arrow behind him before he could release it. The Xeo arrow struck just beside the hole, covering it in ice.

"Hmm. Clever girl..." Zarep noted, his deep voice hauntingly resonant in the tower. "Okay then, you enjoy my plasma bomb!" He threw the device into the middle of the room, where it flashed with a deep explosion, sending bright yellow bursts of plasma into the air.

Gwyn covered her face, but debris still hit her arms and legs, leaving small cuts where it struck.

Zarep approached her, drawing his sword from its sheath on his back. She saw his oddly colored, scarred skin for the first time, as if he were sick. His dark hair matched his black eyes.

Gwyn rolled and dodged his first attack, letting her mind slip as she dodged several more. Zarep's attacks were far faster than she was used to dodging, and she felt a slight fear beginning to creep in.

Zarep's sword was almost as long as she was, making it difficult to get close enough to attack.

A plume of steam billowed up around him, and Gwyn quickly fired an arrow into it. The steam surrounded his leg and side, partially freezing him in place when the arrow hit.

Gwyn reached for another arrow to fire at Zarep while he was stuck, but her mind slipped just before she released it. Zarep had thrown another plasma bomb, about to explode in front of her. She saw herself re-aim and release the Xeo arrow into the bomb, creating an ice barrier that barely blocked the explosion.

Gwyn felt the bomb's shock-waves rippling through her bones as it sent her violently through the air a dozen yards to the north. Sharp ice shards barraged her, cutting her as she flew, leaving trails of blood in her wake. She landed, rolled and slammed into the northern tower wall.

Gwyn's body ached, her good ear ringing as she lay for a moment in pain. She knew she had no time to rest and slowly pushed herself back up. It took tremendous effort to get to her feet. For a moment, she felt nauseous, but as she stood, a warm, wet liquid dribbled from her ear. It had been waterlogged since she awoke on the beach with Jack, and the explosion seemed to have released it. The instant relief boosted her confidence. She looked up and saw Zarep had almost chopped through the ice holding him, somehow out-pacing the arrow's magic, and was nearly ready to approach Gwyn again.

She lifted her aching arm and grabbed another arrow, her heart sinking as she realized it was her last. She considered firing at Zarep but knew he'd likely dodge it.

Gwyn then looked up at the ceiling and saw the giant Xi crystal. Something in her felt she should shoot it. She nocked her arrow, took aim, drew her positive and negative qi together to force as much energy as she could into it, and released her last arrow. The Xeo arrow flashed brightly as it soared through the air. A small plume of sparks flashed as it hit the Xi crystal and bounced straight up, exiting through the tower's smoke relief at the top.

Gwyn's disappointment showed on her tired face. Firing the arrow drained what little energy she had left, certain it was the most powerful Xeo arrow she'd ever shot. She looked down, letting a drop of sweat and blood fall from her face.

Zarep smiled, then laughed. "You fought well, but you're done, child," he said, as if knowing it was her last chance. "I'll have my soldiers collect you—I'll be getting my other princess back now." He then resheathed his sword and turned to leave.

Gwyn placed her hand on the Xi Blade's handle, her fingers aching, hoping it would restore enough energy to escape once Zarep left.

As Zarep walked away, the Xeo arrow suddenly soared back down into the tower and flew into a steam vent near the entrance. It struck the water below, triggering a violent explosion from beneath. The entire tower rattled as giant ice spikes shot up through the grates near Zarep, one piercing his leg. He let out a violent scream that merged with the rumbling echoing throughout the tower.

The giant Xi crystal broke loose and crashed into the center of the large tower room, shattering into pieces. Gwyn suddenly felt its energy and was rejuvenated slightly by its proximity. She tried to control her breathing and let the Xi Blade's energy fuel her. Focusing was difficult as the building continued to rumble and shake, threatening to collapse on her.

Zarep drew his sword and sliced through the ice spike in his leg. He yelled, "Wretched girl!" then leaned down, pulled it out, and turned back to Gwyn, throwing the shard at her. Keeping his sword drawn, he approached her in anger with a slight limp.

Gwyn had readied herself, expecting her mind to slip as she drew the Xi Blade in defense. As predicted, she slipped into a trance again and saw herself throw the blade. It flew straight, slicing through the ice shard and heading toward Zarep's head.

Zarep easily dodged the blade, paused to gloat with a chuckle, knowing she'd disarmed herself, and began approaching again. Gwyn looked at her hand, feeling a palpable bond with the Xi Blade. She pulled at it with a jolt, drawing it back to her. She felt its powerful auras intertwining with her own energy as never before, much like with her mother's.

The blade obeyed, soaring back like a spear into Zarep's shoulder.

Zarep roared as the blade electrified him. Gwyn was stunned to see him resist its power with such strength and took the opportunity to move around him to the east while he struggled. Stones and boulders fell around the room as the tower continued to shake.

A hole in the eastern wall opened from the tower's shaking, and Gwyn ran toward it. Fearing it would collapse, she turned to Zarep and held out her hand toward the Xi Blade. It took focus, but she managed to pull it back to her hand. She marveled at it for a moment, then sheathed it. She saw Zarep kneeling but staring at her from across the room. He stood back up, appearing ready to continue the battle.

Gwyn began to doubt she could beat Zarep, especially without arrows. She also feared the tower might collapse on her and decided to escape through the new hole in the east wall. Knowing Zarep would chase her, she looked down to see a steep hill of stones. She took a breath and leapt, moving quickly, and nimbly, sliding over mossy rubble down the steep hillside, reaching the bottom.

She looked up; the tower now leaned northeast, threatening to crush her. She glanced south, but rubble and the city wall forced her to run north. She ran as fast as she could, occasionally looking back as the tower fell toward her. She heard the rumbling grow closer as she neared the city gate, feeling dirt kick up from giant stones and boulders landing just feet from away. She ran well beyond the city before turning to look properly.

Her legs were burning and she was breathing heavily, surprised at how close some of the tower's stones had fallen, some even making it through the gate.

Gwyn thought Zarep must have been crushed by the tower and bent over to catch her breath, clutching a stitch in her side. She watched sweat and blood drip into the sand from her forehead, the Electric Moonlight glistening off it. She felt around her head, cuts stinging as her fingers grazed across them.

Her heart sank when she looked up and saw Zarep working his way through the rubble near the gate, moving more carefully than Gwyn but still approaching quickly.

Gwyn turned and ran as fast as she could toward the caverns to the north. She reached them and searched for the way back to the hidden tunnels but couldn't find them in the dark.

She heard Zarep saying something just outside the caverns, so she ran up the stairs and decided to hide in one of the upper recesses in the wall. She hoped he would give up, unwilling to search the dark caves, but he didn't.

Gwyn's lungs burned as she tried to steady her breathing. She bent over again, blood and sweat dripping from her head onto the ground. She had forgotten the ice shards had cut her and suddenly feared she was leaving a trail for Zarep to follow. She needed help but didn't know where to go.

The house where Jack and Chele were was southeast of the city, far from the caverns. Gwyn debated trying to run there but knew it was too far. If Zarep followed, she'd be doomed.

Suddenly, she heard his voice echoing through the caverns. "I know you're here... We can work things out, you know."

Gwyn tried desperately to slow her breathing but couldn't. Her heart wouldn't let her, so she climbed the stairs slowly to the rooftop. She lifted a hinged wooden door at the top and tried to close it quietly as she climbed outside.

A large circular opening in the roof, covered by an old leather tarp, allowed her to hear Zarep's echoing voice.

"This would be over if I didn't have my armies out looking for you," Zarep said.

Gwyn wondered where his armies were and feared for the innocent in her mother's kingdom.

"You know, I'm the one who took down your mother... She went crazy after I bombed her tower."

Gwyn suddenly remembered Jade saying something about one of Xess' troops going rogue. Could Zarep be working alone?

"It's only a matter of time before you go with her," Zarep's voice threatened in a deep, dark tone.

Then silence fell. Gwyn's breathing slowly returned to normal as she stared at the wooden door, praying he wouldn't burst through and trap her on the roof.

She looked over the edge and saw the drop was much higher than the ridge. There was no way down now but back through the door.

She waited, fearing the worst, but nothing happened as she stood between the large circular opening and the door. Gwyn began to feel every cut on her body remind her of her mortality as she struggled to hold the Xi Blade drawn in her tired hand. Still, she was ready to attack if Zarep came through.

Minutes passed, feeling like hours to Gwyn, with a haunting quiet filling the air. A slight breeze chilled her and sent her hair flowing. The silence made her believe he might have given up.

Still, Gwyn waited, her eyes burning from sweat despite the crisp, cool night air.

Then a loud click sounded, and Zarep burst through the wooden door onto the roof, wood exploding into pieces. As he burst through, he rushed toward Gwyn with his sword ready to strike.

Gwyn's tired mind slipped once more, and she leaned backward to avoid being sliced by an inch, but the ground behind her wasn't there as she fell into the hole. She quickly twisted in the air to try to catch the ledge. Zarep didn't realize the circular opening was in the roof, and his momentum sent him past Gwyn and through the tarp as he fell, his arms trapped in it, or he would have grabbed her.

She caught a stone in the wall by the tips of her fingers for a second, letting Zarep fall first, but her weakened, bloodied arm was too tired to hold on longer. She closed her eyes and felt her fingers fail, the silty stone slipping from her grasp as she began falling.

Her mind was still somewhat tranced as she watched the stone walls around her slowly fly by. She somehow had time to remember her friends and family: Franz and Delilah, her grandparents—oh, how I wish I'd written them one last time—Chele, Jasmine. She yearned to be with them. Then she thought of her mother's kingdom, doomed to Zarep's armies without her.

She closed her eyes tightly, preparing for the cold stone floor to take her, when something sharp grabbed her by the back of her shoulders and slowed her descent. She still fell, but much slower than before. She landed next to Zarep, somewhat softly and on her feet. Gwyn's mind returned as she looked around. She glanced up at the now-open hole in the ceiling, surprised at how high it was.

Zarep had landed face-down on the stone floor. Gwyn had a strong sense the fall had broken him.

She stood just out of his reach, watching his body squirm in anguish—the air around him smelled of rotten flesh. She looked around, searching for what had grabbed her. She knew something had saved her and wanted to know what it was, but she could barely see in the cavern.

"Ugh," Zarep moaned.

"Is there anything you want to say before you go?" Gwyn said softly.

Zarep tried to turn his head but couldn't. He groaned a bit more. "You can't undo it... She will come now..." his deep voice uttered.

Gwyn stepped around Zarep to hear his words better. "Who are you talking about?"

He groaned in pain before speaking. "The Azerael," he winced out.

"You mean Nok?" Gwyn asked.

"Cindara..." Zarep said, correcting her. "Nok Cindara."

Gwyn paused for a moment, the name sending chills down her spine. "Who do you work for? Do you work for Xess?"

Zarep tried to laugh, but it was more of a gurgle. "Xess... He'll come around. He didn't believe me before, but he'll know now..."

"Tell me about Nok. Who is she? Where is she coming from?"

"I needed stronger blood... The goblin didn't work... But your blood... was perfect." Zarep breathed heavily between words.

Gwyn's stomach turned, recalling how her blood had landed in the water, creating strange patterns and colors. "What did you do?"

Zarep took a while to answer this time. "You'll see," he whispered.

Gwyn stepped back a few feet, her heart telling her something terrible was set in motion.

Suddenly, she felt a firm grasp on her shoulders and felt herself ascending through the caverns toward the hole in the ceiling. She could see where the leather tarp was torn from their fall as she rose 20, 50, 100 feet above it.

She closed her burning eyes for a moment, as if accepting death, if this were it.

Suddenly, her feet softly touched the ground. She slowly lifted her tired eyes to find the giant owl perched majestically before her.

CHAPTER 27
A Guardian's Wings

The owl had brought her far up into the mountaintops and set her down on an isolated peak just big enough for her.

"You saved me!" Gwyn said in relief and with bold excitement. Her spirit instantly felt lighter.

The owl's giant eyes pierced Gwyn's under the Electric Moon as he let out a loud hoot. "I suppose I might have! But I certainly wasn't the only one to do that."

She pondered for a moment, her heart fluttering at the presence of the great owl, which made her feel like a child. As she pondered, she began to question what had happened and looked down. "But... why?"

The owl turned his head slightly before answering. "Just a few years ago, when I met you," he said between hoots, "I saw a magic I hadn't seen in a very long time. I saw greatness!"

Gwyn looked down, unsure of how she felt in that moment. "I... think I'm cursed," she told the owl.

"Oh, my dear, you mustn't believe such things!" the owl said, before letting out a loud purr of hooting.

"Am I not?" Gwyn asked, a slight relief in her voice at the thought.

"You were born with a gift! A great price was paid for it!"

"A great price?" Gwyn asked sincerely.

"Indeed! Just remember, it is how you use it that matters most!"

Gwyn took a moment to let the owl's wisdom sink in. Her mind battled between questions, still exhausted from battle.

"Mr. Owl, I think I've let something terrible happen... I believe my blood was used in a spell of some kind..."

"Yes, it was!" the owl hooted again. "And in due time, you will surely face a darkness."

She held up her hands in the moonlight; dirt and streaks of dried blood freshly stained them from her battle. "I couldn't even beat Zarep on my own. How will I beat someone stronger?"

He shook his feathers before answering. "Do not worry so much, my dear troubled child. There will surely be time before that season."

Gwyn felt relief hearing the owl's words.

The owl looked up to the moon for a moment, then back to Gwyn. She thought his appearance was slightly sad but wasn't sure.

Between hoots, he told her, "My dearest, listen closely," he leaned down slightly. "I've lent you my power because you choose to do good with yours. I've seen the speech you gave Sector 705. No one told you to do that. No one told you to fight for the Glade Goblins. No one told you to save the princess. You chose good on your own."

"...How?" Gwyn asked softly.

The owl then leaned toward Gwyn, his giant eyes feeling as if they saw through to the bottom of her soul. "I did not make this choice lightly, but I do believe you have the right heart to beat it."

Gwyn's heart began racing. "How long do I have?" she asked.

The owl tilted his head. "Could be months. Could be years. Maybe decades. Only one thing seems certain: it will come."

Gwyn thought to herself for a moment, then looked back up into the owl's eyes, her heart mustering a bit of confidence after hearing his kind words. "Thank you, for believing in me."

The owl then told Gwyn to turn around. He instructed her to take a long look across the amazing view of Sterlington and the northern lands. "My dearest, your path will not be an easy one, but try to remember, you're not alone."

In that moment, Gwyn forgot about her aches, the wind blowing her hair and cloak as she gazed at the glory of her mother's kingdom and the lands she ruled. She felt this was her place.

"When you're ready, step off the ledge," he told her. She looked down, unsure how far the fall was, hesitant to follow the order at first, but then spread her arms and did as the owl commanded.

As she stepped off, she heard the owl's faint voice in the wind tell her goodbye. She fell at tremendous speeds at first, winds whipping through her cloak and hair, then felt a sharp tugging from her shoulders that slowed her descent as she glided back toward the cavern entrance.

As her feet touched the ground, Gwyn said, "Thank you," to the owl, then looked up to find him already gone. She turned to walk back into the caverns, pondering whether she should check Zarep's body. When she got there, it was gone. Dark puddles shimmered in the low moonlight, which she could only assume were both her blood and Zarep's.

"Gwyn?" she heard from outside the caverns. She stepped outside to find Jack, Chele and Lily, and ran up to them. She went to hug them but saw Jack was carrying Jasmine.

Gwyn felt a sickening jolt run through her tired mind. "What happened?" she asked in concern.

"Gwyn, what happened to you?" a concerned Chele asked, referencing Gwyn's bloody and tattered appearance.

"I'm not worried about me. Please, Jack, tell me what's going on."

"I'm not sure," Jack admitted. "I got to the overlook just in time, literally seconds before the soldiers found her. But when we were almost to the house, she suddenly screamed and stopped responding to me. I don't know if it was from going into the Hollow or what..."

Gwyn looked at Jasmine and saw her struggling, rolling her head, and unresponsive. "No..." Gwyn whispered, fearful she was realizing what had actually happened.

She pulled the vial from her cloak and threw it on the ground in front of Lily. "What kind of potion is that?" she asked her.

Lily bent down and took it, opening it to smell it. "I'm not the best herbalist, but I think it's a grounding potion."

"It didn't cure the poison," Gwyn said. "It just grounded it to Jasmine instead."

"No... My poor Jazzy!" Lily said with sincere sadness.

Gwyn watched as Jasmine writhed in pain, remembering what it felt like to have it in her for just a few moments. She bent down, forcing Jack to lower Jasmine as she ran her hand over her feverish head. She whispered again, a tear rolling down her cheek as she remembered the glowing vial. "No..." she whispered to her. "Why did you do this?"

Gwyn stared at Jasmine, another tear rolling down her cheek.

"I remember you drinking the potion before we left..." Chele said. "You were poisoned?"

Gwyn looked up to Chele and nodded. "Yes... So was Lily..."

Lily gasped.

They all knelt silently for a moment, collecting their thoughts and hoping some obvious solution to help Jasmine would come.

"We have to find Galanga," Gwyn finally said, urging them back toward the caverns.

Gwyn found herself in no mood to talk, opting to carry Jasmine so Jack could use the Hollow to see where things were more clearly. It still took several minutes of looking for the passage back to where they had come from.

Chele busted a wooden rocking chair apart from the caverns and asked Gwyn to light the board so they had a torch. Gwyn lifted her hand and placed it on the board. She found it painfully difficult to focus but managed to channel enough energy to ignite it.

They traveled through the dark passageways, hoping to remember the way back to Galanga's. The pathway was different in the light. They managed to get through much of it quicker, not tripping on stairs or running into walls.

Gwyn spoke softly every once in a while to Jasmine, telling her it was okay. She had only known the small goblin child a few days but had grown fond of her, almost like a little sister.

They eventually found the tunnel with the blue Xi light. For a moment, Chele and Jack debated which way to go until Gwyn finally looked to the right and directed them to go that way.

Gwyn's mind felt numb. Seeing Jasmine in the poisoned state drained her of what little energy she had left. She wanted to say her body was hurting because she knew it did, but all she felt during the walk was heartache for Jasmine. Her brain had left the rest of her with a dull numbness.

After a walk that felt like hours to them, they saw something in the distance of the tunnel.

"Gwyn..." Chele said, removing her knife and rope.

"Wait," Gwyn said with a soft, dry throat.

Chele looked back down the tunnel, her knife ready in her throwing position.

"Wait a second, I think it's Galanga," Jack said.

"Gwyn!" Galanga yelled from a distance.

Gwyn's heart lightened slightly. As he arrived, she handed him Jasmine. She closed her burning eyes as the sounds around her slowly became muffled. She remembered Jack, Chele and Lily explaining everything, as well as the streak of blood on Galanga's cheek. But she didn't remember anything else beyond that because she fainted.

When Gwyn woke, she was lying in a makeshift bed, still somewhere in the tunnels.

"What happened?" she asked, her voice very weak.

"I think we're all wondering the same question," Galanga told her. "You passed out! Your aura looked like you ran it through a gem tumbler! I'm surprised you made it this far!"

Gwyn moved a bit; she could tell Galanga had done some healing but her body was still aching in various places. She then sat up and looked at Jack, who was leaning against the cave wall asleep, and Chele, who was lying down in another makeshift bed on the hard floor not far from Gwyn.

Gwyn briefly told Galanga about her battle with Zarep. "Since his body disappeared, I don't know if he lived," she said.

"Hmm," Galanga responded with a bit of excitement in his eyes. "A fall that far would kill any normal person... I imagine he's not doing well, if he lived."

Gwyn fell silent, battling a creeping soreness within her.

"How's Jasmine?" she eventually asked him.

He sadly nodded over toward where she was lying. Her condition looked the same to Gwyn, who watched her restlessly writhe around.

"Can you heal her?" Gwyn asked.

Galanga looked down before answering. "Anathema is not just a poison; it's forbidden necromancy," Galanga said. "It attacks in a way that outpaces my ability to heal it by myself, especially this much of it."

Gwyn sat for a minute, then pushed herself against the cave wall. She placed her face in her hand and let her mind process the events a bit.

"Gwyn, I'm sorry I didn't make it to the caverns."

Gwyn nodded. "It's okay," she whispered, not really feeling okay. "What happened?"

Galanga pointed to his face. "They raided my place. They held me—questioned me for hours... I almost had them gone when they saw the tome we left out."

Gwyn thought back to their Christmas morning breakfast. "What about it?" she asked, more concern in her voice.

"They saw the page, and Zarep himself came and looked at it. He ordered the book be burned immediately. They then took me outside and made me answer where I got it. I thought I was a goner!"

"What did they do to your face?" Gwyn asked, seeing Galanga had a streak of blood running across it.

"Zarep struck me. I think it was the handle of a javelin. When I woke up, I had an awful headache. Maybe they thought they'd killed me; I'm not sure, but I healed myself as well as I could and ran to see you as soon as I was back up."

Gwyn suddenly felt terrible hearing about what happened to Galanga. "I'm so sorry," she told him. "You might have saved the princess's life, holding Zarep off for so long."

Galanga looked over at Jasmine, a tear rolling down his cheek. "I wish I'd bound the potion to myself," he said softly.

"Why didn't you?" Gwyn asked coldly.

Galanga swallowed. "Originally, I did. I didn't even tell Jasmine what I was making, but she came up and told me it had to be bound to her."

Gwyn looked over at Jasmine, surprised to learn what Galanga had told her. "So... she knew?"

He nodded. "She did what she believed had to be done."

Gwyn couldn't hold back a tear from forming. "Will she live?"

Galanga was silent for too long but told Gwyn, "I hope so."

"Did she know?" she asked him.

Galanga's sad goblin eyes met Gwyn's. "I... was scared to ask."

Gwyn nodded and thought about it. "I think I would be, too."

A dull silence filled the cave for a while before Gwyn finally asked Galanga something else. "Do you believe I'm cursed?"

Galanga thought long and hard about Gwyn's question. "Gwyn, your aura has something strangely unique about it. Your mother had it, too," he confessed.

"Is it a curse?" Gwyn asked plainly.

Galanga seemed hesitant to answer. "I... I honestly don't know. It's not like anything I've ever seen. There's no Auric text, no cure, no explanation for it. I know that your mother didn't have it, and then she did... and then passed it onto you... which fits the descriptive definition of a possible curse."

Gwyn pondered about what the owl had told her about it. "Would you call it a curse?" she asked Galanga, pressing harder.

Galanga thought about Gwyn's question for a moment before answering. He then nodded to himself. "You know what, I owe you an answer to that. I owe the queen an answer, God rest her soul," he said in a prideful manner. "Now that I know you're alive, I will re-dedicate myself to finding an answer for you."

"Thank you," Gwyn told him.

"No, Miss Gwyn, thank you!"

Gwyn looked over at Jack, who had begun squirming a bit.

"For what?" she asked, sincerely, unsure of what she did.

"For bringing hope to the Northern Kingdoms!" Galanga told her, as if it were already obvious.

Gwyn looked up at Galanga, slightly confused. "I don't know if I've done much. I barely defeated Zarep... In fact, I'm not even sure I've done that."

Jack sat up slightly, smacking his lips and yawning. "Oh man. This stupid place. I was totally dreaming about pumpkin bread."

Chele sat up also, her eyes squinting and her hair a bit messy. "Did someone mention pumpkin bread?"

Gwyn wasn't ready to laugh, so she smiled and felt her spirit lighten at the banter.

They all packed up and walked back to Galanga's place in Clove.

Gwyn was surprised at how much the place had been disoriented. They'd taken pictures down, gone through the cabinets, and messed up random things everywhere.

They fixed up a bed and laid Jasmine down in it before they all helped clean Galanga's house with him, then he did another round of healing before he admitted he was too fizzled to do more.

They all ate a light meal and fell asleep out of exhaustion, Gwyn opting to stay in the same room as Jasmine. It didn't take long before she fell into a deep, but restless, sleep—only to be woken by a soft whisper.

Gwyn barely heard soft whispers that woke her from a deep sleep. They were so quiet that if the room weren't completely silent, she might have missed them.

"Lost?"

As she sat up, every muscle in her body reminded her of her battle with Zarep. She wondered how much worse she would feel if Galanga hadn't healed her. Still, she said nothing of it and fought the urge to express her pain as she looked down at Jasmine's tired, pale face.

"Yes?" she replied softly with a smile, surprised to find her voice so hoarse and dry.

"Where am I?" Jasmine asked with a weak, hoarse tone of her own.

"Clove," Gwyn replied, wondering what time of day it was, as there were no windows to look out of because the city was underground.

Jasmine lay in silence for a long moment, staring at the wall, before Gwyn finally spoke. "Jasmine?"

"Yes?"

"Do you remember what happened?" she asked cautiously.

Jasmine didn't reply but nodded her head very slightly.

Gwyn took a deep breath. "Why did you do it? Why did you give us that potion? I never would have done that to you."

Jasmine lay silent again for a long moment while Gwyn removed herb paper from her cloak. Gwyn tore off a tiny piece and offered it to her. Jasmine chewed the paper slowly as she waited.

"I know... That's why I didn't tell you."

Gwyn wasn't satisfied with the answer, knowing she had nearly taken the tiny goblin's life by using the potion.

"Since I was very young, I've seen things," Jasmine finally said, slowly and softly, her shallow voice allowing her to continue.

"Things... like visions?"

Jasmine nodded very slightly. "I saw... a girl..." she said, taking long breaks between sentences as Gwyn fed her pieces of herb paper.

"With a bow... and long black hair."

She listened intently to Jasmine's words, ignoring the aches throughout her body as she strained to stay composed for Jasmine.

"I saw you, Lost."

Gwyn smiled. "I had a feeling... The bow was a giveaway."

"No..." Jasmine replied, causing Gwyn to tilt her head in confusion.

"I saws you... you were lost."

"Oh."

"Could help the world... but you were lost... So, I always went to... to find you."

Patiently, she listened to Jasmine.

"I told my mom... I knew how to help... Hers didn't believe at first..." Jasmine said with a tone almost too innocent. "Hers didn't want to believe... Then came the Lost."

She looked at Jasmine, thinking about what she said. "You knew this would happen, didn't you?"

Jasmine nodded.

Gwyn nodded back gently. "Thank you, Jasmine," she said in a heartfelt manner, taking Jasmine's little hand in hers. "Please hang in there, you brave little spirit!"

She then heard the sounds of footsteps walking into the room from behind her. She wasn't sure who it was, but she didn't feel like paying attention to them—until they put a hand on her shoulder.

"Gwyn," Galanga said softly in a comforting tone. "Are you feeling alright?"

She lifted her head and nodded slightly. It was a lie, as she was still extremely sore, but she didn't want Jasmine to know the full scope of her pain.

Galanga handed Gwyn a mug with frothy dark liquid in it. "This will ease your muscles and center your shaken spirit. It is a draught, made from the finest herbs across this fine land."

She took the mug and drank from it—the warm liquid was riddled with refreshing flavors that hinted of mint, jasmine, and white chocolate. Galanga sat next to her, drinking from a mug of his own, occasionally spooning some to Jasmine.

Gwyn shook her head. "I don't understand why this had to happen to her."

"No. Most wouldn't. But it's because Jasmine is a seer, one far beyond her years. She's no fool; she did exactly what she believed had to happen."

"But how could you let her do that? It seems so wrong!" She replied, almost losing the whisper in her tone.

Galanga nodded slightly. "Being a seer is a strange and wonderful thing. It's as much a curse as it is a blessing. It's as important for them to see their prophecies play out as it is for you to take your next breath. If I had attempted to stop her, she would have known."

Something about Galanga's tone comforted Gwyn. She was starting to understand what he was saying and respected his experience and understanding of the magical world.

"Gwyn, listen. Jasmine sees more than pain for herself. She sees a greater good somewhere."

She looked at the white carpet where she had slept next to Jasmine's bed. She took another sip from the mug, the contents warming her spirit and easing her soreness.

"Was it guaranteed to happen this way?"

"Of course not. Nothing ever is. But the probabilities were there, and Jasmine's satisfied with the results," Galanga told her with authority. "It took tremendous bravery and courage from each one of you to accomplish what you did, even Jasmine."

The aches in her muscles had nearly subsided as she took another large sip—her spirit lifting as Galanga spoke.

"They're scared of you, Gwyn..."

Gwyn paused, letting the odd phrase sink in, then gave an inquisitive look. "Who?"

"Zarep and Azy-rael," Jasmine said.

"You know this?" she asked Jasmine.

"Hers mad... she knows about you," Jasmine said, her voice getting weaker. "Hers mad at Zarep 'cause hers believes that you're a Great Link, and he tried to... kill you."

"So Zarep lived..." Gwyn said softly.

"...Maybe nots," Jasmine replied.

Gwyn looked at the goblin child for a moment, pondering what happened. "She killed him?"

Jasmine didn't respond again but closed her eyes and fell asleep.

Galanga set his mug down on a table nearby. "That is enough, Gwyn."

The fear in Galanga's eyes sent a wave of fear through her. "What's wrong?"

Galanga became silent and performed some sort of healing on Jasmine's head for a minute before he answered. "When I first started attending classes at the Auric's Guild, the elders shared amazing stories about the ancient world—how several races and creatures shared the surface of the planet."

Gwyn listened and watched in silence.

"Our most ancient texts talk about dark times then. A magical creature so strong—so wicked—with a flaming hatred for the living. Said to have been summoned in a dark ritual, tricking ancient magicians into it."

Gwyn continued to listen, unnerved by the history of Azerael.

"So the story goes. The sky in those times darkened, vegetation withered, and rains became harsh, causing famine and sorrow throughout the planet. The Underworld was a safer place to live, so many creatures went there to escape Azerael's wrath."

She watched as his eyes grow more intense with each sentence.

"Thousands of creatures escaped to the Underworld, building large and vast cities there. Homes carved into stalactites and stalagmites, deep below the surface. I doubt any live to tell the story firsthand now."

"What happened to her?" Gwyn asked.

"Eos knew bringing Azerael into this world was a mistake. Legend has it he used some of his magical mastery and the remaining great wizards to seal Azerael with a blood bind."

"What's a blood bind?"

"A binding spell, typically forbidden because it's weighted in strength through blood. It cannot be lifted unless someone of equal or greater blood value is used to break it."

Gwyn felt her stomach drop. "Like my father and Franz... That's why Zarep wanted my blood. He used it to break a spell..."

Galanga listened, hopeful that she might be wrong. "The most powerful wizards of the time, maybe ever, sealed her. Eos, Michael, Tael, Crux, and Z. She is said to have killed most of them, maybe even all. Too long ago to know for sure."

He then smiled at her, his old eyes revealing long crow's feet. "Before yesterday, you were a rumor. I've missed your family dearly, Gwyn," he said, maintaining his smile. "Now, not only are you real, but you brought one of Azerael's best to his knees... I am proud of you."

Gwyn's day was filled with a mixture of celebration and grief. Her body continued to remind her of her battle, though Galanga was sure to spend time healing her. One scar he couldn't heal was her heart. She felt homesick for Pantheon and missed her grandparents. She wrote them a letter but wasn't sure if it would make it if she mailed it from Sterlington, so she held onto it.

She asked Galanga again about the soldiers, prying him for how these weren't people. He reassured her that they were not. She confessed her spirit was troubled by the thought of killing someone, and Galanga told her that it was a good thing—a reason he admired her.

Gwyn made sure to apologize and thank Jack and Chele for their incredible support and efforts. In her heart, she truly believed she could not have saved Princess Lily without them.

She decided to get some fresh air in the afternoon and went to the surface in Clove. She walked around a bit, surprised how sunny it had become. It felt nice to sit and enjoy the crisp air in the sunshine.

One thing that surprised her was seeing many occasional villagers walking around. She was cautious, as she knew Zarep's armies might return at any moment, so she kept the Xi Blade on her. Still out of arrows, she knew she'd have to rely on her mind to save her—an ability she was starting to learn to lean into, though deep down she was also afraid of it.

She sat on a gray stone next to a poorly tended flower bed and recalled all the moments her mind had slipped, starting with learning to shoot her bow, then the fight in the playground. She remembered the bully, the bandits, saving her uncle in the Shadow Guild, recovering the sheath, the dive into the ocean... She tried to reconcile it all as good, as the owl had suggested—a gift—but doubts still crept into the back of her mind.

The idea that this was a curse bothered her. The owl said someone paid dearly for it, but was that through honorable training and efforts? Studying? Was it a potion her mother found?

Then she pondered on her blood dripping into the water, swirling and evidently lifting a binding spell holding back the Azerael.

She was deep in these thoughts when she heard a familiar voice.

"Gwyn?"

The man sounded too far to be coming from Galanga's home in the mound. She looked up and around, spotting someone dozens of yards away to the south but approaching quickly.

"Franz?" Gwyn whispered, her heart leaping with excitement.

As he neared, she got up and ran to embrace her uncle. They met in an old square in front of Clove, and Gwyn wrapped her arms around him, squeezing him as tightly as she could.

Franz was speechless, as if he couldn't believe what was happening.

After a long embrace, he finally knelt down to speak with her. "I can't believe I found you!" he confessed.

"How did you?" she asked.

"Gwyn, this place... we're in a war zone. We need to get out of here!"

"A war zone?" Gwyn said in surprise. "Zarep isn't even here anymore."

Franz paused, surprised she knew who Zarep was. "How do you know that?"

Gwyn chuckled, a tear of happiness rolling down her cheek. Seeing her uncle brought a tremendous sense of happiness to her burdened spirit.

"Whatever happened here, the council is deeming the Northern Kingdoms unsafe and are working on a plan to get refugees out of the cities."

"No," she uttered softly, a concerned look in her eyes. "This is their home..."

Franz paused, breathing heavily from running. He looked into Gwyn's determined green eyes before nodding. "Alright, we'll tell the council that," he said to her. "But it seems Xess knows you exist now—there's no telling what he'll do if he's willing to level entire cities."

Gwyn's heart sank. "What?"

"Yeah, word reached the council that armies have been wreaking havoc all the way to the east coast of the Northern Kingdoms."

She didn't believe Xess was behind the attacks but wasn't sure what to say. She took Franz back to Galanga, and they talked for what seemed like an hour.

Franz was in awe, hearing what Gwyn, Jack, and Chele had done to rescue Princess Lily.

"We should go back," he told her, but Gwyn protested with a sincere ache in her heart to stay.

"I want to stay," she told him. Then she stopped and thought about it. Part of her did want to go back.

She wasn't sure what was true about the north. She heard Franz tell Galanga that Lily's abduction was the beginning of things, so she assumed the information was fresh.

Franz told them that Delilah had stayed behind the war zone's border line with a summoner. She waited with one of her friends to use it.

"Gwyn," Galanga said. "when the time is right, your kingdom awaits you." He then looked into her anxious green eyes and gave her a knowing nod.

She knew then in her heart that she had to go back to the Western Kingdoms.

They gathered their things quickly. She hugged Galanga and Jasmine in what felt like a hurried goodbye.

"Gwyn," he said softly. "don't expect much from the council. I honestly don't believe the rumors, but if they're true, we'll take cover underground."

She looked Galanga in the eyes and softly whispered, "Take care of Jasmine. I will be back."

"I know," Galanga told her with a smile. "Go home."

Franz pulled two small vials of sand from his pocket and mixed them into a small metal shell, closed it, and shook it. He waited a minute, then told them, "This city is preventing the summoner. We need to get closer."

They left Clove, heading south.

Gwyn saw more citizens walking around than she had before. She wanted to warn them to leave but couldn't. Many of them had looks of relief and surprise on their faces. She wondered if they knew the Northern Kingdoms were in a war zone or if it was even true.

Even using Franz's running aura, it took quite a while to reach the edge of the city and leave it, heading south. She admired the southern entry to her mother's kingdom. It was done in a fairly magnificent way that made her feel a sense of pride.

A mile south of Sterlington, they reached a small town, which seemed slightly larger than most. The people there seemed to be celebrating, almost like a carnival. Someone nearby shouted with excitement about the enemy tower collapsing. She felt a rush of energy but wasn't sure if she should feel excited.

"They must not know about the east cities yet," Jack said with a shrug.

"It's a perfect day to celebrate," Gwyn said, feeling Galanga's instincts were probably right.

Unfortunately, they weren't there for long. Gwyn suddenly felt a tugging in her being. She knew she could fight it if she wanted to, but it also felt quite strong.

"Okay, everyone. If you get a feeling drawing you, just mentally allow it, and it should allow you to be drawn to the summoner."

Gwyn mentally said that she accepted it, and in a flash, she was standing in front of Delilah and a wizard she didn't know.

"Okay, Jack," she said, then Jack appeared next to her. "Chele," she said, then Chele appeared.

It took a minute for them to summon Franz. After he appeared with them, she looked at the smoking summoner and threw it aside. "You blew the summoner," she told Franz.

Franz shrugged. "Just too much wizard for it, I guess."

Gwyn finally looked around at her surroundings. It felt as if she were at an ancient site that was once magnificent. She saw large rectangular stones carved to make beautiful walls and structures. It felt as if there was a town in the center of what was left, but she wasn't sure.

She suddenly felt her aunt grab and hug her. Delilah pulled Jack and Chele into the hug as well.

"I don't know how you guys ended up north, but we're so glad you're okay!"

Gwyn wanted to cry. She hadn't been with her family in so long she had forgotten how great it felt.

As they left the town to the southwest, Franz told her they were in Arcadia. Her heart sank a bit, remembering the stories of her mother's destruction there. She tried to ignore it but couldn't help wondering what had truly happened.

They ran for some time before reaching a city to the southwest, where they bought tickets and boarded a train. Franz and Delilah told her they'd talk when she felt up to it. She honestly didn't, so she rode quietly in her thoughts. She wasn't sure how she felt yet or what she believed.

One thing that kept creeping back into her mind was the Northern Kingdoms. It had only been a few hours since she'd left them, and she already pined for them. Her heart began to break as she thought about Spirit and the fairies, Galanga and Chili... oh yes, and Jasmine most of all. She wanted to do whatever she could to save her, but she was already hours away and couldn't imagine getting back north to help her if her aunt and uncle wouldn't allow it.

There were too many unanswered questions and too many things pulling her to feel okay in that moment, so she closed her eyes and enjoyed the last hour's sun beaming on her face through the train's window.

CHAPTER 29

Echoes of the Heart

The first day back, Gwyn tried to ignore her internal conflicts. Her attempts were met with swells of sorrow, concern, and unprocessed emotions. It would be dishonest to say otherwise, as her heart ached greatly over the coming days back at Franz and Delilah's farm. It became difficult to focus, and she struggled to relax. The happiness that once filled every ounce of her being had become difficult to find.

Franz and Delilah wanted to help, but knew she wasn't ready. Her mind was too consumed with the events in the Northern Kingdoms, especially Jasmine. Deep inside, she wanted to return and help. She had seen the love her mother had for her people and land, and Gwyn wanted to provide a path to victory for them.

She ate but a little and spent most of her time at the ridge. It did make her feel slightly better when she mailed the letter to her grandparents, hopeful to hear back soon, but what she needed most was time—time to process, time to plan, time to heal.

Her sleep was restless, replaying nightmares from her battle with Zarep and the visions of her mother's kingdom that wouldn't leave her. She often recalled seeing the Azerael, the thick darkness that consumed the air around her in fields of Myrrh.

Franz tried to convince her to train and get ready for another semester at the Academy, knowing it would help to clear her head, but she didn't. Her mind wasn't in it, and neither was her heart.

Delilah tried to talk to her but she told her she wasn't ready.

Even though she'd seen the owl for a second time, she still told no one about it. She had planned to, at some point, but her mind was focused on other things. She still felt as if it might have been a dream, his words left an echo of hope when she thought of them, so she did it often.

After a few days of being back, she sat up out of bed one night, bow in one hand, wiping sweat with the other. She tried to shake off the nightmare and walked toward the door. She didn't need to grab her weapons, as she slept with them. She also didn't sneak at all. Since returning, she merely came and went as she pleased.

She looked at Chele for a moment before leaving, who was sleeping in a bed across from hers. She recalled how valiantly Chele fought, bringing down several undead soldiers much larger than she was. She felt a rush of gratitude knowing she had her friends as she stepped outside and looked up to see the Electric Moon in the sky that night.

As she was closing the door, she nearly screamed when Jack touched her on the shoulder. "Sorry, Gwyn. Just wanted to tell you, Chele and I have some good news."

She nodded. "It's alright, Jack. Hard not to be on edge lately—had a lot on my mind."

Jack nodded. "I know. You can't be "princess-sourpuss" forever though, especially when you hear this."

The way Jack said his comment made her chuckle. It was the first time she'd laughed in days and it felt nice. "Maybe later?" she said, eager to spend time alone on the ridge. "Need to clear my head."

"Well, I think we might be able to help Jasmine," he told her quickly.

Gwyn's eye's darted to Jack's, her heart anxious to hear his proposal, "That is good news... maybe the best news since we've been back!"

Jack smiled proudly.

She smiled back, her heart feeling a bit lighter. "Alright, let's talk it over with Chele at breakfast in the morning... You guys are the best."

Jack nodded, excited that she was going to eat breakfast again, "You've got a deal!"

Gwyn dropped Apollo and hugged Jack. She then thanked him sincerely, adding, "I owe you guys. I just need a little time alone to let things process."

"Take your time, Gwyn," he told her with a smile.

As she walked through the field between the house and the forest, her heart was struck with the sincere happiness over her friendship with Jack and Chele. They had done the impossible, battling undead beings, camping under the stars... She knew they'd likely saved many lives in the Northern Kingdoms, including a Glade Goblin Princess, and she knew in her heart they could make things better... somehow. She continued to ponder on how much they had done to help her, and a tear of joy fell from her green eye.

Gwyn made it past the fountain and onto the ridge, enjoying the breeze as it swept across the grass. She crossed her hands on top of Apollo and looked up. She had a sudden urge to play her harp. She sensed it might have the power to heal unseen wounds in the heart and considered going back for it.

She meditated, reflecting on her friends at first, then her mind wandered onto Zarep, Jasmine, and Sterlington, and then on the dire warnings of war plaguing the Northern Kingdoms.

She then wondered how people like her parents could possibly be removed from the world and what evil could have done it. The owl's whisper, "You're not alone," echoed in her mind as she prayed for answers.

Another tear rolled down her cheek just before she heard a noise behind her.

"Please, not now, Jack," she said softly without looking. Her heart was close to reconciling the events and she needed this moment to herself.

No one answered.

Small patches of hair blew across her face as she stood there, waiting for him to say something.

Finally, she turned around, surprised to see Jade standing near the bush Jack had hidden behind. Her opal eyes reflected the Xi Moon in a dazzling spectacle, but it was one she didn't feel like enjoying at that moment.

The two stared at each other before Gwyn broke the silence.

"What do you want?" she asked a bit passively.

Jade stood still, looking at her for a moment before answering. "When Nok comes, Xess will align with her."

"What difference does that make?"

Jade's beauty was as intense as her demeanor as she paused between answers. "War—destruction—She'll make promises, but the world will enter into an age of death."

Silence crept into the conversation for a moment before a certain question bubbled to the surface. "What happened to my mother?" Gwyn eventually asked.

Jade stood there, tussles of hair billowing in a similar fashion to Gwyn's, but she didn't answer.

"Did you kill her?"

Jade's face looked almost upset but still quite passive as she stood. She then shook her head slowly.

"Then what happened!?" She asked again, annoyed by Jade's silence.

Jade stayed still for a long moment before pointing up at her.

Gwyn paused, then felt slighted at the thought of herself being a reason that her mother was no longer around. "Because you think I'm cursed?" she said in a defensive tone.

Jade looked down for a moment, as if in deep thought, then back up to her. "You're sure you want to know?" Jade said in a sobering tone, as if the answer might come with perilous danger.

Gwyn stood still for a moment. The question struck heavier than she expected, and she clenched her jaw as she nodded.

Jade took a step toward her, but Gwyn had grown defensive against Jade and didn't trust her. She lifted her bow and drew an arrow from her quiver, but before she could nock it, Jade flashed up to her and drew a staff from the nether. She swung it, and there was a bright flash as she knocked Apollo out of Gwyn's hands. A violent sting shot through her fingers as the bow spun off, buzzing as it sliced through the air, eventually falling somewhere far off in the ocean.

Losing Apollo angered Gwyn, and she went to draw the Xi Blade but suddenly felt nails digging into her wrists, forcing her ligaments to open her hands. Jade had grabbed her wrists before she could properly wield the blade, and a second later, the scenery around her flashed as if lightning struck nearby. It was an odd, ripping flash, and then it happened again. Unlike other visions shared before, this one flashed a few times and took a moment before she realized that she was on the very same ridge in the vision, staring at a fit, beautiful woman she recognized.

Gwyn paused her resistance to Jade, her heart leaping as she fell captive to the sudden visual of her mother. Selena's eyes were glowing, radiating bright pink and indigo colors inches from her, with irises that were glowing deep greens around her pupils. Gwyn felt her mother's breath hit her face and a chill shot down her spine. The spectacle was surreal—hypnotic—almost otherworldly. A brief thought crossed Gwyn's mind as she wondered if this was how she looked to others at times—powerful—unstoppable.

She was stunned by her mother's elegance and beauty, but something about Selena was different. Even though Gwyn knew she could fight and break free of Jade's magical vision, she had become entranced with seeing her mother. She was so captivated by her eyes she barely noticed the Xi Blade pointing down above her, Jade's hands grasping Selena's wrists to hold it back.

Gwyn closed her eyes, soaking in the view of her mother, and there, under the pale pink light of the Electric Moon, Gwyn relented to a vision that would change her life forever...

End of Gwyn's Kingdom - The Electric Moon

Thank you for reading Book I of Gwyn's Kingdom. I truly hope you enjoyed this adventure.

Please consider giving this book a rating on Amazon, GoodReads, Barns & Noble or any other outlet that graciously carries Gwyn's Kingdom.

Scan the QR code or visit GwynsKingdom.com

Dedication & Acknowledgments

Gwyn's Kingdom began as a labor of love. It has been an incredible journey to write, allowing me to explore my imagination in clever and creative ways.

I never imagined it would evolve into a multi-novel series-worth of content. I poured myself into Gwyn's Kingdom for well over a decade.

At age 11 I learned to play guitar. Even before then I was making up songs and writing. I played in several bands, writing a countless number of songs. When those bands broke up I was left with a plethora of material. I've always been drawn to fantasy. Final Fantasy, Zelda and Warcraft occupied large blocks of my free time. Somewhere along the way, I read The Princess Bride, Peter Pan, The Hobbit and then several other fantasy books. The genre has always had a place in my heart. There's nothing quite like getting lost in some fabulous adventure in a mystical world.

Without a band anymore (circa 2010) I decided to continue writing but channeled my content into fantasy stories. Several stories before Gwyn's Kingdom came and went, most of them lost to time now. I eventually found Gwyn and began to find a style for writing. Over the course of the next decade I wrote and re-wrote the story of Gwyn's Kingdom, partially never believing it would be available publicly.

I was told the story is worth sharing. I hope you find a way to get lost and have fun in Gwyn's journey.

I dedicate this book to my daughters and wife, and to all who believed in me to write and complete this book. Many of them are in the list below.

-- Thank You --

To Jesus Christ, my Savior, for providing me with a talent and desire to do this. I am nothing without You.

To my wife and children for tolerating me while I spent countless hours in coffee shops and stayed up late to edit and write.

To my mother for believing in me and always encouraging me to "go for it." You are a blessing and a wonderful friend—and to my dad for always believing in me and letting me know I can do anything I put my mind to.

To Amy and Heart, and my "bra" Andrew—for taking the time to read through the initial drafts and provide genuine feedback.

To each fan or reader who bought this book or took the time to read it. Even if it's not for you, thank you for giving it a chance anyway.

To all the amazing fantasy novelists out there who have paved the way for Gwyn's Kingdom, producing outstanding content and keeping this genre alive!

I want to give a thanks to the royalty-free clipart/reference art and LLMs out there allowing easier access to base/reference images. I edit and do the artwork in the book but use many sources to draw inspiration from. When I'm in a pinch, these tools can save a lot of time and effort.

Also, thank you so much to Affinity and their amazing community of brushes, tutorials, etc. My cover modifications and photo dev/editing would not exist if it weren't for this amazing program.

This book wouldn't exist without any of you, so, from the bottom of my heart, thank you!

www.ingramcontent.com/pod-product-compliance
Lightning Source LLC
Chambersburg PA
CBHW020914310726
48980CB00011B/875/J